Nightingale

Peter Dorward

TWO RAVENS
PRESS

Published by Two Ravens Press Ltd
Green Willow Croft
Rhiroy
Lochbroom
Ullapool
Ross-shire IV23 2SF

www.tworavenspress.com

ISBN: 978-1-906120-09-2

British Library Cataloguing in Publication Data. A CIP record for this book can be obtained from the British Library.

Designed and typeset in Sabon by Two Ravens Press.
Cover design by David Knowles and Sharon Blackie.

Printed on Forest Stewardship Council-accredited paper by Biddles Ltd., King's Lynn, Norfolk.

About the Author

Peter Dorward was born in St Andrews in 1963. Having been a hop-picker, international aid-worker, pub musician and a runner for a film crew, he now works as a GP and medical teacher in Edinburgh, where he lives with his partner Deborah and two sons. He has published a number of short stories and been a winner of literary awards, including the 2000 Canongate short story prize and the 1997 Fish short story competition.

Nightingale is his first novel.

Acknowledgements

I would like to thank Andy Greig for the years of encouragement, support, whisky and friendship. Slainte!

My gratitude to Gordon, my critical friend, for the example of your life on the wild side. You are so sadly missed.

Thanks to my agent, Stan, whose belief in *Nightingale* never wavered.

Over the years I have pestered innumerable friends for advice and comments about this and other work. For your time, effort, consolation, patience and alcohol, particular thanks to Andrew Dorward, Andrea Joyce, Benito Chakra, and Andrew Canessa.

For guidance on language and politics, my thanks to Martin Rhodes, David Bivona and Dyano.

And finally to Deborah, Jack and Jamie, for everything.

For David Dorward
1931-2003

Part 1

1

'Rosie, this time I'll tell you everything: right to the end... '
I was barely conscious when he spoke. I was half-dead, on a ventilator in a hospital bed. I long now to remember the specifics – his face, the timbre of his voice, the actual words he used – it would bring me such comfort. But the more I try to bring to mind memories of my father, the more worn and insubstantial these memories become.

The images created by that voice, though, and the story it told, persist. They go round and around in my mind like a loop of film, and never stop. I cannot forget them. I dream them. I can almost see them.

❦

Angry, Don slaps the receiver back onto its cradle, but misses. The handset cracks against the aluminium bar; the muffled voice inside its head gabbles on.

He replaces it, gently now, glancing up to see whether his useless rage has been noticed, but the barman has his back turned. He's watching the street: his little niece is marching in a parade outside, and the bar is otherwise empty.

The bells of the *Cattedrale di Santa Lucia* toll and are answered within the moment by the bright keen voices of fifty others. Don checks his watch. Quarter to one. He perches on the black leather bar stool, sips his coffee, sips his water, checks his watch again, plays with the sugar packet, crushing grains of sugar between his thumbnails. He lights a cigarette, wipes sweat from his forehead.

The second of August 1980, fourteen minutes to one in the afternoon: an afternoon in Italy, twenty-four years ago.

He's twenty-one years old, only just. Every day of his life is momentous, this one most of all.

He takes the papers from the breast pocket of his jacket – black leather, coarse wool lining, far too hot but his favourite thing, his best thing, the very last of his possessions still with him – and checks them again. The flimsy airmail envelope, which he had almost torn in two in his rush to open, containing tickets – Ancona-Basle, departing at five past one from Bologna – *an international train,*

3

so bound to be on time. Don't be late, don't fuck up. Just be there! – and another, containing a ridiculous quantity of money. He runs the ball of his thumb across the edge of the filthy brown bills, notes the mark that they make, how their sweating edges come to powder on his skin, leaving a guilty grey stain. Several hundred thousand lira in used currency – though what the fuck that actually means is any man's guess. He doesn't count it. It doesn't matter. It looks like enough to get home on, and his decision to leave is almost made.

So just go!

Glancing at himself in the mirror behind the bar, he sees himself for a moment as others might: dirty, gaunt, haunted – a foreigner in an elegant town, fleeing. *So obviously criminal!* he thinks, then banishes that useless thought, watching it a moment – trapped, fluttering across his reflected image.

He pulls a handful of little coins from his pocket, the last of his own, honest, un-blooded money, and tries to pay, but the barman's back is still turned. He coughs. *'Mi scusi, barista!'* His voice croaks, sounds foreign, a wrong, self-conscious voice – but the man hasn't even heard. He tries again: *'Barista!'* and the barman turns. A slow fat man with grey-on-white apron, black oily hair, he points a scowl at the ragged *straniero* and his rudeness, but takes the money just the same, muttering *'Pezzente!'*, the little coins spilling like grains from his fleshy hands. He counts them out on the bar with his wide forefinger, pushing back a coin or two for change.

Ten to one. The train leaves in fifteen minutes.

It's still hot, but humid now too; the sky heavy with cloud. His head aches and he blinks at the daylight, although it is no longer bright. He walks onto the pavement and faces the carnival: people shouting and whistling and twirling, the sounds of the horns of the cars trapped behind the dancing crowd. He hesitates for a second or two, fearful to cross.

The first drops of rain fall on the pavement at his feet, releasing the season's stink, long locked in the dust. *I've been here one year, today,* thinks Don, shocked by this sudden knowledge. He pushes his way through the first of the crowd, who turn on him, laughing and cursing.

It's seven minutes to one.

$\wr$

She had woken with him at five that morning, to a clean, bright sunrise. They had stood together at the window, hand in hand, facing the dawn, mouths filled with half-formed words, but silent still.

She had made coffee, the first of the day, in a pot on the hob. They had sat opposite one another at the wooden table, taken the coffee in her grandmother's tiny terracotta cups, wincing at its strength. They had looked into one another's eyes then, shying away from what each saw there, glanced down instead at their bare feet, their toes, curling against the cool tiles. She was to stay at the farm. He'd leave alone, walk the hour up to Monte Rosa, pick up the bus to town. They had decided. He had to be away by quarter past five. Time was tight.

He had stood, taken his leather jacket from the peg inside the door, and turned to her. He couldn't find any words, so had just nodded. He had turned to leave, but she'd come after him, and finally broken their foolish silence.

'Donald.' *Tonald,* in her voice.

'Yes.'

'Come back, please. Come back to me. You promise.'

'Yes. I promise.' *Lo prometto.*

And then he had left.

And now, eight hours later, he carries this recent memory with him like a talisman, clasped tightly to his heart, and forces his way through thieves.

'*Come back, please. Come back to me. Promise,*' she had said.

'*Yes. I promise.*'

It's five to one.

The station is at the far side of the *Piazza Medaglie D'Oro,* the bar where he stands on a corner off *Indipendenza.* It's about four hundred yards. He has simply to leave the bar, cross *Indipendenza* and the square, enter the station, show the ticket, join the train, leave. There will be time enough to think about the rest.

But the carnival has brought out the crowds. A parade of children, masked as animals. There are rhino, hippos, lion, zebra, drifting in slow herds down the asphalt. Parents follow beside them on the pavement; the odd, mad car is caught, trapped and squealing, immobile in the current. There are men dressed as beasts, dancers, fire-eaters, jugglers, lorries with open tops carrying bands of men from the south in black suits, swaying and playing drums and trumpets and trombones. A man in denims, brown stack-heeled cowboy boots, cigarette between his fingers, stinking of sweat and carrying a megaphone, blocks his way and calls to a raucous child in the crowd. A section of the crowd calls back and the noise is crushing. Crossing the road, he is immediately carried by the crowds in the direction opposite to the one he wants. He feels himself sinking, drowning under those waves of frivolity, and it takes him a minute to reach the other side.

He faces the crowded square with its lines of densely-clustered Vespas and ice-cream stands, sellers of hot dogs and cones of what smell like almonds roasted in honey. A child in a queue drops her money, cries, calls to her mother, but her mother isn't there. Someone taps him on the shoulder and he spins round, ready, irrationally, to strike – but it's a woman in a bright nylon headscarf, dark skin, violet eyes, a dirty cupped hand held out for change, a baby at the breast. '*Bambino … affamare…* ' she whines in a language which isn't her own, and he wastes more time digging into his pocket, digging out more little coins which he tips into her fist, and she frowns at the smallness of his pity and spits on them.

The air smells metallic. In a moment there will be a torrent of rain. A gust of cooler wind shakes the branches of the oleanders that line the square, giving a little relief from the humidity. A seven year-old girl with long brown hair, olive skin, pale blue checked dress and a sweet smile, hands money to a man who gives her something – a soft toy? – wrapped in crepe and red streamers, and the child, rushing for a train, or perhaps just to shelter from the coming rain, sets off at a run across the square, trips on the cobbles but doesn't fall, picks up her step again, runs up the station steps, under the arches, into the crowd in the station, shouting out '*Mamma!*'

Six minutes to go.

The breeze rises again, cooling the air; and the sound of rain drops is momentarily audible, rattling through the leaves of the trees as the noise of the crowd stills.

He had never wanted to leave, but now he has no choice.

He starts to run across the square, reaches the bottom of the same steps that the little girl climbed a moment before. He wonders for a moment who she might be, her fragile child's smile lodged somewhere in a crevice of his memory.

He gathers himself to leap the ten steps to the station archway, and the bell of the *Torre degli Asinelli* strikes one.

And the world cracks. And shimmers a moment; exhales. The world emits a long, terrible moan.

Lying at the bottom of the steps, surrounded by the densest silence, Don looks up at the now dark, gathered sky; the falling, silver rain-drops. There begins a far-off noise, a whistling or ringing in his ears which will never afterwards leave him. There is a gradual returning of life: of sound; of movement in his limbs; the sensation of pain in his neck and shoulders where he landed, when he was blown, head-over-heels, down the steps.

He stands. He runs his hand through his hair, feeling for blood, but finds only dust. He climbs the steps, slowly this time, enters under a dark arch, feet crackling over what feels like broken glass, his nose and throat now full of smoke, the stink of burning plastic and some darker, uglier scent behind that. He looks around himself, peering through a world suddenly fogged. He sees shifting shapes, movement in the smoke; hears, far off, alarm bells ringing. He hears a long, sad cry, then another, elsewhere, answering. He sees on the ground thick shards of coloured, reinforced glass. He looks up at the roof of the station and finds it gone; sees instead the sky, full now of falling leaves, ash, fragments of paper.

2

The Years of Lead
Rosie Macleod, Feb 2004
Introduction, Draft 1

*O*n *the second of August 1980, at 1pm in the afternoon, a bomb placed under a chair in the second-class waiting room of the international railway station in Bologna exploded, resulting in the deaths of eighty-five people.*

The bomb was timed to detonate at the busiest time of the afternoon, immediately prior to the departure of the 13:05 direct train, Ancona to Basle, at the height of the holiday season, when the waiting room was guaranteed to be crowded. Forty-five people in the immediate vicinity died instantly in the initial blast; a further fifteen over the subsequent four weeks from the injuries they sustained. Of those first forty-five, forty-four were identified. One, sconosciuto, unknown, remains unidentified to this day.

The force of the explosion was sufficient to destroy completely the waiting room and the adjoining buffet. A possibly unintended consequence of the heat and force of the initial blast was the destruction of the lead latticework supporting the stained-glass roof of the main station concourse, which collapsed over the heads of the travellers and their companions below, resulting in a multitude of secondary casualties, the deaths of a further twenty-five people, and the injury and mutilation of over two hundred others.

The date of the atrocity coincided with Bologna's traditional carnevale delle bestie – an ancient Bacchanalia celebrated in the heat of high summer, when the streets become choked with masked and intoxicated revellers and traffic cannot move. Consequently, the first emergency vehicles didn't arrive on the scene for twenty-five minutes, during which time a number of victims of traumatic amputation and laceration by falling glass, bled to death. The first burns victims are recorded as arriving at Bologna's Ospedale della Pietà at 14:30, an hour and a half after the blast. Further casualties were admitted throughout that afternoon and the following night. A group of four station workers who had been refurbishing the second class toilets located adjacent to the site of the blast were found, suffocated by smoke, two days later.

In the immediate aftermath, various contradictory claims for responsibility for the bombing were made and subsequently retracted: calls to a Rome newspaper and to a news agency in Turin claimed responsibility on behalf of the far-right Nuclei Armati Rivoluzionari – the 'Armed Revolutionary Nuclei.' Another, of doubtful provenance, issued on behalf of the ultra-left Brigate Rosse – the 'Red Brigades.' Various other groups were implicated, by various more or less interested constituencies. A shadowy, ultra-militant syndicalist splinter of the Brigate Rosse, the Martello del Popolo – 'The People's Hammer' – was the subject of initial investigations, but no direct connection was ever proven and the group, active in a series of high profile robberies in the area at the time, disappeared from view. Subsequently, attention returned fully to the Armed Revolutionary Nuclei – a diffuse, neo-fascist organisation with alleged links to elements in the Italian secret services, the police force, and the judiciary. Despite indictments and arrests, no convictions were ever secured. The secretiveness and passivity of the authorities, and the inadequacy of the police investigation following the bombing, have led to persistent rumours of state involvement in, and state cover-up of, the outrage.

Whichever interests were ultimately served by the carnage, the bombing marked the culmination of two decades of violence perpetrated by armed groups of both the right and the left. That apparently irremediable cycle of terrorist violence which so scarred Italian political life throughout the seventies is now finished. The foot-soldiers in the various 'Peoples' Wars' and 'Strategies of Tension' are disbanded, either completing long prison sentences, or dead. Some, ageing, have become respectable, with stakes in the society and its institutions that they once affected to despise. A few now occupy positions of respect and authority within their own professions: politics, the law, the various sectors of the state. The Red Brigades are smashed now; the black alliance that existed between the far right, the church, the masons and the judiciary, which fuelled the neo-fascist violence of the time, is exposed and discredited. It is in no-one's interest to remember the terrible events of those years, least of all those in authority, whose sanitised state has ultimately benefited from the calculated horror of those 'years of lead,' and achieved at last a modicum of political stability.

Yet each of those eighty-five victims had a family. Around each of those dead and the two hundred-plus injured are parents, siblings, husbands, wives, lovers, children, friends whose own different worlds were split open by the blast of that bomb. The cries of the victims of the bomb, the terrible noise of the blast, the ringing of bells and the noise of the shattering glass echo down through the generations, and echo still in the memories of those who were there, and those who were affected.

Each of these has their own story to tell, and each in turn deserves an explanation for the events of that terrible afternoon.

As, in a minor way, perhaps, do I.

3

My father, Don, you see, was the first on the scene. He had talked about it with me just once, when I was a teenager, although in hindsight I had sensed since early childhood the burden of this untold story. My Dad had the aggrieved nobility of the veteran – *you weren't there, you can never understand. But put up with me all the same.* He swerved unpredictably between love, rage, grief and humour and then, filled with remorse and self-pity, he drank. Unattractive qualities, definitely, but unapparent to the child that loved him. I had always thought of my Daddy as if he were the survivor of some great, heroic, yet secret conflict. He was a man who had to be protected from his own fragile moods: shielded during the black times, cherished and loved for those rare days of grace and humour. But whatever his mood, it was always to be tended.

We were walking on the sands at Tentsmuir when he told me. It was the day after my fourteenth birthday, and a typical rainy day on the beach. Julia – my Mum – and the dog both chose to shelter in the car. Sheltering, I thought at the time, from the weather; but actually, I realise in hindsight, from my father, and what he was about to say. It had all been discussed, well in advance. Innocent, I had thought that I was going for a walk with my Daddy. I was tricked.

We were skipping along the edge of the sea, dancing between the wet sand and the spit of the tide, laughing. He grabbed a mass of matted wood and seaweed from the tide-line, ran down and threw it out into the waves, with the half-formed notion perhaps that I would run into the water and retrieve it. He joked, said something – that I represented for him the dog that he longed for and had never had – and tried to ruffle my hair, teasing me, making me both smile and bridle in the same instant. It was a typically slightly off-key moment for my father, this kind of jarring, failed intimacy. It was a glorious, dank day. In a sense, it was the last day of its kind.

We stopped together to catch our breath, stood shoulder-to-shoulder, looking out over the grey sea, the horizon barely perceptible, one kind of wet shading into another. The Angus coastline reaches out here, north to the lighthouse at Auchmithie, a fragment of land lodged between the sea and the sky. He took my hand, which was just about okay – despite my age and the new unpredictability of *my* mood – and said, 'Rosie darling, there's something I have to tell you.' And I thought, *Oh God. Here we go...*

'I want you to know,' he said, gazing through narrow eyes at the wild north, 'that everything that is going to happen, is my fault.'

Deflecting my Dad's serious moments was a reflex ingrained from early childhood. I had learned from an early age that the black clouds which from time to time swallowed him contained no prospect of fun for a child. So I used to jolly him along when the bleakness threatened, to make a joke, try to tease out that smile, that pearl buried in the flesh under its dark shell. But that day I had the good sense to just look out at the sea, hold my silence, and wait.

For him to say, 'Julia and I have decided...' and 'It's not your fault, and it doesn't mean that either of us love you any less...' and 'It's just that we can no longer live happily...' and 'We think it's better in the end for you, darling...' Because I knew, from a number of my friends on whom this conversational trick had already been perpetrated, that this is how it begins. But my Dad cut straight to the chase.

'Your mother wants me to leave her because she thinks I'm lazy, self-centred, drink too much, and that I'm dragging you and her down with me. I want you to know that she is right. But I also wanted you to know that I love you, and that I always will.'

Despite his limitations, I have always loved my Dad more than I love my mother. My mother is very serious and disapproves of many things. My mother is a paediatrician, gets up early, saves lives, and is morally unassailable. When he lived with us, my Dad loafed around, read a lot, complained of earache and wrote stuff which he never showed to anyone. He was frequently "unavailable for business" on account of alcohol. He was never unkind. He was always very encouraging. But he was also completely incompatible with my mother, who was at the time, I now realise, just beginning her relationship with Gordon Telford – then junior labour MP for Slag Heap South East, a safe Fife Labour constituency – and now Minister for Trade.

And I realise now, also, that it wasn't my Dad's indolence and alcohol dependence which gave my mother hives and made her hate him, but the fact that he treated her as well as he actually did. That is: although he didn't love her, and probably never had, he was always kind to her, supportive – as accommodating to her needs as a glove, which eventually she was forced to tear off. Julia, despite her harsh exterior, needed real skin-on-skin contact, no substitute. She had finally seen that my Daddy was just *pretending* to love her.

'Why?' I asked in this new, small voice, which the wind whipped out of my mouth and sent scurrying over the dunes like a sweety paper.

'Why am I leaving?'

'No. What I want to know, Daddy, is how did you get like this? Why did you allow this to happen? What happened to you?'

Now, in hindsight, I put these adult words into the child's mouth. In fact I wept, I screamed at him, and then I think I even hit him. I told him he was crap and that I had always hated him, and I think I used the word 'fuck' to him, which was a first.

I loved him, you see.

Whatever it was that I actually said, that was the point at which he told me his story.

His memory. A recurring, waking dream; a conscious act of remembering, over which he now has no control.

It starts in a bar in Italy.

It explains the deafness, the booze, the tinnitus, the *boring* hypochondriasis. It didn't help *me* at all.

When he had finished I gently detached my hand from his, turned my back on him and started walking along the line of the woods, back to where we'd left the car. Mum was sitting in the front, pretending to read. She watched me emerge from the trees, skip the dry, sandy burn, approach the car with a rather rigid smile. Light of heart, nothing wrong, business as usual. But I could see from the colour of her eyes, the passing frown, that she knew, now, that now I knew.

13

4

Fast-forward eight years.

I'm a nervous girl with a Good Idea, going to visit my father, who I haven't seen for a *long* time.

Strictly speaking, it would be untrue to say that eight years had passed without contact between us. There was my Gran's funeral: face-to-face, briefly, when shy Dad flinched away from the vision of the sixteen year-old girls' school sophisticate that I had become, and then left early. My Dad had always loved his mother-in-law. I pretended not to care.

Then there were letters: a one-way correspondence, by and large – my initial fourteen year-old's tears having been replaced in pretty short order by the rage of abandonment – an anger stoked, I regret to say now, by my self-righteous, purse-lipped Mum, and by The Right Hon. Mr Telford, famous step-dad, whose joint purposes it suited. So I got plenty of news from Dad, and he got none from me. Pencil-written accounts of his meandering life; never any reproach. An angry daughter was what he *deserved*, the letters didn't say. But I always knew where he was, what he was doing, the facts of why, without the emotional hinterland. My Dad's letters, when I read them, were dry, funny, factual, and with a level of wit and articulacy at odds with the sad, glazed style that I remembered. It was almost as if they were written by someone else. After a while, I stopped reading them.

But this kind of anger can only last for so long before it turns to bitterness, and life – mine, at any rate – is too short for bitterness. Bitterness is dull. Angry girls with divorced parents are dull. Girls with unresolved feelings towards their absent fathers are the worst.

So enough of self-pity.

My Good Idea evolved from a post-finals conversation which took place under a tree in the Edinburgh Arboretum last May. A cherry tree, I think. Loaded down with late, pink flowers. My friend and I were lying on our backs listening to the bees, drinking white Hirondelle from plastic beakers having a *thank-fuck-we're-leaving-at-last* conversation. A conversation tinged with sadness. Who-we-were, who-we-are, what-we're-going-to-be.

I want to be a journalist. I am a blue-stocking virgin with a head full of books and no life, to date. I only have one story – his, really – and I need the details.

So I re-enter my father's world.

Which is now located in London. A town I do not like. A place with which I am wholly unfamiliar. A place within a place called ... Neasden?

I take the tube to Neasden on the Jubilee line. That's the grey one. I get off; hop through the crashing barriers without letting them sever my legs. I try not to look silly. I try not to blub girlish tears just because I'm in London on my own, privately afraid, trying to be brave, going to meet my Dad for the first time since I was fourteen. I'm *twenty-two,* God's sake! Grow up!

I navigate my way down Neasden Lane using a compass and an A to Z and get lost in a tangle of streets and interchanges, every one indistinguishable, each apparently called Neasden Lane, all full of traffic, dust and vexation. You never escape the noise of the traffic. You never get the smell out of your nose. The only good, homely, ordinary thing about this place is the grey familiar rain. I find myself pitying my Dad, which is bad.

I cross a kind of bridge under the North Circular. On one side, wired in, a basketball court: the lonely sound of a bouncing ball and then some shouts; on the other, a large, stained concrete pillar with 1980s party-coloured revolutionary socialist graffiti that says 'Neasden Garden Project' in great loopy spray-can letters – below which, a picture of a group of smiling multi-ethnic kids brandishing vegetables.

A half-way house for kids getting out of trouble.

Then a late-nineties addition about lottery funding. My Dad's faded name at the bottom, and a date. Which would be a year or so after he left. I try hard to feel magnanimous about this.

There's nothing to ring and nothing to knock upon on the wire gate, but the padlock's off and I let myself in, have a look around.

My Dad has covered a lot of ground. On my left is a hut: two rooms; one windowed, the other a lumber room piled with hoes and rakes and stuff. A sink at one end with flower-pots stacked under it, each bright slate-red and clean. A mud path down the centre, passing all the way down to the reservoir, with allotments on either side – some with little sheds, some tidy, most running to wild, with wire fencing between each of them. To the right is uncultivated ground, marshland, the grey water beyond it. Ducks on the water.

My Good Idea. *'The Years of Lead.'* It's a provisional title. *Anni di Piombo* is Italian media slang, I discover, for the years 1969 (the year of the *Piazza Fontana* massacre) to 1980 (the year of the station bombing). During which period eight thousand people died in acts of political violence. The name evokes the weight, the dread, the colour of that time. The misery of so many bullets, so much heaviness of heart, so many deaths, so much lead. I never intended the title to be definitive, but no sooner had I chanced upon this expression than I thought how apt it was for the state of mind of a time and place – a *zeitgeist* – and for my own state of mind after Daddy left. My own *anni di piombo*. It took me an hour's research and two hours' writing to draft my few hundred words of intro; then another six on the covering letter, three sides long, beginning:

Dear Daddy...

Up all night, but by morning I see that even that wasn't quite right. I had, true, once thought of him as 'Daddy' – when I was a child, when he was there, and there to be played with. Then, after: miserable, self-centred, absent, deserting... Then third-hand, evasive, cool, to friends, as 'yeah, my Dad... ' and occasionally the more distant, *sang-froid* 'Mr Macleod.'

But how about Donald? *Don?* I had no name for this man, you see.

So six hours to write a letter, another two to stare at it, wondering whether I dared ... but I dared not. I have the letter on me, still unsent, stamped and sealed and in my bag, and I plan to give it to him – if I dare; if ever the moment seems right.

But someone's come to see who I am and what I want.

'I'm looking for...'

Black girl, about sixteen, but could be anything; overweight, tracksuit made of what looks like pale blue terry. There's something just a little dead in these eyes. Her mouth is half-open; her tongue plays with the stud in her lower lip. There is not the flicker of a smile.

'I'm looking for a ... Mr. Macleod.'

'Don?' *(Dawwn...)*

'My Dad...'

'What?' *(Waah?)*

'I mean ... Don ... Mr. Macleod.'

''E's ovah theh.'

The sulky girl points with thumb at an allotment halfway down to the reservoir, then shoves past me toward the shed. But I ignore her. I leave her in the past. I think: *this moment I have waited for, for so many years.* My bitterness, all in a moment, is in the past. My heart swells in anticipation of the first sight of his half-remembered face. His kindness. The glitter in his blue eyes.

Leaning into a spade, he turns over a clod of earth. He bends forward in a long smooth action, picks a bunch of potatoes from the ground, bashes the mud from them on the front of his leg, inspects what he sees, then throws them into a wheel-barrow. I hear the dull thud, the clatter of a few small stones. He straightens up, unhurried; looks out at the reservoir, bends, picks up the handles of the wheelbarrow, moves forward a few feet.

He is the same man, but at first I see a stranger. I had expected – braced myself, almost – for a broken old man. My childhood memories are of a man of great age and gravity, although he would scarcely have been out of his thirties, and my friends' fathers and my step-dad are all in their fifties. But this one is thinner and fitter than most. He has a weathered face, good lines: an interesting man. I would talk to this man, I think, even if I didn't have to. I am glad of this opportunity to watch, to inspect him, to size him up like this, to have a little time for my doubts and my second thoughts. I'm glad that the tables aren't turned, that it isn't him, surprising me. I cough.

He turns, sees me, dresses his fine face and blue eyes with a smile. He glances down at my tits, then his eyes flicker back to my eyes, the mouth still smiling. He's probably quite unaware of his habit. It seems my Dad flirts, automatically, with girls his daughter's age. I file this trivia, trying not to let it bother me. So.

17

'Mr. Macleod…'

He takes two steps forward and presents a hand for me to shake. He notices what I'm wearing – sees a smart girl with a short black skirt and black tights, professional shoes, way out of place in the mud – and, with a look I don't altogether like, withdraws his filthy hand, mocking the stranger a little as he does so.

'Dad, I'm Rosie.'

Which changes things completely, in an instant, of course. It feels bad – like a trick I've played on the poor man – but he deserves it. He so richly deserves it. He stares now, smile gone.

'Rosie. You didn't tell me that you were coming.'

I have the letter still in my bag.

'I was going to write…'

The star journalist: I have come wholly unprepared. I expect him to recognise me instantly, to take control again and tell me what's what. I don't expect him to weep. I don't expect to see *any* of those weird emotions working their way like cartoon caricatures across his face; I don't expect to feel them on mine. I haven't done the basic research. Somehow I have forgotten how much he had loved me, and I him.

The moment doesn't last. He forgets the dirt, takes the two paces which separate us and hugs me. He says my name, still weeping a little. We share our tears. He smells of earth.

5

B ut I pull back, recoiling from this intimacy. Too much, too soon. All this sweat; his full, earthy smell.

'I wanted to see you,' I say, uselessly, a little out of breath, a bit anxious. He holds me at arms' length, unaware of my little rebuff, staring at me, admiring me with a frankness which in another man I would have loathed; which in him, touches me. I feel tears rising again, not far off.

'I needed to speak to you...'

He nods, stares, eyes me up and down, *drinking* me. We're interrupted.

'*Dawwn,*' asks a long, slow, thick voice. It's the big girl in the powder blue baby-gro. My Daddy's moist eyes are instantly diverted to hers.

'Cherry-Bee!'

'Wot do I do wiv these?'

Cherry-Bee holds up handfuls of tubers. Long thin muddy vegetables with green, ragged hair. Swedes? Parsnips? *Carrots?*

'Brilliant, Cherry-Bee. Look...' Shoulder-to-shoulder they move away, heads together. My attentive Dad points something out with his finger; Cherry-Bee gets it at last, smiles, lumbers off; Dad returns, shaking his head, smiling to himself. Back to the matter in hand. Me.

'Darling. It's wonderful...'

'So who's she, then?' The words emerge all pointed, barbed and scornful.

Dad is surprised by my question; slightly gored by its tone.

'Cherry-Bee? She's a ... client.'

'A ... client?'

'Yeah. Well, more of an assistant. She's been here for ages. She's got a baby.'

'A baby? How old is she?'

A pause. He frowns. 'Fifteen?'

Dad shows me around. Dad in his wellies stomps off down a muddy path between allotments with a rake over his shoulder, shouting words of encouragement to knots of boys with shaven heads and pointed faces. Everywhere I sense the furtive rustle of

Rizla, the gasps of blue smoke emerging from the doors of little sheds where the kids mutter and plot.

'They get referred by the courts sometimes; sometimes by their probation officers, sometimes by their schools or social services...'

'Do they ever actually *do* anything?'

Dad is surprised by the question. 'Sometimes...' As if that's not really the point.

'Don. Don?'

'Lennie. Tyrone.'

'C'n we go now?'

Dad looks at his watch. 'It's only half-past three.'

Two guys. Fifteen? There's nothing nice about these guys. There's nothing quaint. They do not smile at all, these boys.

'Got to see me Dad,' says one, who has what appears to be a Fleur de Lys shaven into the back of his head. The other boy, yellow-brown hair and orangey skin with blade marks on his scalp, tokes massively.

'But you've got to sign us out first.' He pulls an orange plasticised booklet from his back pocket. *Brent and Harrow Community Liason Div.* Dad signs. 'Cheers, Don.'

'Did you get around to loaming the...'

But they don't listen and then they're gone, and Dad just chuckles and shakes his head. *Well, well! Boys!*

We look at roses. We inspect plots of vegetables. Leeks; courgettes with massive yellow flowers; more potatoes, with some kind of blight which makes the leaves wither and spots the fruit; curly kale; beetroot; carrots; acres of onions. The many terracotta pots diligently cleaned and stacked by Cherry-Bee. The fences maintained by the boys. A wild patch: a briar of grasses and wildflowers sown by some truly remarkable kid called Benny whom my father clearly rated – who did something exotically dreadful to a teacher, then managed to get it together again enough to do this! – but I'm no longer really listening, to be honest. It's getting cold and I'm pissed off. A mass of seething and contradictory attitudes, in fact, none of which I much like or need. And *fucking* Lennie and Tyrone are waiting for us by Dad's hut.

'Hey guys! I thought you were –'

They interrupt him.

'Can you give us twenty quid, Don? It's for the bus.'

They're not quite, actually, *asking*.

Flustered, Dad actually looks in his pockets, digs out a wallet, which I can tell in advance is going to be empty. A mean little Golem in my chest tells me in its cold voice what is going to happen next. Unsmiling, Lennie and Tyrone stand there staring and waiting.

'Ah, Rosie…?' says Dad.

'Sure,' I say, reaching into my bag, pulling out my wallet. 'Twenty enough? Sure?'

'Cheers, Don!' The boys are gone without another word.

The shed, I discover, is where my Dad lives. We come in from the rain. I sit, slightly hunched, on a metal bed with a hessian mattress and a grey sleeping bag. My Dad puts on a Calor Gas heater, boils a kettle, throws two empty wine bottles and the contents of an over-full ashtray into the bucket. If he's embarrassed it scarcely shows, but he makes himself too busy for me to tell. My Dad leaves again. Some business that can't wait; something to do with Cherry-Bee's baby, probably.

A small wooden table where the ashtray sits, and two chairs. *Who's the other chair for?* A wooden floor, an ashy-red once-Persian carpet that I recognise from his study at home. And other things: the fountain pen, the ancient leather jacket, the wire-rim glasses, the scraps of paper on the table bearing what look like scraps of verse.

But sitting, perched as I am on the edge of Dad's bed, it's the photos that engage me. Three, in a line on the table, each of me:

1/ Aged four or five, in my room at home, sitting smiling on the floor, cuddling Dad, my favourite soft toy – a camel, called Camilla, as it happens – in my lap. So far, so good.

2/ On a beach. A sunny day, aged twelve.

I am wearing one of Dad's shirts, to keep the sun off. The shirt hadn't been washed in days: an old, frayed cotton shirt with no collar; his favourite shirt, the one he rescued from time to time from the bin and hid. It stank, and I was learning a thing or two about proximity. In the photo I'm smiling into the sun, trying too much to look good – in a too-thin, big-teeth, limbs-like-broken-sticks, twelve year-old's manner – because it was Dad's last exposure and he couldn't get another film; and besides, this was a special time, and I wanted to remember it.

It was the summer holidays: my last before the beginning of secondary school. We were stranded on the Isle of Lappay and our lives hung on the whim and promise of an unreliable fisherman. For some reason, my Mum wasn't there. This situation – stranded on a desert island – is one she would never have let arise. I think she was working. Or maybe it was Gordon. Who knows? Who cares now? In her absence, though, my Dad had changed – gloriously for the better. Free, we ran and rolled around in sand dunes, cooked together on a fire on a beach, sat till late with the wind in our faces watching the rolling of the sea and the rolling of the weather until I was asleep and didn't even know it, and immediately it seemed it was morning and I hadn't known that the night had passed. The fear, this darkness that always stalked my Dad was gone, banished somehow by the imminence of disaster. And the photo that he took then somehow bottled that moment.

We'd crossed from Ullapool to Lewis, money already low, and hitched down the soggy spine of the Western Isles. A fisherman in a pub in Barra offered us a trip to Mingulay, but Daddy pointed with his bitten finger at the next one along, said: 'What's that one called, then? Is there anything on that one?' The fisherman said in his singing not-quite-Irish accent: 'That's Lappay. You don't want to go there. There's absolutely nothing on Lappay,' and as that thought seized us simultaneously my Dad said: 'Do you fancy it then, girl?' I nodded with my child's bright grin. He dropped us off with a week's supply of food in a rucksack, saying *'Are you sure?'* and then off he went. We stayed in this old shepherd's hut with a wood stove and a rusted padlock on the door for which our fisherman gave us the key; ate baked beans and sardines for a week, and then a week and a half, because the storms had come and the fisherman couldn't put to sea, or he'd forgotten. And then the weather cleared, the sky was blue and we were swimming every day in the sea, down to our last can of beans, Dad down to his last cigarette, and we thought *what now?* grinning at one another like conspirators.

'What now, Rosie, eh?' asked Dad, brown face, eyes wrinkled from squinting, watching the horizon for boats.

But the boat came over the horizon and hoiked us off and that was the end of the story. When we got back to the world, Mum never really asked us where we'd been, and we never really told her, and by accident, almost, it became our secret. In later years, when things were bad with Mum and him and me, he'd sometimes allude to 'the castaways,' mention the gulls or beans or sardines or boats with a sideways look and a yearning smile. It's years since I thought about Lappay. My own years of lead have wiped that memory away.

3/ Aged twenty-two. Photo taken under protest, a month and a half ago. Graduation pic. A First in English Lit. A picture of a proud, uncomfortable girl in her best skirt, silly cap and gown, trying hard to look *ironic*. Someone must actually have sent this picture to Dad. Then comes this gusty realisation: that that person could only have been Mum – which means they still talk to one another – which means that, for all of these years, he might as well have been talking to me. And that's inconceivable.

My innermost tectonics shift and settle, sending little tremors to unexpected places.

I think too much about myself. This is a vice.

At which point in my reverie, Dad comes back in.

'Milk?'

And sploshes water onto two tea-bags, hooks them out, scalds his fingers. No teaspoon. Opens a flickery fridge with nothing else in, takes a quarter-pint carton from the door and hands me a cup of tea with bits floating in. I hold the mug in both hands and blow.

'You've not come because you're interested in gardening.'

'No.' I nod at the table, glance again at the photos. 'Lappay,' I remark, wistfully, and provoke a smile. I bask in the warmth of Dad's smile.

But the Hebrides is only going to get us so far.

'I wanted to talk, Daddy.'

'Yes.' He nods and sits at the table, sips his tea and winces. Milk's off. 'So let's talk.'

We ate sticky Chinese food ordered from my mobile and brought to us by an Iraqi Kurd on a motorbike who seemed to know my father well. We sat on the wooden chairs, one at either end of the table, and drank wine; and because I was nervous and talking too much, I drank too fast. Dad looked down at his mess of food for most of the time, and I couldn't see his face.

The Idea is good. It is the best Idea that I have ever had, and it warms in the telling:

– That Dad, then and there, will tell me again what he told me that day on the beach. That he'll show me again his endless film: that *thing* that wakes him every morning, interrupts his daydreams; that tale that loops around and around inside his hot skull and won't let him go, that makes him drink, and makes him angry, and made him unable wholeheartedly to make love to his-wife-my-mother, and eventually leave the daughter who he *(he said)* once loved. But this time we'll hear a few more details please, Dad. How did you come to be there in the first place? What did you actually *see* in the wreckage? Whose dying head did you hold, cradled in your hands, as you looked, baffled, around yourself whilst you waited those twenty-five long, slow minutes for the sirens? Did you save any lives? *Would you ever consider ... hmm ... going back there?*

– And that with all of Dad's knowledge, and my own life experience, my own story, I will then go there myself. The bang happened twenty-four years ago this summer – in six weeks' time. So I will speak to some of the relatives, and some of the survivors, who will tell me their stories. I will speak to the police and hear *their* perspective too. Did the bomber *really* die in the explosion? Who were his/her confederates? Why did (t)(s)he(y) do it? Why is the **truth** not known?

– And that then, perhaps, I will march with the relatives from the station to the church where they go every year to lament the loss of the ones they once loved, or the people they once were, before their slaughter. Perhaps I will weep with them. Perhaps afterwards I will go with them to drink and talk, and reminisce. Perhaps my Dad will sit at my side there, too, participating, weeping, even, and be healed by this, *my* intervention –

How warmly I had anticipated telling him my plan.

Dad crunches beansprouts and chow-mein, drinks thirstily to the bottom of his glass, cracks another bottle. I begin to talk. I still can't see his face. What a fool for a daughter this man has.

About half-way through the second bottle of wine, I become aware that mine is the only voice in the room.

Dad's plate is empty. He picks it up, carries it across the room, places it carefully in the sink. I have scarcely touched mine. But a glimpse of Dad's face makes me stumble. In fact, the expression on his face causes me instantly to fade out. I say something hesitant about the march of the relatives. I haven't got round to the ultimate and best suggestion – which seemed so fine to me when I pondered it in bed last night – that he might see his way to coming with me – but my words have become a stony track indeed, and peter out altogether. He sits. My mouth goes dry and I push my food away.

'Look, Rosie,' he mumbles, almost to himself, after a *very* long pause. 'You need to sort your own life out.'

'What?'

'I said sort your own life out. Leave mine alone.' This time he holds my gaze. Daddy's face has changed; Daddy's face is grey. Daddy is being *very* hard. He wears a long, bleak, frown.

'So you're not interested, then?' I say, my voice colder than I had intended.

'No. Forget it. Leave me alone.'

Dad's, on the other hand, is expressing exactly what he feels.

'Tell me. Why?'

'No.'

He holds my gaze. The thing is, the sudden change is, that Dad is now waiting for me to leave.

'Dad! I'm trying to communicate with you, here!' My voice yelps and swoops like a child's. 'What exactly has gone wrong? Daddy!' I lapse into Opra-speak. Faking it, somehow. He still makes no response. He just waits.

'Well … well, bugger it then…' Under the duress of his silence I try to swear, but it's still a little too St. Trinian's to be credible. I stand, pick up my bag, put it back down.

'Look, Daddy, please!' I say, a little panicky. I really *can't* leave like this. This is too stupid. I've waited so *long*…

Something about his silence, though, propels me toward the door.

'Right. Right.'

Stifling a sob.

But hung from a hook behind the door are so many woollen jerseys, scarves, hats and oilskins that I can't find the doorknob. And all his stuff falls down at once when I try to move it out of the way, and I'm scrabbling on the floor amongst odd pairs of my Dad's muddy wellies, trying to pick it all up, in order to put it all back, and it's this little irritation, together with his appalling silence, which breaks me.

'Look, Daddy, I haven't seen you for ... I don't know ... years ... it's like you've run away from me, like you're hiding...'

I begin to rant.

As I rant I pick up, one by one, these precious framed photos, look at them, contemplating my different faces and my different ages, and think for a moment about throwing them to the ground, longing as I am for the tinkling of glass, for violence, for some more tangible evidence of the rage and resentment that I feel.

'Okay, I'll leave you in your hutch in your garden with your booze and your fags and your vegetables and your *lovely happy, family...*' (this last at full volume).

It was *his* voice which first called me here, to search him out, but it is my mother's that I hear now – the same voice that I heard from under my pillow as a child in bed, listening to the shrill, broken, posh voice, directed at a pissed, silent Dad, who just *took it* – and this realisation, that I am now yelling and singing *just like my mother,* makes me *even* angrier – 'So, *Dad,* you can take your *fucking* ridiculous *floozies* and you can...'

At which point I stop. I run right out of steam. I'm just standing there in the middle of the little wooden room, in front of the door that I'm about to walk through, and I start to cry. I'm like a four year-old that's just peed herself and gone into total breakdown as a consequence. Standing there crying, whilst paralysed Dad watches me. Then I stop crying and sniff a bit. And then, when the coast's clear, Dad says, a little husky in the voice:

'Rosie, don't go over there. *Please* don't go.'

I shrug. I sniff. I blow my nose.

I go.

6

The Years of Lead (Cont.)

*G*ianmaria Forteventura *of the* Lega Anti-Violenza *of Bologna is sceptical that the truth about the bombing will ever emerge.*

'*Too much is at stake here,' he tells me over a latte, taken in the* Caffè Nettuno, *opposite the League's offices on the* Piazza Uffizi. '*What you have to understand is that despite their valiant words about the violence and terrorism of these years, the authorities have always been extremely reticent when it comes to actually bringing the people – the really responsible people – to justice. They get a few ugly sociopaths, frame them up: that's good enough. Doesn't matter whether it's the violence of the Right or the violence of the Left – arrests are made, investigations are launched, but when it comes to actually convicting anyone serious...' He smiles despairingly, hands up, palms out, in that characteristically Italian manner which says,* Well, how could it be otherwise...

Forteventura *himself is a product of these years. His father, he tells me, was a trade unionist active in* Turin *throughout the sixties and early seventies; his mother active in* Lotta Continua, *a left anarchist splinter from the Italian Communist Party. There is something very marked, very final, about his use of the past tense here, and when I ask him he nods, grows sombre.*

'*They were both victims of* stragi *too.' For a moment he loses his relaxed, urbane surface, grows serious and angry, and the day darkens a little around our heads. 'There were over eight thousand victims, in four thousand, two hundred and ninety-eight acts of terrorist violence carried out during these years. My parents make up just two. I am their only child. They were caught in the bombing of a peaceful protest in* Turin *in 1976. I was twelve at the time. They were protesting, as it happens, against the treatment of mainly right-wing political prisoners. A non-partisan demo.' He laughs, bitterly.*

'*Our left-wing terrorists used to go in for targeted assassination: kidnaps, shootings – mainly of politicians, the children of the rich. Our fascists, on the other hand, planted bombs. The reason for this is only partly ideological: the masses travel together and so are vulnerable to bombs; the powerful go alone in cars, and so can be picked off one by one. The Right has always had access to explosives, large amounts in dumps all over Italy, left behind by the Americans after the war for use against the communists. The Left makes do with hand-guns. You see, Italians are very pragmatic when it comes to politics.'*

But there is peace now in this country. There is a degree of political and social stability that wouldn't have been dreamt of only ten years ago. The Italy of today is a prosperous, normal country with a GDP similar to the UK, a health and educational infrastructure that is better, and an attitude to food, culture and fine clothes which we will never have.

'This organisation exists,' says Gianmaria, 'in order that we don't forget. We always forget unpleasant things in Italy – this is the Mediterranean part of our culture, and it's good. But not this. The reason that we do this unpopular work is to remind people, to make sure that they don't lose their anger and forget the dead. Because if we forget our dead, then our peace will be in vain.'

Visiting the offices of the organisation, there seems little possibility of that ever happening. Surrounding the plaster-board walls of the small, attic office are the haunting black and white photos of the eighty-five victims: photos of the diverse adults, children, elderly, young, Italian, stranieri, who happened to be in the station that day – with the words Non Dimenticare! – Don't Forget! written in a dominant red font below them. Despite the heat and the oppressive stuffiness, the rooms buzz with activity: three-quarters of the organisation's twenty-four volunteers are under the age of twenty-five; Forteventura himself is in his mid-thirties, and has worked for the Lega in his spare time for three years. They produce a monthly pamphlet, Proiettore! and maintain a high-end website detailing the activities and movements of known neo-fascists in Italy and elsewhere, with updates on police investigations of right-wing and other terrorist violence. This is a vibrant, highly dynamic organisation, run on air, devoted to maintaining the memory of this country's violent past.

'It seemed, almost from the very first day after the bombing, that the forgetting had begun,' explains Forteventura. 'On the evening of the bombing there were two separate calls made to the press: one, implausibly, on behalf of the Red Brigades, which was later

withdrawn; the other on behalf of NAR. *Four left-wing terrorist suspects were picked up early the following day – they had been under surveillance for weeks – but by the following day they were all dead by their own hands, before they confessed, say the police. Or suicided, as we say. They then conveniently let another forty-eight hours pass before raiding the known* NAR *hideouts. You'll be surprised to hear that by then the* corvi, *the crows, had flown.*

'In the week after the bombing, the area was combed by forensics for evidence of explosives. They said initially that nothing was found, but the report was suppressed. Segreto di Stato – state secrecy for cases of terrorism. Ostensibly for the protection of witnesses. But this was a forty-four kilo bomb! The Lega couldn't accept this, and in 1990 commissioned its own studies on specimens of some of the remaining rubble. We were distressed, but not surprised to find a substance called T4. This substance was found on every stone which was examined, after cursory analysis. T4 is an explosive material used by the allies, the Americans, in the latter stages of the war. There was a lot of it left lying around in Italy, as you can imagine. It was collected, spread around in many safe locales, in churches, NATO bases and private property. It was kept under the strict control of the security services. It was also the weapon of choice of the neo-fascists. None of this is secret, none of this information is hard to get hold of, but none of it makes any difference to anything. You see, we have forgotten.'

Forteventura speaks with quiet, dispassionate anger. Although clearly a man committed to his mission of memory, there is nothing fanatical about him. He is neither a conspiracy theorist nor a monomaniac. The office which he runs is relaxed, well-organised, with the level of humour and banter that one would expect in a hot office full of youth in Italy. What strikes one, in one's conversations with Forteventura and his colleagues, is their never-ending sense of amazement: that all of this happened, and so recently, and that the perpetrators of violence are known, and that some of them enjoy positions of power – and yet no-one seems very much to care.

'It is a kind of madness,' *he tells me, when I confront him with this impression.* 'We are so wedded now to stability, to being a normal country, that we will accept any kind of lie in order to avoid having to confront the truth. For example: of the fifty-seven right and left-wing extremists who at various times have been indicted on *charges relating to the Bologna station bombing, three of these have been linked to the security forces. You might think that this would ... I don't know ... interest people. But no. This is all forgotten.' He shrugs, chucks his hands, mimics indifference.*

Collusion between the security services of the state and Italian terrorist organisations, both red and black, has long been suspected. In the words of Roberto Cavallero, a 'stay-behind' operative working for the CIA in Italy after the war: '...I chose to work in and therefore infiltrate neo-fascist movements because I have a rightist background. But others of my colleagues worked in left-wing groups, using the same techniques. I had specific knowledge that many of the terrorists – both red and black – were acting on the basis of directives or suggestions from the secret services...'

Although secret service operators were indicted in connection with the bombing, in keeping with a long-standing judicial pattern their convictions were later reversed, other suspects went free, a few Italian espionage officers had their wrists slapped for muddying the waters and deceiving investigators...

7

Forteventura speaks with a quiet, dispassionate anger. Although clearly a man committed to his mission of memory, there is nothing fanatical about him. He is neither a conspiracy theorist, nor a mono-maniac. There is nothing *loud* about this man...

§

I am happy now. I have taken a small room in the attic of the *Pensione Apollo* on *Via Drapperie*, the tiny, winding market street in the ancient centre of the town. My room, indeed the whole *Pensione* – with its narrow central stair, its age, its sloping roofs and floors – is as I had imagined it had to be when I planned this trip, for the trip to be a success. It had to be an old place; it had to be a cheap place; I had to feel comfortable there. It must be as I imagined it, else my trip would fail.

I have struck up a friendship with the owner, Floria, a middle-aged woman in creaking black nylon who sang her Italian over her shoulder at me as I followed the shadow of her vast widow's bottom up the dimly-lit stairs to her room on the top floor. I speak my new Italian with Floria, and Floria responds, and this makes me almost shiver with pleasure.

'*Si, parlo Italiano...* ' I say to myself under my breath, into the mirror above the stained little corner sink, practising the accent, saying it like Floria. I have a small mullioned window with six panes of old, uneven glass and a view over a narrow street where pigeons flutter at dawn. At night it is quiet; by day there is a flower market, fish stalls – dripping *merluzzini*, twitching *scampetti, branzini,* transparent *bianchetti, polpi* with big, ugly eyes. I write the names of fishes in a book, say them to myself in my mirror. There is no traffic because the street below is narrow, and the only noises at night are the shouts of prowling boys and cats, chasing and fighting over scraps from the market. The church bells call in the morning. My room is too hot during the day to sit, because the sun beats directly on the red tiles of the roof and air becomes too dense to breathe by ten and opening the window makes it worse – but none of this matters, because I am busy. During the day I interview, read, simply walk the streets; in the evenings I sit in a café in the streets below and write up my notes, collecting my impressions in the journalist's ring-bound notebook which I bought, as a momentous afterthought, in a shop at the airport.

At night I sit and write my journal at the little desk in the bay of the window, looking out at the ochre-coloured wall opposite, composing my thoughts, trying to get it down, trying to find a voice and a version good enough to carry my idea.

§

I write:

> *Although clearly a man committed to the preservation of the memory of those, unlike my father, who didn't survive, Gianmaria...*

I stop, start writing again, stop. I cup my hot wet face in my hands and groan.

The truth is, you see: I'm not as happy as I had hoped.

I have this cold stone sitting in the centre of my chest, weighing me down, knocking against my ribs if my heart beats too hard, whenever I breathe too deeply. Dad. Yes. The things I said to him; the things he should have said to me. I try hard to put him out of my mind, back where he belongs, back in his garden shed with Cherry-Bee, but the memory of our last meeting colours everything I do.

It is the memory of my argument with my Dad that makes me so unhappy. Tomorrow I will shrug it off. I tell myself: tomorrow I will be just fine.

But it's not quite as simple as that, is it, Rosie?

No. No, it's not... says my unwelcome inner voice.

My room is too hot to work in, even when the window's open. The cats miaow and fuck, miaow and fuck all night long, and their rutting makes my head ache. I'm drinking too much coffee to compensate for my lack of sleep, and so spend the whole day with a headache, wired and nauseated.

I don't understand a *word* of what anyone says to me – least of all fat-arse Floria. Who has put me in this very hot room and charged me just a little more than I can afford if I am to stay here until the anniversary. And I resent this, though I try not to, because I have imagined a friendship with this gravel-voiced widow, and that's how it *ought* to have been...

Still not being quite honest with ourself, yet, are we, Rosie?
No. Not yet. Not quite. Give us a mo.
Okay.

I write:

> *Gianmaria is neither conspiracy theorist nor monomaniac. He is practically always serious, and in these rare moments when his hauteur cracks and his eyes do glint with something like humour, when he says something which could be irony, or even a joke, one's laughter is brief, one checks his face for confirmation. Is it all right to laugh, then? Is it okay? He has brown curly hair which he wears long, down to his collar, in a way which could never be credible now in Britain – where baldness amongst young men is currently the fashion. And piercing. Gianmaria does have an earring, and that's just about okay, but I strongly hope and believe that there is no other unexpected metal work there to surprise one, to take one off one's guard, as it were. His manner is curiously dated: he is courteous, though distant; gentle, willing to spend time with me, yet impatient of foolishness; he tries hard to understand my Italian, masks – just – his irritation, then we lapse back to English. He could crack me open like an egg; scoop me out...*

Just cut that last bit, will we?
Okay. Try this:

> *I still can't quite work out why Gianmaria, who is very far from being the kind of total div I'm accustomed to, is as patient as he is currently being with me. He suddenly seems to take me seriously. I am fraudulent. He makes me feel a fraud. Tomorrow we interview a man whose wife and daughter died in the bombing that I am trying to write about. The daughter,*

*who was seven, would have been nine years older than me
had she survived. The interview will be conducted in Italian,
which is a language I only pretend to speak. Gianmaria is
coming along. Why? Why is he helping me at all?*

*Like a child, I have kept nothing from him. In the first
moments of our meeting, as I stumbled through my (prepared,
Italian, crap) introduction, wishing he'd take off his shades so
I could get a glimpse of the colour of his eyes, he sat behind
his desk, reading something else. While my legs were turned
to Blu-Tac by the bright lights in his brief introductory smile;
while I reverted to being ten years old and got all hot and
confused in my attempts to impress, he was scanning his
e-mail and taking calls on his mobile. He gets a lot of folk
like me. I used up all my alibis all at once: famous step-dad,
writing prizes, editor of university newspaper, First class
honours degree, the Fifeshire point-to-point horse-riding
championships, the A-level results, distinction at grade four
on the piano, swimming badges, practically all the way back
to Brownies. Ummm ... God. Dull ... gabby ... cow... He
just yawned and yawned. Glacial. Distant. Bored.*

*But filleted by the man's good looks, I did my awesome
best. I played my last, best card. My Dad was a survivor
too, I said, and was rewarded at last by the first flash of real
interest. The mirror shades came off. (Brown eyes – almost
hazel.) What did you say your second name was? His interest,
snagged. But then, poor me, I had nothing much left to
say...*

So, how was that, then?

Bit better. Almost. But we're not quite there. Try again. Let's
hear the worst...

Okay.

I write:

*'It is a kind of madness,' says Forteventura. 'We are so wedded
now to stability, to being a normal western democracy that
we will accept any kind of lie in order to avoid having to
confront the truth. This is our national disease: we have*

fascist retired porno stars in our government, our prime minister is a corrupt newsman, an ex-cruise-line crooner who has altered the law so that he's not corrupt any more; our Christian Democratic governments for the last twenty years have been suborned to organised crime; we have no judiciary left with the coglioni *to deal with this, because they have all been systematically wiped out – but let us not be too disturbed, we are a normal western democracy... But let's change the subject, Rosie. Let's not talk about this any more. Let's talk about you. Do you have a boyfriend?'*

It is the middle of the day, they have no money to run the air con and the office is very hot. Gianmaria has lost interest in his subject. He stands, crosses around the desk where we sit, sits on the corner above where I am, looking down at me, arms folded across his chest.

I notice that he has some red in his brown hair. He has this habit of shaking his hair out of his eyes; running his hand through his unruly curls. He wears a ring, but on a neutral finger. He smiles at me. The dark brow lifts, his whole face changes. I have never seen a face so lightened, transformed by a smile...

'You are very young to be a journalist. And yet you are very good. You ask good questions. You are well ... prepared.'

I am automatically on my guard. I am a journalist: a serious professional. Beware of flattery! I attempt to return to the matter under discussion.

'Thank you,' I say, 'but can we talk a little more about threats to political pleuralism in the modern Italian State?'

'Ah, Rosie, bella, not until you answer my question!'

He winks, roguishly.

'Which question?'

'You know. Do you have a ... never mind.' He laughs, smiles. 'A girl such as you could never be alone.'

'No! No,' I say, 'I have no-one but my work, my devotion to finding out the truth... '

'I'm sorry, Rosie; forgive me. I have offended you... '

'Please, please, Mr Forteventura, you are sitting so close to me!'

The office is empty. It's lunchtime. Every day the others

go to the café opposite where they eat, meet friends, chat for an hour before returning. Gianmaria glances around us, checking whether there's anyone else watching. He leans over the desk, gently takes my hands in his, then, almost as an experiment, kisses me on the mouth...

'Mr Forteventura! I must insist...'

'You are so beautiful, Rosie! Tell me, please, put me out of my pain! Tell me that you feel ... something...'

And *what* do we say now, Gianmaria? Even if you *had* said that? Even if you ever, possibly, would? What do you say then, Rosie? That you are a lovely man, but no, sorry, I'm sworn to a life of journalism and celibacy? That, though I can't write two sentences without your imagined smile intruding, actually I'd really prefer to stick to the politics? That I long for you with a yearning I have never felt for anyone, but, no, I can't – I'm too frightened? That the warmer your smile, the colder my heart will become? That this girly you've met may *look* twenty-two, but as far as matters of the heart are concerned – why, she's only twelve? That she can't so much as *kiss* you without freezing?

It's too late. It's night, I can't breathe, my thoughts run around like a little mouse in a cage. I have nothing to say. I have a heat in my belly that won't go away, I am only half a person and I am homesick. I stand, fling down my pencil, throw away my notes, swear, wipe away a tear. It's *far* too hot for work. I have no concentration. I need to sleep. Tomorrow I will start again.

8

A nd by morning, as things turn out, I *am* better.
Brave once more, I take coffee in Floria's kitchen. Through
the hatch she passes buttered Italian toast and jam, and her boy
Toni, who's twelve, picks it up and serves me, chatting away about
football (I think) and I get about two-thirds of what he says. The
radio plays in the background: music and news. I eat off a terracotta
plate on an oily red and white checked tablecloth with pots of
olive oil and vinegar. At one end of the table in a stack is the boy's
homework; next to it, a pile of his Mum's glossies. There's an
ashtray, which is always full, but no evidence anywhere of a man.
There are no other guests, and these people are not simply out for
money: they are friends, and they want me for their family. This *is*
where I want to be.

I have slept well. Torrid, over-ripe dreams with a predictable
ending. Today I have a busy day. There's nothing wrong with what
I am doing.

And as I leave, refreshed, I warm to these narrow lanes with
their filthy, shitty cobbles; the cool air of this particular morning,
with its little breeze and the hope of an early summer storm. So
this morning I like the high-smelling streets, the scent of Etruscan
squalor; the old man who lives next door who every morning stands
on the step of his house with a hosepipe, hosing the pavement, the
cobbles, the dust and rubbish, the silver quality of the morning light
which glints through the haze, the pigeons.

'*Buongiorno!*'

He smiles, throws his hand up at me, splashing me with water,
half a greeting, half a waved farewell.

I have been here for two weeks and have begun to understand
the rhythm of the place. I know that today, Friday morning, there
is a flower market in *Pescheria Vecchia*, and I have started early,
clearing my head of the dark ruby thoughts of last night, to look
at flowers, to languish in their bright colours, to achieve the right
frame of mind for the day ahead.

It's eight-thirty. I have plenty of time. I admire a stall of wreaths,
think about ancient, brick-built churches, think how orientated
toward death these lively people really are, and wonder in the

same instant whether this is true? And who will tell me if it isn't? I exchange a smile with a woman of my age selling lilies and think about *her* life: to be selling lilies in a market stall in Bologna seems good; a life simpler, I imagine, than my own. I pause by a cart of sweet stock, breathe the mixed scents of thyme, basil, oregano, lines of pots of tarragon and other herbs too which I don't know. The woman there smiles at me and says something in a thick voice which I can't understand. I smile, move hurriedly by. The stall holders tip water over their plants and it drips between the trays and the wooden carts they stand on, marking paths and rivulets across the dry cobbles and disappearing between the stones. It's too early yet for the sun; the buildings surrounding the tiny square are tall, leaning in, and so we're in shadow here, all still well wrapped up, the morning air glassy. A man beside me lights a cigarette, breathes in the black tobacco smoke, argues a point with his neighbour whose cart stands too close to his, and has stood like that, too close, annoying him, I think, for twenty years.

We are meeting at nine. Last night I drafted my questions, made them solid, thought through the likely answers, my responses to these answers. I have nothing to do now other than prepare myself, be confident, be brave enough to face this man, and ask him what I need to know.

I wander under the arcades on the *Piazza Maggiore*, buy an English paper, sit on a bench, watch the litter in the square and the birds playing in the dust in the dry fountains, just waiting until I have to go.

Gianmaria is there and waiting. I ring the bell, hear his voice calling me up, find him there in the open-plan office, first to arrive, sitting at that very desk over which he'd had me, in my scarlet dreams of last night. He glances at me, and I blush and smile, wondering for an uncomfortable moment whether he's able to read my thoughts – conclude that, like most blokes I fancy, he probably can. I push on anyway, bold, as if it doesn't matter. He's wearing a jacket. Suddenly my Gianmaria is smart: Italian man with fine-looking shoes and well-made clothes. He looks about ten years older too, and ten years (even) better. He's smart. For my part, I've dressed down, tried to loosen up. Fatally. I'm in jeans.

He looks me up and down. I sense some surprise. It's a question

of respect, say his eyes. If in doubt in Italy, dress up. But it's too
late.

'So are you, ah, ready, Rosie?'

Scorn and sarcasm lurk, dangerous and close, behind that
question. I want to go home and start again.

'Yes. Ready. What time are we meeting?'

He looks at his watch. 'I said after ten. It'll take half an hour
to get there.'

'Let's go.'

'Are you sure?'

'Should I be?'

He raises his eyes, looks seriously into mine.

'You seem very committed to this story, Rosie.'

If it's a question, I dodge it.

'It's important. As you say, there are some things that people
shouldn't be allowed to forget.'

'Even English people? It's not such a big deal in your country.'

Scottish. Let it go.

'These things affect everyone. They're of *universal* concern.'

'Hmm.'

'I appreciate your giving me Mr. Galante's name, Gianmaria. If
you prefer I can go alone.'

He pauses, smiles to himself, shakes his head.

'Let's go, Rosie.'

He opens the door to let me pass.

Galante lives at the edge of town: far out via Saragozza, in the fat
belt where the bankers live and every second shop drips with pig
lard. A bus ride and a walk to get there. Gianmaria has no car,
and my budget doesn't run to hiring one. It should give us time to
talk. More time, informally together, away from the noise of the
office. I sit the trip out in anxious silence, paralysed by Gianmaria's
proximity, checking my notes, practising my lines, while he, half-
asleep, watches the street passing outside as we make our long way
to the hills above Bologna.

Galante's villa is on a hill set in large grounds surrounded by
trees. It takes us a little time to find an entrance. I had no idea this
man was rich. As Gianmaria presses the bell and a female voice
bids us enter, I grow nervous. My doubts grow as we push open the

door and make our way up a long brick path towards the pillared front door.

'Galante's family owned a tyre company,' Gianmaria had said. 'For years he was benefactor to the Families' Association. He kept the pressure up when everyone else wanted to forget. He's a bit of a saint. He's retired now, but he still knows everyone and everything to do with 2nd August. I'm sure he'll talk to you. He's the one you've really got to see.'

'Will he talk to me?'

'He's a sad man. Very private.'

Thanks, Gian.

Irrationally, I had imagined this man with an oily shirt, black hair, balding, thick hairy arms with Popeye muscles, developed over the years from working monkey wrenches. Danny de Vito in his *Taxi* days: funny New York accent, lovable fat guy. Easy. I'd imagined a flat in some poor suburb in the north – a younger second wife perhaps, smiling, gap-toothed, in her eighteenth pregnancy and embarrassed by her print nylon dress; a second wife, herself unable to fill, quite, the gap left by the first; a kitchen table where Galante the tyre-man sits with his head in his hands pouring out his heart to me. An overflowing ashtray like Floria's; chewy Italian bread; a Pyrex tumbler with the remains of last night's wine.

Not this long path, though, through these beds of hibiscus and camellia, these mature cypresses and lawns, the walls tumbling with ripe wisteria, the child's swing next to the swimming pool in the garden below, the fountain, the French windows opening from the rose-coloured villa onto the stepped terrace, down which strides this long-legged sixty-four year-old with brown cotton trousers, an ironed white shirt open at the throat with a red cotton neckerchief. A fit man, with pale blue, deep-set eyes, very short, perfectly white hair, a hand held out to greet us, but no smile.

'Don Francesco.' Gianmaria greets the man, solemnly. They talk together, he indicating me with his palm, says my name, the words '*Giornalista, Inglese*.' I try, hopelessly, to look the part. Brisk smile and a 'how d'ye do.' But Galante just looks at me – too polite or too saintly to do the usual inventory: no tit check, no bum check, no total all over parrot-puss check, followed by the all-inclusive invitatory smirk that most blokes do unconsciously – Galante is content to notice the important, simple indicators: my little age, my bad clothes, my apparent lack of basic credibility – then he simply shakes my hand, nods, turns to go back indoors without asking us to follow. We follow.

'He lost his wife and daughter. Like so many others, they were in the station, going off on their family holiday. Francesco Galante was delayed, by business. He had decided that he would follow them, after the weekend.'

Gianmaria had stood, turned to the wall of photos (the words in red, *'Non Dimenticare!'*) and walked the line of faces, pointing to one, then another.

'That's them. Her, and her.'

He had carefully pointed out a photo of a woman in her thirties.

But what could I have said about a black and white photo? She held a little dog on her lap. She was laughing at the camera, responding to something wildly funny that the photographer, probably Francesco Galante himself, had said to her, engaging with the viewer – me – in that uniquely poignant, lively way that those destined for short lives and bad deaths can have. And then there was the daughter. The shy girl in the blue checked dress with a finger in her mouth, a seven year-old coquette.

I thought, I imagined, that I saw the shadow of some kind of knowing in *her* eyes.

We sit around a low hand-chipped, rosewood table in the large room overlooking the terrace. Bricked floor with bright kilims. There are oils on the white walls – bright originals of sixties and seventies art; majolica tiles by the door and big window; a grand piano in the corner with music open on the desk. The place smells of furniture polish and lilies. I look for photos.

'*Mi scusi…*'

I fumble in my bag, take out my tape recorder, place it between us on the table. I try to find the Italian word for 'tape recorder,' stumble over a word that sounds a bit like 'magnet,' look at Gianmaria, who frowns and starts to translate. The word is *registratore* – nothing to do with magnets at all – that's French – but I don't imagine just at the moment that I'll ever need this word again.

Galante raises his hand, also frowns, says: 'It's easier in English,' in his perfect, smooth English.

'Oh. Okay. Thanks.'

He nods, sits back, waits for me to begin. I sit, watch the little spools on my Dictaphone going around and around, and wonder what I can possibly find to say. Galante, embarrassed perhaps, interrupts my silence.

'Which paper do you work for?'

'I...' am about to lie. To make something up. Something which sounds believable. Credible. Good. Gianmaria looks at me, waiting. I find I can't.

'Freelance...' I say at last, before the silence covers us again.

'Ah,' he says, 'freelance,' and nods.

'Your English is excellent, Don Galante.'

'I am an anglophile. I have worked in England for many years.'

'Oh,' I say, chatty. 'Where?'

'In banks. Italian banks.'

'Oh...' I say something wittery about tyres then, feeling unsure, stop. He stares at me with his empty face, his blue eyes unsoftened by my sterile chatter.

A lady, a servant dressed in black uniform with white starched pinnie, comes in with tea. Sets out china tea-cups, a white teapot with little roses on and a gold-rimmed spout. Matching milk jug, a silver sugar tray with tongs. A little dish with cut lemon, for Gianmaria.

I am finding that I hate this anglophile with his manners and *tea*. I am surprised at how much I can hate him, and his suffering, and his dead wife and child, so quickly. This is not how it was meant to be. I look around for ideas.

And there they both are, on top of the piano. Which of course is where they would be – not hanging from the walls, staring blatantly and pointlessly across the same comfortable room – nor, say, on the coffee table, muddled with the newspapers or the magazines or cups – but sitting on the piano, faces discreetly half-hidden by a pile of sheet music. And they are the same ones that Gianmaria showed me in the office. These are clearly the images that Galante has chosen of his lost family: the ones he released to the press; the woman who laughed, twenty years ago; the daughter with the finger in her mouth, the distant look in her eyes; the daughter who, somehow, knew. Every morning before he starts the day, Galante sits at the piano, sits by these pictures, plays something under the gaze of his family, often the same sort of thing, I think – a little Baroque: Scarlatti, tinkling music, difficult to play, made perfect by years of habit and practice. It settles him; readjusts him, first thing in the morning, to sit beneath these photos, to play for them.

Shockingly, I feel suddenly sick. I swallow. I attempt a question, but need to swallow again. This nausea is real. Not some game my stomach plays, but imminent. My mouth feels dry, my chest is tight. I attempt to find cover. To buy swallow time and hide the appalling silence I reach into my bag again, pull out my notebook, open it at my notes, my list of clever things to ask if things get sticky. Like:

1/ Can you tell me a bit about your wife. What was she like? What did she like to do? Try hobbies; clubs; friends.

2/ Daughter similar. Check – how old exactly was she? Was she at school?

3/ Tell me how you found out about their deaths. Were they amongst those who died in the primary blast, or subsequently from injuries?

4/ How do you feel about the bomber? How do you feel about the legal system which has failed to bring them to justice?

5/ Do you believe the theory that the government was implicated in the bombing? If so, why? What were your politics before the *strage?* Have the subsequent events changed your perspective? What do you think about the question of forgetting? What do you feel about the current peace?

6/ Did you marry again? Find out whether he has a girlfriend, look for photos etc. – Note to self: make sure you have a mandate for this question!

7/ Do you have contact with any of those in the police force who were involved in the initial investigation? Can you give me contacts?

8/ Do you stay in touch with other relatives of the victims? Can you give me contacts?

N.B. Don't forget to thank him. Bring presents for any second wife/children.

But none of this is any help to a girl who is about to vomit. I try tea – I pour for myself, rudely, watching the urine-coloured liquid shimmer and twist as it emerges from the spout. I swallow, burn my throat, run out of time. The grown-ups watch on, baffled. I stand, hand to mouth, try to say 'I'm sorry, I'm so, so sorry...' and rush from the room.

Into the corridor of a house which I have never previously visited. With a polished parquet floor – doubtlessly of the sort greatly susceptible to damage by bile acids. More of these bright, new-looking but I suspect ancient Kilims. A vase of lilies – neck too narrow to risk for my purpose – and also too many stems in the way, and dripping yellow pollen, the source of that heavy scent – which is making things *so* much worse. I try a door, surprise the maid making a bed in Signor's bedroom. My stomach muscles are contracting, my mouth fills, which means I have about three seconds to go, and the next door is my last.

Bursting in, I puke, mainly in the bath. Again, this time in the white, antique porcelain toilet with pale blue fake Ming dynasty style printing round the bowl. I stand, all the evil now gone, and think about the damage.

Which will not be simple to undo. I run the bath, let it empty. I do some scooping and dropping into the toilet. I flush the toilet. I look at the (marble, tiled) floor and remember something my Mum once told me during a lecture about stains, and realise that the situation is *still* not perfect.

I take a (white, ironed) towel from the rack, wet it, mop the marble floor. Never a mark. No-one will ever know. I flush the toilet again. Aware of the passage of time I look for a place for the soggy towels. A basket, for instance. The kind of thing that you might use for laundry, dirty stuff, sicky towels, just supposing for a moment, that you were an extremely rich, widowed banker ... but I see nothing of this sort. With this failure of the imagination, I place the towels back on the (heated) towel rail, try to smooth them out, hoping the maid will find them, blame Galante... I take a mite of solace from the fact that, whatever happens, it is unlikely that I will ever have to see this man again.

Crisis over, I return to my interview. Which is not going at all well.

The room has chilled since I left it. My Dictaphone recording yards of silence; my notebook, with its large and legible handwriting, still open on the coffee table, sat a dreadfully significant inch or two to the left of where I *think* I left it. Gianmaria looking at his feet, Galante staring straight ahead, the window open, the hot air shimmering. I sit.

'I'm so, so...'

'1/,' says Galante, interrupting me, in his tenor, smooth, perfectly-accented voice: 'she was thirty-two, very *gentile* – that means kind. She liked little dogs. That was her only *hobby*, beyond her family.'

I wonder what he's talking about.

'2/ She was six. She was very *nice*. She could already read.'

I begin to realise. I now occupy a place *beyond* mere nausea.

'3/ From the radio. I knew immediately. I was in my office. I went first to the station, which was, of course, quite impossible. The streets were ... jammed. Then the hospital, which was equally impossible. There were many hours of waiting. I like to think that it was instant, but I know in fact that this was not the case. I cannot talk about this further.

'4/ No feelings. I do not know who this man or woman is. I am deprived of even this little shred of comfort.

'5/ There was no *government* at the time. There can be no doubt that there was knowledge of the bombing by our security services. No-one, other than the perpetrators, can know more than this – because such information as there is, is corrupted by lies. I have no interest in politics, and less now than ever. I do not understand what you mean by *forgetting*: for me there can be no *forgetting*, ever. I have no *peace*.

'6/ You have no mandate for this, nor for any other of your questions.

'7/ No.

'8/ Yes, of course. I was the chair of *l'Associazione Famiglie delle Vittime della Strage* for fifteen years. I know all of these people. No, I don't think that I should give you their names or contact details.

'There will be no need for any presents. There is no second wife; there were no further children.'

All delivered with eyes looking straight ahead. More *quiet anger*, words which I could write down in my book if I chose, but don't. I switch off the Dictaphone with a loud *click*. Gianmaria, calm, looks at his shoes. I cough. Galante is waiting. I stand, Gianmaria shrugs his shoulders, stands too.

I turn to leave. Galante says: 'You forgot to say "thank you."' I turn again. 'You have also forgotten your book.' Which he lifts with fingertips and tosses back onto the table, where it lands with a snap.

'Thank you,' I say, hoarse, picking it up.

Then Gianmaria and I leave through the French windows, not another word said between us.

9

A nd now I am thinking, perhaps, that the time has come for me to go home.

Mid or late afternoon, I'm not sure quite which, but the heat is intense and I have a dreadful headache – brought on, primarily, by indecision. This little room in the attic of the *Albergo Apollo* is once more loathsome. The noise of the traffic is incessant. There's a man on the pavement beneath my window who never stops smoking, and the stink of his black tobacco snakes into my room, stinking it up like a guilty conscience. Last night I would have found this smell romantic. The noise in my head never ends.

I think of myself as someone who never gives up. I am a persistent, tenacious and ambitious person. These are qualities which I have discovered in myself, which I value. I have a lot invested in this trip/ my father-his daughter/ the slaughter.

But thinking about it all now makes me want to put my head under the pillow and sob – and this is what I would do, without any shame, were it not for the pillows here, which I must now acknowledge smell strongly of the heads of others; and confronting the odours of the hair of my predecessors now would, I fear, make me vomit once again.

This is how the disaster played out:

The journey from Galante's house back to the centre of town passed slowly. I was silent. Still nauseated. Very ashamed. The beginnings of this bad, bad headache.

Look, I thought:

Everyone with whom I have discussed this project, who has the remotest interest and connection with it, thinks it's rubbish. Apart from inscrutable Adonis on my left here, who once upon a time took it seriously. So go home.

I had thought that when it really came to it, this interviewing/ research thing is something that I would be very, very good at. I believed this deeply: a sensitive, intuitive, feminine interviewer who deftly navigates the fine line between friendship, journalism and catharsis. *Ha Ha Ha.* I am not. I am naïve and clumsy and offend everyone. So go home. Re-think. Everything. And *never again* wear jeans!

My research has run dry. My leads have boiled down to two: Daddy, Gianmaria. The first you squandered. Pursuing those of the second, just supposing there are any – which is unlikely – is unthinkable. So go home. Train as a nursery nurse instead. Go and work for Gordon.

I don't speak Italian. I make a tit of myself when I try. So go home.

Just go home.

On the other hand:

Consider those who I will have to tell, when I get there. The climb-down.

Consider Mum, who, in an epic gesture of trust, as a reward for daughter's First Class degree, funded this trip, its destination and purpose unseen, on faith. She'll need to be debriefed. She will almost certainly require a refund.

Gordon's *I told you so.*

Dad.

So all in all, everything considered, weighed up, balanced...

Conclusion: just go home.

At which point Gianmaria glanced at me again, opened his mouth like a fish and shut it. I looked at him, strained face. He raised his voice above the rattling bus.

'What's on your mind, Rosie?'

I gave him this silent, pop-eyed, care-in-the-community look. It's such a daft question, I can't immediately think of the answer.

He shrugged, made a *so, hey, we all make an arse of ourselves from time to time* face. Kind man. He shook his head, forgiving me.

But exactly what are we talking about here? I thought. This was no Sunday School picnic fuck-up. I haven't just bought the wrong bus ticket, or mixed the coloureds with the whites in a hot washing-cycle. No no no. This is vomiting in the bath. Not stuff you can just sweep under the carpet. This is leaving a towel soaked in sick to warm on a heated towel rack in July. Leaving your banal interview notes just lying there, where that kind widower with the grey blue eyes can lean over and read them...

'I think I'm going to go home, Gian.' This last was unplanned. But the words became true as I said them, my decision made.

Any warmth that there was, ebbed. That sympathy, that little sustaining kindness, squandered. Wretched Rosie.

'What?'

My voice became a little hoarse. A child's voice. I was frightened. I can't bear the disapproval of others. Particularly not *this* other.

'I said, I think I'm going to go home.'

'You can't, Rosie... You can't just go home.' He seemed almost angry.

'Gian...'

'Rosie, look: you threw that interview away. You turned into a kid, you made fools of both of us. But it doesn't matter, we can try something else. I'll call Galante, say you were sick...'

But by then I think he already knew that I was sick.

'Thanks, Gian. But you know, no. I'm finished here. Job's off.'

'But what about your father? The book? Are you going to just forget about it?'

'Gian!'

'Well?'

I looked straight ahead, wanting for the little row to be over. But Gianmaria wasn't finished yet.

'What, Rosie?' he asked, as we stood together. 'I don't understand. You had a project. A book. You believed in it yesterday. What's changed? You can't just give up!'

Our stop was just coming up. The *Piazza San Pietro* on *Indipendenza*.

I stood, hand on the rail, swinging. 'Gian, I can understand why you're so ... bothered. You've put a lot of time in. But it's *my* project. I can't do it. I mean – thanks and everything, but ... I can't.'

I scarcely know this man. Perhaps that's an excuse. Perhaps not. Gian looked fully angry now: big brown eyes flaring, his hand, resting flat over his heart, turning into a fist for moment, then relaxing again.

Other passengers were looking at us. *Get away!* I thought. *Run for it!*

I jumped off the bus but the man followed me, damn him, now raising his voice. He searched carefully for his words, found them beautifully. Very Italian. Exactly the right words.

'I took you for someone better, Rosie.'

I stopped, silenced.

'You insulted this man, who has suffered, and didn't deserve your insults. I thought that you were serious, and I gave you my time. Lots of my time. I thought that you were worth this effort, Rosie.'

'I didn't want your fucking *effort!*' I yelled, in this stupid falsetto shriek, trying to stifle my tears, my credibility dissolving in this always-fatal blend of rage and self-loathing. 'You're a patronising *arse-hole* and I never wanted your stupid *effort...*'

But he backed off then, thank God: his hands up, something of kindness still remaining, a smile now on his face – which was meant to soften the blow, I suppose, but it was that smile, at last, that finished me off.

'It's up to you, Rosie,' he said, shrugging his shoulders, hands up to quieten me, his anger stilled. I sniffed, turned my back and fled.

Back to the hot room in the attic. The second-hand black tobacco smoke wafting through the window. The headache. The indecision.

Perhaps it's becoming clear by now that I'm a bit crap when it comes to blokes. The evidence is becoming overwhelming. And I'm afraid that things in that department are coming to a head.

I roll onto my side, sit up, my cotton tee-shirt clinging to my sweaty skin. I put my head in my hands, wipe the sweat and hair from my temples, groan and snuffle, a few sobs emerging here and there. My nose runs with all those tears that have been suppressed; my eyes are swollen; my hair streaked with sweat, tears and snot. I have been lying down, motionless, for an hour and a half. Thinking: *This vile afternoon should soon be over.* But that's no comfort. There's still the evening, and when the evening's spent, the night. Then there remains the question of the next day, and then the day after that. I have decided, pretty much, to go home, but even with that un-brave decision made, I still have too much time by far to kill. A lifetime, in fact, of resentment, spent alone with my thoughts, which squabble like little rats in a cage.

It all needs to be sorted. *Now.* I stand. I pull myself together. I pull a long smile in the mirror, shake the tears away.

I shower. Dry myself, feel cool, take a long draft of water from the tap, pull on other, better clothes. A black skirt, wrapped around my waist, held by a tie. The tight white top I haven't worn until now. This day will end well for me, I tell myself. I'll make it so.

Back out into the narrow lane of the *Via Drapperie*, I pass the oily-headed bloke who's been standing in his checked shirt smoking under my window all the long afternoon and driving me nuts. But I smile, cheery, and he crushes his cigarette butt under his heel and scowls back. I don't care. The woman on the fish stall recognises me at once and calls out *'Buona sera!'* which means it's pretty late. I think of buying my boy a garland of fish, but the joke could too easily go wrong. No tricks and jokes. Settle instead for flowers. Be direct. Back to my market. Roses. Marigolds. Something.

It's cooler now, and from the shadows of the winding streets, from somewhere cool, there is a breeze now, which ruffles the paper that my thin girl uses to wrap the flowers. I am almost certain that the gesture that I plan is highly untypical for this country, with its layers of atavistic Mediterranean values. But I am nearly certain, too, that my gesture will be welcomed – by Gian, at least – and that the end of this day is a time to be brave.

A fat woman in pink passes me, pauses, looks over my shoulder at my flowers, sniffs, says *'Belli, belli,'* and her little pink mouth makes a heart as it smiles.

To the office. A short walk under arcades, through the cool evening. The streets here are too narrow for the local *ragazzis'* car and killing obsession to really get going. There *are* guys on scooters, there always are, but you generally hear them coming, with their shouting and their tooting; and I can skip onto the pavement to avoid them, and they leave me well enough alone. An old guy under some painted roofs plays an accordion – badly, wheezing his way through the remains of an Eastern European tune, with lots of blurred, badly-played quarternotes, barely really trying. I give him money anyway – half a Euro, whatever that might mean – and he halts his playing, smiles, tips his hat and shows me his brown tusks, thanking me.

I think of Don, here, all the time. I think about where he stayed, who he talked with, where he ate, where he drank, what this place offered him. I imagine meeting him – wonder whether we would get along, what he was like in these days before the trouble. I think about him: his time, how he spent it, however long it was, whatever it was brought him here, whatever it was that made him stay. I think about my father all the time.

A pause before the bell at the door. The *Lega* occupies the top floor of a minor *palazzo* off *Piazza Galileo*. Grandiose title. It's an ancient brick building, with weeds growing under the carved and decorated eaves. Moss grows on the rust-coloured pantiles and the ochre walls are smeared with generations of graffiti. There's a portal with a wrought iron gate, a courtyard, a pulley lift in a cage in the corner.

I ring the bell; a girl's voice answers. Renata? Gloria? One of the chicks that helps him. They're all girls in that office, I realise. But do it anyway. Don't blank out now. I say my name into the grill and ask for his, and the girl pauses – embarrassed, I suspect, but the lock buzzes anyway, the gate swings open, and for the second time that day I enter the lift, feel its bracing and heaving and squeaking as it makes its busy way to the attic.

I present my pitiful bunch of flowers, which work, wonderfully. He smiles. Second time that day. Seems … touched. Gentle. Charmed by my peculiar little gesture.

'I wanted to tell you that I didn't mean what I said earlier. I'm sorry. You didn't deserve it. You didn't have to help me. I don't really know why you did. I don't want things to end this way.'

He raises an eyebrow. Renata and Gloria, sensing intimacy, gather round.

'So … thank you. For everything.'

This is turning into a farewell speech. It's sometimes strange how these things play out. I try not to be too disappointed. But he's still looking at me as if he doesn't quite know what to say. I think: *after another three seconds of this, I will turn my back and leave.*

One elephant. Two elephants. Three … very … slow … eleph…

'Perhaps we should talk in private, Rosie.'

Yes!

I nod. I think I even go a little pink. Okay. Baby, if it's talking you want, you'll get it. Talking.

He gestures back towards the lift which waits for me still, metal cage still open, machinery silent.

'I will buy you tea. I know a place.'

'Okay.'

Renata and Gloria look pissed.

The place is a bar, or a bistro, or a café, or I don't know what; down some steps, off a narrow, cobbled, ochre-coloured street in the warren that forms the ancient heart of the town. It's called the Nightingale: *L'Usignol*. Above the door hangs a hand-painted sign, wrought on thick, cracked, oak: a picture of a plain brown bird with bright eyes, sitting on a tree, singing. A nightingale.

We leave the day, ducking our heads as we go down the steps into the dark bar-room. A long dark, narrow room with a sawdust floor and a black wooden bar down one edge. Old posters on the wall, yellowed by smoke, some behind glass. An old man behind the bar looks up as we enter; looks past us, smiles anyway. He wears dark glasses. It's plain that he's blind.

'Sammi!' says Gian.

'Gianmaria!' says the old man, with a strange, thick accent. *'Buongiorno!'*

We sit in a wooden stall at the back, below some steps which lead to a raised area where a pinball machine blinks on and off, bright colours, silently.

'Weird...' I say, weakly, as Sammi, who seems to be missing half a leg as well as his sight, stumbles and claws his way to our table, pulling out a ring-bound notebook for our order.

The poster above our stall shows a shadow of a man in a full-face balaclava, aiming a gun at a group of steel-faced soldiers in Tommy helmets. There's something very familiar about the image. Below, in green letters, words in a language which looks like Scots Gaelic. Below these, in English:

'The Derry Brigades salute the martyrs of Sunday 18th January.

Let your sacrifice not be forgotten.'

Next, behind glass, a black and white photo of a dead man: long hair and beard, emaciated face, teeth showing behind stretched back lips, bone-like fingers clasped over the spotless white tunic on his chest. He looks like a religious martyr; some kind of saint. The logo's in German, which I don't understand. The man's name is Holger Meins. That's about all that I get. I make a note to myself: *Who's Holger Meins?*

Beside that, a photo of a barbed-wire fence, behind which stand women in veils; murderous looking men with black and white skull caps. A *Star of David = Swastika*. Writing in a language that looks like Swedish; a date. Message pretty clear. Advertising was simpler in 1972.

Gian's eyes raised in a question. Sammi's pen hovering over the note-pad.

'I've no idea what the time is, Gian.'

He shrugs. 'Neither have I.' Turns to Sammi. '*Vino Rosso*.' I settle back into my chair. The evening is just beginning. I sense that it will be long.

'This place has a history.'

'You notice the posters?'

'"We salute the Martyrs of Bloody Sunday!" Yes.'

'This place used to be the spiritual heart of Bologna Rossa. Red Bologna. It's more of a museum now. During the war it was a meeting point for anti-fascists, then anti-Nazi partisans. It retained the connection. After the war it became a hot-bed for all kinds of groups. *Lotta Continua. Autonomia! Martello del Popolo.* Even splinters of the *Brigate Rosse* are said to have hung out here.'

'Anarchists?'

'Definitely. Lots of anarchists. Red and black. Pragmatists and idealists. Stalinists, Leninists, Maoists, Trotskyites. Pacifists, killers. They all mixed up, they all seemed to get along. The only thing that they had in common was that they didn't believe in the State and they didn't believe in God. These groups in the seventies, they weren't quite as separate as you might think. People would jump from one to another. It was often more fashion than belief.'

I smile. I prefer this Gian. This more relaxed man. Something has definitely, definitively changed. The magic of my gardenias.

'What about NAR?'

He laughs. 'What, the other side? The crows? Only God knows. Maybe the crows too. Maybe even they were sometimes here.'

'And now?'

'Times change. Now it's a museum. A lot of posters. A few tourists. A quiet little place.' He nods towards something very tattered above the bar. An inauspicious thing, red surround, grey-white centre, the broken cross too damaged really to make out.

'That flew above the town hall. Partisans tore it down when

the Germans finally fled. They brought it here. All this stuff's very valuable. But now it's all just hanging there on the wall, falling apart. Sammi won't sell them. Won't even put them behind glass.'

'Why not?'

'Because Sammi doesn't accept that this *is* a museum. Thinks it's all still real. He thinks they'll all come back. He longs for a fascist resurgence, so that he can have someone to fight against. You should ask to see his gun collection.'

All this said for the old man's benefit – who grins and shows a gold tooth and probably understands nothing other than his name. He pours a glass for Gian, one for me, deftly finding the glasses with the neck of the bottle, never spilling a drop. He places bread on a basket, a little oil, a little vinegar, a plate of olives.

'*Buon appetito.*'

'*Altrettanto.*'

'Now tell me more about your father.'

I take a long draft of this smooth red wine that Sammi's brought. Gian breaks off a piece of hard, salty bread, dips it in his, looks deeply into my eyes. The time seems right at last for Rosie to talk about Rosie. I have no fear.

'I don't know very much. He left when I was fourteen. He only talked about his time here once, the day before he went. I've always been curious to know more.'

'But he was in the *strage*. A survivor.'

'That's what he told me. He said he was the first one on the scene, after the bomb went off. He saw it all happen. I think he saw a lot of … terrible things.'

'I'm surprised that I've never heard of him. I thought that I knew everything there was to know about the *strage*. You should be careful who you tell this to.'

'Why?'

'You know he's a witness? Did he ever testify?'

I shrug.

'And now? What does your father do now?'

'He's a gardener.'

'In Scotland.'

'No. London. *Neasden.*'

'Neasden. It sounds beautiful.'

I laugh. So does Gian. Briefly.

The accordionist is back. Seems to be an old friend of Sammi's, judging by all the hand-shaking, the back-clapping, the laughing. Directed by the blind owner, he makes his way between the bar and the stalls, stumbling between them as if he's drunk. Stops at our table, grins, shows us his terrible teeth again, and starts to play. But better this time: perhaps with more certainty of a reward from us, his trapped audience, he puts more feeling into his dirge. But it's soft, sweet music to me, and the wine is already going to my head, and this time I give him four Euros in small change and a smile, my best. He seems aghast at the amount, shuffles away again, grinning and thanking me under his breath.

'You like accordion music?' Gian laughs – at my smile, my insane generosity.

'Yes. Not particularly. I liked *him*. I ran into him earlier.'

'Do *you* play anything?'

I shake my head. Funny question.

'No-one in my family plays. We all have tin ears.'

Gian raises his eyes. He says the new expression quietly to himself, as if he's memorising it. *'The Tin Ears.'*

'I wanted my Dad to come here with me. That was my plan, to see it all through his eyes. But he wouldn't come.'

'It's a shame. I would like to have met him. He sounds a very interesting man. Perhaps you could persuade him?'

'Not a chance. Not in a million years. He seemed really angry when I suggested it. We had a terrible argument. I said some terrible things to him.'

Gian nods at me, pulls a deadly serious face. 'You … *shouted* at him?'

I laugh – a little embarrassed. And after a moment, so does he.

'You do this a lot? Have arguments like this?'

'No. That's the funny thing. I never argue with people. I never, ever complain. I'm not that sensitive. I can usually handle stuff.'

'So, Rosie, that must mean that you will stay and finish what you've started?'

Maybe. Maybe. But I don't answer that one.

The evening is long. We share two bottles of wine, Gian and I, and start and finish many conversations. We eat well: salted bread, salad, tortellini, fish; drink the *grappa* which Sammi brings us, unasked.

We watch the place fill and empty again. We share our stories and our lives and at some point make that startling leap into friendship. And then, very soon, it's time to leave. And this is a moment that I have been putting off all evening. Actually, this is a moment that I have been putting off since I was about fourteen.

We pay. We stand, staggering a little, pushing ourselves out between the chairs and the table. We wave farewell to Sammi, who waves back, almost in our direction. We stand outside, in the hot air, breathing the night. I have that cold, scuttling feeling in my belly once again. But this, I have vowed, is the last time that I will ever feel this way.

'So, Rosie,' says this man who warms me so, whose occasional, hard-won smiles I am coming to love. He holds my eyes in his.

'So, Gian...'

'Thank you, Rosie.' He bows his head, a little, formal bow. 'I have had an ... enchanting evening.'

I giggle at that word. His use of the word, which is ... enchanting. But I can tell: Gian is not going to say the next bit.

'Thank *you*, Gian. For more than I can say.'

Pause as we smile.

One elephant. Two. Three ... very ... slow ... eleph...

But no matter how many elephants, he's *still* not going to say it.

'Gian...' I help him along.

'Rosie.'

'I would like it very much ... if you were to invite me to your house. Tonight.'

He never wavers, bless him. Never an anxious look. And I feel a rush of pure elation, just to have got these few words out.

'I thought that English girls were reserved.'

'They are. I'm Scottish.'

'I see.' A pause. Then: 'Rosie. I live very close to here. I have a little flat. It is my grandmother's really, but she lives away. Would you like to come back with me?'

'Yes.' No bother; no hesitation.

It's a short walk down dark cobbled streets to where Gianmaria lives. I stumble a little on the stones and he takes my arm, and I seize the day and put mine around his waist. We stop a moment

at a corner under a lamp, and he folds his arms around me and so
we kiss. I have never felt like this before. This is my first time. I'm
almost twenty-two. I lose myself in the warmth of that first kiss.
And it's not old mother crab that I feel in my gut, with her tight
claws, her pointed, scuttling feet and bright little malicious eyes,
but something new and warm which melts me, which makes me
happy. I look up at him and smile.

'I'm glad I met you, Gian.'

He says nothing, smiles a little, then nods his head across the
road. 'I live just over there.'

For die-hard militant leftists, Gianmaria's family weren't half
well-off. The flat is not as I expected it. On the first floor of a block
on the *Via Ravennese*. With marble staircases and brass hand rails
which someone has taken the time to polish. He opens a heavily
decorated oak door, steps in, snaps on the light.

I stand on a tiled, black marble floor, a fake chandelier overhead.
There's a wooden sideboard along one wall with a crystal bowl
on top, filled with cream-coloured rose petals. The walls are clean,
white-washed, hung with luminous oils, authentic-looking pictures
of saints.

'Wow.'

'I borrow it from my grandmother. It isn't mine to change.'

'No ... I love it. It's just not quite what I had expected...'

'Changed your mind?' Asked kindly. Offering me an exit. I'm
nervous, but it's nothing like usual. It's not the angry little crab.

'No. Have you?'

'No.'

I cross the three paces which separate us. I take his hands.
Squeeze them. Say, a little breathlessly:

'I don't do this often, Gian. You need to give me a little more
help.'

'*Cara* Rosie!' He laughs now. 'I'm a lazy man.'

'You're a good man.'

He shakes his head, takes my hand. 'Come with me.'

He leads me across the floor, through a white double door, into
the bedroom, where there is a made-up double bed in the middle, an
embroidered counterpane, thick hessian carpets on a wooden floor,
floor-to-ceiling shuttered windows opening out onto the balcony

above the street.

'We are both a little drunk, Rosie. If you like, we can shower first.'

I nod, despite the pounding of my heart, my dry mouth, my tingling nerves.

We go through a smaller door of the bedroom, into the bathroom. A shower in the ceiling, a drain in the middle of the terracotta floor, a mirror along one wall; bright lights angled from the walls, candles in bowls on a shelf which Gian lights one by one, then turns the bright lights off. The mirrored room is alive – a Pentecost of flickering lights.

'Okay, Rosie?'

I nod. Yes.

The choice of clothes, tonight at least, was right. Light things, easily removed, a minimum of straps and levers and zips and buttons. I am elegantly naked and so is he; he turns the golden shower taps and we stand together under warm water, examining and admiring one another's skins. I was nervous and drunk before, but the water on my skin, Gian's light, expert touch on my back, my belly, my chest, washes that away and as the water runs through my hair and face, and I feel Gian's lips again on mine, I'm sober once more, and yes: feeling good.

The shower off; proud Gian offers me a towel (thick, white, freshly-laundered) from the rail on the wall. Earlier memories banished, I take it; start to dry the hard body of my new lover, and he dries mine.

'Do you want to go next door, Rosie?'

'Yes,' I whisper, a little too harshly.

We sit on the bed. A little pause. Not embarrassing. Tender. I'm nervous. But ... okay.

'Rosie?'

'*Cara* Gian.' I try these words in *my* mouth; find that I like their warm taste.

'Rosie, is this ... how can I say it ... is this your first time?'

I pause before I answer. *In a sense. In a sense, not.*

'No, Gian. No...'

And I put my arms tightly around him. I squeeze him hard to me. I pull him down over me, so that I can feel his splendid weight.

59

It's three or four in the morning. There's a moon shining through the open windows, and it's quite cool. I need to drink. I need to think. I rise silently, trying not to wake the man who's sleeping at my side. Gianmaria. Mysterious Gianmaria, with his cascade of brown curls, his greater age and confidence, his flattering interest, his rough chin and cheeks where he needs to shave, the gold crucifix I found hanging from his neck when his shirt was off. A man who understands what I need and want before I know it myself. An elusive, distant man. A man who is kind, in so many different ways. A man who will harm me, I sense, if I let him.

His back is lit by moonlight, his skin is luminous, shadows form under the ridges of his shoulder blades. He is strong. At the moment, he is vulnerable. I could spend a night and a day and another night contemplating the form of this body: how the right arm lies across that indentation in the sheet where I lay a moment before. How that bent arm had lain across my chest as I slept, and how gently I lifted it, so that I could leave without him waking.

Silently, I go next door, drink some water, bathe my face; examine my new self in the mirror by the dying candlelight. I like what I see, though it could scarcely be worse. Mouth bruised and swollen as if I have been struck. The sweat has made rats' tails of my hair. Skin of my chest and neck red and raw. *Stubble-burn* is what I've heard them call it. But also: that look of grace in the eyes; that transparent quality of the skin which I have only seen in the faces of other girls. *Rosie my girl: you were fucked within an inch of your life.* I smile and my reflection smiles back, complicit.

So thank you, I think, as I pull back on my clothes, murmuring to myself something like a little prayer to the man that sleeps. Who, hearing my thoughts, turns a little, says a few words, sleeps on.

But proud of what I have done, I shall return now to the *Apollo*, put my stuff together, leave my room in the dead of night with the money I owe in an envelope on the reception desk. I'll go straight to the airport and find a flight out today. *'Sort your own life out. Leave mine alone.'* That's what Dad said. And, by this mysterious, indirect route, I think I can do that now. It's better. When Gian wakes, which will be late, he will be surprised to find me gone. He will wonder why I didn't leave a note. It will be a mystery for a day or two – perhaps he will even be a little sad – but then he will forget.

But I will always remember *you*, Gian. I'll always remember this mysterious lover of mine, whom I chose to leave when the loving had scarcely begun.

Part 2

10

'What?'

He catches his breath. He has run from the other end of his garden. He heard the first ring, cocked his head like a deer scenting risk in the breeze, dropped his tools, knowing in the instant of that first ring that there was something badly wrong.

'When did this happen?'

'This morning. Very early this morning.'

This quiet, well-spoken messenger, with his almost un-accented English.

'What happened to her?'

'She was attacked. It looks as if she was attacked.'

'Is she ... is she all right?'

Silence. The crackling of the ether on the line. The breathing of the man that has called him. Then: 'I'm afraid not. She's very, very sick. The doctor says that you need to come. Straight away. Someone at least from her family needs to come.'

'Bologna? I ... I can't ... I can't possibly...'

'The doctor said that your daughter might die.'

'She might ... die?'

❧

He looks like a tramp. Wherever he goes he draws glances. People notice him, murmur caution to one another, draw back from him as he passes. The air around him crackles with rage.

He jumps from the airport bus, strides across the lanes of traffic, ignoring the horns, the smoke, the heat, the mad risk he takes crossing like this.

With the torn leather jacket, the gardener's kit-bag over his shoulder, his soldier's boots and khaki trousers, he looks like one of the beggars from the arcades, sitting on his knees on a sheet of cardboard, with a dog on a string, a little sign: 'Ho fame...' 'Sto malatto con Aids...'

He leaps up the steps, piercing the crowd which recoils from him, enters the swinging doors which open with a hiss, looks around himself, cursing at the sky.

Scares the girl at the desk as he approaches. Breathless, asks: '*Cerco mia figlia. Dov'é? Si chiama Rosie,*' and the girl's finger hovers over the red button under her desk.

'What is her name? What is your daughter's *full* name?'

'Rosie. Rosie Macleod. She's English.'

Girl raises an eyebrow, pouts, checks a screen, still an inch off calling the guard.

'No. Not here. No Rosie Macleod.'

The man looking at the roof. Thinking: *She is already dead.* He swears to himself in English. He swallows hard. The girl is pinned to her chair by that look from his pale blue eyes. Just to break his gaze, she checks her screen again.

Then: 'Oh … Rosie … Telford?'

'Rosie Telford. Yeah. Okay. Fuck. That'll be her.' Leans right over the desk to try to see the screen. Security man has noticed now, comes a few steps closer, bringing out his radio, and the English man clocks this and backs off. 'So where *exactly* is she?' he hisses.

'Who *exactly* are you?'

'I am her *father!*'

The girl thinks for a moment. The man sweats. Breathes like a dog. Waits on her decision.

'*Reparto Terapia Intensiva. Eeentenseev…* The lift. Third floor. Follow the…' But the man has already gone.

She shakes her head, sighs, returns to her magazine.

While he marches down long, bright corridors following the signs. Stops at the secure door, rings the bell. A girl in a face mask and theatre greens answers, is startled by Rosie's father's wretched appearance – but softens when she hears his name: she's seen many torn men like him; she can understand. She handles him. She leads him gently down a corridor lined with cubicles, past the nursing station with its banks of lights and flickering lines on screens, opens the door with the name on the front – Rosie Telford – the wrong name, the one she chose. That choice which, massively irrelevant though it now is, he still cannot quite swallow.

But she is not the same person. Only the colour of her cheek remains unaltered. Hair's all gone, head wrapped in a bandage. A drain emerging from the bandage: thin, pink fluid. Mouth obscured by ventilator tube. Eyes taped closed. Chest and body covered by a sheet, which rises and falls with impossible, slow regularity. The clicking and hissing of the ventilator. Venous access at hands and neck, fluid pumped into her body. A bag containing urine hanging from a frame clipped to the side of the bed, the clear tube snaking from under the blanket.

He crosses the floor in two steps. Takes the free hand, clasps it in his own, collapses on a chair, holds her hand to his own, tear-streaked face, says her name – 'Rosie!' – twice; sobs.

The nurse sees all this – that pattern thus made: by the father, the older man, who weeps his daughter's name; the daughter, just emerged into adulthood, who will die; the lover, a few years older than the girl – the one who brought her in, who sits opposite now, in shadow, watching. The nurse wonders – *how did this all come to be?* But too busy to think, she leaves.

'So who are *you*?' he asks, lifting his thin face from his daughter's protective clasp, seeing the younger man opposite, who flinches at the sheer *hatred* which he encounters.

'Gianmaria. Gianmaria Forteventura.' Husky voice, tired man; been up all night. He stands, letting the light fall on his face, presenting his hand across Rosie for her father to shake. 'I am Rosie's ... friend. I called you this morning.'

After a pause – after two slow breaths of the respirator, whose flat music counts the tempo of this slow, angry encounter – Don takes the offered hand, barely squeezes it, lets it fall.

'What happened to my daughter?'

'She was attacked.'

'Who by?'

'I don't know.'

The clicking of the exhalation valve. The gasp of the concertina bag which fills, empties. The sigh as the girl's chest is filled again.

'She'd left my apartment. Checked out of her hotel. Three, four in the morning, I don't know exactly. I was sleeping. I woke to find her gone.'

You lying cunt, say Don's eyes.

The two men stare at one another, information hanging like gas in the light of the closed space between them. Don can see the man's age. Thirty-three? Thirty-five? *You're ten years older, at least.* His startling looks, the manner of his dress, his *seriousness.* Don nods, finally acknowledging what he has just understood. *My daughter is grown now, after all. She slept with this man. I have no right, at all...*

'I followed her. I was worried about her. She was ... naïve. I found her on the steps of her *pensione*. She had been attacked from behind as she was leaving. She was unconscious. A head injury.'

Rosie can hear every word that we say. Hearing is the last thing that goes. Sometimes they wake, even after the most terrible injuries, and they can remember every word that was said. Watch what you say.

'Some kind of weapon...'

He shrugs. 'Not known.'

'How is she?'

'She's very sick. The doctors are very worried...'

Something rises in Don's belly, expands in his chest, bursts in his throat. He swallows hard.

'How did you find me?'

The man called Gianmaria doesn't answer. Thinks a moment, fixed still by the implacable look in the eyes of the older man. Why *that* question? Why *now?* Then reaches into the breast pocket of this jacket, passes over an envelope.

Don's name and address on the front. British stamp/Queen's head. No frank. A letter which was never sent.

'Someone has opened this already.'

Gianmaria nods once. *Of course I opened it.*

Still staring, Don opens the letter, pulls out the sheets of handwritten paper, narrows his eyes, squints as he tries to read his daughter's scrawl.

Dear Daddy,
I don't even know what I'm supposed to call you now...

'This was written a month ago...' Trying to make sense of that fact. As he reads, his legs tremble, and he sits, frowning, eyes boring into the paper in his hand, which begins to shake. He stuffs the three thin sheets of onion-skin into his pocket. He puts his face onto his daughter's shoulder, longing to feel her fingers curling in his hair. The nurse enters, looks at a machine, writes something on a chart, leaves. There's a moment of calm. Gian, still standing, watches, says nothing. Don lifts his head then, twists his wet, angry face into his daughter's, hisses, 'You *stupid* girl, you *stupid* girl, you *stupid…*' and Gian, shocked, tries to push him back, and the father, inexplicably and dangerously angry, rounds on him, seems about to shout, or strike, but silences himself instead; turns his back, paces to the foot of the bed, looks again at the girl, his face red, his eyes masked by angry tears – then leaves. Gian, left alone, looks down at Rosie, smoothes the starched white counterpane, now marked by her father's tears; follows the man out.

It was a spanner, in fact, that was used. She was attacked from behind, but something – a noise, probably – had caught her attention in the instant before the actual impact, and she had partly turned her head so that the blow had caught her glancing, just off the temple. She hadn't seen her assailant; she knew nothing of what happened. She was immediately unconscious. Falling, she had hit her head for a second time on the step of her *pensione*. From the original blow she had sustained a fracture across the parietal-temporal suture, the overlying skin broken – technically an open-skull fracture. No intra-cranial bleed on the first scan despite the territory of the fracture; but very marked, diffuse cerebral oedema as a consequence of the secondary injury. She is paralysed and ventilated, heavily oxygenated and sedated, with a mannitol drip to bring down her intra-cranial pressure, which is threateningly high. Even when gathered in private, her doctors and nurses are sombre when they discuss the English girl.

Don stands a hundred metres up, on the balcony of the visitor's area. It's eight-thirty in the evening, and the sun is going down. He looks across the roofs of the red town, the silhouetted city towers, the leaning tower, the dome and the steeple of *San Pietro*; lets his eyes follow the arcades winding and climbing the low hill opposite, the *Santuario San Luca*. Watches as the sun sinks, as the blue sky turns to pink, the shadows growing long across the old town. He stiffens a little but doesn't turn when he feels the presence of the other, the man, his daughter's lover, who stands with him behind and to his left, sharing the view.

'Tell me what's going on, Mr. Macleod.'

Don watches the chimney swifts hunt insects in the early evening; specks in the distance, darting between the windows of the towers and the eaves of palaces. He listens for their thin voices which will carry to him across the still air.

'You read the letter. *My* letter. You already know.'

'Rosie talked a lot about you. She came here *because* of you.'

Don turns from the burning image of the town, stares at the man at his side.

'She came here looking for you. There was something that she was searching for, trying to understand, but she would never tell me what. She was writing some kind of book – about this town, its terrible politics, how things would have been when you were here; about you and her. I didn't think that it was very good. I didn't listen to her at first. I am a busy man. She told me that you wouldn't speak to her about it; that you threw her out when she asked. So she came here instead, looking – and then this happens. I don't understand, Don.'

Who stares deeply into Gian, thinking *Who the fuck are you to ask me...?*

'When she first came to see me, I thought that she was very naïve. She is certainly very young. But despite the difference in our ages, we became friends. Then ... more than friends. She was a very lonely person, Don. I hope that you don't mind my saying that. Rosie is very dear to me. She was very gentle. She was a very good person.'

'Was.'

'She *is* a good person, Don. But the doctor thinks that she might die. She needs your love. Not your anger.'

'You don't know anything about my *anger*.'

'But I know Rosie. I know her well enough to know how much you hurt her.'

'You only knew her for two weeks.'

'Three. And that's three weeks longer than you, *Don*.'

'Fuck off.'

He turns abruptly away from the sunset, disappears inside. Gian watches the town a little longer. He smokes a cigarette, blows the smoke across the face of the green hills; watches for the first of the street lights at his feet. He waits a time, until it is almost dark, throws the butt of his cigarette out into the night, then follows the father indoors.

11

It is as if neither wishes to be the first to leave. They sit silently through the night, one on each side of Rosie, each hunched forward on a chair, hands clasped, each mimicking the posture of the other, listening/watching for the rhythms of Rosie's attenuated life: the ventilator; the whizz-click of the drip pump; the rising/ falling of her chest; the alarms that jolt them, which the quiet nurse attends to; the mesmerising green flicker that her heartbeats make on a screen.

❦

They are sitting in silence when the nurse returns at six, this time rushing; the tired nurse, just about to go off duty, ties her hair back again behind her head, hair band in her teeth as she squints at illuminated electric numbers on a machine, shakes her head, presses a button, mutters something under her breath, resets the machine, frowns again at the numbers which haven't changed, turns to leave, hurrying now.

'*Che succede?*' asks Gian, urgent, half-standing. Don jolts awake, unaware that he had ever slept.

'*Niente … la pressione … chiamo il dottore.*'

'What's happening? *Che…*'

'*Devo andare…*'

And she's off. Don looks at Gian, who raises both hands. They both look at Rosie, sharing a last moment of her peace as she lies there, quite unchanged.

There are urgent voices behind the door, which swings open, ending this brief, quiet moment. The doctor pulls a white coat on over his greens, blinks at the same lights and the numbers, clearly still asleep, addresses urgent, angry questions at the nurse who answers rapidly, defensively. Neither look at the two men; neither glance at Rosie as they appear to argue, then leave. Don follows. The doctor is at the nursing station, speaking rapidly on the phone, impossible to interrupt; the nurse is gone, returns a moment later with two others – a man, senior, and a young man with a pony-tail, who may be a porter. The doctor finishes his call, awake and quick on his feet, returns to Rosie's cubicle.

'*Aspetti!*' calls Don, but is ignored, so follows back to Rosie. There is a crowd now gathered round her bed, gathering electrical cables, placing instruments on the cot, unplugging instruments from the wall.

'*Pronto!*' announces the porter in the pony-tail, standing now at the head of the cot, one hand up on each bed-head, ready to push. '*Andiamo!*'

'*Andiamo,*' calls the doctor, opening the double doors, making way for Rosie to be taken away.

'What's happening? Where are you taking my daughter!' Don shouts now, but is ignored by the serious, concentrating faces who manoeuvre Rosie, still quiet, still unchanged, still breathing, from the cell she has occupied.

Don tries again to follow, useless and angry at being ignored, now at the limit and just about to hit someone. Gian places a hand on his shoulder, steadies him, stops him, as they take Rosie away. It's *Gian's* hand that brings him comfort.

'Wait, Don. There's nothing we can do. Wait.'

Don sits again, stares, dry-eyed, at the floor.

❧

The tableau is the same, except there is now a void between the two men where the girl once lay. At the head, a corrugated ventilator tube still attached to the machine, now quiet and dark, ends, open on the floor. Drip-stands, three of them, empty, like abandoned cranes. A black and white tiled floor. Wires and leads coiled there and waiting. A thin layer of dust just visible in the new light, where the bed had stood. The *absence*. Gian sits still, eyes half-closed, hands clasped, head bowed. Don, for the first time in many, many years, wants to pray, but can't. Wants to cry, but can't. He is seized by restlessness; he stands, paces, sits, playing with his fingers, crosses to the window, looks at the town – a misty day, nothing to see – returns, sits. *Oh God. Oh God. Oh God.* But for Don, at least, there has never been anyone there to hear that cry.

❧

The doctor, sitting behind his desk, his face glazed and grey with sweat, stubs out his fourth cigarette, wishes he'd had time to shower. The doctor, aware that he stinks, looks from one to the other, wonders which to address: the younger, the clean Italian, with the sunglasses hiked above his forehead, half-buried in his hair, the stubble, the clear, brown eyes; or the older one – the smaller, English beggar-man with his weird Italian and piercing grief. He chooses the former. Both men clock that decision.

'We think that Rosie is going to live. She has been very lucky.'

He begins badly, setting the wrong tone for what he really has to say. He looks from one to another, waiting for some meaningful response which he can use to hang the rest of this dreadful speech. He faces the same wall of antagonistic silence. *One's the lover, one's the father. They don't get on,* Laura, the nurse, had told him. She said she'd spent the night trying to figure out the deal, but hadn't gotten it at all. Soldier on anyway.

'She had a blood clot. Putting pressure on the brain. They can appear very quickly. In this situation, they are usually fatal. We removed it just in time. We think. She is still heavily sedated.'

The father is stone-faced. He seems to understand, perfectly, but doesn't respond in the usual way to this kind of information. Perhaps this is cultural. Perhaps, for him, to be so *frozen* is to be normal. Perhaps this is the English way. According to Laura, he seemed more angry than upset or sad. But people are dreadfully unpredictable in this situation. If her father had been Italian, there would be tears and oaths by now. An Albanian would be swearing revenge, polishing his knives. He'd have brought in security before even beginning. If she'd been an African, there would be a tribe of mothers outside, pacing up and down the corridor, wailing and praying and slaughtering goats. It could be worse. It can always be worse. The lover is still the safer of the two. This is better done quickly. He leans forwards, giving some punch to the last words.

'But we cannot tell how she will be. When she wakes.'

The father nods, once, abruptly. The lover turns away. The doctor thinks he sees a tear, at last.

❦

In the relative privacy of Rosie's quiet and shadowed room Gianmaria does, indeed, seem to weep. Don can't bring himself to return to that claustrophobic circle, but dances instead on its periphery. Can no longer bear the presence of Rosie's lover; wants him *out! Now!* But he cannot bear to stay here himself, either. He can't cry, but can't stop himself from trying, and his eyes ache. He can't pray, but he can't unclasp his hands – he can't stop this pleading: these sterile, twisted-dry, hopeless thoughts which scurry around, gnawing away at the inside of his skull. He wants to bury his face in his daughter's hair, and whisper in her ear the words he used to comfort her when she was a child. But her face is masked by tape; her hair is gone; he can't remember any longer how it had felt, when she was a child, and he had loved her.

So, after three or fours long hours of this emotional coming and going, this doing and not-doing, being *there,* and yet elsewhere – with Rosie still utterly unresponsive and Gianmaria apparently asleep – Don drifts silently out, and for the first time in twenty-four hours retraces his steps, back down those clean, well-lit corridors, the air-conditioned entrance hall; is wafted through the automatic doors, back into the sunshine, the heat and noise of the late afternoon. Thinks: *How did I come to be here?*

Navigates by the falling sun, by the sextant of his memory, through dusty outskirts towards the heart of the red city. With neither planning nor any thought at all he follows the curve of the right street, finds the right, painted arcades with the same roofs and tiles and broken flagstones; turns left then right, finds the sign with the dun-coloured bird, the steps down into the gloomy interior – now quiet again – where he stands, blinking, sniffs, clocks the blind, one-legged owner who, hearing him, shambles up with a nod and a smile, then frowns.

'Hi, Sammi.'

'Ah...'

He sits in a corner right at the back, half-hidden, his back to the wall. Salty, sour bread. Last night's. The first gulp of wine. Wersh in his dry mouth; it goes to his head. He hasn't eaten for over a day and he's suddenly starving.

Don drinks wine, eats the bread and olives, smokes. He waits.

One glass into the second bottle, the door outside opens again, a glint of silver light, instantly gone, a shadow by the bar, the murmur of voices. Don's heart thuds. He waits.

Delicately, Gianmaria pulls the chair out, sits opposite, pours himself a tumbler from the wine, lights a cigarette. The two men stare, unblinking. A moment passes in silence.

'So tell me, Don,' says Gianmaria eventually, staring through slitted, cold eyes. 'Did you ever see her again?'

Startled, Don looks away.

Part 3

12

I should never have let things reach this stage, thinks Don, one afternoon in late August, 1979.

Picture him, aged twenty-one: long, sandy brown, unwashed hair tied back behind his ears, three days' growth on his chin, an earring in his left ear. Pale blue, bright eyes, white collarless shirt, baggy green army surplus trousers with 'anarchy' and 'peace' written on the knees – left and right, respectively. The same black leather jacket, twenty years newer but still looking its age. A light rucksack on his back; a small, coffin-shaped case with a brass handle in his left hand.

Then, twenty yards behind him, the woman who, in a year or two, he will marry, and who he will then eventually abandon – to almost everyone's relief. But this is all far, far in the future, and there's a lifetime of experience in between.

Don strides ahead, marching bold and arrogant down *Indipendenza.* Behind him, Julia struggles. She's being crushed under the weight of a massive rucksack; she's pushing her way through large numbers of better-dressed people, all going in the opposite direction, all irritated with her.

She always seems to be trying to catch me up these days, thinks Don, ungraciously.

She keeps knocking things over; keeps bashing into people and having to say she's sorry. She looks, and feels, inelegant. She's doing all of this for Don. She's very sweaty. She's having a miserable time, and she can no longer pretend. It's incredibly, unbearably, *fucking* hot. She wants more than anything to go home. Don has been aware of all of this for three weeks, but has done nothing about it. Feels *powerless* to help. He wrecks her with his indifference.

Young Don is still looking for adventure. Julia's cramping his style.

I don't love you any more, Julia.

Julia, who is approaching him now, sees him waiting for her there beside a traffic light, and in order to make *him* feel better, she summons up for him a suffering smile.

But actually, it's even worse than that. You see … you see … I didn't ever love you, Julia.

Guiltily, he smiles back, giving encouragement.

I just thought I did. It was an illusion. But now, you see, I'm really ... bored! Sorry!

Sorry.

You lying cunt.

Poor Julia treads softly wherever she goes, fearful of irritating him, fearful of making his moods worse, fearful of his scorn.

And when DID you become a bully, Don? How did you let this happen?

Julia treads on a pavement display of plastic beads. An Arab guy with no front teeth swears at her in sibilant Arabic, Julia apologises in English, and the guy shakes his head then ends this otherwise irresolvable conversation by spitting on her sandaled feet. Julia goes pink in the cheeks and says sorry again. Don writhes but doesn't intervene; then feels bad about this, too.

⁊

Once, it had seemed to him, Julia had some unique moral quality, like purity. Julia was *good*. Julia was a pale-skinned, finely sketched Leonardo, with a finely wrought, mischievous and enigmatic half-smile, more St Ann than Giaconda, more holy than whore – and for him, then, entrancing. She had a weight, a moral substance to her – some soul or spirit which Don completely lacked, and found magical.

Or possibly it was merely his exultant self-pity at being rejected.

Julia, unlike the others – the many others – that Don had bedded whilst frittering away his short and beastly youth, didn't give in too easily. In fact, she'd mocked him when he'd tried, and mocked him when he'd tried again.

They met at a party at a friend's. Don was playing – jamming in the corner with the little band he'd formed in the first months at university, whilst the little room, packed with students, wet with spilled Liebfraumilch, danced. They'd played well and now he was pissed. He'd been glowing with self-satisfaction when this girl had swum into view. Less sparkling than the others, perhaps; but more serious, with her dark hair, her light skin, her little hovering, quizzical smile which mocked. She had clever, bright eyes and a glass of fizzy lemonade in her hand. Not. At all. His type. But the engines of destiny whirred around, little wheels clicking, propelling Don to *her*, and not to her (much frothier, much *easier*, much more *suitable*) friend. Sal.

Thus changing everything.

'Don,' he'd said, ignoring Sal, hand thrust out, wearing his best, sequined smile. 'You're...?'

'Just leaving, actually,' Julia had said, glancing knowingly at her slightly disappointed friend. *I have no time for arse-holes like him*, being the meta-text. In spite or because of which, Don was caught. Don wriggled like a wee trout on a baited hook. He pursued her. He pursued her, for *months*.

1/ The gentle way:

A week or less later, he ambushed her outside the hospital with a posy of freesias, stems wrapped in tinfoil. She was standing on the street outside Edinburgh Royal Infirmary, white coat, stethoscope, tendon hammer leaking from her shoulder sack, beside a fretful bloke with a bush of curly hair and 'respectability' written all over him. The skulking boyfriend: easily vanquished by the scent of these deliquescent little flowers. The flowers that won him his first *proper* smile.

2/ The romantic way:

He introduced her to poetry. *I may seem dangerously chaotic to you, but really I am sensitive, serious, an artist...*

One Saturday morning in autumn, friends now, almost close, they were walking in the Edinburgh Botanics, feet squishing over mud and melting leaves. He was walking just ahead of her under the bare trees, reciting Marvell:

'What wond'rous Life in this I lead!' he cried, his metaphysical arms above his head, invoking the luscious blessings of the heavens.

'Ripe Apples drop about my head! The Luscious Clusters of the Vine Upon my Mouth do crush their Wine; The Nectarine, and curious Peach, Into my hands themselves do reach; Stumbling on Melons, as I pass, Insnar'd with Flow'rs, I fall on Grass –' he heard himself babbling as, tripping on the roots of an elm, he fell in grass, then looked up at her, appealing – *Fall too!* Patted the sward of damp grass by his side – *By me!* – and she laughed, but didn't quite fall.

3/ By means of a kind of accidental intimacy:

After a long, windy, after-lunch walk in the dunes near Arbroath. They'd had lunch with his father. Don now feeling the need to blow the stink of pipe smoke out of his hair. Don had sat in blank amazement as she had made common cause with the old grunt. They had medicine in common – he'd forgotten that, and so could speak in a language which he couldn't understand, whilst Olive, his father's receptionist, now *(and he still finds this one almost impossible to accept)* bed-partner, dished out silver spoonfuls of steaming mashed potatoes which tasted to Don of snot.

'You're *so* wrong about him!' said Julia later, taking the first bold step into new and dangerous territory. They'd never talked before about anything that *mattered*.

'How can you say that? He's my father! How can I be wrong! I'm the one that had to *live* with him!'

'You think we can't be wrong about the people we love? You just argued, that's all. Everyone argues with their parents. Most people grow out of it. Why can't you forgive him? It's stupid, Don!'

'I *don't* love him. That's the point. It's not even just him; you know that, it's the witch he lives with...'

'But your stepmother's lovely...'

'She's not my stepmother!'

'She's your father's wife, Don; she is!'

It's a wild afternoon. They'd walked for a mile and a half down the beach toward Budden Ness, heads down into the wind, faces sprayed with the rain and sea-spit cut from the grey waves. They'd shouted to make themselves heard. They'd shouted because they were angry. They'd taken shelter from the wind in the rough grasses, found a warm, dry spot beneath a sandy bank. Don found that his eyes were suddenly full of tears, no matter how he blinked them away, and ascribed those tears to the fierce wind howling above them.

'I'm sorry, Don,' said Julia at last, taking his hand. 'It's none of my business.'

'No,' he said, after a pause. 'It is. And you're probably right.'

This was the first serious conversation they'd ever had. Don was caught off-guard. Up until this moment, Julia had been a game. Nothing more. He'd thought.

And, mysteriously, this was the moment she chose to kiss him. A look of mystery passed across her eyes when she saw the tears in his, and in an instant the crystal of ice buried in her heart reached melting-point, melted, and she leaned forward over the angry boy, put her arms around him, and kissed him.

He had anticipated this kiss for weeks, and so had she, and in a moment their anger, his grief, her forgiveness, the many weeks of waiting, were sublimated into an instant's simple, feral lust; the walls of restraint built around them, already dry as dust and crumbling, tumbled down, and the two kissed and squeezed one another, hands running over each hidden part of their hot bodies, and they gasped, and gasped and ... stopped.

'What is it?' asked Don as she pulled away, lifting a hand from her breast, the other from her thigh.

'I ... really like you, Don,' she'd said, red in the face and breathless. 'But you go too fast. And you're not ... sincere. Most of the time you're just mucking around. I need someone serious. I'm sorry.'

'I *can* be serious...'

'I'm sorry...'

4/ So, by being serious:

By laying down for a season the drugs, by cancelling the reserve and the second-reserve girls, by not joking about her in private with his friends, by cutting his hair, straightening himself out, becoming someone else.

5/ By waiting:

Until she had finished her exams. By showing her that he could wait, and even then not rushing. By taking her away for a month, before she had to start her first job. She wanted to visit Paris, Munich, Vienna, Venice, Florence, Pisa and London.

They'd (finally) got it together in a cheap room in a hotel in St. Germaine which smelled of drains and french-fries, on a double bed with sagging, heaving, gasping, shrieking springs, where the sheets were crumpled and bore still the stains of the passions of others, under a Renoir on one wall where the pastel pinks and blues had faded to a uniform ochre brown, and a window on the opposite wall with a view over the Seine and the South transept of Notre Dame.

And now? Presented with an abundance of every square inch of the body of the girl who's occupied his dreams forever, his interest has started to flicker. On/off, like a dodgy telly.

Don: you are a dishonest, mean, lying, inconsiderate, ungracious cunt! (He deploys the word again, for extra effect.) *You* have *to tell her!*

'Okay, Jules?'

He starts to cross the road. The green man blinks. The traffic revs up to kill them. Jules stumbles.

'Oh, Don, *please* wait!'

You *cunt!*

''kay, Jules.'

They had intended stopping in Florence. Julia, starved of it, wanted the art, but on an impulse – his impulse – they had left the train two stops early. As they had left the plains of Romagna and approached the low foothills of Toscana, they had arrived in this smaller, less crowded place and Julia had said 'I thought Bologna was in northern France...' and Don, casting around for any excuse to get out of the *Uffizi,* the *fucking churches,* had said, 'Let's just check, then;' stepped on the seat, pulled down two rucksacks from the luggage rack, emerged out onto the station concourse.

A town with a reputation for violence. Don has always wanted to visit this place. Militant red graffiti on walls and buses. Stubby medieval towers, one leaning like a broken stick in the centre ('Fuck, this isn't *Pisa,* is it?') red pantiled roofs, the domes of churches.

Their budget is tight. They stay in a far-off hostel which smells of laundry soap and has dark stairs, and the owner scowls as they count out the money between them in advance, checking and double-checking the amount. They carry their bags – two rucksacks and a fiddle in a case – up the brown sloping steps, scraping the walls of the narrow stairwell, plunged into thick darkness when the timer clicks off.

A narrow double bed with a greasy counterpane and a yellow light from an almost powerless light bulb. The funny thing about this bedroom, which actually explains why they can afford it, is that it has no window. The other funny thing is the smell. It's somewhere a long way off, in the distance, but it's there all right. An animal? Vegetable? Just drains? But there always, unidentifiable and lingering, a harmony and counterpoint to their bickering...

Julia lies on the bed. Moans. Picks herself up, throws the bedding on the floor, lies on the mattress where at least you can *see* the stains, shuts her eyes again.

'I'm so tired, Don. I'm so tired, I can't move. Lie here for a moment.' Pats the mattress beside her. 'Just for a moment...'

'I'm going to shower.'

Don scuttles off. Has a cold shower under a dribbling tap in a cubicle off the corner of the stairs. Washes away the muck and the heat of the day, wanks guiltily, turns his face to the showerhead, telling it his troubles in a low voice:

'I'm sorry. I really am. It's not anything to do with you. We just want different things. I just don't feel the same as I once did. I still want to be friends...' *Yeah, yeah.*

The shower wheezes and spits. The pipes groan. Somewhere far away outside he hears someone laughing. Don dries himself, feels cold for the first time in weeks and likes it. Feels his spirits rise. *Now is the time. Tell her now. Don't wait. Don't practice the words, just say them. 'Better perhaps, for both of us, if we travel home separately...'* (At which thought his corrupted spirits lift a notch.) *Now is the time to do it.*

Pulls a damp cloth round his waist, gathers his clothes in his hand, climbs the creaking steps in darkness, finds Julia, book *(The Magus)* lying unopened beside her, sound asleep on the mattress.

Tell her tomorrow, instead. Tomorrow. Definitely.

¶

He dresses. Tee-shirt. Canvas trousers, the jacket. Takes the fiddle, which he has scarcely touched in three weeks; leaves Julia asleep.

He leaves the darkness of the hostel, blinks in the afternoon sun, breathes freely again. She will sleep for an hour. An hour to gather his courage together once again. Don, off the hook, sets out to survey the town.

He stops when he has found the perfect place. A narrow, cobbled street, *Via dei Poeti,* busy with travellers and tourists. There's a café on his right, folk sipping the first evening's beer, a thin waitress his own age with a glint in her eye, who he knows won't move him on. He's distant enough for his presence not to impose, but close enough to catch the ears of those who are susceptible. Drifting, slow-moving people mingle: youth with nowhere to go; passing lovers. The sharp scent of dope mixes with the smells of summer. A pavement arcade shelters him from the sun; the shops there in its shadow are all closing for the night. The sound of a drummer, playing out of sight in the piazza at the end of the road, gives him the confidence he needs to stop, to place the violin case opened on the pavement in front of him and stand up to an indifferent public. But this arcade will give resonance to his music. This is the perfect place. The fiddle tucked under his chin, his shoulder rises slightly to accommodate. His fingers adjust to the delicate weight of the bow between them, the way it springs into life when the hair grips the strings. He checks his tuning, tests the acoustic, the soft full tone, the gathering melody returned to him from the shadows of the wall behind. An elderly couple stop, expectantly. He winks and smiles.

It's only when he plays like this, exposed, public, yet at the same time anonymous, wrapped in his own private meditation, that his hopelessness – the slow, rambling chaos – leaves Don. At least, when he plays well. Sometimes, often, it feels more like a shovel there under his chin; a pickaxe handle balanced in the fingers of his right hand – then everything's worse, sometimes for months at a time. But despite those weeks off, today he makes music. It's the resonance of these ancient arcades; it's the sound he makes, which shimmers in and out of the arches, resonating with the black and white ground tiles; it's the ochre walls, the dark roofs with their worm-eaten ancient beams and the smoky images painted and long-forgotten, just visible in the eaves. It's something to do with the evening temperature of the air, the end of a casual day. It's the perfect place. It has something to do with the girl he has left behind, the sense of relief to no longer be lying; it's the joy he feels to be at last alone.

It's not as if he plays anything much. Doesn't need to. Just warming his fingers and his instrument, really; running through an arpeggio, testing and softening his tone; a couple of scales, reacquainting himself with the tender voice of his beloved: his demanding, and yet uncomplicated love.

He finds a tune: over-sweet, rapturous, syrupy. Wonders whether he dare. It's illuminated, vaguely Italianate-Baroque, emerging, as if already formed but buried, and waiting to be found. B-flat minor. A dangerous place to be for a fiddler who's out of practice, inventing it as he goes, exposed. Joyful, he goes with it notwithstanding; follows its tail, chasing the tune to its roots, the truth of it. Liking it, he plays it again; tries it in D, pings the melody off his open strings, spends a half-hour just lost in it, emerging every few minutes to acknowledge the chink of small change in the case, that hesitant smile and nod which is always offered too.

It was his mother that was the musical one.

His father, the family doctor from Auchmithie, had seemed an old man – even in his early fifties. A man with a thick tweed button-down coat and a shiny black leather Gladstone with drawers inside, with glass vials which chinked and were only ever glimpsed; a man who was always working; and when not, was sitting by the fire in the grand Victorian sitting room, smoking his pipe and drinking Scotch whilst the child, from the age of six or seven, stood in the curve of the grand piano picking out melodies on a quarter-sized fiddle while his mother clapped and sang and played with him.

She used to sing, she used to play the piano, but mainly her love was the fiddle: her own an old French piece, thickly varnished and dark with years, the name *Veillaume 1888* written in quill pen on the label stuck on the inner belly – just visible with the light of an angle-poise tilted through the f-hole to illuminate the dusty interior. Don had never been allowed to touch his mother's violin, but had sat and listened while she stood playing, worshipping in his childish way at the edifice of sound that she built – four strings, a bow, her two hands – head tilted, chin resting gently on the black chin-piece, a far-off gaze in her eye, a look of rapture in the boy's.

But his mother had grown ill. Over a month or two, beginning just after his twelfth birthday, when Don noticed those changes in his own body – his voice, his skin, his hair. When his face pricked with new hair and acne, his mother's had changed too – grown thin and sallow, bruised too easily and bled in the night – from her nose, her teeth. As if her body had become porous, leaking like soft rock so that in the mornings her bed clothes were coated in a thin watery blood which would never quite dry, and whose stains would never quite wash away.

She had died, thin and jaundiced, in a nursing home in Dundee; and after the manner of the time, Don didn't see her for those last few weeks of her life. *I don't want his last memories of me to be like this...*

He was translucent with loneliness and grief. His father, absent at his mother's bedside, had left no-one to care for him but a square-built medical receptionist with grey, scraped-back hair seconded by his father to the purpose of caring for the son, and quite inadequate to the task. She had sat in the kitchen downstairs drinking tea and ringing her hands whilst the boy sprawled alone upstairs in front of an unlit fire in a cold room which smelt of ash, doing his lessons, waiting for his parents' return.

His Dad had looked grim as he walked up the drive in the rain. Something of the colour of his skin had changed with his wife's: his own face had taken on that sallow, lemon-yellow tone. Don had known immediately what the news was going to be.

His Dad had said nothing. Tried, failed, to conjure a wet smile for the boy.

'I'm afraid that your mother...' Didn't ever finish that crucial sentence.

Casting around himself, looking for something, he had found it under the piano stool – the coffin-shaped wooden case with the brass handle which held his mother's treasure. He had laid it on the carpet in front of them, in front of the unlit fire, and opened it. Don had wanted to say – 'Don't!' – fearing in some sense that his father's touch would corrupt it – but had held his tongue. His father had opened the case; the instrument was shrouded in a sheet of thick, navy blue silk – something original and old. With his forefinger, his father had exposed an inch of the red-brown skin of the instrument, and quickly covered it again.

'She asked me to tell you ... she would like you to have this.'

This is mine I will treasure you ... he had thought all at once, all in a jumble, lifting it by the neck from its silk wrap, from the wooden case, stroking its skin, running his fingers over the strings.

In the intervening years Don has cared for his mother's gift, nurturing also the talent which prompted it. He sees himself as the custodian of the instrument, plays it as he believes it wishes to be played, and when he plays well, his music is a form of prayer. He treats his violin with more consideration than he does a person. Cleans and polishes it, wraps it in the evening in its navy blue silk bag. Knows its moods and seeks to please it.

He plays a long, golden thread of a note. Low D, sustained, *son-fillé,* second finger on the G-string, a rich, diminishing vibrato, and the music dies. He notices for the first time that it's dark. There's money, a little, in the case. He needs to get back to the hotel; he needs to finish what he has to finish. He's ready now. Relaxed. Balanced. Resonant and in tune. But now there's someone watching him.

'*Continua! Mi piace la musica!*'

Been watching him for a while. So let's play some more. See how things develop.

A dishevelled bloke, same age (give or take a year or two) as Don. Dirty. Ragged hair, violet-blue eyes, the right eye dead and turned inwards in a squint, a face with something of the gypsy. A bruised look. A slight man, thin, boyish shoulders, wearing a khaki soldier's jacket, second or tenth hand, itinerant boots. In his hand he carries a guitar in a hard case. A rhapsodic look on a face whose expression moves constantly: a shifting screen of moods, as if the face concealed behind it ten others, each wrestling for control. He indicates with an open palm the fiddle in Don's hand. '*La musica!*' Face settles into a copy of Don's own: for an instant Don sees himself reflected. The effect is … strange.

'Hey!' he says, startled, as if his pocket's been picked.

The other presents his hand to shake. '*Marco.*' An open, welcome smile. Don warms.

'Don.' Still suspicious though, he touches the man's filthy paw and withdraws.

Marco opens the case, takes his guitar, hangs it from his neck by an embroidered strap, picks a note or two, twists a peg, tries again, nods, looks at Don with an expectant smile.

'What?'

Don's little belligerence is ignored by Marco, who turns his finger around in the air, making little circles.

'You play, I play too. We can make more money together.'

But I have to get back…

'Play … what?'

'Anything.'

And that's how it began. With a few broken chords picked out by

Marco in the base and a crude first melody coloured with blues from Don – something new and sweet, getting slowly good. A few grating non-starts provoking the first of decades' worth of laughter, and then the pleasure of the first little money that the two made together. Beginning a friendship of no words; a strange shared humour conjured in an instant from the music that they made, and just as instantly gone. A collision and a merging of two voices and two talents. An understanding.

They spend an hour together in that first and favourite place, then another on the steps of the fountain in the *Piazza Nettuno* where the youth skin up, strum, and beat on drums, and where new music is welcomed.

They rest. They share a joint: powerful medicine bought from a guy with spread-eagled hair and a nose ring; bought with a few of their very own, earned, *lira*. They blow blue smoke between their feet, each feeling electric, and neither wanting to stop.

'I know another place to play,' says Marco, suddenly leaping to his feet, crushing the roach under his boot. He picks up his guitar, skips off without waiting for Don, who stumbles after, happy to be stoned, and led, for a change.

❧

That was the first time Don went there – to the cellar bar, half-hidden down some steps, marked by a sign: the picture of the brown bird painted on an old bit of wood, hanging above the door.

The first time in the *Usignol* they forge down deep through a dark crowd of voices and smoke to the bar and pull down a bottle of brandy with the handfuls of little money that they've earned. Two glasses filled to the neck and then they toast one another for their talent.

So who *is* this Marco?

It takes Don several goes to find out, what with all that noise and the limitations of their shouted pidgin: their Italian, French, English; their made-up, improvised Euro idiolect. And still, even after the entire span of their brief friendship, there were many details which were never made clear at all.

He is talented: rich with quirks and a twitching improvisatory skill which turns on a pin-head and leaves Don standing, gape-mouthed, wondering: *how?*

His nails are bitten down to ragged flesh, and when he plays, they bleed.

He smells bad. He doesn't wash. His clothes are rags.

His speech seems as scrambled and improvised as his music.

Don gets the words *sorella* – which he doesn't understand; *prigione* – which he does. *'Due fuckin' anni en prigione'* – two scabbed fingers jabbed under his nose to make his point, and a shudder. And *'eroina'* – a guilty smile and a shrug which refers, almost certainly, to the drug which put him there, the *punctate stigmatae* of which Don immediately sees when his new friend peels off his shirt, showing the old bruises on the forearms, some needle tattoos; or, just possibly, to the woman whom Marco is pointing at insistently, at the other side of the bar. *Per* his *eroina*. Maybe. But probably not. The fragments of his story, as yet, make no sense.

But for the moment Don ignores the seedier side of Marco, and fixes his gaze instead on this girl who occupies so much of Marco's constantly shifting attention. Marco watches her: who she's with, who she's talking to, what she does. It's as if the girl can never leave the arc of his predatory eye. Don wonders that she doesn't seem to notice this. Between the deep slugs that Marco pulls from his glass, the snatches of disconnected, often unintelligible conversation, the shuddering, deep tokes from the cigarette which he has just effortlessly stolen from the open packet in the back pocket of a German guy with a crew cut, who half-sits, arse on their table – his eyes never leave her. All of her gestures and movements – the pointed way she waves her hands, tosses her hair, throws her head back to spit her point or argue – are mirrored in the mirrors of his new friend's fox-like violet eyes.

'Now we play.' He points at the girl. 'Something sweet. A love song. Now. You. For *her*.'

Me! Jesus fuck. Marco sets his sights *too* high. The girl, his *eroina*, is deep in serious, frowning conversation with three others at her table. She's in her mid-twenties at least – long, wavy dark brown hair down to her shoulders, a cigarette in her long fingers which she uses for emphasis, her grey-blue eyes alive as she talks. *Where have I seen these eyes before?* She neither laughs nor smiles, but talks constantly, jabbing some point home to the older, bald guy with drooping spaniel eyes who sits opposite her. With each thrust of the red-hot tip of her cigarette, he flinches. Her voice, which is raised, carries over to them, and although the words are lost, the content isn't. It's *war*. She speaks rapidly, throws her hair back out of her eyes, waves her left hand, says it again, whilst bald man nods, flinches, raises his finger and grunts, trying to get in.

'Play her a love song. Something sweet.'

'A *love* song? You must be fucking joking.'

She's not my class, brother. She's simply not my type.

'No. Not *ah* fucking joking. We play. Then we speak with her.'

That simple, eh?

Don tries the cigarette trick – pulling one from the arse pocket of a pair of tighter-than-tight black Levis which intrude on his living/sitting/breathing space. It's a neat trick. He need never buy smokes again.

'So, how?' Leans forward to accept a light – but the cigarette trick must have failed – he must have guddled too much around Crew-Cut's slim arse for, feeling the rapid tug from his pocket, Crew-Cut has spun round with a dog-like ferocity, barking: *'Was machst du, arschloch!'*

This guy is really savage. Don, scared, flinches. He leans back, out of range, hands up, palms out, shrugging his eyebrows, trying to look innocent.

'Il mio amico pensa che il tuo culo e' un distributore di sigari…'

'Was sagst du?'

'My friend he think that German ess-hole make ceegarette come…' Marco leans forward, smiling with open-handed sympathy, and then in a lightning gesture tweaks the German's nose – who, enraged, leans across the table and responds with a bunched fist, but misses as Marco twitches his bright face out of the way like a little scarlet hankie.

The innocent party wriggles porpoise-like across the table smashing glasses and covering himself in ash and sticky beer, whilst his girl – a thin blonde chick in tight white jeans, pointed tits thrust up under a half-transparent cheesecloth blouse – giggles behind her hand. Two friends lift him by the shoulders, saying: *'Nein, Horst, ruhe dich…'*

As if a switch has turned, Marco loses interest; wanders off, leaving Don in the firing line of Horst's rage. Who fixes Don with a long, piercing, glare. Moving his arse from their table, wiping stuff from his tight white tee-shirt, he points a finger at Don, says: 'You. Esshole. Later.' Don breaks the gaze first, looks for the relative security of his dodgy new pal.

'Horst, you understand, is really my friend,' says Marco from elsewhere, ignoring the rising tension. 'He is *German*. He is our *comrade*. He is cool. He minds nothing. He *loves* me.'

'No, he doesn't...'

But in the far corner, *Eroina* has noticed the jostle: that spark of violence, the backing down. The whole café had sensed it; silenced for a second to accommodate the row. Now heads are turning back, conversations re-starting at a lower, muttered level. *Eroina* is calling: 'Marco! Marco!' – *To heel!* – in the kind of voice she might use for her dog.

'Maria!'

Maria frowns. Like two guilty poodles the two cross the floor towards her, fluffy docked tails drooping between their hind legs, weaving their way through elbows and leather to the table at the back. Maria shouts at Marco – high-pitched, high-volume – and Marco hangs his head in a pantomime of remorse. Don, shrinking before her rage, looks at his feet. Spaniel-face, Maria's companion, tipping the flame from a *Zippo* into the bowl of a Meerschaum pipe, looks at them with sardonic watery eyes, unsurprised.

'*Don't fuck with Horst, Marco, you ess-hole,*' she says finally in English, then looks, at last, at Don.

'And who the fuck is that?'

More alive, wired to a higher current than the others and the air crackling around her, Maria sits, radiant and sparkling in the centre of a darker, muttering group of men.

Now staring up at Marco who, however improbable it may seem, is some kind of friend – Marco being a smelly, twitching, feral old dog, Maria the opposite in every way – silky-sulky, fragrant, bright-eyed, energetic, beautiful. She finally half-stands and kisses him, once on each cheek, and Marco grins, forgiven.

'Don't bring your stupid friends in here,' she says in her bad English.

'He's a musician. He's English.'

'Scottish,' says Don, embarrassed and feeling very young, very foolish – and tries to shake her hand; her long fingers get tangled for a second in his before she pulls them free.

'Maria. I'm sorry,' she has the grace to say before turning back to Marco, tilting her head at the guitar. *'Suoni anche 'sta sera?'*

Behind her sit three companions: the younger, with black greaseball hair combed back in a duck's arse and a beautiful, glassy, elfin face; the older, the bald one, mid-forties, with the pipe, a collapsed, tobacco-stained face, sitting back in his chair and examining Don through half-closed, soggy eyes, saying nothing. Lets Don's offered hand hang in the air; lets it drop untouched. *Cunt,* thinks Don. Then the third amongst them emerges from the shadow where he has sat half-hidden beside Maria, and holds Don's eye for longer. 'Manu Boccaccio,' he says in a quiet voice – which rises, nonetheless, above the background café noise.

'Don,' says Don. Manu smiles. A diffident smile. An island in turbulent seas. 'I heard you play earlier, as I was passing through the *Piazza Nettuno*. I came back a little later to listen, but you were gone. I'm glad to have caught up with you. You play well.' He bows his head a little as he shakes Don's hand. 'Bach. The Prelude and Siciliana from the E-Major Partita. *Hai coglioni!* You have … balls.'

He speaks in good English, with a soft American accent. He is in his mid-thirties, has deep brown eyes, a fine, aristocratic face, black hair brushed back, a face too deeply lined for his years, a notched chin. He is sober, drinking mineral water, but the ashtray in front of him is piled with the butts of many white-tipped Italian cigarettes.

'You live in Bologna? I have never seen you here before. Are you … *del martello?*' he asks, with something like a smirk.

A space closes off around them, walling them off in a tight, yet transparent intimacy where the noise of the bar doesn't penetrate. They speak, somehow, without raising their voices.

'No,' says Don, not understanding, and confused by the steady gaze, by the man's film-star good looks, his patrician kindness. 'I'm just … passing through.'

Maria whispers something urgent to Manu, frowning and angry, but Boccaccio smiles his calm smile, nonchalant and ignoring her; squeezes her hand.

'A holiday…' he nods, waiting.

'Yes! No! I plan to live here,' blurts Don, trying to fill a silence.

'Good! Let's talk one day.'

What? Talk? Why?

'Okay.'

'*Ton!* Love song! Something sweet!' Marco is plucking at his sleeve. He has opened the guitar case and is looking at him.

'Please! Play!' says Boccaccio, inviting and dismissing them all at once with a wave of his open hand.

'Okay,' says Don, blinking, slightly disorientated by this man's attention. 'Tender and sweet, Marco, tender and sweet.'

The *Usignol* is Marco's regular last pitch, and this habit the habit of every night: he rises to his feet and stands up the same broken chords again, and a glass of wine and a cigarette appear as if from nowhere at the table by his elbow, and the noise around them diminishes. *Fuck*, thinks Don, suddenly exposed as the bar goes quiet: *oh, fuck!* But he tunes up too.

Don could not normally do this. His music is often hit-or-miss. He is too aware of how bad he can sound, how paralysingly thin his squawking can be, how disabling it is for a fiddler to be pissed. But there's something about Marco; something about the atmosphere of this place…

So he drinks some more of the wine, picks up his instrument, tries a note or two, thinks *oh fuck* again, plays.

And the magic, somehow, still works. Marco's telepathy, too. His instructions – *tender and sweet, Don* – merge with feelings engendered by the place itself: the darkness and the smoke, the faces which look up at them one after another as people start to listen, the last shiver of threat from the cigarette man, who still skulks angrily, waiting – and Don finds himself in a slow, sweet, soaring tango – unlike any of the music they've played before, but Marco adjusts to it anyway, and the thing builds in momentum and complexity and style until the *Usignol* is filled with their music and it feels to the two boys that their music will go on, like this, forever. Or that this moment which they are creating between them, which cannot be other than transient, will somehow survive them when they stop.

Or perhaps it was all illusion.

But there is calm and silence for a second when they *do* stop. Don thinks *that was special*. Then, *I'll never play quite like that again*. Marco smiles at him. There's no clapping. But even Maria-the-aloof smiles for an instant, says under her breath: 'Heh! Bravo! Bravo.'

Her three confederates return almost immediately to their talking. The first of many pushes through with a drink for Don, a hand-shake, words to the effect: 'That was fucking brilliant!' Don drinks. Don, too full of himself and too wired to be entirely safe, becomes shouting drunk.

Marco is lost in conversation with an emaciated Dutch woman with crew-cut orange hair, a skeletal arse, little tits and a tight simmet which shows off her needle tracks. Don has no money. He cruises drunkenly around the periphery of the bar, thinking the evening too young to die, yet unsure how to breathe life into it again. He considers pestering strangers for money or cigarettes, wishing that he spoke Italian or German – at least *one* European language – and is all unaware, or perhaps just dimly aware and simply not caring, that he is pursued by enemies.

'I love your music,' says a smiling, petite blonde woman with a bearable Prussian accent, confronting him suddenly with a cigarette and a glass. 'What is your name?'

'Don. You?'

'Stephie,' says Stephie.

Scenting the sweet smell of sex, he retreats instinctively into a quiet corner, under the platform where the pinball machine stands, letting the minx-like Stephie follow him into the shadows. Something about the shape of her hips under the tight white jeans is familiar. Something about her pointed breasts, the almost see-through cheese-cloth blouse, warns him, troubling something at the back of what remains of his super-ego, which is whispering to him with some urgency but being drowned out by a louder, coarser, more insistent voice, saying *fuck her fuck her fuck her*. Yet what is it? What?

'Horst! *Nein! Bitte!*' cries Stephie.

'Uh?'

He feels suddenly sick, and at the same moment more definitively afraid as, turning, an elbow finds his throat, the force of the body behind it pushing him back, a vision of those same, dog-like, snarling lips, the sound of Stephie screaming whilst his head hits the wooden wall behind him, ringing through his senses.

The elbow cracks right up onto his larynx, strangling him, and a lit cigarette is applied an inch in front of his left eye, and though his arms and legs are free, he knows that the moment he twitches, he will be blind.

He is sober, and suddenly alone. Though the heat from that cigarette burns him, he feels no pain; he tries to swallow but can't; he tries gasping for air, can't breathe.

'You. English. Ess-hole... ' says the voice of the man that will blind him, and behind that harsh whisper is the memory of a laugh.

'Horst!'

Then a squawk and a grunt; and a strange vision from hell...

...the whites of the eyes of his assailant; the bizarre sight of a gold fountain pen thrust into his nose and pulled sharply back; one hand placed on Horst's forehead pulling him away, the other gently twisting the pen, and blood gushing in a bright pink arterial torrent from the middle of his face, accompanied by a howling of anguish. Don pulls himself to his feet, says, 'Eh?'

Horst is standing, comically, with his arms spread wide, an expression of terror on his face; disabled by the power of one man and the nib of his expensive pen. Don's saviour whispers confidentially in Horst's ear; Horst nods, terrified, says '*Ja*' in a desperate and pleading voice, is then released, and scurries off, holding his now blood-purpled tee-shirt to his nose. Stephie has quite disappeared.

'Are you hurt?' asks the god that saved his sight.

'No,' says Don, mysteriously unhurt, though still blinking the stinging heat from his quite undamaged eye. 'Ah ... thank you, Manu.'

'Horst is not a good enemy,' says Boccaccio confidentially, wiping blood and ink from the blade of his gold pen with a handkerchief. 'We must apologise in the morning. You are shaken. Let me buy you a drink.'

*

He leaves as it's getting light. A cool, clear day. There's no-one else around as he emerges from the cellar, his mouth tasting of ash, head miraculously clear, eyes blinking. Hoisting the fiddle on his shoulder, he sets himself toward the dank hotel room, somewhere in the north or east.

It takes a pleasant hour or so, but despite his yearning for sleep, Don's in no great hurry to return to his life. He rings the night bell – rings it half a dozen times before it is answered by a fat bloke in a vest rubbing his eyes and looking at him with rage.

Climbs the greasy steps and is surprised to find the door unlocked. None of his stuff's been touched, but all of Jules's is gone. As is Jules.

Don braces himself for the note leaning on the mirror. It's not the screaming howler he'd feared though. Just:

> **Gone home. Don't follow. See you,**
> **Jules**

Oh. *Oh.*

❧

Freedom tastes of stale tobacco. Freedom is a headache and nausea. Freedom is being rescued at the very last moment. Freedom is new enemies, and strange new friends, made in dangerous places. Freedom is bitter, and sweet. Freedom is penniless.

But just for the moment, Don sleeps.

13

E merging from a long, disturbed, hung-over sleep, it takes Don an hour or two to adjust to the new reality.

First, he badly needs another shower. A change of clothes. A shaking-up, a brushing of teeth, a good gargle, a clearing-out, a new persona.

He shaves his face. Impulsively, he shaves his head. Carefully he packs his kit, sensing that he'll be a long time out of the ordinary swing of things. Pays a silent, un-lamenting farewell to the crap, dark, unlived-in room he didn't share with Jules; to its bare, passionless mattress; its bad smell.

Poor Don has several immediate problems. In the only really spiteful gesture of all the long years they will spend together and apart, the normally saintly Jules has left with the remains of their cash. It's actually all *her* money. But still…

But still, in an inexplicable act of mercy, she has left behind his passport. And even now, during this low moment of discovery, some shadow part of Don's subconscious acknowledges this inconsistency: the significance of The Act, only partly carried through.

She fucked me over! he thinks, raging.

Then: *Almost.*

So, dog-like, his personal live-in Satan wags its tale, cocks its little red penis, licks its master's ear. Don has correctly interpreted all this as a sign. Like: *come back you bastard, but only when you're well and truly sorry* is the only thing Jules could have meant. And, inevitably, Don's subconscious takes this as license. To do whatever the fuck he wants, forever, with the option always open to come on back home if he fucks it up.

Another life-altering mistake on poor Jules's part. She should have taken everything: his passport; his clothes; his toothbrush. She should have pissed on his underwear, too.

He leaves the hotel, skulking under the cover of the owner's long afternoon sleep; loses himself in a sultry afternoon.

He returns to the *Usignol*, first port, a place with happy, recent memories.

He asks the owner, Sammi *(Adib Shishakli)* – coprolingual

Egyptian, not yet blind but half a leg gone, having been shot through and through by an Israeli sniper on the Gaza strip in 1952, tourniquet left on too long, amputated in the field by an eighteen year-old Zionist/pacifist called Yol – for a job. Gets one. A bad one. Cleaner. 7AM sharp every morning. *You steal from me, I fuck you in the ess* – says Sammi, miming the act in slurpingly lascivious detail, drooly tongue half-out, swearing appallingly as always.

The job is not enough to live on, but it's better than nothing. It's cool, and besides, Don now thinks he knows how to sing for his supper.

He has an appointment at five.

The last thing he remembers of the night before: the wolf-like man with the violet eyes, gleaming and ready to feast; the Dutch girl, strung out now and barely conscious, supported on his arm, ready to be borne off.

'Where were you when I needed you?' he'd asked, aware of the ludicrous impropriety of this question even as he uttered it.

'*Chto?*' Marco had replied in the wrong language, further gone than he looked, face mimicking Don's face: his own terror of being left behind, his unendurably English-looking desperate uptightness. Appealing to Marco was like begging before a mirror.

'Where…? Forget it. See you.'

'Tomorrow!'

'What?'

'At five. Same place. *Arrivad…*' Marco, stumbling over the polysyllable, said '*tschus*' instead.

It wasn't what you'd call security, but it *was* something to get up for.

So there's an hour or two to kill before five. Using the very extremes of the last of his money – pulling handfuls of worn coins from various countries from the very bottom of the pockets of his canvas shoulder-bag: a half-torn Clydesdale Bank one-pound note, his lucky ha'penny, a marble he won once in primary school (*bully twa'*) – Don orders a double espresso from the thin-hipped and pretty waitress he'd noticed first almost twenty-four hours previously. He thinks how glad he is, how joyful a thing it is to choose this mad poverty, this freedom, as he waits for the jolt of the first caffeine rush. It's a shame he hasn't money for another, he thinks, moments before the waitress (Tania) brings it to him with a smile.

'You a musician, then?' asks Tania, in a surprising Mancunian accent, pointing with her cute retroussé nose at the fiddle case. 'No. Yes,' says Don, who sees his friend approaching from the other end of the street, finding their spot, laying out his gear, case open, guitar hanging from his shoulder, plucking a string or two, testing it against another as guitarists do, checking his tuning.

'How d'you know *him*, then?'

'Met him yesterday. I was playing his pitch.'

'I heard you two. It was brilliant.'

'Thanks.'

'You playing again later?'

'Yeah.'

'Where?'

In about five seconds, thinks Don, *I'm going to ask this girly out...*

Then, seizing himself firmly by the moral lapels: *Don't be a trunt. Just ... don't.*

'The *Usignol.* I suppose. D'you know it?' Don's two eyebrows arch like bows, eyes twinkle like little arrows.

She nods. 'Not really my kind of place...'

'Don't blame you. '

'*Ton*!' calls Marco, seeing them.

'Got to go!'

'You haven't paid.'

'Christ, you're right; fuck, sorry,' says Don, clutching at his many pockets, trying to look like a guy who actually has *real* money.

'Only joking,' says Tania, smiling, taking the piss.

The powerful thing he thought he had had with Marco is more than imagined. They greet one another with a handshake, a pat on the shoulder which is almost a hug, then, from Marco, on impulse, a real, full-contact bristly kiss: warm, Mediterranean-style macho – a style quite new to Don, whose genes come from way up north. They unpack their kit, Don glancing for Tania to see if she's watching, but she's disappeared inside. Marco sets up a riff – something quite radically different from the night before; Don makes a few false starts; they pause, skin up, then find a melody – something restless and fast, percussive, discordant, angry. Marco shakes his head.

They start again.

They break; Tania brings them coffee, water and a smile.

Marco: 'You and I – we work on this. We play every day.'

Don: 'Can't. I've nowhere to stay.'

Marco: 'No problem, *amico*; come and crash with me...'

Don: 'Yeah?'

Marco: '*Come no?*'

Why not?

Marco lives in a shit-hole. Don gags at the reek of the place.

But it's not too far from the centre of town; a place which, despite the obvious lack of facilities, has style. The stink: it's just freedom. Drugs. Laundry. This lack of order, this absence of any real need to wake in the mornings – it has its own smell, thinks Don, *which I can bear...* His friend shows him round the dusty shop-front in the quiet, southern end of the old town, which he had squatted a year or so ago with a mate, a maker of constructivist abstract sculpture – and also a scag-head who's back in prison now.

'You've got a sleeping bag?'

'Sure. Sure.'

A grimy smile. A handshake. 'Welcome, then!'

There's a stand-pipe in the back shop and a bucket, and the water still works. There's no electricity but there are candles, *and Italy, by and large,* thinks Don wrongly, *is warm.*

There are cardboard boxes taped to the window, with two hinged flaps if you want light. There's a camping stove. There are a lot of empty soup tins and packets. There are cockroaches which rustle in the night and do not die, no matter how you stamp your feet and crunch upon their brown shells. There are a lot of ashtrays piled with butts and twists of cardboard. There's a mattress on the floor in one corner with a sleeping bag eviscerated on top, opened and exposing its grey insides, curled there like a dead animal.

There's a lot of dusty floor space. Avoiding the tacks in the hardboard, you can pace up and down. You can play music. There's not a lot of clutter. On a plank and some bricks on one wall there's a bookshelf with stacks of paperbacks and mags.

'Where do you...'

'Shit?'

Don nods.

'There're places.' Marco winks, enigmatically.

And so, after a bit, Don settles to the rhythms of his new life.

𝄌

Six weeks later, on the first cold morning of the year, Don has another of his early starts.

There is condensation on the window glass. His breath hangs in spirals in the air in front of him as he groans, sloughs off his sleeping bag. He leaves his hangover behind with Marco, who turns and farts and groans, still curled tightly in *his* bag, snoring, holding his head. He hasn't washed in many days.

So Don stands alone this morning, cold and naked, rinsing his hair in the freezing water from the standpipe, yelping like a baboon; then his neck, his chest, soaps his arse over the bucket, slops the grey water out in the drains at the back of the shop. Leaves at six-thirty sharp, walks through a clammy autumn morning to the *Nightingale*, greeting Sammi there at seven. Who checks his watch, grunts a taciturn half-welcome.

Don slumps at the bar, pulls the day's first cigarette, hangs it from his lower lip. Sammi, who is basically a good man, sets him up a coffee and lets him chew through a basket of last night's bread, listening to his moans.

Seven-ten, and there's a clattering of mops, the rushing of water into the bucket, the beginning of an hour of washing of the wooden floor, the prising off of gum from the tables, the sluicing of vomit from the toilets as he holds his breath against the stink and tries not to think; the wiping of the tables, emptying out a hundred ashtrays, dusting and polishing the bar, washing the glasses, stacking them on the gantry behind while Sammi sits and watches, squinting through a half-closed eye, smoking, glancing at the paper, drinking grappa and coffee, grunting.

Generally, it takes Don about an hour of this kind of work before he's ready to throw in the towel for good. Always the same old thoughts:

8:00: thinks – *I am not cut out for manual work. I am an intellectual.*

8:15: thinks – *fuck anarchy and freedom.* Thinks – *I want a hot bath. I want a bed with clean sheets; a girl in it whose language I share. I want to go home.*

He's already hung up his pinafore, stowed the buckets, the vomity mop, the rancid cloths and pre-war dusters. He looks critically at Sammi at the bar, wondering how to ask for the money he's just earned, which he needs, immediately, to eat –

'I think I'm finished, Mr Shishakli... '

– wondering how many more days he needs of this, to scrape his fare home. Or, perhaps: *How long, in fact, would it take to walk, from Bologna to Edinburgh...*

'*Non hai finito fottuto cane d'un inglese...*' says Sammi ('Are you fuck finished, you English dog...') wrinkling up his nose at the lingering beery smell, the dust, the evident half-arsedness of Don's morning's work. Jerks his head, not bothering to lift his porous nose from the paper, recites: 'Wipe shit off tables up-a-stairs, clean the steps, sweep dog shit off pavement, clean up pigeon shit, then mebbe I pay you two pennies, *esshole...*'

Don, thinking already *fuck, that's it, I'm walking!* walks up those same mucky steps to the pavement, broom, mop, cloths once again in hand, stopping at the top for a moment to catch his breath, wondering whether just to throw the stuff away...

...but no. Today will be different...

You see, there's this tiny child-god hovering in mid-air, invisible above the little oleander tree growing from the pavement opposite, insect wings fluttering just so, to keep him steady enough to aim. God shuts one chubby baby eye, squints down his sights, lets loose an arrow...

Don, wincing at a sudden piercing in his chest, has recognised the woman sitting there alone at a table: the curve of her long neck, the shape made by her hair over her shoulders, the round shapes of the tips of these shoulders, her breasts, unexpectedly full ... he notices all of this. The curve of her back, the shape of her hips on the chair (*big hips? Or ... little hips,* he thinks). Her legs. The boots she wears. Don staggers with vertigo. Suddenly weak at the knees, burning inside with the first little flame of love, he wants to see more. So stands there foolishly, staring, sensing the passing of a marvellous opportunity *(she's alone! Alone!)* yet with not a clue how to take it.

She senses his presence and ignores him.

She is reading: a magazine, making busy notes in tiny writing in a ring-bound notebook beside it, her hand over her forehead, shading her eyes from the morning sun, perhaps, or the flaming gaze of the sexually incandescent cleaner. 'I'm *trying* to concentrate,' says her frown. These little wrinkles around her eyes, which disappear in tiny lines behind her dark glasses. Don would like to trace them to their source: to see these eyes again – what colour *were* they? – just once more, before he dies. An open bag lies at her feet, full of books. A pile of newspapers, unread. Manky polishing cloth at the ready, Don takes a step closer.

She squints over her shoulder. The magazine is a pamphlet, black and red cyclostat. The cover: a picture of a fist, all muscle, sinews, power, wielding an industrial sized hammer. *'Il Martello.'*

She shifts in her chair, using her back to try to obscure his view. Wanting a closer look, he cleans the table next, eyes drifting over to hers. Then, seizing his opportunity:

'Trade mag, is it?' he offers. 'DIY?'

Maria slaps the paper down. *'Fuck it!'* – forcing the ugly sibilant between her tightly-closed teeth. Don shudders at the scale of his arsedom, and at the sheer force of this woman, who's giving it to him hard now with her angry face, flaming him with her intimidating beauty. She gathers her things in her arms, stands, picks up her bag, stares at Don, then turns to stomp down the café steps back into the dark before he can even say he's sorry.

'Sorry…' he says in a voice too tiny to be heard, squished, like a bothersome fly.

Two steps down, though, Cupid intervenes again and miraculously she turns suddenly, takes off her sun-glasses.

'You … you were in the bar that night. You were with my brother.'

Violet, they are, of course. Violet, like her brother's…

'Your brother?'

'Marco. You're Marco's friend…'

'He's your brother?'

'I liked the way you and he played. He needs a friend. You're staying with him, right?'

'Yeah. I'm staying…'

She climbs back up into the sun. Her eyes. The little frown lines traced to their source. She smiles at him, puts her things back on the table.

'You're *Ton. Tonald.* I've heard of you.'

I like how you say my name.

'Yes.'

'I would like to ask you a little favour...' Said suddenly, quite business-like.

Somewhere off, like a startled bird, the whirring of wings; the bell-like, delighted giggles of the tiny, winged child-god.

'You see, my brother is very sick.'

That's an understatement...

'Oh?'

Don, casual as fuck as usual, has changed his mind. Swapped his day's pay – his lunch, his supper, the first instalment of his ticket home – for a double espresso, a cappuccino, two pricey little biscuits in cellophane wrappers which Sammi lifts from a glass barrel with a grand look – half-ridicule – *You arse! You can't afford these!* – half-admiration – *Yet you forsake your lunch? For ... the chanciest, most improbable fuck?* – restoring to Don in an instant, with this glance, his pride.

'We have always looked after one another. He is very ... vulnerable. I have to care for him. We have always tried to help one another.'

Maria sips her cappuccino – leaves a little froth on her upper lip, purses her lips with appreciation.

'You *care* for him?'

She nods.

Something hard and brittle shimmers on her surface, from which Don flinches.

'Maybe what I ask is unfair. I'm his sister. I shouldn't be his mother too. You're his friend, yes?'

'Yes...'

'What do you think of him?

'I don't know. I love him. He's a mad fucker.'

'Yes...'

The corners of that sad and serious mouth twitch in response. She softens.

'I love him too. A mad fucker. As you say. But he's not stupid. Don't make the mistake of thinking that he's stupid.'

'You have a little froth.' Head spinning a little, he hands her an immaculate little folded tissue from under the tiny cup, a picture on its corner of a little brown bird, sitting in a tree, singing its heart out. *Usignol.*

'Thank you.' The full smile blossoms for an instant, then disappears. 'Would you watch him for me?'

'Watch him?'

'I am very busy, Ton.' Indicates again the big leather bag at her feet: the papers, the magazine with the red and black fist logo. 'I run this magazine. I do a lot of organising. I'm very *involved.* I would like to see my brother every day but I can't, and I can't trust him to look after himself. He needs to be ... watched. He has suffered a lot; at times he...'

'The drugs?'

'You know?' Surprised. Then a hesitation: *Maybe you too...?* To which Don responds with his best, open smile – the one he thought he'd not be needing again, the one left over from years ago, kept from childhood to placate his Mum's friends.

'Not me! I'll watch out for him, Maria. Don't you worry...'

And unexpectedly she puts her hand on his, just for an instant – *Christ! She just put her hand on mine!* – smiles, says *'Grazie!'* and then looks up, startled – because there's a third, now. Manu. The handsome boyfriend with his black hair, the deep cleft in his chin – standing above them, smiling, looking down, *So glad you two could have a chance to talk!* – as Maria quickly lifts her hand from his.

'Don,' he says, plucking the remembered name from nowhere. 'You're good?' Meaning not 'good,' but *'well? alive? unharmed?'*

'I'm good.' Don tries to force a smile for the man that saved his life, but covering up all the same that little part of his hand where her hand had lain on his, as if seeking to preserve a little of its warmth.

'And ah, thanks again for...'

'No!' he says, raising his hand modestly, an enigmatic look directed at Maria, winking at Don. *Our little secret, eh?* Maria, irritated, doesn't return the smile.

'So! Maria? *Innamorata?*' Looking at the thin silver watch on his wrist...

'Yes,' she says, abruptly, gathering her stuff.

'So *ciao!* Oh, and *Ton?*'

'Yeah?'

'Let's talk music someday. Yeah?'

Music?

'Sure. Let's.'

Maria, interest gone, looks away.

Don watches these two enigmatic love-birds as they flutter off. Grinds his teeth and goes back downstairs to ask Sammi for a loan on his wages.

But this is how it is, every morning afterwards. 8:30AM, he's hanging around, hoping that she will be back. Sitting on the bar stool reading Sammi's paper, trying to chat, drinking coffee if he's got the money, water if he doesn't: waiting. It's his only chance in this new, squalid life to show off his better side. His intellect and style. His credentials. Waiting for an opening, he strikes a quite transparent pose: the leather jacket, the tightly-rolled cigarette on lower lip, *La Repubblica* open in his hand, beret on his head, toying with his espresso, a few practised phrases ready to roll off his tongue. Don is living financially and intellectually beyond his means. If only his friends could see him now…

'Maria!'

'Hey *Ton!* What do you think?'

Casually she hands him the latest of *Martello*. That first chill between them now long-dispelled, Don posts his serious revolutionary face and examines dense columns of prose and blurred black-and-white photos on the front page. Guys in tee-shirts with guns hanging out the windows of a big church. *'Siempre hasta la Victoria!'* reads a logo on a big flag. *'Baja a la Imperialista!'*

'Cool.' Then: 'Chile?' he offers, vaguely.

'Nicaragua. How's my brother?' Taking the paper back.

'He's … okay.'

Which is a total lie.

Quite a few weeks have passed, and the source of his sister's concern is becoming very clear.

Marco disappears from time to time, and when he does he can be gone for days. The cause of his absences is a thing not spoken of. But when he returns, in the middle of the night, half-dead, thin, slept rough, often bruised, stained and raked with vomit, Don sees that his new friend is marked for an early death. He can see it – this death – stalking Marco like a hungry shadow, and doesn't want to have to cope when it swallows him. Particularly, he doesn't want to have to tell his sister. Don spoke the truth that first day: he loves Marco – the wild and chaotic man, the simplicity of his foul-tongued, rough violence: this teeth-chatteringly wired man who never sleeps. Or, indeed, the suddenly calmed, kindly man – his new brother, who sometimes places his hand gently on his shoulder and steers him with the tips of his fingers as they descend the steps to the bar in the evenings for their first drink of the night, for an hour of pinball before the place begins to fill and it's time to play.

Don is caught on the tines of several conflicting commitments:

A week or two after that first conversation with Maria, Marco made him promise too. Drunk and elated after a hard evening of successful beggary, instruments laid down, having a smoke, committing more fully to the grappa which Marco pours for his friend in thimblefuls: glug glug glug, slugging his own back, he asks suddenly:

'My sister. She, ah, aska you to spy on me yet? Yes? No?'

'Ah, no,' said Don, caught off-guard, mouth half-open, clearly lying.

'She will. When she does, don't, yeah?'

'Sure. Of course not. Sure.'

So, the answer to Maria's question can only be:

'He's … okay. Yeah. Okay.'

Knowing, in fact: *The mad fucker's stopped his tablets, been gone for three days … he's probably dead somewhere under a layer of onionskin and fishbone, head-first in a wheelie-bin…*

'Good.' says Maria. Then: that hand on his again. 'Thanks for watching him, Don.'

'It's nothing… '

But just touch me one more time, I beg you…

And then there's the problem of her lover, Manu.

Lonely, half-destitute Don, who hungers for intellect, for company more *verbal* and a little saner than Marco's, is surprised to find himself a little stiff, a little uncomfortable at first when dealing with the open-handed warmth of the older, much smoother, gentler, much cleverer, lover of the woman Maria, whose barbed little dart is still lodged somewhere in his chest, perilously close to his heart.

Perhaps it is the remnant of some shame at having had his sight, face and probably life saved by such a delicate, finely-manicured man. Perhaps it is fear at the casually brutal manner of the saving: Manu hadn't even broken sweat when he'd disabled Horst. Don remembered still the terror in the German's eyes, his gratitude when Manu had let him go, and most of all the economy of effort: one twist upon the blade of the golden pen, and Horst had shrieked and bled fit to die. Or perhaps it was simple ingratitude which made Don flinch when they had met, early one Sunday morning when Don was walking alone in the *Montagnalo*, washing away with fresh air and the light morning rain the traces of last night's wine, watching the progress of two old men playing chess with large wooden pieces at a café table, comfortably smoking their pipes under a drooping parasol. He'd felt an arm placed lightly on his shoulder, was surrounded by a cloud of expensive and instantly identifiable aftershave, and heard Manu's soft, educated voice: 'Coffee, Don! Let me buy you coffee!' It was Manu, it seemed, who'd sought out *his* company.

And they play most Sunday mornings now. When the rest of the world is either half-asleep or gathering for church, they place the board on the unsteady wooden tables stacked outside the tourist café, play until the place opens, then drink coffee and eat pastries, feeding crumbs to the sparrows which hop between their feet. Manu plays a slow, strong, evasive game. Don, an intermittently brilliant, usually crap, chess player, almost always loses; knows enough too to know when Manu should be thrashing him, quickly, every time. Often wonders why he is kept alive for so long.

One morning in late October:

'She has such talent. Such ... *power*, so much beauty. She does so much. She achieves so much. In spite of ... so much...'

He is barely talking aloud; mumbling his oration in half-swallowed sentences, as if he is talking to himself. The words are left dangling like a baited hook.

'She is, it's true, an amazing woman...' answers Don, embarrassed and a little tongue-tied.

Manu treats him with a respect he doesn't deserve. He flatters

Don with his friendship. Scatters confidences like curious, brightly-coloured baubles in Don's path, to be picked up and examined, or simply cast away, as pleases.

'Why does she look after Marco in the way she does?'

'Orphans. Older sister. She did everything for him: brought him up. Looked after him like a mother. Force of habit. The boy's an ingrate,' says Manu, now a little distracted. 'Or perhaps it's just guilt. Check.'

'Why guilt?'

'Because he's the one that really suffered.'

'Suffered?'

'She is a very private person. Although I have known her for four years, at first as a student, then as her lover, I do not really *know* her, Don. She lives in my flat here in Bologna, and when I am here we spend every night together. Yet when I am away, our lives are separate. I have my work: my research, my travel and my students, and she has her paper, and her *friends*. We live in separate worlds.'

Don nods. Staring at the board, feeling trapped.

'Her parents were murdered, you know.'

'*Murdered?*'

Moves his knight to create space for his black bishop. Seeing the error in the move the instant that he's made it, he seeks to take it back, but Manu's hand is there before his. Without a moment's pause, Manu's black bishop fucks his knight in the ass.

'It's the story of her life. The thing that makes her what she is. She never talks about it...'

As the two finish their game, some images, fragments of a tale, are conjured for him by Manu from Maria's past:

Of an office, circa 1967, a guy with long curly hair, a glinting eye, an affectionate smile and a beard. He wears leather sandals on his dusty feet. Her mother: her long flat hair and her eyeshadow, her suede shirts and flowers. The bedsheet, tacked over the window, on which there is a blotched painting of a fist, the words in scarlet: 'Il Martello;' the circled anarchist's 'A.' Electric fans churning around the thick, smoky air. A hand-cranked printing press, the guy who was her father – a man who never grew old – turns the handle; her

111

mother gathers the still-wet prints from the cyclostat, gently, so as not to blur the print. They murmur affectionately to one another. He glances at his watch. It's growing late.

(A gust of wind blows over a parasol at the next table, dragging it a yard or two across the concrete café floor. A waiter drops a tray with a crash that makes Don flinch, and the chess pieces are scattered on the green-painted wooden table before their game is ended. The king and queen and the great pieces roll across the board; the little pawns fall between the slats and get lost amongst the ash at their feet. Manu says *'ecco l'autunno…'* and shrugs, and continues with his sad tale.)

The aftermath of a bombing. The perpetrator lies dying under a heavy doorframe, the glass of which has shattered outwards with the blast. His confederates have escaped – the fire which will consume the building will destroy all evidence of their involvement, and so they will never be caught. There is blood on the floor. The room is already filling with suffocating black smoke; a flame curls around the table leg; the sheet tacked across the window catches light, and there is a moan from the floor, rapidly choked off. Maria's father is already dead. Her mother will die in hospital within a week, stripped of her skin. Their children, thank God, are both at home.

The daughter, aged ten, over-burdened for her years with responsibilities, thin and tall, dressed by her impoverished parents in clothes too large and too adult, sits reading. Her little brother plays at her feet. Five and a half, wild-child and one of God's innocents, clearly – for despite his energy and cunning, his mischief, his thieving, the simian confidence with which he climbs or wriggles free, his gift of mimicry and his musical ear, he doesn't yet talk.

There is an urgent knocking on the door downstairs, and instinctively the two children are silent, Maria's hands clasped over her brother's mouth in case he squeals. She has been taught not to answer the door when, as is often the case, their parents are away. The hard knocking again, some adult voices, then silence. It is a day or two before the two children are found…

'It would be better if you don't tell Maria that I have told you all of this. I have told you too much. She is a private person. She prefers for these things not to be widely known.'

From the beginning there has been something clandestine about these meetings: the time, Sunday morning, when people sleep; the place, a park frequented by no-one but the old, and occasional tourists; the games – a private game of chess between two friends, who talk, in low voices; the subject of their talk – which tends always to the intimate, the tender, and the secret, as if Manu needed to unburden himself of these private things. Don is flattered. Although Manu is quite unlike any other of his close or intimate friends, and seems in all other respects quite un-needy, he responds, thinking:

He tells me this because I am anonymous; because he knows it will go no further; because he sees me as a friend.

Don is flattered.

'I understand.'

'Check. Mate.'

'Well played.'

Was it fuck.

They shake hands.

❧

Usually, Don would hate someone like Maria. So committed. So fiery-icy. So *serious.* So morally unassailable. His first impression was correct – she's *not his type.*

'…The autonomous organisations *cannot* ignore the challenges posed by leftist feminist organisations such as *Rivolta Femminile,* or *Lotta Femminista* – the fate of the 1977 youth movement – remember? – teaches us nothing if not the need to harness *every* element of protest, wherever it is found, if we are not to become *irrelevant,* if the whole concept of workers' autonomy and *praxis* is not to be consigned to the dustbin of…'

Don can pick out only fragments and phrases, clichés which sound the same to him in *any* language; odd rocks and pebbles in the white flood of Maria's long discourse.

They have been joined by the older guy, the one who'd sat with Maria the first night: the pipe smoker with the watery eyes and the pallid face – he's just passing, has taken a coffee, said something in a mumble that Don didn't quite catch. Now Maria jabs her fingers

113

at him, narrow, bright eyes, voice high and angry. He's smiling quietly into his little clipped beard, a patronising twinkle in his washed-out eyes, the blue smoke rising and twisting like serpents from the bowl of his pipe.

'…you know as well as I, Maria, how peripheral these issues are. How the distraction of *particularism* threatens to undermine the true struggle, which is the universal political and economic struggle by the *operai* for the ownership of the means of production. This is irrelevant *deviationism…*'

'…Abortion? Family planning? Rape? You call these *irrelevant*? Deviationism?'

The old git chuckles and smiles and shakes his head and waves them farewell as he leaves.

'*Esshole! Esshole! ESSHOLE!*' says Maria, her hands now fists pounding the table, her head in her hands, black curls spilling between her fingers. Don offers her a hankie to wipe away these tears of rage.

'So why do you bother talking to him?'

'What? Why-do-I-talk-to-him? Jesus, Don. So why do I talk to you? Fuck it.' She lights a cigarette, burns half of it away in a single draw, looks away.

Don, sliced off at the ankles by this mercurial change in mood and with nothing left to say, says:

'But he's boring. Patronising. Why do you give him time…'

Enraged, Maria stands and struts off. Disappears into the café to get away from him, to be alone a moment with her cigarette.

Urgent to recapture his cool, Don, heart hammering, picks up a copy of *Martello*. Something to leaf through as he's waiting for the next act. As if *he* cares.

Ah, but he does. He cares. Of course he cares.

A black and white portrait photo of a man in a tie, smiling into the camera, cross-hairs super-imposed on his high forehead, the caption '*Bersaglio del Mese*' – 'Target of the Month:'

'…Francesco Galante, Presidente of Galante tyre company, financier and banker, implacable enemy of workers' and unions' rights within his three factories in Emiglia Romana, has been selected as *Autonomia Operai's* 'Target of the Month.' He is to be found at 478 Via Saragozza, before

9AM and after 8PM. There is a locked gate, a dog and a guard. Don't be deterred!'

Fucking weird joke.
Don puts the paper down.
Maria sits. A long sigh.
'You're probably right, Don.'
Thank God!
But she's tired and grey. She's iced over again. She's full of sorrow. She's not laughing at all.
'I don't understand.'
'It's like ... my personal struggle for control,' she says enigmatically. 'If I lose, if people like *him* win, people like me are fucked. I talk to him because I have no choice, Don. Like ... I'm trapped.'
'No *choice?*'

♪

'Why *no choice?*'
Manu pauses, choosing his words, his voice filling with affection and regret.
'Because that is how she sees it, Don. She was violated by the evil of her childhood: this sepsis; the fascist violence which eats through the heart of our society and threatens to destroy it. For her – for Maria – it isn't a question of political choices, of beliefs which might be modified by thought, or discussion, or experience: it is something that she lives and experiences. The intellect for her does not exist as an objective entity. There is no separation with her between the political and the personal: she *is* what she believes.' He sighs.
Gazing down at the formations in front of him – the ziggurat of pawns, the bishop placed ready to occlude the threatened knight, the knight upon whose fragile vulnerability the whole of his over-stretched attack rests and his mind immersed in the solution to this constantly changing and ineffable problem – it is possible for Don to talk more openly about things which, were he obliged to meet his opponent's sorrowful brown eyes, he may have hesitated to raise. To say more difficult things. Like:
'She doesn't seem to me like a fanatic. There is kindness to her, too. Sadness. Gentleness.'

Fearful of betraying himself, Don stares at the board as he talks.

'A great gentleness. A great sorrow, which not everyone understands. She is hated by many of those whom she sees as friends. Many in her group tolerate her with great reluctance. They see her *gentleness*, as you put it, as weakness. It puts her in danger.'

And that's what hooks me, thinks Don. *This mixing of the strong and the vulnerable; the tender and the hard…*

…Glancing up at Manu, who is waiting for his next move. Sipping his coffee, his mineral water, pulling another white-tipped black tobacco cigarette from the pack and lighting it, for a moment their eyes meet.

'And that is why I *love* her,' says Manu, wistfully, *implausibly*, as if he is reading from lines of text buried in the deeper parts of *Don's* mind:

– *When she smiles, it is as if that impulse to smile has taken her unaware; as if the light mood that holds her, holds her hostage; as if her laughter contains within it the seeds of risk. She laughs, then looks around like a fugitive, wondering whether her laughter has been witnessed –*

But Don says nothing; averts his eyes from Manu's gaze, returns to the game, loses.

*

At ten sharp every morning, whatever he's doing, Don's got to leave. Other commitments. Business. Tania, in fact. The slim-hipped waitress.

What a relief to speak English again. What a relief to be in uncomplicated apolitical company. He picks her up for her break, laughing loudly at her scabrous morning jokes, turning the air blue. He flips from the brooding mysteries of his new friends to the bright, daylight surface of this other: Tania.

She gets half an hour off between morning cleaning and the day's serving. Their timing has to be *absolutely* precise.

'Morning, chuck.'

She hangs her pinnie up behind the bar, and together they skip off into the street to Tania's grandmother's house, two blocks down the *Viale Occidente*. Out of sight of either café they link arms, chase down the street, kicking stones and telling jokes in their loud English. Tania is eighteen, brought up in Bolton, hanging out between school and college, working to make some money: she's going to be a nurse. Meanwhile, poised between this moment, this *now*, and her future, she's having a laugh. She kisses him on the corner of the road, her tongue flicking like a minnow between his teeth.

Her grandmother, though, takes the charge of her virgin *nipote* seriously, and passing the half-open kitchen door where the old woman, wrapped in wool, sits with her cats, Don has to dart silently, hidden by shadow. Tania enters the kitchen while he waits outside, talks to her grandmother in her rapid Italian, her singing Bolognese accent. Makes the old woman her breakfast – her coffee, her pancetta – lays food for the pets. Then, five minutes passed, finger at her lips, telly turned up loud because the old woman's deaf, the two tip-toe up the brown-wood stairwell where the light never filters to Tania's attic bedroom, and pull the mattress from her rusted single bed onto the tattered hessian mat that covers the wooden floor.

10:12. If time and temperature permit they strip; if the mood takes them, they don't; then giggling and ardent, they fuck. At 10:23, lying flat, bathed in one another's sweat, her head cradled in the palm of his hand, they gaze together at the eddies in the dust; at the light filtering through the thick air of the room. They talk in whispers, saying nothing, sharing kisses, smothering their laughter. Though the old woman is deaf and can no longer make it up the stairs, it still fits better to be secret, to whisper, to make no sound which could betray them.

10:28, and Tania looks at her watch, gasping with a faked outrage at the time and how they've wasted it; giggles again, says '*slut!*' or something like it, and pulls on her clothes. Don would like to lie there for longer, but of course he never can. At 10:29 they slide like shadows back down the stairs, Tania crying out to her grandmother: '*Arrivederci, Nonna!*' her grandmother crying out in a sad, cracked voice, because she adores her: '*Nipote!*'

10:32 on the street and Tania ties her pinnie, spreads her fingers in a little wave, a little half-smile, a kiss in the air. 'Bye, love.'

'Bye,' says Don, sauntering off.

✿

Most afternoons he sleeps, then lives for the nights in the *Usignol*.

What had, at first, seemed a tangled and senseless world to Don, with its noise and darkness, its rank smell and peculiarly attenuated mix of violence and sudden laughter, reveals itself after a month or two. Despite all the *libertá e anarchia*, the *uguaglianza e giustizia*, all the brave, wild talk of *pistole e bombe e azioni giustificate*, there's order here. There's a structure. A strange group of almost-friends. A hierarchy. It's Manu that explains:

Start with Horst, the deadly German. He has strong bones, short blond hair, deep-set blue eyes, hauteur. He seems, even after many weeks, to resent the theft of that cigarette, the fight, the subsequent humiliation. His is the loudest voice, the greatest muscles, the brawn. He turns away, wincing, whenever Don approaches – to Don's eye like a child in school, excluding the new boy – muttering in near silence to his main and trusted friends, viewing him through slitted eyes, through a curtain of smoke. This is funny, but frightening, too.

Late one evening, deep in the black depths of the bar. The musicians have finished playing. Marco makes straight for his sister – source of action, source of cash. Don bounces just behind, keen, a little uneasy. Surprised to see a little glint of gun-metal grey, for a moment unwrapped, glimpsed on the bar table.

'Show and tell, is it, Horst?' says Don, who can't resist sneering.

This *thing* is wrapped in an oily towel. Horst keeps it *almost* concealed. Allowing just his two best friends a keek and no-one else. Don is definitely intruding. He arches over to get a better view.

'Ach, it's our *non-violent* friend,' mocks Horst, hiding the thing hurriedly when he sees him.

'Got a gun there then, lovey?'

The boys close ranks. A giggly secret hangs around the comrades like a dense fart.

Horst's beautiful greaseball friend Fioravanti scowls. *Fuck off.*

This is just like being at school, thinks Don who, currently a pacifist, tries to work up an Italian phrase to encompass this complex concept of:

Horst – a horse – its big wooden penis – largeness –

– but times out, contenting himself with saying lamely: 'Baader Meinhof, eh?' then realises by the sudden plague of frowns and silence, by Horst's vituperative *'Ess-hole!'* that he has said, again, very much the wrong thing. Stung, Don retreats to drink alone.

Days later Manu explains. The whole story:

Horst, like many, does indeed retain a loose connection with the murderous organisation in question. It all starts with his dead father, who was a pilot in the Luftwaffe: a war hero for a year or two, in '41-'42. Who almost single-handedly, according to the old man, had lifted the blockade at Stalingrad, kept the food coming in and the sick and limbless coming out, for four frozen months before freezing his own hands off on the controls of his Focker-18. So the raging, handless father, who never accommodated himself to the loss of status after *his* side finally went down, drank himself to a lonely death when little Horst was still in nappies, and was followed, not so long after, by his widow.

'So you don't need to be a shrink or a priest to understand Horst's hunger for certainty,' says Manu. 'His great bitterness; his anger against the machine. His violence.' Don nods, solemnly.

Though you still probably need to be one to actually like *the guy.*

Horst was brought up in a children's home in Hugelstrasse, Frankfurt, which in 1969 became one of the 'people's nurseries,' liberated by a wild young man in denim called Andreas Baader, and a girl with thick glasses and a southern accent called Ulricke Meinhoff. Horst knew them first as occasional parents, and then, as he grew, as comrades. So Horst has been the *real thing* since the age of about twelve. And Horst reveres the dead – his many foster-parents, murdered by the capitalist state on 'Death Night' in Stuttgart-Stammheim...

Horst has done many bad things which he doesn't at all regret, and will do them again and again. He is justified, by *history,* in everything he does. He likes for all of these things simultaneously to be known, and yet never referred to. So, quiver with fear. Watch where you tread, lest you step on one of his shattered dreams – and

119

there are bits and pieces of Horst's dreams lying everywhere. Don, by mentioning those names without respect, has just shat on Horst's brothers' and sisters' graves.

'So, Don, it's better perhaps not to talk about it any more, eh?' says Manu, winking and mocking as they take coffee. 'Horst – he has the tender bollocks. You understand? *Coglioni sensibili.* So say sorry, no? Make your peace.' He looks at him with large, not entirely serious eyes. *Do this little thing? Eh? For me?*

Why the fuck should I apologise?

Don thinks that Horst is probably just a cunt. But he fears him still, and is both indebted and drawn to Manu. So, a few days after, he says he's sorry, just in case.

'Ah, sorry, Horst…'

Who just frowns back, ungraciously refusing his hand.

'Fuck off, esshole.'

In contrast to Horst, Fioravanti – whose first name Don *thinks* is Valentino – is almost wordless. He's another enemy, Don senses; though why this should be he can't tell, because nothing is said.

Fioravanti is remarkably, magically gifted with beauty: he *wears* his sheer elfin face like a garment; he affects a sulky manner befitting a boy no more than half his age. An almost-transparent skin; short, thick black hair, oiled back; deep brown velvet eyes. Thin-boned, a heart-shaped mouth. Fioravanti is so beautiful, there is something in him that repels. He sits by Horst, in Horst's shadow, says almost nothing, supplies his bigger, older friend with smokes.

'Is he … are they…' Don shuffles around for a balanced, kind word like 'gay.' The concept, only recently invented in the north, hasn't yet evolved in Italy, so the word still doesn't exist. Maria, who understands anyway, shrugs, shaking her head.

'When he was a child, he was a lot on television. He sang songs to housewives. At Christmas. He was very popular. He had big hits. He was called *Tino Teeny Tino.* He is very ashamed of all of this. He doesn't like to be reminded. He is still very vain.'

Don banks this baffling information too.

Then there's the older one: the one with the pouches under his eyes, the pipe, the tin-grey hair, the pointed little beard, the lined skin which has seen too little of the sun. Giuseppe Mariotti. A man also well under-cover. Been on the run too long. He is the dullest man that Don has ever met. Once an academic at the University of Bologna, a political historian. Implicated in many evil deeds and now contributing clandestinely to *Martello* – long arcane articles about the eternal workers' struggle, the dialectical process in a post-industrial age, the *Marxian Destiny* – this kind of shit, written in a dense jargon which plagues Maria's mornings. These articles are becoming a great source of sterile laughter for the two growing friends. She lets him read them; explains the difficult bits. *Curare* prose. Words like darts from a blow-pipe; words which can paralyse. The man talks like his writing, smokes his pipe, talks, while the world goes on around him, never aware, never listening. Giuseppe the inevitable. Always there. Attended to. Yet never quite liked. *Why?*

Manu soon lets him further into this secret too:

'... the political left in this country has been emasculated by the phenomenon of red terror. Our ... resistance ... expends its strength in murder, and the political-criminal class continues to profit. Terror simply furthers the corrupt interests of the state. Their masters are quite conscious of this. So one must thus question which constituency these people ultimately serve...'

Manu has lowered his voice to something nearer a whisper. Don leans forward over the chess board to follow him.

'What has this to do with...'

A waiter brings them coffee; Manu tips him and makes him disappear.

'...the person we're discussing?'

'Mariotti was, is, a leading advocate and perpetrator of the kind of violence which we are discussing.'

'And Maria?' Don, his mouth wide open, a pantomime of shocked innocence. *Faaaaking 'ell...*

Manu gives him a long, hard look; hesitating, as if to ascertain whether he can be trusted.

'Maria has been involved in some terrible things. Things which she will discuss with no-one. She sees herself as a woman who can never be forgiven. She devotes her life to trying to make amends.'

Don is awed.

121

'So what did she do...?'
'I cannot tell you that.'

And then there's Manu himself, of course. With his smooth face, his cleft chin. The quiet and unassuming friend who Don still fears. Who passes silent and unnoticed like a gas through the fissures and cracks between these people. Who turns up unexpectedly, looms over them silently in the mornings, cutting like ice through Maria and Don's long morning conversation, making them startle with a kind of suppressed guilt. Who Maria then looks up at, smiling thinly, irritated already by his silence and wishing he were gone. He offers her his hand, with its long, tapered fingers and well-kept nails, which she takes, reluctantly. He seems to lift her from her seat, as if she were made of coloured paper and nothing more, folds her crumpled form over his arm and bears her off home to wherever it is they live, leaving Don alone with nothing but the memory of an apologetic smile painted on her paper face; a glimpse of what looks to him like sadness, anger or even shame.

It is as if there are two versions of this man, occupying the same flesh. There is his Sunday morning friend, who seeks his company, earnestly asking at the end of each match whether they might meet again the following week. Manu who, with his deft, gentle questioning, the bestowing of confidences and irresistibly intriguing fragments of information, has cultivated Don with such subtlety that the innocent is *almost* unaware that he is seduced. A comfortable, safe, Sunday morning intimacy, which yet feels like vice.

And then there is the lover, the rival who joins Maria briefly, sometimes, as she works. Greeting her, ignoring Don, he sits without being asked, takes one from the pack of her cigarettes, calls her *amore*, seems quite unaware of the coolness of her response.

Don, always uncomfortable in the presence of both of them together, immediately leaves, turned by witch-magic back into the cleaner and wielding his mop like a wand, sloshing grey water around Manu's soft, brown leather shoes, clearing him up and making him go. Which he does, soon.

Don waits a moment to let the colour slowly return to Maria's face, for her to breathe freely, deeply once again, to inflate her collapsed paper-self so that she's a woman once more. She smiles at him hesitantly, recognising him as if it's only just now safe once more to do so; laughs a little, vaguely, as if she's waking from a dream.

You see, Manu casts a shadow over Maria. *She hates him,* thinks Don, *and yet she is his lover too. Why?*

And the air always seems a little clearer, the light a little brighter, after he's gone.

Don takes guilty solace, from this, tiny thing:

When Manu leaves, he sometimes kisses her. He'll lean over, scarf her neck with his hand, stamp her lips with his dry kisses, saying '*Ciao, amore.*'

Once, just once, when Manu's back was safely turned, Don thought he saw her shudder; was sure he saw Maria wipe that kiss away – like a child, furtively, with the back of her hand. Then their eyes had met briefly and Maria smiled – a little, complicit smile, the tone and wistful mood of which had pierced him somewhere close to his heart and given him hope – and then she had looked briskly away: ashamed, perhaps, of her disloyalty. Don treasured that little intimacy, but also thought: *what is the glue that binds these two people?*

It is not friendship. Neither is it love. Nor necessity, nor pleasure, either. *What is the glue that binds these people?*

❦

One mellow, precious Sunday afternoon Don, Marco and Maria sit in a stall at the back of the *Usignol*.

They've been there an hour. A moment's peace while the seasons turn. A low afternoon sun slanting through the skylight high in the wall behind them finds a passage through the smoke and motes of dust, filtering a little of its bruised light through to a place usually in shadow, where it picks them out, illuminating the faces of all three. Perhaps they have been here for days: perhaps they have been sitting, suspended in this moment, forever; perhaps they are figures in a painting – the dark, greenish shadows for background – the pearl-coloured light, the light from a painted angel, picking out the faces of the three – the varnished colours of their faces cracked with age.

Sit back. Watch this scene develop, as if from a distance:

A young woman sits reading and smoking, sipping coffee, at first comfortable and silent, listening with half an ear to the others. Half of her face is in shadow; the subtle light, the pale light, plays with the colours in her dark brown hair.

An angular young man sits with a fiddle on the table at his elbow, frowning, his body half-turned away from the woman, but his attention nonetheless entirely directed towards her.

The other man – tangled black hair and olive-coloured skin; strange, lilac-coloured eyes, looking blankly into the dust on the table, strumming without intent on a guitar.

Sounds:

The wandering of the music of the guitar; the movement of broken chords, seeking resolution.

The scraping of a match on a matchbox; the nearly silent flaring of the tobacco on the tip of the girl's cigarette. A pause, a long exhalation.

The sharp red light of the cigarette as she inhales; the bluish smoke drifting across the table, reaching its long tendrils upwards towards the source of light; eddying almost imperceptibly. The glass is cracked; there is movement in the air.

Sounds:

The hollow knocking of wood against wood as the first man picks up the fiddle, tries the tuning, plays a phrase, a bar or two of a spiked, dotted semi-quaver rhythm.

The guitar, in turn, adapting its voice to that of the fiddle. The beginnings of a dialogue between the two, which soon breaks down. Muttered voices exchange views, a whispered dispute overt this or that, before they start afresh.

The girl, her attention now wholly directed towards the two musicians, smiles wistfully, her head on one side. It is rare for her to smile like this, and the fiddler is distracted by her pleasure; the music breaks down, the guitarist, in a parody of irritation, snaps his fingers to attract the fiddler's attention. The girl laughs at his rudeness.

Sound:

The girl's laughter, which sounds to the fiddler like clear water running over round, worn stones – and to the guitarist, like mockery.

Seeing the effect her laughter has, she stops – but still, this rare smile is not yet replaced by the usually sad cast of her expression. The guitarist, in a childlike pique, plays once again, filling the dusty air between these people's heads; and the fiddler too, and this time the melody is more refined, richer in its colour, consistent, repeatable.

And if this melody were to have words, what would they be?

The fiddler and the guitarist sit at the table, heads almost touching, wrapped in concentration over this song which they are shaping together. Their respective faces mimic one another – the fiddler bites his lip, closes his eyes; the guitarist does so too, and the movement of their music follows this same synergy: they sway in time together like two snakes. One taps his foot, sharply, twice; the rhythm of the thing is altered, a beat or two faster. 'Yes!' one mutters to himself; the other coughs. 'Yes.' They no longer notice the girl, who watches them both, her wide, violet eyes pricked with tears.

Or later, when the guitarist picks out three soft, ripe cords, which hang and shimmer there, twisting slowly in the dusty light between them, ready like fruit for picking.

Sounds:
The guitarist's chords
The fiddler finding his tune
A voice, singing:

> Ay, ay, ay, ay … cantaba
> Ay, ay, ay, ay … gemia
> Ay, ay, ay, ay … cantaba
> De pasión mortal … moria

A voice which billows, filling up the spaces between them. A loved instrument, neglected and long-untouched. A textured, deep alto; a voice which longs to be used.

His throat stopped, Don can say nothing as the echoes from her untrained, amber-coloured voice fade. Marco places the palm of his hand on the strings of his guitar, bringing about silence. His eyes are wet with tears. His face is a caricature of puppy regret. He wipes his nose on his sleeve, casts around with blind eyes for a hankie.

After a moment:

'I didn't know that you sang,' says Don.

Maria laughs again: a short, rather bitter laugh.

'There is a great deal that you don't know about me.'

Marco has wandered off. To piss, to cry, to buy cigarettes – to leave the two together, even. It doesn't matter why – for the moment, he's gone. The thick air and the shadow enfolds these two that remain; just two heads leaning in together now in the pale, late afternoon light.

'But you sing beautifully. You should sing more.'

She shrugs her shoulders. *There is much that I should do, but don't.*

A look of passing regret.

'It's a waste. It's a terrible waste.'

A thin smile. 'Now I have no time. I have nowhere to sing. I have no-one to sing to.'

'Yes, you do...' Meaning: *me! ME!*

She shakes her head, but the smile is still present. She may discount such frivolities as music or song, but yet she is flattered.

'Our parents taught us when we were little. Marco had the talent. But still, I loved to sing. That was one of our songs. Our mother taught us. She died a few years ago. Both our parents did. In ... an accident.'

'I know,' said Don, the image of the violence of their death conjured for him once again by its mention.

'How?' asks Maria, sharply.

'I...' and Don is suddenly dizzy with uncertainty, for the source of everything that he knows is Manu, her lover, and what he has been told he has been told in confidence. And he feels ashamed, too: somehow contaminated by those sticky threads of secrecy in which he has allowed himself to be wrapped.

'Marco. Marco told me.'

'Marco?' says Maria, astonished, for in that common, narrative sense, Marco never talks.

'Yes ... I think so,' says Don, seeking to obscure the lie with a little cloud of uncertainty. 'Or maybe...'

But Maria has moved on.

'After they died, all the music stopped. I didn't see Marco again either, for years. You know him better than I do, you know. He is almost a stranger to me. It is good that the two of you are friends.'

Don looks at his feet, then glances up. Their two heads are very close. She looks at him, gazing through him with a wistful, distant expression on her face. *Manu lies, then. Everything that he has told me could be a lie. And so I hardly know a thing about you*, he thinks, and tries to find the words to communicate this last, but can't. He smiles instead, and she returns his smile, and between them they hold this mystery for longer than they should.

ℓ

'I would like to ask something of you, my friend,' says the voice of Manu, the lover of the woman whom, just three days previously, he had almost kissed.

'Sure, anything,' says Don, eyes staring through the depleted row of pawns which form a perforated line on the board in front of him. A *frisson* of anxiety. No protection there. He shivers.

They had – *almost* – kissed, you see. Maria. And the memory still makes him tremble with joy.

They had almost sealed that long smile when their eyes, their hearts, had locked; that long moment of profound communication and understanding that can occur between two quite dissimilar people – with a life-altering kiss. *Fuck.*

Manu looks at him with his open, friendly eyes.

'Over these months I have come to trust you.'

Don swallows nervously.

'I would like to ask your help.'

Me, help you?

'Of course ... anything.'

Fuck. He shivers with guilt and fear.

She had said to him – 'It is good that the two of you are friends...' Meaning he and Marco. And he had replied, after a moment, 'And that we are friends too...' And she had said (distant voice, edged with melancholy): 'Yes, I think that that is really what I meant...' Her eyes on his, his on hers, the smile between them blossoming, and she had touched his hand and he had leaned forward, closer to her, so that he could feel the warmth of her body and smell her scent...

Hush, memory! Listen to what is being said! This matters:

'...I have to leave here,' says Manu. 'I have to leave Maria alone.
I will be gone, certainly for some weeks, perhaps for months. I
will probably be abroad much of the time – London, mainly, and
New York, and certainly hard to contact. I shall be very frank with
you...'

Don braces himself. He now fears this lover's confidences.

'I dread leaving her alone, Don. Maria is deeply involved with a
group of people whose true danger she doesn't properly appreciate.
She believes that she can influence and control them, but she can't.
I have tried to warn her, over and over, but she will not listen to me.
Her *comrades* do not trust me – I am not one of them, and they see
my presence as a threat. I do not want you to become *involved* – I
don't think that they would permit you in any case – you are not
liked – but I would like you to remain close, and I would like you
to keep me informed of what the group's intentions are. I would
like especially for you to watch Maria, for her safety, but I do not
want her to know that I have asked you to do this.'

'Are you asking me to spy?' asks Don, melodramatically.

Manu slides his white bishop from A to B; pins Don's last
remaining rook to the king. All looks lost.

'Why?' Then: 'Who do you *really* work for?'

Brave words. Don, cutting through months of artifice. Manu
evades the question, tellingly.

'The only person that matters to me is Maria,' he replies,
eventually. 'Whatever I do, I do for her sake. Whatever happens,
whatever you tell me, I won't let her be harmed. I promise this, Don.
But I *can* help. Do you understand?'

Yes ... I think so...

'But she mustn't know anything about this.'

'Of course not.' *Stupid question, really.*

'Why me?'

'Because you are a virgin.'

'A *virgin*?'

'You have never been *involved*. You aren't known to this, or any
other organisation. No-one is watching you. No-one is suspicious
of you. You can move freely, practically unseen.'

Which explains a lot.
'Will you do that? Stick around. Let me know what happens?'
Flattered, frightened and curious, Don nods.
'I will give you some numbers you can use to contact me.'

14

A few months later. It's nearly Christmas. Manu is now gone. No-one seems to notice his absence. Marco, his unreliable guide through this hard new world, has also disappeared again: been gone now for four days. And Maria seems to be avoiding him.

During the long afternoons and nights he tries to sleep, but can't. He's depressed, though doesn't yet know it. *He* thinks he's just hiding; attributes his pewter-grey mood to the weather. It has rained forever. Without Marco, he has too much fear, to earn. The dreaded grey of the mendicant musician has closed in on him. His life has no purpose. His sweat smells rancid. The exotic all stripped away, his new world now merely terrifies: there is no joy to be had any more; no compensations. It's too cold to go out; he has no money to keep the shop-front warm, so it's too cold to stay in, too. He worries he may have pubic lice, and spends hours with a flickering torch hunched under his sleeping bag, looking for tell-tale little crabs – which he imagines, flat and clawed, clicking their little pincers and scuttling for cover when he clicks on the yellow beam.

He has nothing to eat, and no friends. He lies there awake, days long, shivering and scratching. Tania's gone home to Manchester for two weeks and anyway, even she's grown tired of his long moods. No solace there. He hadn't imagined that Italy could ever get so cold. He hadn't imagined this possibility: that freedom could make him so miserable.

Four days into solitude, and he can tolerate it no longer. Desperate for company, he emerges thin from his sweaty sleeping bag, wets his face and body in grimy water from a pail, smears himself dry again with his oily grey towel before the water freezes on his skin, wraps his jacket around him, makes his way to the *Usignol*.

Sammi nods, and seeing the state he's in, says nothing about his absence those past few days and stands him a drink instead. He's not wholly bad, Sammi. In fact, he's not *bad* at all. The *Usignol* is almost empty, but for the *compagni*, deep in their smoke, warmth and conversation. Don has never approached this group on his own, but today he's hungry, and steels himself. He needs to talk to *someone*.

Horst and Tino, Spaniel-Eyes, a horrid hog-faced student from

Bergamo, who he hasn't previously met. Maria's not there. He realises as he turns, despairing, to leave, that only *her* help will help today. And then, reflecting on this and his otherwise near-total absence of friends and comfort, thinks she's the only thing he's staying on *for*. Which is daft. This realisation, taking him unaware, makes him hesitate. Then Horst sees him. To his great surprise, the *Feldwebbel* raises his hand, cracking his teeth on a kind of smile.

'You. Eenglish.' Beckons him over.

When Horst speaks to him, it's always like this: in German high school exam English. Irritated, because his Italian's now *good,* and thinking that the *Feldwebbel* is just taking the piss, he responds in best comic-book Kraut – *Jawohl mein ubergruppen führer, donnerwetter!* – realising much later, of course that irony is beyond Horst's cognitive range. Horst has never read a *Commando!* book. Horst has never even been a child. Don is simply making an arse of himself.

But today he is too tired, hungry and cold to play games. He stands at the periphery of the group, hanging around, wanting to be asked in.

'Ve vant you to help. Zeet.'

Jawoll.

Don: torn between this desire to smoke and drink, to huddle down in the foetid warmth of these people's company, and the sense of revulsion – and self-revulsion, too, at the company he's now forced to keep.

'What?' He sits.

'Read zis. Please.'

Four hand-written sheets in turquoise ink, big letters, an 'Introduction' followed by six bullet points, written in distinctly dodgy English.

'What's this?'

'A … communiqué. You don't need details. Read it, zen correct ze English. Zen forget everyzing zat you hef read, and everyzing zat you may hef discovered. From zis.' Horst looks *very* serious.

He sits. The others wait.

Workers of the World Unite!

Oh oh oh. Fuck. Cunt. Shit.

131

He stifles a yawn, a groan, and sips some borrowed wine.

We, the comrades and friends of the martyrs of the night of 14th August, constituted by will of the vanguard of the proletariat into the organism known as 'The Peoples' Hammer,' hereby serve notice on the representatives of the Multi-Nationals' State, the SMI, that a state of war now exists between us, and will continue to do so until our demands, to be issued in our forthcoming communiqué, are met. We demand:

—The immediate dismantlement of the Multi-Nationalists' State and its instruments, and the formation of the New Italian Peoples' State-Collective (NIPS-C).
— The peoples' unconditional support for the unending fight against International State Fascism.
— Immediate withdrawal from the so-called North Atlantic Alliance.
— The smashing of American hegemonic interest everywhere.
— The total destructuralisation of the capitalist, mercantilist, Imperialist-Zionist system of oppression.
— The unconditional solidarity with workers' proletarian states everywhere.

We arrogate to ourselves the right to use any means, violent or otherwise, in the pursuit of the above principles.

He struggles through. Tino brings him another drink. Horst *gives* him a cigarette. His bones begin, slowly, to thaw.
'Well?' Spaniel-Eyes raises his eyebrows.
'It's very ... good,' he says, lying. 'Very, *very* interesting. What is NIPS-C, in Italian?'
'S-CNPI.'
'Good.' He nods. 'Almost ... SCAMPI.'
'Vot?'
'Nothing. Nothing.'
The others nod.
'And the English?'

'Good. In parts, very good. Give me a little time.'

It takes quite a lot of time – a glass or two of table wine, more of Horst's American *(multi-nationalist)* cigarettes *(Camel),* a bite of salted bread, and another – to straighten out the strangled syntax, check and re-check the spelling, review the thing for content.

'It doesn't say anything about Iran. It doesn't say that you support the legitimate aspirations and autonomy of the Islamic revolutionary students' movement of Iran.' Don, two glasses of wine in, is getting chippy.

The others look surprised, and frown.

'*They* are proto-fascists,' explains Spaniel-Eyes, almost kindly. 'We don't support *them*. Their revolution is *premature*. They will *suppress* the legitimate aspirations... '

'Oh. What about Afghanistan? You need to say something about the right of the Peoples' Republic of Afghanistan to request Soviet assistance in their struggle against American imperialism. Don't you?'

Some nod. 'Maybe... That's true,' says the one from Bergamo.

'Your communiqué lacks ... scope. There's nothing about the Jews. You need more about the threat from the Jews. The Jewish-American banks. The multi-national conspiracy. Israel. The *Bilderburg* group. Something about that.'

Teeny Tino nods, fervently.

'And prisoners. There's nothing about the release of prisoners. What about the murdered prisoners of war in Stuttgart Stammheim? What about the Red Army Faction martyrs? The victims of German state terrorism?'– this dialectic *trompe de parole* directed at Horst, the most intelligent and eloquent of them, it seems, who frowns and squints, questioning for a dangerous moment his sincerity. The Englishman draws deeply on his Camel, exhales in their faces, keeps his own dead straight. 'You forget your comrades too easily.'

This gets them. The cadres frown a moment, chastised.

'Ve don't esk for your advice,' says Horst, slitty eyes staring right through to the back of him, making his spine tingle.

'You ought to,' says pissed Don, seeing a new career as a kind of double-agent opening in front of him. 'Politics is my thing. What do you intend to do with this?'

They look at one another, deciding whether to trust.

'It is a declaration of war,' says Horst.

'We will have it delivered to the embassies of all of the countries from NATO,' says the student from Bergamo.

'We will *post* it,' says Teeny Tino, irrelevantly.

'It is a first shot. A salvo. A *definitive* statement of principles,' says Spaniel-Eyes dismissively, an angry light for once in his grey face.

It is good to be drunk again, despite the absence of laughter. It's good to be warm, too, despite the chilliness of those surrounding him. It's good to smoke other peoples' cigarettes, drink their wine, eat their food. All of these things are good. Don goes home happier. Feels he has a place again in the world, however strange, insincere and contingent that place may be. But Don's fragile new happiness is not going to last.

§

Cold again next morning, he drags himself to work.

I always seems to have more time to think *at work,* he thinks, as he sloshes the piss off the floor in the Gents, scrapes crystallised snot from above the urinals, disperses the obstinate and furtive turds which lurk deep in the lavvie pans. These introspective, morning thoughts, they ambush him: gathering all around him, always, all at once, when he's feeling sad.

Don lays his life out flat on the oak-wood bar, wipes it down with a wet then a dry cloth; then, because it's filthy, does it twice more. Finds it – that life – all spread out there, a thin, transparent and insubstantial thing, and wishes for the first time in months that it was different – that he'd just gone back home that day in August, and done his sodding exams.

This bad step, this throwing everything in the air for a life of anarchy and music – it's too bad – too cold, too … dirty, he thinks weakly, as he manipulates his broom behind some stools in the shadows of a cubicle and brings out a thick clotted wad of dust which he realises, seconds later, is a tampon. *Perhaps Jules wasn't so bad …* he thinks, chinking the ashtrays, wiping a smear of lipstick from the rim of an otherwise clean-looking glass, before stacking it. *Anything is better than this loneliness. Discounting Tania. Of course. Who doesn't count. For some reason.*

Bucket and mop, he lathers the wooden floor into a thick grey soup. *And cleaning is a really bad job. And Marco has been gone for five days, and is probably dead. And there is no reason to stay here. Back in Scotland I can gather together again the shards of my shattered life...* Collecting with his fingertips the fragments of a broken glass from a table, picking up a blood-stained hankie from the floor, finding a razor buried in it. *Become a male nurse. Or something.*

Excepting ... the face of Maria, which pops into his mind, wearing just *that* look – his favourite – the one that dawns on her face when he's just said something that has touched or amused her. That moment of surprise or delight, before she smiles. *Maybe...*

And now it's 8:30, and she's right there. Incarnate, sitting outside, adjusting her papers at a table. Keeping her jacket tight on against the cold. Don sees her shiver. Taking off his pinnie, he goes straight out to join her. *I shall lay my troubles at her feet, and* she'll *care.*

'Maria! Good morning! *Buongiorno!* I'm *so* glad to see you! It's been ages!' A fresh new voice in his mouth today: a big adult's voice, the voice of one friend talking to another.

She looks up. He sits with her.

'I wanted to speak to you. I've been wanting to speak to you for days. Marco's gone. I don't know where he is.' He smiles wanly. 'I'm really worried...'

But today she isn't smiling back. She looks at him with flat eyes as his voice trails off into silence.

'Why did you write this?'

Taps a sheet of printed A4 with her forefinger.

'Why have *you* got involved with *this?*' A little tremor behind her rising voice warns him that things are bad.

'What?' he says. Feeling like a bad child suddenly, he has to swallow twice to control his voice. 'What?'

'This ... *shit* of Mariotti's. Why are *you* involved?'

'I'm...' He looks over at the paper. The communiqué. The English version. Sees the word 'Jew' a couple of times. A couple of extra bullet points too, which weren't there before.

'*Horst* tells me that you wrote this. Tells me I'm to publish it. Why are *you* writing *this* shit?'

Maria seems very angry. He has let her down. He has betrayed their embryonic intimacy; blabbed out some precious secret. But she's also close to tears – and so, suddenly, is he. So where has all this come from? This excess, random feeling? How can a friendship, which seemed one day such a warm, growing, important thing, veer so suddenly off into such cold, unlit, unmapped territory?

'It was a joke,' he says, bewildered, in a new little-boy voice.

'A joke?' Wide-eyed, not believing what she's being told. *'A joke?'*

'I didn't take them seriously. I was just teasing…'

'You weren't taking them seriously? Teasing? Mariotti? *Horst Kleber?'* Names said as if these were names that any fool would know. *Mariotti. Horst Kleber.* Names that any fool would flinch before, before taking them in vain, before mouthing them so lightly.

He shakes his head. An anguished pause. Maria talks slowly.

'You are only a child, Don. You don't understand a thing. Don't dabble. Better that you just … go home.'

Fuck you.

'Fuck you!' says Don, hurt and incautious, in English.

'You don't understand,' says Maria with hard, steely patience. 'They are *dangerous*. They have principles. *You* may not be serious, but they *always* are.'

'I *am* serious.'

'About what?'

That soon shuts him up. But: *You*, says a dissident voice, angry and lost somewhere, deep in Don's head. *You, just you, all along.* A voice, struggling to surface, which he daren't use.

Aloud, he has no answer. Stares into the woman's sad face. Which, in Don's eyes – though he misinterprets – pities him. Whatever it is he reads there, he is stung by the insult. As a dialectic, as a man, you may think, Don urgently needs some synthesis. But at present, rodent-like, he uses his sharp teeth, his razor claws, to tear things yet further asunder. He becomes angry.

'My friends. My music. I *am* serious. I don't surround myself with people I hate, for the sake of a catechism of moral principles which would freeze the balls off a polar bear. For example. *That's* serious. I don't bore myself and the rest of the world with my fantasies about the perfect world – that's a principle. I don't take orders from anyone, apart from Sammi, and I wouldn't ever sleep with a person whose touch I loathe.'

There. Said.

She looks shocked. Stares at him, bug-eyed, thinking, no doubt: *what the fuck is he talking about...*

'You are very *young*, *Ton*, to be so smug.'

He stands, shoves his chair back with a rasp on the stone pavement, trying like a turkey to swell his craw, his belly; trying to be bigger and strong in her eyes, in everyone's eyes...

'Perhaps. But I don't rely on children to make me laugh, or indeed, to make me feel as if I'm alive.'

She's silent. Her silence enrages him further.

'And because I make you laugh, doesn't make me less than serious. Just because your friends – Horst, Mariotti, Teeny – have no joy, doesn't make them *more* serious. And because they claim to want to kill for what they believe, doesn't make their beliefs any better. It just makes more dead people.'

Maria blinks. Don is now shouting and crying, both at the same time, spittle flying. He's like a child that needs his mother. Jabs his finger at the table, not making any sense. Enjoying himself. Hating himself. She shakes her head.

'*Ton*, you don't understand...'

'Don't I?'

But he's out of steam now. The pressure of all this rage vented, he now just feels sad and stupid. He never wanted to say any of that, and now she'll hate him.

She's looking at him still: shocked, hurt, angry. The crap communiqué still, absurdly, gripped in her left hand. Don has nothing left to say; no idea why he has just said what he has said, where all that feeling came from; no idea at all what to say now. And in that moment of silence, the little lost boy pokes his head out one last time:

'So. Do you *love* Manu, then?'

What a total arse.

She blinks, stunned; shakes her head, gathering herself for an answer.

Which doesn't come. Because Maria's now looking over his shoulder, frowning at something/someone just behind him.

'Don! Don, I'm really sorry...'

There's a hand pulling at his elbow, pulling for his attention. Been there for a bit, in fact, but he's been ignoring it. He turns, fails for a moment to recognise her: her child's purpled, tear-smeared face.

'Don, it's me Nan. I think she's … sick.'

Tania. *Fuck. Fuck.* Freshly back from Bolton. Tired and drawn, her long unwashed hair making rat-tails on her new raincoat. Tania, who is looking at him in this very new way: anxious, frightened, apparently needing his help. She looks about twelve years old. Desperate. Unimpressive.

'Tania…!' He doesn't quite say, *Christ! Not now!*

But nonetheless, his eyes flickering from one face to another, he compares. Maria the adult, attention now diverted, her eyes wide with concern for this bedraggled child; the child herself, now plucking at his sleeve, begging him to be gone.

'Please come, Don!'

Don looks from one face to another, then flees with Tania, without saying goodbye.

₰

'I just got in this morning. I was on my way to work. I was going to go straight to work. I just went home quickly, on my way, to say hello to Nan…'

They hurry together through the street, skipping between the cars and scooters parked on the narrow pavements, dodging traffic.

Nothing silent or secret this morning as Tania lets them in her grandmother's front door, runs up the narrow steps to the old woman's flat, crying 'This way!' to Don.

'I just didn't know what to do.'

They're standing in the old woman's bathroom, just inside the door, neither quite ready to go any further in. Then: 'I'm sorry, Don. I just didn't know what to do…'

Don hadn't seen the old woman before – not more, at least, than the back of her head: a grey bun tied tight in a net, a crescent of scalp peeping over the top of the back of the chair where she sat in the mornings waiting for her *nipote* to bring her breakfast.

She lies in the bath, skin yellow and vivid through the clear, now cold, water. Her boxy hips, the thin legs with wax skin, purple bruises down both shins. Her hands grip the handles, braced and ready to pull her out. Her mouth – thin lips, translucent orange like the beak of a fledgling – is open, as if she had suddenly cried out, gasping something – a name? – at the moment of her death. Her tongue lies small and blue in the floor of her mouth. Her grey hair is still bound tightly in its net. Her face is fixed in an expression of surprise, as if the door had opened suddenly and someone had walked in, interrupting her, naked in her bath.

Tania quietly hides the old woman's underclothes, which are folded over the back of a chair, under the corner of a bath towel.

'What should we do?' she asks Don in a small voice.

Don, in truth, has no idea. No-one has ever really asked him to *do* anything before. He leans forward, touches the old woman's hand as if to take it, to offer some late comfort, to help her over the moment – but then flinches at the coldness of her touch. He makes himself take her hand, detaches her grip from the bath handle. She is light and stiff as a little bird, caught dead in the morning by the frost. If he chose, he could lift her himself from her bath, but her limbs are stiff and delicate as dry sticks. Don is fascinated at first, and frozen for a spell by this first encounter with death. The strange violation of her dignity. And those ordinary, insoluble problems: how she should be moved, whether they should attempt to dry her. Whether this problem will be easier or harder to manage if they empty the bath. Enough. Tania needs his help.

'I'm afraid she's dead,' he says in his quietest, most tender voice. Tania nods, solemnly. Obvious enough, perhaps; but words like these do need to be said.

He puts an arm across Tania's shoulder and she places her head, seeking warmth and comfort, on his chest. He leads her out of the bathroom, saying 'Let's make some tea. Then I'll deal with it. In a moment or two.'

Don makes Tania tea – strong, brown, sweet, Lancashire – and she huddles in the corner, opposite the chair where her Nan had sat in life, hands around the cup, blowing onto its surface, wrinkling her nose at the condensation which forms there.

Don calls for a policeman and a doctor. They both arrive within an hour, as Tania sits in silence in the corner, drinking more tea. The doctor signs forms; the policeman interviews Don, then Tania, with Don translating – for, strangely, Tania has lost her perfect, singing Italian, preferring to communicate through his – slow, stumbling – while he sits on his haunches and holds her hand, choosing the right words, the kindest ones, while the policeman, impatient, smokes and takes brief notes in a little black book with the nub of a soft pencil.

The undertakers are a pare of *sgerri* – rough, muscular boys with white plastic overalls and black, greased hair – clearly the undertaker's sons, to whom the hard work has been delegated: the lifting work, the dealing with moisture, the potential for mess. They've brought the van. Don closes the kitchen door, sparing Tania the bumping on the stairs, the yells of *Easy does it on the bend!*, the curses and shouts, the words and their sounds, which sound the same in any language.

And after they've gone, Don goes back upstairs. Pulls the plug on the bath and lets the cold water out. Mops the wet floor and the drips left on the stairs. He clears away the clothes, disposes of towels, and even flushes the toilet where the uncouth undertaker has left the butt of a cigarette floating in a pool of his oily pee. He clears things up and makes things right.

It's almost ten at night by the time he finishes. Tania, over-wrought and exhausted, has fallen asleep where she sat by the gas fire, the eighth cup of tea empty on her lap. Don picks her up, cradling her in his arms; he carries her up the stairs to the attic where she sleeps and lays her on her bed fully clothed, pulls the duvet over her so that she will be warm in the night.

'Please stay,' she says, half-opening her eyes.

'Of course.' He lets himself under the covers, folds Tania in his arms so that together they will be warm, squeezes her tightly to him as she sleeps.

15

For a while, Tania, at least, will need him. Don grasps at her thin, reedy love.

The old woman has neglected herself in recent years, and her callow *nipote* has failed to notice this. There is much cleaning to be done: much moving of heavy pre-War chairs and old divans. Generations of cat litter has been turned by the action of moisture, heat and cold to concrete. Paintings and statues and stuff to do with God need to be shifted. There is decades' worth of settled dust; thick, pungent encrustations on the grill pan. He scoops black roasting-fat from the floor of the smoky oven with his nails. He beats the carpets and dusts the shelves and wraps ornaments in newspaper; boxes and labels everything so that the family will know what, and what not, to sell.

Tania sits watching him with heavy eyes from the corner, a cat or two in her lap, fingers twined in the soft neck hair, sipping her tea, wondering, perhaps, who he really is.

There are boxes of letters to be filed; yellowed photos of a younger, still glamorous thirty-five year-old wartime widow with a child; younger-still pictures of the dead woman with her dead man – a sharp-faced, thick-haired boy from the south with a black suit and wild eyes who died fighting with the partisans in '42. The same black and white picture that hangs, fading with the others, in front of the town hall. A picture of a grave with flowers. The same dried flowers, sixty years on: treasured, wrapped in crepe, kept in a box. Don casts their rustling stems into the bin, while the petals turn to powder in his hands.

He speaks to a priest in a church to arrange a funeral, then phones Bolton to tell them what he's done. By now they know his voice, know him as 'Donny, Tania's new boyfriend,' and are grateful to have him around.

It is a relief no longer to be free.

One morning, a few days later, he goes back to the squat and notices that Marco has been back – a shift in the dust, an odour of fresh, stale sweat, Marco's irrepressible socks – but the author of the smells is not currently there, and Don is relieved not to have to explain his absence to his friend. He pulls together his stuff – sleeping bags, fiddle, a few clothes, a few books – packs it all away in his rucksack, leaves.

He stands with the family at the funeral. Tania's mother, Angelina, an implausibly glamorous woman in her forties with raven-black hair and a glossy face who greets him with a steady eye, sizes him up, and slightly fancies him. Her Italian accent almost replaced by that of the north-west of England – she's not been home for *years*. She runs a café near Chorley. Her husband's a big bloke with tattoos and a gut and a hod-carrier's shoulders. He's a builder from Farnworth with a thriving business. You meet him and know him in an instant: he's a *good* man. Her little brother, Steve, a young thirteen years old, fidgety and bright tangled red hair, looks at him curiously – my big sister's got a *boyfriend?*– along the pews as they sing hymns for his Nan, whom he'd scarcely met. The uncles and the aunts, all in Australia, send cards but stay behind. Don bows his head, but can't kneel for the prayers; sits alone whilst the others queue for the wafers and the wine, and the family, and everyone, respects him for his principles.

After the service and the graveside and the gathering over cakes in a café, the father takes Don aside and shakes his hand, saying: 'Thanks for everything, son. Thanks.' Don grows in his skin, meets the builder's eyes.

'It's the least I could have done, Stanley.'

Over four days Stanley, Steve and he use their muscle to clear the flat – throwing out most of it, packing the rest in a white van – and the days of labour make them friends.

'I hope we'll be seeing more of you back home, Don!' says Stanley, the evening they leave. The van's all packed – Don and Tania will set off a day or two later, taking it easy because there's no rush. The family and cats are packed in the car. Steve in the back looks at Don with bright, glad eyes; imagines the two of them hanging like brothers in Bolton; sees him as a kind of social capital which will float him through his gathering adolescence. The mother, in the front passenger seat, smiles a promise. She has enjoyed, vicariously, Tania's man. Her daughter's new femininity – her hunger – her cat-like lust, in fact; those secrets and passions which the mother instantly recognised, alight and flickering behind her daughter's new eyes.

Stanley just likes Don – sees in him the kind of honest, straightforward, hardworking lad *he* would have chosen for his daughter, and doesn't trouble himself with the rest.

Don and Tania watch them go. Don has one arm around Tania's waist; waves with his other hand. Tania lifts her head from his shoulder; looks a little curiously at him as the big blue family car rounds the corner and disappears.

§

10AM of the fourth day on which Don has intended to leave. Every morning he wants to make an early start, but Tania's not bothered – she turns and buries her face in the pillow and weeps, and Don doesn't want to push. So hours and days have drifted by. The truth is – and Don will never quite realise this – she doesn't *really* want to go. She's not even *that* sure about the new Don, in fact.

Another day squandered, he thinks, irritable as an old husband. Irritable as his *Dad*.

He set off that morning with the simple intention of wandering. A mental farewell to a place where he has had a strange but happy time. An appraisal. A time in his life that has been grand, in its own way. Creative. He has made strong friendships, which he will never forget. He will boast about this, in future. About that sniff of violence. The day he was almost recruited as a spy. Horst and his gun. Mariotti. The lot. He will invent. How he begged and busked for a season, lived on his friend's floor in a shop-front, hung out with the reds – the urban Indians – the *guerriglia*; went wild. So: this little walk, to straighten out his story. To remember the time as it really was, before it becomes an imagined time, before it becomes his past. A moment to anticipate nostalgia. Prolepsis. A time to blow away regrets; a time to move on.

I have done everything that I desired. Soccia! Me la sono succhiata tutta. He can think in Italian now. *But what did I want…? Why did I come here? And why did I leave?* He knows that he'll never forget this time.

Already he is forgetting.

Walks north to the squat to say farewell to Marco, hoping that Marco will not be there. Presses his nose against the window, squinting through a crack in the cardboard, sees Marco's sleeping bag; makes out – just – his friend's shape lying in it, slug-like. Says goodbye, whispering it to himself. The condensation runs down the inside of the window. He could knock on the door, force him up; he could leave his friend a note... But he does neither. He visits their pitches instead; remembers a few tunes they played, some hot days, guys with bead bracelets and braids, their sweaty girls... A hot summer, and the tunes from a long while ago. He walks around the *Piazza Nettuno*; inspects the façade of the town hall where they hung the greying photos of the War dead, picks out again the face of the grandfather – two rows from the top, three grey photos along. He walks the arcades, looks in the windows of shops, thinks of climbing the hill to *San Luca*, changes his mind, has a beer instead on the pavement outside a café on *Indipendenza*.

But the last, big farewell he orbits – avoiding it, yet unable quite to forget. It's a responsibility to one friendship which he cannot duck. He stubs out his cigarette, pays for his beer, drags his steps over the quarter-mile of arcades and narrow streets to the *Usignol*.

A bright, glittering cold day, clear after heavy rain the night before. It seems she's been waiting for him. She's sitting alone at her usual table – the only person outside, so late in the year – her scarf wrapped around her neck, jacket tight about her. Her paper folded, unopened on the table in front, coffee in her hand, cigarette burning down in the ashtray. She frowns when he appears, bag over his shoulder, dressed for travelling. He stands before her, one foot in the gutter, the other on the narrow cobbled pavement. He returns the frown. That sharp, private thing, still buried in his chest, pricks at his heart.

'I've been wondering whether I can trust you,' says Maria suddenly, with neither warning nor artifice, holding his eye in hers as if their last conversation had never ended. 'Can I trust you?'

Don nods, then flinches, looking away. 'I came to say goodbye. I have to leave.'

She raises her eyebrows, squints into the sun to see his face more clearly. She looks tired.

'Why?'

'I'm taking Tania home. She's going to train as a nurse. I think I may too.'

'Ah.'

This new plan, thought up these last few days and said aloud for the first time, withers and dies in the instant of its uttering. *Am I fuck going to be a nurse.* 'Or something.'

'I'm sorry. Our friendship has meant a lot to me,' says Maria finally, with a struggle, a look of sadness, missed opportunity – a tear, even – swelling in the corner of her eye. Don feels suddenly, vividly, like someone else – some other, better, bloke – the man he *could*, or *ought*, to be. Suffocated by regret, he sits.

'Yes. And to me, Maria.'

'When do you leave?'

'Today. Tomorrow.'

She nods. Smoothes the surface of her paper with the back of her hand, stubs out the butt of her cigarette on the table, grinds it under her heel, lights another, says:

'I was going to go to the beach today. The seaside. Would you like to come?'

'The *beach*?'

She nods abruptly.

It's a funny kind of day for the beach.

'Okay.'

'Right.' She stands, slings her little leather bag over her shoulder. 'Let's go.'

A strange, tense, changeable girl, Maria.

16

Her car is a rusted, once-blue Diane, parked in its own little space outside an imperious and gated *Palazzo* on *Garibaldi* where Don, surprised, supposes Manu must live.

She startles and fidgets, ducking her head when cars or people pass. She wears dark glasses against a thin winter sun, warding off the stares of hostile strangers, and so drives half-blind, hiding behind the wheel, wrapping her scarf around her head, covering half her face. They drive the rattling little car too fast, sliding over greasy wet cobbles, passing through the smoky morning streets without words. Maria shrinks back into the canvas seat, muttering under her breath at the red lights, rattling her impatient fingers on the steering wheel. But once out of the city, heading on the south-west road to Rimini, as if a shadow has lifted from her, Maria relaxes.

'We're going to a little town called San Lorenzo. My parents used to take us there when we were very small. It will be a long drive. A few hundred kilometres south. Many hours. I think you will like this place.'

Out in the countryside, the day feels early still. They drive a long straight road lined by poplars, through grey fields and their cracked, red-stone farmsteads, plumes of mist drifting like smoke between out-houses. Later on the wind rises, and there's sand in the air, and the air smells of the sea. They pull the car roof down and play music for a while to drown their silence, drumming flat hands on the thin chassis, the wind snatching words from their mouths. Don hangs his arm over the car door, lets the cold air run like water through his numb fingers, as if they were sailing in a boat.

During lunch she points over his shoulder at a branch in the road: a narrow track snaking up into the grey-blue Apennines, rising to the south.

'I was raised not far from here. My grandmother had a farmhouse near a village, an hour or two that way. She looked after me when I was very little. My father was in prison. He was a writer. A pacifist, like you, but also a man who fought for his beliefs. I am a country girl – *una paesana* – in my heart. They took me back when I was six, after Marco was born. We lived in Turin. This is a terrible country, Don. It's beautiful, but it's the most evil country in the world. It's a long time since I came this way. You asked me a question. Do you still want to know the answer?'

A darting look; a thin, uncertain smile.

'Yes,' says Don.

'Okay.' Deep breath.

They sit for a while side by side on the cold dust of the roadside, resting on pine needles and sand, their backs against the car door, glimpsing patches of sea between the dark green branches of the roadside pines. Don has stolen yesterday's bread, left by Sammi on the bar before they left. He breaks it now, handing half to Maria, keeping half to himself, letting the crumbs fall on his lap. The bread is sour and tough; it hurts his jaws as he chews.

'Manu saved my life. He made me what I am, and yet he has destroyed me too. He has been the beginning and the end of everything for me. I would have been lost without him.'

Hunched in her coat against the wind, she looks at him with big, tear-smeared violet eyes. She recites:

'I loved him. Once.'

Shivering all the time against the cold, her face paper thin.

Brave Don stands, blows in his palms, buries his white hands under his arms, stamps his feet.

'And now you don't. Let's go, before we die.'

❦

They descend a long, hair-pin road on a cliff above the sea. Winter olives writhe from their banked clay terraces, sticks reaching across the road, silver-green leaves trailing and slapping across the windows of the car; figs, out of season, bare-branched walnuts and almond trees ranked in orchards on the hills above the road. In summer the fruit will be crushed and slippery on the asphalt; wild hogs, come from the hills at night, will descend to gorge on the fallen fruit; the fields will sing with the sound of cicadas; the air will shimmer with insects; the thrumming heat of the sun will still everything that moves. Today – this afternoon – the cold morning mists have cleared, the sky is brilliant, the sea deep blue. A steady east wind blows and their faces begin to numb.

It's late by the time they come into San Lorenzo. A little castellated citadel reaching to the cliffs above, below which lies a village on a beach: a cluster of fishing houses on pebbles, a jetty and an ancient, cracked church, clinging to the steep sides of a narrow bay as if once washed there by the sea, cast up after a storm and held there, gripped by the jaws of the headlands – the ragged black cliffs to the north and to the south.

The sun sets early in winter on this cliff-bound village, and by four everything is in shadow. The narrow road winding down from the hill is deserted. They're in the shadow of the wind here, and the air in the trees is just a whisper; the houses are shuttered, the one or two shops are closed; there is complete silence but for the engine and the drumming of their tires over cobbles.

They leave the car in the tiny square, shut and lock the doors, whispering for fear of breaching the winter's silence. They warm themselves in a café on the corner opposite the church. The owner – beetle-browed man, black, oily hair and pencil moustache, filthy grey apron – frowns at them as he pours them beer. He has a room, he says: only one, two single beds, a small price. 'Do you want to see?'

Later. Later. As if hesitating on the brink of love, these two won't be rushed by *details*.

They drink beer at the bar. They are strangers here, warming themselves in the thick, old air, the stink of tobacco, the drifting voices.

Her voice:

'After our parents were killed, Marco and I were separated. I stayed at school. I became educated, and channelled my anger into politics – what I thought of as the continuation of my parents' work. He lived in a home – an orphanage, run by the Christian Brothers. I did well; he got into trouble. He stole cars. He has a great talent for theft. I'm sure you can imagine. He ran away from the home when he was thirteen. We lost contact for many years.'

At one end of the bar there is a machine which dispenses nuts. A thin young woman with a child comes in, feeds the machine a coin, takes a handful of nuts which she gives to the child. The two disappear through the saloon doors, leaving behind a drift of cold air which slowly dissipates. *Junkie*, thinks Don. A poster advertises a local concert, the star of which is a local girl, singing from *L'Elisir* and *Norma*, the date passed years since. Two old men in torn white shirts, greasy black jackets, berets – both once fishermen, both now without boats – gamble with dice in the dark in the back corner, smoking their pipes, arguing quietly, like the living shades of their grandfathers.

'I met Manu when I was nineteen. He was a professor of law and politics at the University of Rome. I was one of his students. I saw him as the only gentle man in a violent world. Rather unworldly. He was my only safety. He was the only person that I trusted.

'I was very angry then; very uncompromising. I had known nothing but politics since my teens. My whole world – my friendships, my studies, every moment of my spare time – was bound up in the hunger I had both to continue the work of my parents, and revenge their deaths. Manu was something quite new to me. He can be very kind – you will not have seen that side of him. He is not political in the sense that I was, and my ... friendship ... with him was a refuge from that.'

They sit at the bar, perched on their bar-stools. She with black curly hair spilling over her shoulders, a strong face, slightly hawkish, sharp, bright eyes; belted coat and a tasselled bag at her feet; staring into the eyes of her companion, her left hand up, fingers coming together in a cone, moving her hand briskly forth to make her point. Dry-eyed now, every word she utters carries force. She's nervous; she darts little glances at strangers, lowers her voice when they enter, lest she be overheard. He, a few years younger, with his wiry frame, shaven head, blue eyes; he looks at her with a face like awe. A leather jacket collapses over a canvas rucksack at his feet; a cigarette is wedged between his fingers. His Italian is broken but improving; his accent is good. Poised to tell him her secrets, she hesitates.

Lovebirds. Adulterers, thinks the barman with the oily hair and rancid soul, sampling the air with his fleshy nose, sniffing out the alluring scents of sex and money.

The girl talks.

The barman with his thin black moustache sits munching pretzels, scratching his arse, watches soccer on the TV propped on one end of the bar: a black and white set, the aerial balanced squint on top, a tinny roar from its speakers covering the couple's furtive conversation. Mad for Lazio, he punches the air – *Goal!* the fans scream. The two at the bar lean closer. Their glasses are empty, their ashtray half-full. The woman talks in a rapid, quiet whisper; the man strains to understand, to catch every word, because every word matters.

It's getting late. The café owner leans towards them. His words are barely audible over the chattering TV – *you wan' da fuckin' room or not?* – and like guilty lovers the two spring apart. The woman nods, *yes*, and they follow him from the bar through a side door, from where he lifts one of three sets of keys that dangle there. He hits the time-switch on the narrow yellow stairway, switching on a yellow light, and the three make their way up the worn steps.

He insists he only has the one room. A narrow slot with a lino floor and tiny window overlooking the bay. A livid green-skinned picture of Christ on the wall with a crown of thorns, blood budding from his forehead wounds like tiny purple berries. Two single beds on either side of a string of pink carpet; wallpaper stained yellow-brown by decades worth of smoke; a sink with a green stain around the plug-hole; a chain with no plug. Nothing like soap; nothing like a towel; a powerful, sweet smell of mildew. The young man shrugs his shoulders, uncertain; smiles a question, looking at the girl, who laughs at him. They take it. Fine. The barman smirks, clocking the timid *ragazzo's* hard-on, the girl's diffidence. Sensing sex, their *delicate dilemma,* he palms a handful of notes and leaves them to it. The two, alone in the cold room, look at one another embarrassed as each drops their little bag on their respective bed.

'Let's see if his food's any better than his accommodation.'
'Yeah.'
They flee.

Four square tables with greasy, red and white checked covers in a room next to the bar; a silent kitchen. The barman snaps on the light, calls to his tired wife who stands above them, arms folded over her bosom, mouth like a clipped purse, taking their order. She brings them rancid wine, a basket of bread, shuts the kitchen door behind her.

'I'm sorry now to bring you to this place, *Ton.* It is horrible. You see, *my* memories are the memories of a child, and in summer, too. That man was once a young man and he used to joke with my father; his sourpuss wife used to give me sweets. They had a son, our age, who we played with.' Maria glows for a little with nostalgia. 'It's strange and terrible how things change. But I'm sorry. Now it's all horrible.'

Don looks up at the pictures on the wall. Four dogs dressed as men in a smoky billiard room: a fat dog chalking a cue; a thin dog with long ears, mournful eyes and a pipe in his snout that reminds him of Mariotti; a sleek hound in a dog-toothed jacket potting the blue; a small fat round dog in a business suit. A bitch with a ribbon in her hair and a cute arse brings the men-dogs beer. On the wall opposite, behind Maria, a calendar with a pair of lorry tires. A hatchet-faced girl with a steel grin and blond hair turns her tail to the camera, spreading herself with ruby-varnished finger-tips. Don stares; Don flinches guiltily away. Drinks his harsh wine, smokes, chews his bread, looks into the face of the real girl opposite him, considers her seriousness – the weight of the things she has told him; the weight of those things yet untold. He longs to touch her; holds back, sensing the distance they still must travel before he can touch *her*.

He thinks of the cold room upstairs with its narrow beds – how will they negotiate these beds? Both in one saggy cot, clinging together under thin, damp sheets, clinging for warmth? How will it end? He thinks of the breakfast they will have the morning after, and the journey home again, and wonders who they will be, the two of them, tomorrow? Looks again at the girl: the lost expression on her face, a face she wears only for him and which he can never adequately read: the wide eyes, the *hope* he sees written there. The smile, the habit she has – which he cannot reciprocate – of briefly placing her hand on his when they are alone: a comfort. And of withdrawing it, as soon as there is another there to see.

'It's *not* horrible, Maria,' he says after a pause. 'This place is … special. I think I'll remember this *horrible* place of yours forever.'

And then she does it again. Tentatively touches the back of his hand, drawing her fingers gently across his skin, thanking him.

'But there are things I have to tell you.'

'I know.'

The café owner's woman brings them more bread.

'He was my tutor, at university, in Rome.'

Don places his glass to one side, puts his chin in his hands, looks up at her, feels himself pulled into the slipstream of her story.

'He picked me out from all the others in my class. I slept with him almost in my first week. I don't know how he knew.'

Knew what?

She answers the unspoken thought:

'That my rage was the result of hurt, not belief. That my parents were both dead, and my brother, whom I promised I would protect, was in prison. That I was alone in the world. He saw that it was love and protection that I yearned for, not revolution. My only family were my partners in the struggle. I had been politically active from my school days; when I arrived at university, I already had a reputation amongst my fellow students. He saw all of this and cut through it by offering me a kind of material and intellectual comfort which I despised even as I grasped for it.'

A *frittata* is brought, with a thin, yellow skin, a vinegary green salad, pickled vegetables, tomatoes, more bread. *Fettuccini* with meatballs in a thin tomato sauce. Dusty old *pasticcini* soaked in syrup, lifted by the lady from a varnished case with a net to keep the flies away. Rank coffee.

'I spent my days in the university building barricades and organising strikes. At night I swapped this for the comfort of his flat in the Monticullo, with its Modigliani prints and the harpsichord, where I would drink his wine and relax. He taught me about hypocrisy, and eventually the nun in me rebelled and I broke with him.

'He didn't appear to notice. One day I failed to come home. We were organising something big. A noble, trivial thing – a demonstration protesting against the withdrawal of subsidies from the university canteen, which meant that the poorer students would no longer be able to eat – but it was important. Back then, political meetings almost always ended in violence: that was part of their purpose. Demos were a sort of *audition* for students like me to perform, to demonstrate our commitment. And for the ones that wanted to take their rage a little bit further: to show off their talent, and become more involved, too. They were always looking for more talent. I was making my choice.'

❧

This girl, though, has great talent.

Those whose work it is to watch her, see these things: the purity and strength of her anger. The simplicity of its source. The diligence and skill with which she organises others. Her ability to be soft when appropriate, yet ruthless too. They see and note how confidently she moves in this harsh, masculine world which she shapes to her own ends with such perfect efficiency. Few are as talented as she.

She marches around like a quarter-master, inspecting, lending a hand with a sandbag, the odd barricade, the smashing of desks and other furniture to build the pickets. She holds the matches when the tyres are set alight in the campus square. She coins and paints slogans on red flags, fills glass bottles with petrol, stoppers them with rags, lines them up behind doors torn from hinges and set on their edges. She soaks pillowcases in water to use as masks and, in an emergency, bandages. She has her eyes about her too: she knows that she is noticed, but not yet by whom.

While her friend Prospero holds the little hessian sack open at the neck, she uses a trowel to spoon in sand. Outside, the noises of battle grow. The police have always been armed, and now some of the students are too. The air stinks of tear-gas – though the two comrades wear damp hankies tied around their mouths, their eyes still run.

Later this evening there will be some, pitifully young, left bleeding on the pavements, but they are never the real brigatisti. *The one that catches the bullet is always the least in rank.*

But Maria is ready to die tonight. Her anger is high and she is ripe for martyrdom. But as the forces of the law gather outside, Manu moves in – deft and unseen, he crosses the muttering barricades. In the distance, the first sound of gunfire, the smell of tear-gas. Manu leans against a coffee machine, sips a coffee, smokes one of his unlimited cigarettes, waits to be seen. Prospero the friend nods over Maria's shoulder, mutters darkly, suspicious: 'Your professor's here…'

'Fuck.' She looks up, angry. His presence undermines her credibility – makes her seem complicit. He just smiles at her, innocent, and beckons to her. She hisses: 'How the fuck did you get in here…!' But he silences her, turns his back and leads her away until, at a safe distance, he says 'Keep your face hidden,' as they pass three comrades in leather who nurse a tiny hidden camera.

'*So what is it?*' *she asks him, in the safety of his study. He smiles.*
'*Once your face is known, you can no longer be useful.*'
'*To whom?*' *she asks, still suspicious.*

§

'Laugh at me, but I hadn't realised until that moment that Manu was involved. I regarded him with a little contempt. He was a vice: a source of compromise and hypocrisy from which I needed to be free. *He* just needed me for a job. They wanted a new face; they'd picked mine out months before.

'In March 1978 the movement took a hostage. A politician called Alfredo Collina. You may have heard of this man. He was the *architect* of the Multi-Nationals' State, and as far as we were concerned, he was the devil. He sponsored the historic compromise with the Communists, the offer to them of a share in government, in return for their principles. The great collusion. He was the brains and the conscience behind the corruption that we were committed to destroying. His party, the party of compromise, was the political black hole which sucked in our country's idealism, all belief, all possibility of a just future for everyone. When this man's head was offered to us, although it was clear to many that it could only be trap, there were others of our comrades who couldn't refuse it. Orders were passed down the long chain. We acted. My friends acted.'

§

Half-past two on a busy Tuesday afternoon on the Via Fani *in Rome. It's early spring, and the cherry trees lining the wide, imperial streets are heavy with pink blossom, the last of the winter rain just past. An un-armoured black Fiat limo passes, cutting scales of water from the puddles on the road, the light of the new sun refracted in the scattered drops of water. Passers-by stop to watch the makeshift motorcade – police car in front, outriders on the flanks. A sombre man, heavy after a full lunch, sits dozing in the back of the limo, gazing blankly out of the window. He thinks he recognises one of two men who stand on the corner of the street reading a paper, looking up with dark, malevolent eyes to trail the car as it passes.*

He thinks to tell the driver that he suspects ... something. Decides not. The motorcade moves slowly off into the traffic.

Two forty-five; the motorcade is delayed and the passenger grows anxious. They move off again, intolerably slowly, and he looks back at the papers he is reading. Is startled by the sudden application of the brakes, the jolt and noise of metal upon metal – looks up, swears quietly: a little red car – a Renault 4 – has pulled out in front of them from a side street, and they've hit it. Swears again as the doors of the car in front open and two men emerge – grim-looking faces, hands buried in the folds of their bulky jackets. He shouts, but the words are torn from his mouth by the silent after-shock of gunfire. He blinks in horror and surprise as the head of his chauffeur explodes into fragments of glass and bone. His bodyguard lies slumped against the door. His passenger door opens and already he stands outside on the road, hands up, pleading mercy as his coat is pulled over his head and he is forced – the cloth over his face muffling his cries – into the boot of the car behind.

Two minutes, fourteen seconds. Good work, thinks his captor.

'We were presented with the dilemma, once we had him, of how best he was to be used. Whether we should try him and sentence him for the crimes of the party he represented; whether we should exchange him for money, or prisoners; whether, as some favoured, we should make him recant, become *our* tool, *convince* him – or whether we should simply execute him. Hang his head from the window with a placard, and watch as the crowds gather to cheer. There were so many possibilities open to us that summer – such a *bounty* of possibilities.'

'*Make him your friend, Maria. Find out what he likes – what makes him laugh, what makes him weep. Whatever it is, give it to him. Make him confide in you. Talk to him; listen to what it is he believes. Soon he will do anything to please you. You will find him a civilised man. He will talk to someone like you. But do not let yourself be fooled by him.*'

The kitchen of an ugly flat in a high-rise outside Rome. She has been hiding out there for two weeks since the hostage was lifted. The man who was her lover stands behind where she sits, talking. Two other senior cadres whom she has never seen sit opposite her at the table. The third, gazing out through a gap in the newspaper covering the window, smoking his pipe, saying nothing, is Mariotti. She has heard his name before; she is overawed by his presence.

'Are you prepared for this? You do not have to do this.' A reassuring hand, gently placed on her shoulder. Manu. For the first time she shivers at the man's touch.

'I'm ready,' she says, in a small, uncertain voice.

❦

'I was told over the phone where to go, in code, by a stranger's voice. No-one but Mariotti knew the location of the people's prison: the address was a flat in a lane off a street only three blocks north of the *via Fani* where he had first been lifted.'

❦

She hurries down the busy street. She stops in the middle of the pavement, studying an address that is hand-written on the back of a bus ticket. She is blocking the way, and two heavily-built men with oiled, black hair and expensive dark suits step around her, staring and swearing. She stares back, is about to shout – Cornuti! – give them the finger – then stops herself, wondering: are they watching me? Do they know me? She stares back, finds herself meeting the eye of a policeman – his light machine gun cradled in the crook of his arm; mirror shades in which she sees reflected her own, scared expression.

She stands on the pavement opposite while crowds wander by, looking up at the block of flats from the street below, counting – second from the top, on the fifth floor, the corner flat, and there it is: sheets tacked over the window frames all the windows occluded despite the hot, hot weather. All windows tightly shut. It seems so obvious. She swallows her fear. Even from where she stands, from the level of the street, the place reeks of captivity.

She rings the bell, speaks briefly in a low, suspicious whisper to the concierge, who directs her up. She knocks on the door and after a brief silence, they let her in.

To a widow's flat. A front door darkly varnished, a knocker and a name plate; a widow's front hall with a wrought iron stand for umbrellas, and pictures of Jesus and The Virgin on the walls. The guard in the hall is a rat-faced boy with a gun, who she's never met – looking serious with his combats and oily hair and the walled-off eyes of those ready to die for their beliefs.

The second guard she does know. Marco. They haven't seen one another since his release from prison three months previously. He is naked, but for a towel around his waist and an Uzzi over his shoulder. He is ragged and unshaven. The widow's flat where he prowls, with every window tightly closed, filled with angry or frightened men, stinks like a tigers' cage.

He isn't expecting to see her. His eyes pop with shock when they set upon her face and he swears. Grim-faced, the joy has been burned from him. He's been in this second prison for almost thirty days. He's hardly slept, hasn't washed, lived on nothing but bread. He swears when he sees her – then: 'Maria. We're fucked.' She doesn't understand. Then he nods to a door, says, 'He's in there. Wear this.' He gives her a stocking for her head, to cover up her face.

❦

'The door wasn't locked. Another odd thing. I walked in. Collina was sitting on the floor. A man in his fifties – once a dignified man with a face the whole world would recognise – a lock of grey hair across his forehead, big, soulful eyes, his full, catholic mouth. Feet stretched out on the floor, he was leaning against the wall. There were floorboards nailed across the windows and sheets nailed over these, and the place was lit by a single light-bulb. He was wearing the clothes he'd been picked up in: black suit trousers; a crumpled white dress shirt, unbuttoned at the neck and the collar off; the cross which he'd worn, which he always held, grasped in both hands. The jacket and the collar and the tie were lying on the single bed, waiting for when he needed to be smart again. *His* room didn't smell.

'He looked up at me when I walked in, with this completely expressionless face – his mouth opened to greet me, but no words coming out. He was trying to be polite. I could tell: he was trying

to greet me. To put me at my ease. But it was the look in his eyes
– that infinitely miserable expression on his empty face – that made
me understand the significance of what my brother had said. We
were fucked. This man would be the downfall of us all. This man's
misery would swallow us up.

'Faced with his face, I took the stocking from my head so that
he could know me. Why? It was my first violation of the rules – my
first doubts; my first step away. I was motivated by kindness, I think,
but if it was meant to gain his confidence it failed, because he asked
me immediately, in a quavering, fearful little voice – so much at
odds with the rest of his great dignity – whether this gesture meant
that he was to die that day. And so I said no. Not today. Not *that*
day. And he started to weep, and so I stood and waited as the man
pulled himself together, as he wiped the tears from his eyes with a
sheet. Then he stared back at me, and held my eye until I looked
away in shame. I asked him if he wanted anything, if there was
anything I could do. He shook his head, angry, and so I asked him
again – kicked him, I think, to my shame – and he said a word
that I didn't hear first time. So I asked him to say it again, and he
said, "Risotto." I nodded. He said "With porcini. Chicken livers.
And white wine."'

'Mariotti had instructed me to do anything necessary to gain
his trust. We needed leverage. I left the People's Prison unobserved
– marched out through the front door, swinging it shut behind me.
I bought provisions: the rice from an *alimentari* on *Via Montalcini*,
white table wine for stock, some chilled Frascati to drink; dried ceps,
vegetables, a chicken for stock. I cooked his mother's risotto in the
widow's dismal little kitchen. Peasant food. The scent of the country
– his country. I knew what it was that he wanted. I *sympathised*.
And that was how I befriended him.'

'Let's walk.'

Suddenly she breaks off her story, looking around with an
expression like fear as if the walls were closing around them. The
brown side-board with the remains of cake; the yellow walls; the
ghastly pictures.

'I *hate* this place. Please let's walk.'

Don nods, empties his glass, follows her onto the dimly-lit street
outside. They walk on the harbour wall, listening to the sea breathe;

they watch the white sea-spray, picked out from the black by the street lights. Maria takes his arm, pulls him close to her as they go. She's shivering.

'I haven't spoken about this before.'

'That hostage. He was killed, wasn't he?'

They walk together to the end of the bay, beyond the reach of the street lights. They lean against a stanchion, smoke cigarettes one by one, and watch the stars – Andromeda, high in the winter sky; the Sheaf, the Great and the Little Bears; the black line of the horizon, barely perceived; the dancing lights of fishing boats out on the blacker sea.

'Although he knew that he was destined to die, the hostage was entirely without rancour. His anger he reserved for his friends in the party. When I brought him his food, he thanked me with the grace of a priest; he insisted that I feed his captors with the remains.

'He had been a politician all of his life; he was famed for his deviousness, his ability to compromise, his tactics, the obscurity of his language and motives, his extraordinary ability to sacrifice principles in the pursuit of power for his party. His moral sleight of hand. Yet he was not evil. He couldn't possibly be. Although in fear of his life, he still found it in his heart to treat *us* well.

'On that road which led downward toward his death, he was always three steps ahead. He knew the route better than we. He understood perfectly the inevitability of the outcome, and our powerlessness to prevent it. In fact, he *showed* us the way. When we attempted to reassure him – that a deal would be made, for example; that there would be some kind of compromise that would permit his release – he would merely smile, graciously, sadly, humouring us for our naivety, and explain – "They won't treat with you. My *friends* want me dead." Then handed us, unsealed so that we wouldn't be *embarrassed* when we read them later, sheaves of his letters: to his wife, these *friends* in the party and government, the press, pleading for his life.

'When we told him that, whatever happened, *we would not kill him*, he would jab his forefinger at the front pages of the daily newspapers that we allowed him, and say: "It is not *you* that will kill me. They have invented this *fermezza*, this new politics of *not giving in to terrorists* especially for me. It is the political instrument which compels my execution. When the time comes, *you*, my friends, will have *no choice.*"'

Maria, saying these words, shivers. There is a breeze coming off the water, coming from the east, cutting up waves, lifting spray, and their skins stiffen with salt. Don puts his arms around her shoulder, pulls her to him, and briefly she rests her head there.

'I like that,' she says simply.

Their eyes become accustomed to the dark; they watch the rising, falling sea.

This is it. If she has said nothing to discourage me before I count to three, then I will kiss her. One. Two. Three ...

He moves to turn to her. She resists.

'I have to tell you what happened first. I can't be ... happy ... until I have told you.'

'I know,' said Don, dread lying like a stone in his belly.

'Your enemy, the one you so despise, Mariotti, was the judge in the People's Tribunal which tried and sentenced the hostage. I kept the record. I wrote the press release which announced the death sentence, and its date. I posted the letter which he wrote to his wife and his daughters, saying his last farewell. I was there, at every step, *involved*.

'His trial was a tactic – to put pressure on the government to make a concession; to get us out of this hole in which we had found ourselves. I took his photo: our banner behind his head, the copy of *La Repubblica*, the headline *Collina Assassinato?* on the front. I asked him to smile, and he smiled bitterly for us, and when we developed the picture to send with our press release we thought that that face he wore – so sad, so bitter, so resigned – would make the world so pity him – pity *us* – that they would pay, and let us let him go. It was a tactic. I truly believed that it would work.

'Only he *really* understood. Two days after the announcement of the death sentence, we were still waiting for a response from the state. This was the worst time in the entire fifty-four days of his captivity. We had a deadline two days hence. We all knew, though said nothing about it, that there was no plan after that. The hostage, unusually, hadn't eaten. I was worried for him. It was at the back of my mind that he had been locked in the flat for more than seven weeks; that he was going to get sick if the situation wasn't resolved. It made me very angry – that the forces in the government which were keeping him there were so casual about their responsibility.

'I flung his uneaten food in the bucket, said something about the fact that he would die if he wasn't released soon. Marco whispered, "Listen to me, Maria..."

'There was something quite uncharacteristic about the tone of his voice: such urgency and bleakness that it startled me and made me turn. We were alone in the kitchen, which was very unusual. The people's prison was a very crowded place – by and large Mariotti and I were the only cadres ever allowed to leave, and we minimised as much as possible the amount of coming and going – which meant that after all this time, five or six guards had accumulated. It was a rats' cage.

'"Maria, they've told me *I* have to do it."

'"Do what?" I said, impatiently. Stupidly.

'He just looked at me, eyes terrified, completely powerless. A child, practically in tears. Why, of all of them, did they have to choose him?

'I didn't say anything; I just stared at him. Hopeless. Then Martino – the rat-faced gaoler – came in, saw that we had been talking, gave us this long, hard, angry, suspicious look, and left.

'So I made a call. That same morning, I let myself out of the prison, went to the café on the corner and phoned the police. They put me through to a special department, and I gave them the address of the people's prison. I didn't tell them who I was, but they knew anyway. It was as if they already knew everything, always a step or two ahead.'

'What happened?' asks Don.

'Nothing. I returned to the prison. I waited, resigned and ready, but nothing happened. Two days later, Marco shot our hostage – the order came and he had no choice other than to obey. He and I put the body into the back of the same red Renault 4 which had been used when he was taken, and left him with a note around his neck, in the boot at the side of the street, a quarter of a mile from his Party's headquarters.

'We locked the car and walked away. It was four or five in the morning, but the streets were still busy. We parted at the street corner, and didn't see one another again for months. He was soon back in prison for other, unrelated things. I have told no-one this, apart from you. If you ever tell anyone, if anyone finds out, I will be killed. The hostage is always on my mind. I cannot forget his face.'

'Did you ever tell Manu?'

She looks at him with an odd mixture of pity, affection and contempt.

'You don't understand anything, Don. I haven't told *anyone* this. After Collina's murder, the cadres dispersed. *He* moved to Bologna, and I followed. I had nowhere else to go. Now I do whatever he tells me. I live in his flat, I share his bed, I suck his cock. He *owns* me.'

Don stands in frozen silence, trying to understand the implications of what he has been told. *Your life is at the whim of whoever you spoke to that night when you betrayed your friends. And you can never escape this.*

'You asked me, when we last spoke, whether I loved him. I didn't answer. I would not have been able to. I hadn't considered it, until you posed the question. It didn't matter. Now it does. But I am not free.'

'Why have you told me this?'

'Because you said that you were going, and I don't want you to. You are the only person I have who is uncontaminated. I wanted you to stay.' This last said with enormous struggle.

But he can't look at her. His heart beats so hard that it hurts; his throat is so tight that he feels he will suffocate. He stares out at the waves.

She waits. Though she says nothing, her silence is eloquent: *If you think that you love me, first you have to know me.*

She stares at the sea. Then she turns to face him, pulls him round, forcing him to meet her eye. She puts her cold hands under his jacket, pulls him in towards her warm core, raises her face to his and waits.

Don looks down at her face, feels her breath on his cheek. Does nothing.

You see, he can remember, from the British papers at the time, the face of this man. Looking up from where he lay, twisted around in the boot of a Renault 4. He can even remember something of the expression on that dead face. And now, though he can run his fingers through her hair, breathe in deeply and smell her scent; and though he longs to with his whole heart; and though he may desire her with all the longing that his twenty-one years can muster, he cannot bring himself to touch her. So he lets his hands drop, and gently pushes her away.

She looks at him a little longer, then the hunger in her face dies, her expression freezes over. Okay. And it's another, less familiar, colder voice that says: 'I've said too much. I'm cold. I'm tired. I need to sleep.'

He nods and lets her turn away.

He will stand there a little longer. He will watch the lights of the fishing boats riding on the swell of the deep, black sea and think of all the life that lurks down there, the large and the small, the sprats and the swordfish, the fishermen's nets straining to hold them all; then, later, he will watch these boats come in, watch them unload their catch, the darting of the red tips of their cigarettes, their harsh voices carrying to him across a now-calmer sea, just before the dawn. Which comes, now many hours later: a rim of pink on the horizon, a bright star rising just before the sun; then a little colour on the sea, some blue in the early sky, the loss, one by one, of those passing constellations; then a lightening of his mood, the thawing of his bones when at last he tries to move.

A chatty note, tied by a red ribbon to the handle of the locked door of dead *Nonna's* little flat. A bag of Don's things left carefully on the step outside. The van he'd left parked carefully with its tyres mounted on the pavement, now long gone. Don waits until he has his coffee before he reads the note.

Dear Donnie...

...it begins, using the nickname which had always irritated him, the use of which he had never quite got round to stopping:

So long! I've gone to Bolton. Thanks for everything. I know, sometime, we'll meet again.
Your,
Tan

Cut adrift again, Don feels himself begin to sink. Something in him struggles, briefly, then stops struggling; something makes him gasp for breath, once, as he reads and re-reads her note.

17

22nd March 1980, three months later. Late at night in the *Usignol*, and all the cadres are gathered together to hear what the new comrade's got to say:

'The *Banco Di Roma* on *Rizzoli* has four tellers, two of whom are always occupied. There are never less than three others working in the back shop. The bank closes for an hour between twelve and one, and again at two-thirty. During five visits at various times of the day I have never seen fewer than eight customers, even just after opening, and just prior to closing. The safe appears to be in the back right corner next to the door to the manager's office. I haven't any real idea how access is controlled, but its position at least would suggest that this would have to be through the manager. The street outside is always busy, there is no reliable parking during the day; leaving a vehicle at night would certainly attract the attention of the *Vigili*...'

'*Ja;* next...' says Horst, tapping his fingers on the table.

'The *Banca Nazionale* on *Via Zambroni* has many of the same problems...'

'Next...' says Horst.

'The *Banca del Lavoro*...'

[*Yet each sneers so differently,* thinks Don...]

'...on the corner of *Ugo Bossi* and *Saragozza* is blah blah blah...'

Horst, without effort, automatically – as if by right – by the slightest, sceptical inclination of his head, the quizzical slitting of his yellow eyes; by the rattle of his pencil on the wooden table, by the hissing interruptions which issue from his snake-like mouth before Don has even half begun – he does it all *so* well.

Teeny Tino is more obviously hostile. More simian than serpent, he skulks in submissive silence when alone, but when surrounded by other, bigger baboons he somehow swells, preening and showing off his bright purple Mandrill's bottom, soliciting the favours of the other monkeys by his chortles and farts and his chewing of long strings of indigestible Parma ham, the remains of which he picks from between his teeth with the long nails of his manicured thumbs before examining and discarding them like bogies, wiping them furtively under the wooden table. *Very* distracting.

'...the safe is on a timed, automatic lock protected in turn by glass partitions *blah blah blah*...'

Mariotti just looks bored. Breathes too loudly, stertorously through the revolutionary hairs in his large, dog-like nose.

The beast from Bergamo snorts through his flat, porcine face, acne scattered like millet seed across his wide forehead.

'...on the other hand, the *Banca Comerciale* on *Zambroni*, although large, has the advantage *blah blah blah*...'

Even Marco betrays him – for he is there now, too – by being drunk, always.

But hush! Horst speaks:

'Ve esked you for a leetl, qviet benk, vis leetl ah ... poleez. Zees benks are all very beeg, vis meny possibilities of poleez. You undahstend? Yes?'

Gli sborro in culo a quella puttana che t'ha cagato, thinks Don, in fluent Italian.

'Yes, Horst. I totally understand.'

'Good. Try again. Try harder.'

'Right-oh.'

'You can go now.'

'And Don?'

'*Ja?*'

'Speak to anyvun about this, and ve vill kill you, yez?'

'Oh yes, oh yes. Okay. Right.'

Don stands. Tries a careless *ciao*; tries to look brave and unhumiliated; more like, ah, one of the group – an equal, almost – but no-one notices. Marco talks to the student from Bergamo; Mariotti stares deeply into the flaming bowl of his briar pipe. The cadres close around the space where once he had sat, accommodating rapidly to his absence.

So what's it all about?

An elaborate, but doomed strategy for staying close to Maria. He is doing this entirely for her. To try to re-light that damp, dead little flame. Don, a veteran of rejection and failure, should know better by now: he should know that there are never any second chances;

that once blown away, love never returns; that he has *no fucking hope at all*. But the colder the object of his passion grows, the more his passion flares.

I love her, he thinks, during those long, lonely, sweaty nights. *I will not give up until I know for certain.*

Since that night on the harbour wall, that cold night spent apart, and the next day making his own cold way home, they have scarcely spoken. If Don is present, she leaves; and if she can't, she is elsewhere, talking with her comrades – Horst or Mariotti – about other, more important things: their heads together, dark hair touching, murmuring stuff he can't hear in the dark at the far end of the table, searing him with jealousy.

So, was everything she said to me a lie? Did I imagine it all?

When he speaks she looks elsewhere; leaves when he enters the room; looks down when he tries to meet her eye. Don wonders in despair whether this woman whom he thought he'd loved, was imagined. Whether she'd ever offered him her mouth to kiss; her life story and then her warm body, all for him, on a harbour wall. Her love. Or whether he'd imagined all that too.

One night, at the end of a long and turgid meeting, he tries to force it. He'd left to piss, and when he returns the others have gone and she is alone, hurriedly packing the last of her things into her bag. She looks up, startled, when he says:

'Maria, I want to talk to you.'

Startled, but only for a moment. Then with her canny eyes wide, she glances around, seeking her escape. But he's blocking her way. She ices over. The Ice Princess says:

'What?'

Freezing him out.

'Why won't you talk to me? Wait!' he says, voice cracking, as she tries to pass him. 'These things you told me ... that night in San Lorenzo ... I wanted to say...'

'Don't!' she hisses, white-faced and a look of fear rising behind her eyes. She tries to push him out of the way. Don, raising the stakes, blocks her.

'I *have* to talk to you!'

'Please don't make me harm you,' she says, in a suddenly-calm voice. The quiet malice combined with just that hint of pity – *please!*

– piths him. He sits, collapses, whines:

'You don't trust me?'

'I have never trusted you.'

'I don't believe you. That night…'

She raises her voice – her loud, public voice, drowning him: 'You are new. You're untested. You're a virgin. That is your only value to us. So just do your job and keep your mouth shut. Do you want it or not?'

Someone, eavesdropping, has stirred in the background and quietly left.

Don looks hard into her face, searching it with narrowed eyes, looking for any little sign of purchase on its slippery glass surface. There is nothing left there at all.

But where have I heard that word – 'virgin' – in that context, before?

'Maria, you're the only reason I stay here,' he says, in this fucking desperate, sad little voice.

Nothing left there for him at all – except perhaps anger. A little flicker of anger.

'Then go,' is all she says, before pushing past him, and leaving.

How did this all go so awry?

§

By April the weather has grown warm and wet, and the tourists have returned. Each afternoon, when he's not working the banks, he stands under his portico on *Via Dei Poeti,* where the painted arches flatter his music the most. He plays unaccompanied Bach – long, clean lines of polyphony, the echoes under his favoured arch returning a rich, round sound to his now-demanding ear. His touch is truer now, and every day he plays better, more in tune, with more understanding. In the absence of love, music is his only consolation. He pours his heart out to the pavement, where his fiddle case lies open in front of him.

He plays, and with half his eye watches the chimney swifts flit from their nests in the brickwork, hunting insects in the low, evening sky. Now the season's starting once again and he plays well, every time, and he does good trade. He makes enough to eat lunch every day at the pavement café where Tania used to work: soft bread, *prosciutto,* coffee. He avoids the new waitress's eye, tips her only modestly, refraining from speech. A bleak, friendless time.

Don has been promoted by Sammi to the early evening shift behind the bar. So after a morning cleaning, in the evening he gets to be the guy that pours his own beer, spreads his paper over the wooden bar, running three cigarettes at a time as he moves between the espresso machine, the tables and the pinball when the evenings are quiet. He cuts dried bread for sandwiches for the tourists, replies in clipped Bolognese to the loud questions of angry Americans and short-changes the pink-skinned language school English girls who, mistaking him for another, flirt clumsily in Italian, and then speculate coarsely about his manhood behind their soap-smelling hands in their horsey English. They get dreadfully, giggling drunk, and on the worst, most lonely evenings, he sometimes takes them home to his and Marco's bear pit where he shares out the shocked adventuresses with his uncouth, but not unattractive chum. In the mornings he surprises them with the fluency of his English and shoos them out, before their blurred faces have time to register anger at the wretchedness of his fraud.

Half-past five one afternoon, and the phone rings. The first time, he can't be bothered to answer it. It's never been for anyone that matters before. It rings again a few minutes later, and this time Sammi takes it with an irritated glance at the indolent barman; speaks in increasingly frustrated, simple Italian, before looking up at Don:

'For you. London.'

'London?'

Tania? My Dad??

Don hurries over, suddenly anxious. No-one knows that he's there. In fact, he doesn't know *anyone* anymore. Any news must be bad news, any contact made, made after considerable effort. *God. He's dead, and I never said those things I meant to say...*

His hands sweat as he picks up the receiver.

'Don,' says a perfect, slightly American, English voice, blurred slightly by the long-distance crackle.

'Who is that?'

'Your brother.'

'I have no brother...'

169

'You do. Why haven't you phoned me?'
'Oh.' *Manu.*
'You promised to.'
'Yes. I did.'
'Nothing to tell me?'
'Ah, no.'
'Good. And my, ah, sister?'
'Who?'
'My sister. *Mary.*'
'Mary?'
'Yes.' His voice becomes a little testy.
'Oh Mary? Yeah, she's ah, fine, too.'
'Nothing happening then? Nothing planned?'
'Ah, no.'
'What about the bank then?'
'Oh, yeah … the … ah … '
'Did you forget to mention it?'
'Ah, yeah, ah, how did you know?'
'Just knew, Don. Ah – Don?'
'Yeah?'
'Stay in touch, okay? Like we agreed?'
'Ah, yeah, sure, Manu…'
'Not Manu. In future, call me Mike.'
'Right. *Mike.*'

§

'Why banks, anyway?' asked Don once, late one afternoon. It's been pissing down all day. He's spent another hard day working for the comrades, the evening walking home, returning from the periphery of a town he hadn't thought could be so large. Marco's just up, percolator on the stove just spitting, half in shadow, face flickering in the light of a candle stub, pulling languid chords from the loose strings of his guitar.

'Uh?' says Marco, looking up, stoned as always; looking at Don, managing all in an instant to seem as drenched, as miserable, as he. He shrugs magnificently, plays an extended diminished seventh arpeggio across three octaves, finishing with a 'ping' at the very top of his E-string. Looking amazedly at his hands, he grunts with satisfaction.

'Banks!' says Don loudly, momentarily fed up of having this talented retard for a squat-mate. 'Why do they want to rob a bank? Why bother?'

'The money?'

Marco reaches from the couch (where he lies now, collapsed) to the stove, tips a fingerful of tar-black coffee into the ashtray, drinks it, ash and all, slurping the tarry broth-like soup. His muddy eyes clear a little. He lights his tightly-rolled cigarette from the candle flame; the dry tobacco flares, shrivelling the little hairs on his chin. He wrinkles up his face, blows out a stream of blue smoke – *poof!* – the candle flickers, recovers. He smiles like a conspirator, pushes papers and tobacco over to Don, who echoes:

'The money?'

Marco nods. 'I know. It's shit, my friend. Play this game a little if you want, but don't get burned.'

Which is the nearest thing to an answer that Don has ever squeezed from him.

'Why do *you* do it?'

Marco lays smoking on the couch now, examining the stained roof through slitted eyes.

'The money.'

'And?'

He rolls over, fixes Don with a rare, dark look.

'Maria. I keep watch over her.'

Don pinches a little tobacco and a paper for himself, smoothes out the skin with his cold fingers, leans into the candle-light for warmth.

Each spying on the other.

'Why banks? Three reasons,' says Manu over the crackling long-distance line, after a little thought and with just a touch of irony. Don can hear him, a thousand miles away, drawing on one of his white-tipped cigarettes, blowing out a plume of smoke as he considers his answer. Perhaps it has something to do with the special quality of his voice, but even at this distance, Don catches a whiff of the man's aftershave, as if it is emanating like the last guy's breath from the earpiece of the receiver – and it makes him sweat.

'Firstly, the ass-holes need the money. They always need more money for their struggle. They need a lot of money. They like to eat well. Valen*tino* has his clothes, Mariotti has his whores, Horst has his BMW. Even Maria – even she has a lifestyle. *Banks* have large amounts of money. Banks in Italy are very easy. Everybody here robs banks. You simply go in and ask. The younger comrades sometimes even forget to bring their guns. They use bananas wrapped in plastic bags; they'd use their *cocks*, if cocks went "bang."

'Secondly, they need the practice. They talk so much, they forget how to fight. That is why they must plan it all so carefully. That's why they are armed. They mustn't make it seem too easy. If it were too easy, it would undermine the moral legitimacy of their case.

'Thirdly, the more they steal, the more quickly they bring down the edifice. If everybody robbed a bank every day, they would have no need to do anything else. The *Stati Multi Nazzionale* would collapse. Poof! Revolution. No more capital, no more capitalism.'

'Right…' says Don, feeling mocked.

Pause.

'So who's your driver?'

'Look, Horst said he'd kill me…'

'Who's your driver, Don?'

'Marco.'

'Marco! *Marco?*'

The Banca Agricola di Emilia Romagna *on* Universitá *is very quiet and very small. It usually opens at some time between half-past nine and ten. It remains closed after lunch. There is one female teller who is always on duty. She appears frequently to be alone. There never seems to be more than two customers there. There is ample parking, without restriction, outside and round the corner. The area itself is very quiet. The safe, in the middle of the back wall, appears to be left open much of the time. It is emptied only once weekly…*

Early April. Still casing banks. He jots all the details down in his little book.

His technique is simple. You present a personal cheque, for cash, for, say, a hundred pounds sterling to the teller, and insist she honour it. You don't take no for an answer. The teller – in this case, Emilia, a nice middle-aged lady whose own wild son Don reminds her of, which is why, in fact, she is so patient, so kind – has to phone your local branch (Bank of Scotland, Lochee, Dundee, in Don's case) for authorisation, which is never forthcoming. This takes time. This gives Don a great deal of scope for sitting around, mooching and observing, making notes, sometimes for hours, in a variety of financial institutions, without attracting attention.

Don sits alone at a little varnished wooden desk in the waiting room of the *Banca Agricola di Emilia Romagna*, making notes in a black-bound spiral notebook. He thinks, at long last, that he's found his bank. An elderly security man with a baseball cap (logo: *B.A.D.E.R)* and a shotgun across his lap slumbers disgracefully on his uncomfortable chair by the entrance, a filament of drool from his purple lips blotting on his blue collar.

> *There is one security guard by the entrance. He is armed, but appears to be asleep. Even awake, I think he would pose little threat...*

The guard snores loudly; the dog asleep at his feet beats its tail rhythmically upon the carpet. Emilia returns to the wicket, face mortified. 'They say no! They say you have *no money left at all...*' Emilia the Mum even offers to lend him some, but Don will have none of it. 'I'll try again tomorrow...'

'Mike! Hi!'

He tries to muffle his voice with a dish-towel clasped over the mouth. These calls hurt. Though the bar isn't busy – mainly unknown, anonymous Europeans, an American family with two fat children, an old bloke with a dog – and the noise is sufficient to cover his conversation, nonetheless, when he hears that voice, Don is paralysed with fear.

'Got your bank yet?'

Manu's tone is almost light-hearted. Mocking.

'Ah ... yes...'

'Which is it?'

'It's…' But now there's a girl, standing at the bar. Don tries hard not to be distracted.

'It's…'

Thin, blond, tight top, small, pointed breasts under a cheesecloth blouse. A familiar-looking chest. *Where have I seen this girl…*

'Can't tell you just now…'

'Why not?'

'Hi, Don…' she says, a foxy look on her thin face. She wears bright red lipstick, but no other makeup. Her eyes smile winsomely. She has a thin, little, unlikeable mouth, which doesn't. Without recognising her as such, Don becomes aware of old urges; of their dreadful aftermath. The voice starts up again. *Fuck her fuck her fuck her…*

'Stephie!' he says, dish-towel pressed over the earpiece. 'Look, Mike, I'll phone you back…'

'No, you will not. Which is the bank?'

'Can't, ah, just tell you that now, Mike…'

Gently replaces the receiver, enjoying for a fraction of a fraction of a second the relief.

'Stephie! Hi!' *(Fuck her fuck her fuck her…)* '*Che ti do da bere, bella?*' Fetches her her spritzer, looks around the bar-room for her friend, sees him in the corner, watching, watching.

'Here to see young Horst, then, yeah? That's just, ah, great…' *(Fuck her fuck her fuck her…)* 'See you around then, yeah? Cheers!'

A moment later, and the phone rings again.

'Mike!'

'Don't-put-the-phone-down-on-me.'

'Sure Mike, sure, great to talk, eh?'

The shaven hairs on his neck stand up like little cactus-spines.

'Keep me informed. Watch Mary.'

'Who?'

Horst appears at the bar, taps his long nails on its varnished surface, orders with one slanting eyebrow.

'Listen Mikey, I've really got to go…' But the phone is already dead.

❦

July 4ᵗʰ

'This is the plan,' says Horst, glancing first at Mariotti, who nods support. He leans over Don's large, hand-drawn plan of the Banca Agricola di Emilia Romagna, covers it in charcoal Xs, cars, running stick-men, other stick-men in uniforms carrying guns, coloured lines.

'Every player wears one of these.' Horst takes from a plastic bag four packs of black stockings and four masks. Mickie, Minnie, Donald and Goofy. Gives Minnie to Maria. 'Fioravanti and I are the main players. I take the teller and carry the money. Fioravanti covers the guard. Valentino?' Tino nods and simpers. 'Maria will cover the door, prevent anyone else from gaining access. Maria?'

She nods too. Face looks grim.

'Marco will be in the van on the corner of *Tribunale* and *Francesco Cilea*. He will drive us to here...' [*points with pointer to the effluent of the* Canale Santa Lucia] 'where we dispose of our masks and hardwear. We change vehicles – Marco and Maria take vehicle A' [*marks the spot on the map*] 'to their safe house. Fioravanti and I take vehicle B' [*marks another little spot, on the other side of the road*] 'with the money, to *our* safe house.

'We call *this* number, in Rome, next day, at 7PM. If that fails, July the 22ⁿᵈ or, at the latest, the 31ˢᵗ, to receive instructions. Any questions?'

The cadres look one to another, timid little beads of sweat appearing on foreheads. It's the practical *details* of the game which scare them, and its imminence – three days hence. Only one hand is raised from the corner. A pale face, half in darkness.

'Ah ... yes,' says Don. '*I* have a question.'

'Vat?' asks Horst, in English.

'Where am *I*?'

Horst's eyes say '*For-fuck's-sake.*' His mouth making just a harsh little slit. Mariotti lights his pipe and beams a good-natured inoffensive smile. Marco looks at his feet. Tini giggles. Maria looks at him, little pebbles in the pupils of her eyes. Horst says, eventually, 'Ah ... Brighton?'

'Brighton?'

'You hef finished, no?'

Don looks wordlessly around the table.

'No?' says Horst.

'This was never *your* fight,' says Maria, quietly, pointedly – with just, perhaps, a trace of … regret?

'No room for passengers,' says Mariotti.

'You can read about it after,' says Tini, and giggles.

Something inside Don, bent too far out of shape, finally, silently snaps. He feels enormous relief. A new sense of freedom. Suddenly pleased to be going home at last. He takes a long farewell look around the group and, despite the small defeat and humiliation involved, feels a great, warm joy that he need never again play their mad, grandiose games again. *Bank robbery, my arse!*

He considers the denunciation – the grand gesture to fill out this deflating moment – *Your best gun can be disabled by a fountain pen in the nose; his mate giggles like a porn-star and has a crush on him; your grand theoretician is so dull that the songbirds fall stone-dead from the trees when he speaks; your driver is so strung out on heroin most of the time that he doesn't know what day it is; your leader is a woman dogged by the shameful memory of the face of the innocent, murdered man whose life she couldn't save* – But … no. He stays silent instead, fastening his eyes on the woman.

Who finally looks up at him. Don, bracing himself for the impact of her indifference, is surprised to see, instead, fear. She flinches. Reading what is in mind, she makes a small, involuntary shaking of her head. *Please, don't!*

And then the penny finally drops. *It's fear. It's just fear. No more than fear. She's frightened of what I can say,* Don realises with wonder as he leaves.

❦

'I'm *out*, Mike. I'm off. I'm not coming back. They can go and fuck themselves. They don't want me, I don't want them. It's not my fight. It's a pile of shite. You're all a pile of shite. You'll have to watch Maria yourself. She's your bird, after all, not mine; she's your problem and I'm glad to be seeing the back of her.'

'Fine, Don. We'll see. Bye.' *Crackle click crackle click*
brrrrrrrr...

𝄞

Don drinks hard.

Don contemplates the swastika hung above the gantry behind
the bar as he empties a glass of Grouse and asks for another.

'Low flier, Sammi.'

Sammi, who knows him well now, hands him a quarter-gill of
grouse.

'Ice? Water? Piss in your glass?'

'Fuck off.'

All of this time, she's been frightened of what I might have been
going to say...

He lets that amber thought sink to the bottom of the glass; lets
it turn and dissolve there, like ice-water through spirit.

Just frightened. True? Or false?

What I took for indifference was actually fear. All these weeks
I've been wriggling like a wee trout in a burn at the end of her hook,
wondering what I've done wrong. But all this time, she's just been
frightened. True? Not true?

Nah ... not true...

''Nuther low flier, Sammi.'

'A little virgin's milk? Dog spunk? An *olive*, perhaps?'

'Fuck off, Sammi.'

She was always way out of your league. You never had a chance.
She's playing some kind of game. She and her boyfriend – some
kind of game, the climax of which is you getting fucked. Get well
out of it, boy...

But...

But when she told you about the man that was killed she was
telling you the truth. She wasn't faking. She took you all the way
to the beach to tell you something she was too frightened to talk
about at home.

'And ... I *love* her... ' Hiccough.

Fuck, did I say that out loud?

'Hey, I know, *Ton*. But you know, she's lost. She's lost. Hey?
Fuck.'

A kind hand rests gently on his shoulder.

'I thought I was in with a chance. I really thought...'

'Two more' *(hic)* 'of these,' says Marco, bilious and pissed, holding up two fingers, pointing at Don.

'A little ... pus?'

'And take' *(hic)* 'one for yourself.'

'You know I don't drink, you infidel cunt.'

'You black devil. Can't you see our friend's in pain?'

Marco rolls two tight ones, keeps one for himself, hands the other to the wilting friend.

'Go home, Don. Take a holiday. Go somewhere else. Leave her. She doesn't care about any of us. We've lost her to these dog-fuckers.'

'These *dog-fuckers!* These *murderous* sons of... ' Hiccough. Stops himself short. *Is it my imagination, Marco, or are you fluent, suddenly, in human speech?*

'It's going to be fine, Don,' says Marco, making perfect sense. 'You just need to go-somewhere-else now.'

Don swings and sways in his drunkenness, stares at his friend, stares at the torn swastika hung above the gantry behind the bar. *'Don't underestimate Marco. Don't make the mistake of thinking that he's stupid ... '* someone had once told him a long, long time ago...

'She loved me, you know...'

'I know, Donny, I know. We'll get our own back. Everything will be okay. *You* just have to LEAVE.'

'Nah... Too late... We're fucked...'

'We're not. You GO, *I'll* stay, and sort these cunts out...'

Don drinks. Loses self in an extended riff off the germ of this self-pitying idea:

That I, Don, am the partisan (Tania's dead grandfather) who wrenched this German flag from the dying grasp of whichever Nazi soldier (Horst) it was who guarded it; that I, Don, then presented it into the hands of the lover who waited for me at home (Maria), who betrayed me to her former Gestapo lover (Manu), who had me shot, wrapped in this same flag. Now the flag with its bullet holes hangs above this bar, where every day grief-stricken Maria will pray before it and remember me ...

Don starts to weep a little at the sheer, pure beauty of this tale...

Pull yourself together, you self-infested whore-dog...

Don is startled into consciousness.

Marco (who was behaving very oddly – that is, normally) was trying to tell you something important.

'Did I imagine it, Sammi, or was Marco here a moment or two ago?'

'He was. He left when you fell asleep. Now get off my bucking far and let me wipe away your dribble, you uncircumcised whore-bitch-spawn... '

'Gone... ?'

Like a puppet with tangled strings Don jerks himself from the barstool, collapses on the floor in a heap of wooden arms and legs, staggers to his feet once again, wiping snot from his face with the back of a wrist, misses.

'Gone?'

Sammi nods, shakes his head as Don leaves, turns to close the bar for the night.

'Marco!'

Shouting his friend's name out into the night. 'Marco!'

But he's not gone too far. He's waiting, sitting half in water, fifteen feet above the cobbled square, arse over the side of Neptune's fountain, kicking his heels and knocking chips of stucco from its decorative sixteenth-century edge. Looks down when he hears his friend's voice. His face and his hair are wet. Water's running down his legs in little rivulets, collecting in pools on the stones beneath his feet.

'Climb up! Wash away your sins! Clear your head. You are too too drunk, my friend, and we need to talk.'

'Marco!' gasps Don, breathless from running. 'Listen! Maria told me about ... the man you killed. She told me *everything...*'

Marco looks down at Don with his violet, squinting eyes. Then he shrugs and kicks his heels against the lip of the fountain-bowl.

'Mind who you tell that to, *compagno*. You could get yourself into trouble. You need to wash. Climb up here. Clear your head.'

He falls back into the water. Legs make a V-shape then disappear over the edge. He crawls back over the side, shaking his hair like a dog and spits a jet of water at the cobbled square.

'Marco, listen. It's because she's frightened. She's frightened of what Horst and those other wankers might do to her. I have to stay and *help* her! I have to *save* her from them!'

Marco jumps from the side of the fountain, lets out a yell as he falls, lands in a mess of tangled limbs on the cobbles, lies there a second as if he's dead before picking himself up, arms out, advancing towards Don, saying in a pitying voice: 'My friend!' and folds Don in his arms, holds him in a tight embrace, wet hand gripping his skull...

'You stupid, fucking, fucking, fucking...' but kisses him, hard and wet on the mouth, before the sentence is even properly begun. 'You don't understand anything! You are too much of an *esshole* to understand! This is not your fight! You're a virgin!'

Third time. That word. 'Virgin.'

'What's a virgin, Marco?'

'An innocent person who is about to get fucked. Don, when you are no longer useful to them, they will kill you. You have to leave! Just fuck off and leave! Leave them to me.'

'But I love your sister.'

'My sister loves no-one. Least of all you.'

Don prises himself from Marco's grip. Looks at him very hard through dense clouds of strong, tender feeling; through half-obscured signs and meaning; through all the alcohol. Thinks he sees light, somewhere, shining dimly through.

'No. You don't understand. She does.'

It's a hot night in early summer. A clear night with a full moon. A beautiful night. Already the town is filling with the summer's tourists, and even this late – it's almost three – there are still well-dressed and respectable folk wandering before bed, who drift from the noise and the shouting to the safety of the arcades at the edge of the square, muttering about *teppisti, ladri, delinquenti, terroristi...*

For these people's public safety a police car sits, empty, yet threatening still, on the edge of the square, two tyres mounted on the kerb, the driver's side window left open to let in the air. The two *Vigili* are absent; wearying of their vigil, they have taken coffee in a late-night café two blocks to the north. One, the senior of the two, is delayed by a crisis of piles – by the sudden and unexpected climax of two weeks of hard constipation – and is smoking and huffing in private agony. His partner, Giuseppe, worried lest the two *delinquenti* whom they have been trailing on a tip from the

SDI might flee, has discreetly hidden himself in the shadow of an arcade, glancing anxiously at his watch as he sees this, the following evil scene, unfold – and wonders what the fuck has happened to his mate:

The two drunk men, the *drogati,* are arguing: tripping and sliding, sloshing arm in arm around the square. Shouting. They are loathsome. They come to rest by Giuseppe's empty car (Giuseppe, twitching, wonders whether to go it alone), one leaning on his back against the side, the other, hands around the open window, leaning forward and gazing into the empty driver's seat.

One shouts drunkenly: *'Maria, ti amo…!'* at the moon, who turns away her pale virgin face in disgust.

('He-loves-Maria,' writes Giuseppe painstakingly in his little black book, then activates his short-wave radio with a little crackle.)

The other suddenly leans his head into the window of the police car, makes muffled puking noises there.

The lover pushes his friend away, the friend objects – *'Hey, Ton, I think I have been a little, ah, sick…'* – and the lover then stands, hips akimbo, pelvis thrust forward to the open car window, shouting *'Libertá e giustizia…!'* and hoses manfully, loutishly, lusciously, through the open car window…

At which point Giuseppe breaks his cover: yelling, he wheels into view, followed by the other, older one who is holding his radio and gun belt in one hand, buckling his tight blue-grey *vigili* trousers with the other, now wracked by the peri-anal itch which always starts the moment his BTM leaves the toilet seat, muttering angrily to his junior about his lack of vigilance…

The two *vigili* turn the corner and see this terrible sight. They shout. They give chase. Then the *terroristi* run, one shouting – *'Ich bin Horst Kleber. Ja, HORST KLEBER bin ich! Ich habe nur ein klein PINKEL gemacht…'* The *vigili* chase, puffing, through the arcades. Giuseppe, in front, the younger and fitter of these two unfit men, slips on dog shite, skites across the polished marble pavement by a smart leather handbag shop, cracks his head on a stuccoed arch and swears. The other catches him up, stops, hands on knees, gasping.

Horst Kleber, eh? He writes the name in his little policeman's notebook.

181

¶

The two wake late, haunted by bad dreams – ghosts, still present, of the bad things done the night before.

They pass the morning hiding in their sleeping bags, shunning the sun, which is shut from their hovel by cardboard pasted on the windows. The perpetrated act awaits its consequence. The knowledge of this clings to their flesh and their clothes like last night's smoke.

They brew coffee at four; gather themselves at five to leave.

'I'll be going tonight, then,' says Don soberly, grey-faced, wasted.

'Where?'

'Naples? Sicily? Brighton? I don't know.'

'Will you say goodbye to my sister?'

'There's no point. You say it for me. You were right. The dog-fuckers have got her. Better I just go.' Don explores his self-pity, rubbing at it like a patch of eczema. 'Perhaps in a month or two I'll write to her. Perhaps in the future she'll remember me differently. I still really love…'

'Yeah, I know. Let's play pinball.'

Packed and ready to go, Don has his old canvas rucksack and his fiddle by him. They play pinball. Don's on. Marco lounges, back to the wooden rail, drinking *Peroni* by the neck. He's racked up a score of forty million and three bonus balls. Despite almost a year's commitment, Don has never approached his friend's skill at pinball. The nipples of Botticelli's Venus barely flicker on and off as the steel ball rolls across her large pink bosoms, flashing four thousand points apiece; then over her shell, the deep blue sea which bears her; then bounces twice between the faces of Leonardo's Virgin and St. Anne, lighting briefly the golden lights of the halo on the suckling infant Christ for another thousand; rattling in the paralysed death-jaws of Don's immobile flippers before being swallowed in the narrow throat of Bosch's hell.

'Nudge! Fucking Nudge!'

The machine goes *Waa-ooh Waa-ooh*.

'Isn't that Manu down there?'

'Can't be, he's in London…'

A dark man is sitting alone in a corner stall at the back, smoking. Don tries to catch his eye, but is ignored when he does. *Is* that Manu?

'Perhaps he's come to say goodbye?' says Don.

'I think ... not,' says Marco in a flat voice, looking over Don's shoulder towards the door.

'What...'

They are four. The two *vigili* from last night in plain clothes, one with a bandaged head, black hair oiled down hard over tough Calabrian skulls; jeans; white tee-shirts pulled over their dome-like bellies; gold jewels – lots; black zipped jackets, polished black shoes. Two friends, similar outfits, accompany them.

'Oh ... oh shit...'

And these guys know where to look, too. They've been told. The pinball machine stands on a platform above the bar. Narrow steps lead up. The four *vigili* advance, slowly...

'They're going to...'

'Yes, I know...'

One by one they ascend the steps, the first leering and smiling like an idiot. Marco backs off, is blocked by the still-singing, still-twinkling pinball machine.

Waa-ooh waa-ooh...

Don, surprising himself with his bravery, tries to kick the first man in the belly, but he's only got his plimsolls on and the policeman simply catches his foot, twists it round so that the rest of Don rotates, then pushes him forward so that he too collapses face-first at the feet of the blinking machine. Big man number one then leans over, grips his head by the ears, smashes his face twice on the wooden floor, kicks him twice, hard, effortlessly in the belly, once on the back, then leaves him for Marco.

Marco is now surrounded by four, who take it in turns to stamp upon his hands, breaking each of his precious fingers, kicking his stomach. Don, too dazed to move, in too much pain to do more than groan and stay alive, nonetheless feels it as the men kick his friend, who now no longer even moans. Feels it too, when, after the other three have stood aside a little to let him in, the fourth – the youngest, thinnest, most vigorous – takes from his jacket a silenced little snub-nosed pistol, buries its blunt snout in the back of Marco's knee, and shoots. Winces with regret when, in a last, pathetic gesture, they take his mother's fiddle from its case, break its neck and its varnished red-brown belly with a twang over the rails, snap the bow, throw the lot to the floor then, laughing like crows, leave.

Don is sure that it is Manu he sees, tightly wrapped in a black overcoat, leaving too. Walking briskly past the bar where Sammi cowers, saying '*Prego barista – ambulanza?*'

§

His face hurts like fuck.

He can just about see her through his swollen eyelids. She has tied her hair back. Her black hair; her curls spilling from a hair-band. She moves rapidly between the wooden table and the kitchen sink, gliding through her narrow kitchen. She's no expert at this, but she's trying not to hurt him. A bowl of boiling water left to cool, cotton wool balls held between her pinched fingers. Though agitated, she tries to be tender. His head is tilted, his face inclined toward the roof; on the wall is stuck a yellowed poster, a Frenchman scowling under a beret: *Gauloise, le cigarette de France,* the corners of the poster peeling from the walls. This place is home to her. This is where she sits. Her fingers touch him lightly in the face.

'Shut your eyes. This is going to hurt.' Where did she learn to nurse? The cotton-wool is soft, the water warm, at first soothing. *This is the most tender moment...* He flinches, suppressing a whimper as the water runs into his wounds.

He had watched the pool of purple blood advance slowly across the wooden floor towards him. His friend's leg crooked, lying twisted under the other; his friend motionless, his face turning grey, his short, gasped breaths. *He's dying.* The long, long wait for help. Two guys come with a gurney – they bind Marco's legs to a splint, put up a drip. There's the hiss of oxygen, the crackle of radios, off he goes.

But get this: as they'd raised him, Marco's head had rolled over to face him. He'd opened his eyes, seen Don lying there, and he'd smiled at him – a thin smile painted upon his blue, transparent lips – then he'd raised a fist, gasped '*Ciao, compagno!*' and collapsed again. So Marco's going to be okay. Don, overwhelmed by sudden love for his friend, forgets his own pain. He refuses help for himself, discovering that he can stand. Wobbly, but sober, he makes his own way from the empty bar, staggering into the night, the one possible destination fixed in his mind.

It hurts, but her touch is soft and he would, he realises, have done anything – even this – to feel her soft touch again, her hands bathing the wounds on his face.

He'd hammered on her door, rang upon her bell, shouted out her name until eventually she appeared, angry at first, then shocked when she saw what they'd done.

'Where is Marco?' Her voice tightening with fear.

I would do this again, a hundred times over, to have a reason to hammer like this on your door, to fall down dead like this at your feet...

'He's still alive. Don't worry. There's something I have to tell you...'

'Maria, why did they just go for Marco? Why did they leave me?'

She says nothing. Shakes her head – *be quiet.* She towels away blood from his hair, wringing out the white towel in a bucket of steaming water at their feet. He's leaning forward now, naked but for a cloth around his waist. She bathes his torn face, his bruises and his cuts.

'They must have followed us. I don't understand ... they knew just where to find us.'

'Shh.'

She places the soiled towels and the cotton wool in the bucket, lays the lot in the sink, passes him a tee-shirt and some fresh clothes, watches him as he dresses. She makes coffee for them both, lays his in front of him at the wooden table, sits on the stool opposite.

'What was it that you wanted to tell me? Be quick. The others will be here soon.'

Faced with it, though, the words don't come. She's too impatient. She's too icy. The woman that he'd loved is gone for good, and this new one fills him with fear. She dries her hands on a dish towel, throws that to the floor, uses her foot to mop a little of the blood and still warm water which have fallen there.

His head has begun to hurt again. Great pulses behind his eyes, rocking him. He braces himself for the next wave.

'So what was it?'

What indeed?

There's a knock at the door.

She shrugs her shoulders, face still hard, and turns to leave.

'Maria.'

'What?' Her voice is growing impatient. It's now or never.

'Manu was there in the bar tonight. He saw everything. He didn't try to help.'

She looks at him through half-closed eyes, as if from a great distance. She says nothing. There is another knock at the door; the sound of voices outside.

'It was as if he was there to watch!'

She closes her eyes; turns away without a word to answer the door.

'Maria!'

'What!'

'There is something else.'

Impatience. That frightened/ frightening look again. More knocking at the door.

'What?'

'I wanted to tell you that I loved you. That's the only reason that I'm here.'

She turns and looks at him again. Pauses, staring at him again from somewhere deep down within her unfathomable eyes. She turns to open the door.

It's become an interrogation. Don sits alone in the centre of the room, face bruised, a little blood running into his left eye where the bandage has leaked again. The light from a desk lamp is shining directly into his face and its effect, to block the angry faces of those that question him, is disorientating. A chaise-longue opposite where two sit, one of them Bergamo, the other unknown. The air stinks: sweat, fear, aftershave, the breath of his captors. At his feet a parquet floor onto which he's dripping blood and water. Behind him and out of sight, a round antique French-polished rosewood table with a vase of lilies and piles of papers on it, where Maria sits. There's old, hand-painted English patterned wallpaper on the wall, ornate fake-crystal light-fittings, paintings. Someone is rich.

Horst paces round and around him, offering him smokes and a light, firing questions.

'You say you were drunk, but *last* night. You attract the attention of the *vigili*. What were you doing?'

'Shouting. Stuff. Arsing around.' Schoolboy Don bites his lip.

Horst's voice opposite: 'Fuck. English *esshole!*'

'You were playing *pinball*, and these same *vigili* just happen to find you?' says Mariotti. '?' say Mariotti's voice and eyebrows. 'How did they know where you were? *Who* you were? Did you *talk* to them? Did you give them *names*? Did you make *any* connections?'

'No,' lies Don.

'*Esshole!*' says Horst.

Don recalls ruefully, for the first time, his little joke of the night before, which had seemed *so* funny when he was pissed. *Ich bin Horst Kleber!* he had shouted as the police gave chase. *Ich habe nur ein KLEIN pinkel gemacht... Fuck fuck fuck...*

'He's lying,' says a voice next to Horst. Horst's voice says: 'I think we should kill him. Straight away.' Silence from behind him, where Maria sits.

'The policemen last night. Did they catch you?' asks someone.

'No.'

'So how did they know where to look for you?'

'I don't know.'

'Have you been spying on us?'

'No.'

'Are you working for the police?'

'No.'

'Can you think of any reason why we shouldn't cut your balls off and feed them to you whole until you choke?'

Horst slips *so* easily into this role.

'No. I mean, yes!'

'Who is "Mike"?'

'Who?'

'Every evening you talk to someone called Mike on the telephone behind the bar. Who is this Mike?'

The interrogators look down at him with cold dispassionate faces. Terrifying, staring eyes.

'Tell us the truth. We know when you lie.'

'He's my brother. He phones from London. My sister ... Mary ... is ill...'

'You're lying, cunt!' says Horst, triumphantly, raising a hand to strike him, but held back by Mariotti, who asks:

'What time did the *vigili* first come in?'

''Bout seven-thirty.'

'Was anyone else in the bar?'

'Yes, *Manu.' Cunt.*

'Can't have been. He's in London. Was anyone *else* in the bar? Did anyone else *see* you there?'

Pace, pace, pace.

'No. Yes. Sammi.'

'Okay. Anyone else?'

'No.'

'Hmm.'

ℰ

'Call the action off. We're compromised,' votes Mariotti.

'Call it off,' votes Tini, who's squeezed himself tightly onto the chaise longue beside the Beast from Bergamo.

'Call it off,' says the beast.

'Yesssssss,' hisses Horst. 'Call it off. And ah, let's not forget to kill the Englishman. Maria?'

Her nervous voice, from behind Don's head, speaking for the first time:

'No.'

Silence.

'You're not compromised. They wouldn't have left a job like that in the hands of a pair of traffic cops. If you were compromised, they would have picked up the Englishman too. And you wouldn't still be here, either – they would have picked you all up at the same time. But they didn't. They just beat up Marco and let the Englishman go. It's a vendetta. They know Marco as a thief and nothing more than that. They recognised him. It's personal. A little traffic-cop thing. I think we should go.'

'So who drives?' asks Horst. Another silence. As everyone thinks...

'The Englishman,' says Maria, finally.

'What?'

'Unreliable,' says Horst.

'Bad move,' growls the Beast.

'He's not one of us,' says Tini.

'I ... can't drive...' lies Don.

'The Englishman,' says Maria, finally.

A long and thoughtful silence.

'Okay. Don. Let him drive.'

Fuck.

Mariotti turns off the desk light. Don blinks.

'Just. Don't. Fuck. Up,' says Horst.

'Here. Tomorrow, half-past ten,' says Mariotti.

18

Tomorrow at half-past ten.

It's eleven-thirty. Don sits alone.

They're late. They're fucking late!

Each titchy hair-like fibre of Don's autonomic nervous system hums with electricity: a high-pitched hum, complex harmonies, just south of B-flat, three octaves above middle-C and rising. Press your ear against the tin skin of the stolen white van where he sits and you'll hear dissonant harmonics of distress, breeching the spectrum of the audible. Dogs bark a mile off then, cowering and whimpering, bury their heads in sandpits. Bats, asleep for years in medieval towers, ovulate. Fleas flee their hosts, gnashing their complicated jaws, sharp little teeth aching. Mosquitoes fall, twitching and dazed from the sky.

Bathed in his caffeine-adrenaline-rich internal sea, wired Don stares out of the windscreen at a sun-bleached street, at the ochre-coloured walls, the red graffiti, the suburban villas half-hidden behind, shrouded in wisteria, alive with insects. His beating heart gripped between his dry back teeth, his lungs gasp for breath in the hot air, his head spinning. He thinks *no! fuck! no!* The little muscles in his hands twitch uncontrollably and the steering wheel is greasy from the sweat from his palms; the air inside the cabin is close and stale from his panting breath; his back, cold and moist, itches intolerably as he rubs it against the plastic back-rest. *I've been waiting an hour.* So much can go wrong in an hour. *The comrades I depend on are arseholes that want me dead.* Dread squats like a toad in the centre of his chest.

But it's a curious state of mind he's in: flipping in an instant between panic and boredom and then back again.

He sits in the driver's seat of a stolen white van, staring.

He nurses an indolent erection. An hour ago, some girls passed. He strings out a once-vivid, now over-used and frankly washed-out sex dream, to try to stay awake.

Girls his age with thick folders pressed to their pointed bosoms walk in pairs, chatting and giggling carelessly.

It was a roaring-dog dream. In which a demon axe-swinging Don had burst from the confines of his van, rendered caveman by the license of his fantasy, animal pelts and sharpened stones swinging from a thong at his waist, loping after these well-dressed girls who, hearing his unmistakeable grunt, turned to flee (giggling with anticipation) and not unwillingly allowed themselves to be run down by the savage man-he, who tore their tightly applied clothing away from their firm behinds, went 'Grrrr!' and mounted each of them then and there, three of them simultaneously with his triple-pronged penis, somehow, on the pavement...

...They'd walked past his white van, these girls, chatting in their little groups, parting around him like a flock of skittish goats, then closing in front, tails up, their voices cast like party streamers behind them. One of them started and turned, a frown painted on her pretty oval face, as if she had seen the goat-predator behind the wheel, his red eyes piercing the gloom, his *heat*. Don, cast in shadows, watched them pass, wondering, not for the first time, whether his thoughts were audible to others...

Don: you're sleeping.

The comrades were due an hour ago. Something has definitely gone wrong. Nothing can possibly go wrong. *Wake the fuck up!*

Perhaps it's just because he hasn't slept. He hasn't really slept for three days – has kept himself going with a combination of caffeine and fear. Pain from his bruises, worries left over from the day before, this dread emanating from the day ahead, made him twist and turn in his sleeping-bag all night so that the sleeping-bag threatened to strangle him. The mosquitoes, too, were bad. He'd scratched all night, so that his wrists and ankles bled.

Wake up!

After the girls had passed, the wealthy old came with their dogs. Ladies in camel-coloured suits, little scarlet mouths and flesh-coloured makeup, long leads, scampering little dogs attached, their cocked, docked tails, their furry little penises squirting against trees. Retired men in checked trousers and beige pullovers, a few over-groomed, undesirable married young women looking older than their years.

One woman, well into her eighties, stops outside his near-side window, waits for the others to pass, then lifts her little deformed in-bred dog up so that it sees him through the window. The mutt winks at him. Don thinks *whaaat?* Old woman talks all the time to her slavering *bambino*, muttering *'Facciamo pee-pee leetle doglet...'* and, not seeing him there inside, a foot or two away, squeezes on the thin, curly grey wool on the dog's belly, so that a thin stream of pale, straw-coloured dog piss washes the glass an inch or two from his face.

The old woman, giggling over her many transgressions, hurries off.

Concentrate! Bastard-cunt! Stay awake!

When he was growing, aged thirteen or fourteen, after his mother's death, his father sometimes used to take him into the Angus glens at the weekend to paint. His father's weekends off were rare, prepared for months in advance, little islands of pleasure in the heavy grey sea of sadness and over-work which always threatened to drown them.

The weekend keenly anticipated, his father packed the car on Friday evening – a Hillman hatchback with rust on the blue body work – with canvas bags smeared with oil colours and pastel; a heavy wooden easel with butterfly nuts to adjust; cardboard cases with pastels, each stick in its slot, each colour in order, the darkest blue through yellows, greens and reds, each in order and each colour clean and uncontaminated by its neighbour.

This was my father. An ordered man, a man better by far than me, a man who could keep the colours separate...

They set off in the morning before dawn, to catch the first of the day's light. They would drive an hour or two into the hills. His father laid out the tartan travel rug on which he would place thermoses, the cases of paints and brushes, beside it the easel, paper, watercolours for the boy. Or on cold, wet days Don huddled for warmth under his waterproof and the rug, and his father would simply sit with a pad on his knee, smoking an acrid pipe, working on images of brown hills, silver birches with their long, imploring branches, leaves like little claws, clouds blown like rags between them, the smoke-like hedges billowing between buff-coloured fields.

Perhaps it's because I have no siblings that these weekends have formed the substrate for the memory of my childhood. Everything else measured against such as this:

Quickly getting bored of painting, yet not wishing to hurt his Dad's feelings, like his father's puppy dog he wandered off in widening circles, coming back every hour to check the old man was still there. Then he explored the fields round where his father sat; the burns which ran in their sinuous little glens, up between the low hills; the dry dykes with their lilac-coloured mossy stones which came loose when you tried to climb them, and scuffed your knees; the colours of those wet days, each colour bleeding into another – from the leaden grey skies, spitting throughout the long hours; the brown fields, the hedges between them; or those spring days when the winds blew from the west, and the sky was blue and the clouds were high; the yellow, pink and violet of the sun going down, and the dark blue quality of the night sky as they packed up their boxes and rugs at the end of the day and left. They would stay there till nine or ten at night, and still scarcely know that the day had passed.

Longed-for times, now scarcely ever recollected; separated from him now by the treacherous chasm of his adulthood.

I'd forgotten about him. That I once loved him, he thinks, yearning. And: *When I get home, I shall tell him that.*

His thoughts, cast over the brown hills of his memory. The windy days.

If I get home from this, I will make my peace with my father. Tell him that I loved him, that I can love him again…

'Don, wake up!'

Minnie Mouse appears to be hammering at the window with the back of her hand, screaming at him in the voice of a girl he once knew…

Don, assuming that this is all part of a dream, yawns and grunts something to himself in a sleepy voice.

'*Ton,* wake up!'

The dog-piss has all gone, leaving just a moist, evanescent film on the surface of the glass.

'Go go go!' he hears himself/someone else shout, like a character from a film heist.

There's a hammering at the back of the van.

They'd agreed that they'd keep the van locked. That the driver would open it from the inside. Can't quite work out why, now, that had seemed like such a good idea. Don, blinking hard, leans over, opens the passenger side; Minnie Mouse leaps in, screams in an uncontrolled falsetto – 'Start the engine!'

'Need to open the back first...' *Duhh.*

Jumps out, sorting between the unmarked keys Marco has cut for them – ignition, front, back, dimly aware, somewhere far-off, of the sound of sirens...

Micky and Donald are standing with their backs to the van pointing guns at the street; Goofy, a large, heavy-looking black canvas bag in one paw, is hammering with the other upon the van door, screaming something in a Bergamo accent about some whore-son-dog-fucker falling asleep...

'Okay okay okay,' says Don, opening the back door, jumping around to the front, starting the engine – which turns once, twice, three times before catching. 'Let's go...!'

Off to the left, a gun-shot, then another. Something pings off the side of the van, and again, and Minnie ducks so Don picks up speed. A police car turns the corner, right in front, sirens and lights, sees them (and death) not ten feet off and gaining speed, and mounts the kerb and hits a wall with a crash to avoid them.

Minnie screams 'You're driving on the wrong side of the road!'

'Yeah!' says Don, veering left, then right, then left again – suddenly feeling like a god. Don, discovering something unsuspected, something totally new about himself, has ruptured the fear barrier with a bang, and now just wants to go faster and faster. He fills the narrow streets with his blue exhaust smoke and the gravel roar of his engine. Heads turn as they race the lights. Minnie Mouse grips the window-sill and whimpers as he screams down *Vittorio Basso*, turns left and heads north, singing under his breath: 'Row, row, row the boat...'

Three police cars pass them, heading in the opposite direction. Minnie Mouse tears off her mask, takes the stocking from her head, shakes out her curls as Don turns onto the main road by the station, pulls to a halt by the bridge over the river, between two parked cars, one green, one blue. *Yeah!*

Jumps out, releases the three cartoons from the back, who tear off mouse and dog masks and overalls and throw them, plus two Uzis, into the rushing blue-green waters of the river. Then take a set of car keys from a side-pocket of the canvas bag, jump into the blue parked car, gun the engine, roar off.

Maria stands in front of him, panting, as if she has run a mile. Don nods at the green car.

'That's ours. You got the keys?'

She looks at him with wide, frightened eyes. Fear has its own smell, acrid and sexless. She shakes her head.

'The keys are with the money, in the side-pocket of the bag.'

Fuck.

They look at one another. There are sirens very loud, very close. She looks at the van, its four doors open, bullet holes raking one side, a deep blue scratch down the other where the police car hit.

'No. Bad idea,' says Don.

I am masterful. I am merciful. I am God... he thinks, as he takes her arm gently.

'Just walk. Don't run. Walk with me.'

He guides her across the road. They wait in the centre, blinking and coughing, dodging traffic: more police cars, a fire engine, a flock of angry, honking Vespas, bungling commuters. They make the other side. Somewhere, far-off, the sound of gunshots once again.

'There is nothing to be afraid of. We're going to get away. Where did you leave your car?'

They walk, arm in arm, innocent like lovers, like happy tourists, through the busy centre of the town.

19

Nine and a half hours later:
'It's here. Stop here.'

The car hushes to a halt. They kill the engine and the lights, and the bat-filled night presses in on them: the whispering wings of countless insects – cicadas, crickets, mosquitoes – the dense, velvet solitude. Don puts his forehead on the steering wheel, and for a second lets his heavy eyes close.

'Wake up!' She shakes him like a child. 'We have to walk from here. Hurry, and be quiet.'

He opens his side-door, stands stretching outside, twigs cracking underfoot on the dry sandy ground. He breathes in the heavy air, stretches out his arms as if embracing the sky, fills his lungs with the night scents: thyme, mountain sage, something ancient and resinous from the valley floor.

'Come on!' she whispers. Her voice hisses at him, full of urgency and fear.

'Wait,' he says in a half-voice. He doesn't want to leave this place. Already sick of running. He breathes deeply in again. 'There's no-one around.'

Just total darkness: the peace of an infinitely-layered night – then, as his eyes adjust, the silence of the ranked, unblinking stars. And at his feet the pale glow of fireflies, blinking slowly, on and off, each with its own slow rhythm.

'*Lucciola,*' he says quietly to himself, retrieving the word from somewhere, proud to know it, to have a cause at last to use it.

'Please, Don! Come on!'

They stand on a hillside above a deep valley. By its darker shadow, Don can make out rocky slopes and crags on the opposite side – the sharp teeth of a summit just picked out by the silver light of the moon rising behind his shoulder. He stands a minute, then takes the sack of food from the back of the car, hoists it on his shoulders, and follows the stumbling shadow of the girl down the hill.

'It's not far from here. Just follow the path,' she gasps, trying to run. She is exhausted. She trips and falls forward in the darkness, tumbles on the path and suppresses a sob.

Silently he helps her to her feet, places a gentle hand under her elbow. She shakes him off.

'There's no-one here, Maria! We're safe!'

But she runs ahead, still trying to escape, her shadow weaving and stumbling through the darkness.

Don has been driving for almost ten hours. In strange solitary silence at first, following the little roads and driving with exaggerated care, avoiding the sirens, the blue lights, the rushing police cars, the horns of other traffic, fearful of being seen by the world.

Maria says nothing. She doesn't bother to hide her face when they are stopped at a road-block, just looks at the floor with tear-smeared eyes, arms wrapped around herself, shivering, as the turnip-faced *vigili* looks in the window, glances cursorily around the inside of the car, waves them on. Clearly, the man's still looking for Mickie and Minnie. Their white van. Doesn't notice the strain on the face of the girl, her teeth chattering as if on that hot day she risks dying from the cold.

'Are you all right?' he asked once, later, but she said nothing other than: 'South. Keep driving south.' Her face was a frightened mask. She pointed out with her finger a branch in the road.

They stopped for food and petrol in a little town two hours south of Bologna but Maria wouldn't wait – just sat in the car with her white, frightened face; wouldn't eat, but wouldn't let Don stop either, urging him on with her silence.

'What happened?' he asks eventually, once they've left the world behind. They are heading up a winding narrow road, high in some wooded hills, where the air is cooler. 'What's gone wrong?'

She says nothing – avoids his question, gazes out the window at the air, the wisp of smoke rising from the valley below. Then, after a pause:

'Horst shot the guard.'

He feels something like a fist bury itself hard in the pit of his stomach; he catches his breath as if he has been winded.

She glances at him. Her face reads anger. And bafflement. As if: *how could this thing be?*

'The old man? The guy with the baseball cap and the dog?'

She nods.

'Why?'

She shrugs. Then the story. The humiliating story:

Don had dropped them as planned outside the bank. He'd

parked just round the corner, as planned. He'd waited and fretted, watched girls, thought about his old Dad, felt bad, started guiltily awake, thought: *they're late! they're fucking late!*

But meanwhile, elsewhere, this morning, just this once, the bank hadn't opened on time. The comrades had stood for twenty minutes on the pavement outside, spooked by their Micky, Minnie, Goofy and Donald masks, trying furtively to hide their stumpy little guns from passers-by, trying to look *normal*. Passers-by giggled. A child popped a pink, cherry-flavoured gum-bubble in Horst's face – *pop* – waft of sweet, cherry-flavoured breath – and almost got wasted.

When the old man with the baseball cap and the hundred keys swinging from the heavy chain at his waist had snapped back the bolts from within, opened the door in a rush, a bit hung-over, not suspecting that this day was his last, the comrades were already fidgety, nerves thrumming, stomping from foot to foot as if it were cold, wanting to piss. *Remember this: if you're off to rob a bank, go to the bathroom first – you never know how long you'll be...*

And everything immediately went rickety-wrong. Old man, despite the keys, had no access to the safe. The teller, the sweet lady with the generous nature and the son at university, was in the bathroom so couldn't help. More waiting. When she appeared, drying her hands, a little embarrassed to be caught with her knickers down, so to speak, she'd thought at first that it was a joke. She'd started off by giggling, seemed to believe that the robbers were friends of her boy's. Then, finally convinced by Horst's barked commands, by Tino's sharp little boot planted in her ribs, and with a little yelp of understanding, she'd tried to cooperate. But with her fumbling, muttering anxiety, her sausage-like fingers, her weight, her sweat, the creaking of her tight, patterned nylon dress, despite the gun at her head and the vicious threats bidding the contrary, she accidentally set off the alarm. The guard was frozen with fear but his dog, terrified of the sudden noise, the intrusion of these strangers, went for Horst, who shot him. The old man, who loved the dog, went berserk, flew at Horst with his fists. Horst shot him too, once, in the head. Then the comrades took the money and ran.

So what did you expect, Maria? What did you honestly, bloody well expect?

But he contains his rage; says nothing. He just studies her angry/ baffled face, wondering how anyone can be both so clever and yet so stupid both at once.

'Here.'

A rim of silver moonlight, risen above the hillside opposite, gives enough of its light to make the farmhouse just visible: a pantiled roof, squat above some twisted olive trees. A path winding through the undergrowth. Maria reaches in her bag for keys, traces a wrought iron gate with her hands to try to find the lock. The key jams, scrapes, turns slowly, and the gate yields and opens with a scrape and a shriek that tears through the silence like paper. The door beyond, heavy, studded wood, opens with a grunt and a shove and the cool blackness inside swallows them. There is a rustling and scratching within which quietens, a breathing and a settling as the long empty house accommodates to their presence.

'Candles...' she says, and Don holds his blazing petrol lighter aloft, illuminating cobwebs and dust while Maria runs her hand across a shelf above the door, finds what she seeks – lights four big catholic candles, and spreads them around the room.

Flickering silence. A low roof with heavy beams. A long oak table down the middle of the room with a bench on each side. A fireplace with a huge stone lintel at one end, chairs placed around it, poised, as if still occupied by the spirits of those who last sat there.

'I need to sleep,' she says, flustered by her exhaustion. She indicates a couch by the fireplace: 'There's a blanket there. Cushions. I'm sorry...'

She takes a candle, disappears through a door at the opposite end of the long room, shuts herself away inside, alone.

Don wraps himself in a blanket for warmth, lies on the hard couch by the empty fire, falls into a dreamless sleep.

❦

The walls are whitewashed stone; the floor pink, terracotta tiles. The sweet scent of wood-ash, persisting over years. Black, low roof beams above which heavy tools are stored – two-handed scythes for hay, sickles with rusted blades, a long-handled axe, broad-headed shovels, a store of logs and hay in the eaves. Above him, the apex of a high pantiled roof, deep shadows pierced by shards of the silver, morning light. Stillness; the jostling of bats, settling for the day; stillness and quiet once more.

Twisted and aching, he chooses not to move: lies there instead bathed in sweet, old scents, watching the slow twisting of the columns of dust in the air above him.

There are two small, deep-set windows on either wall; the glass, long unwashed, lets in little light, and there is vegetation outside pressed in hard against it. In an alcove above his head is a crudely-painted wooden statue of Our Lord, his right hand raised in the sign of peace, the wooden eyes long since dried of their tears, face worn flat by veneration. Beside him, half-blackened pots and pans; a kettle by a wood-burning stove sits in the fireplace. He yawns, stretches, pulls himself to his feet. The door where Maria went is still shut; the place is silent.

He walks across to the front door, bare feet cool on the stone tiles, stands in the porch by the open gate and looks at the morning.

Opposite him, far away, the marble summit of the mountain, picked out pink by the dawn. He breathes in the cool air. Blue-grey hillside clad in dense pine, the bottom of the valley obscured by cloud which rises slowly, warmed by the first sun. The house is in shadow and it's still cool where he stands; he shivers, his bones still cold. The ground at his feet is a reddish, sandy brown, stamped flat by generations of feet, and the hillside above and below him is covered by weed-choked olive groves, a few fig trees, the fruit already fallen and rotting on the ground, a grove of citrus over to the left, the fruit still green. Around the house itself are the remains of a garden – tomatoes running wild, some herbs: rosemary, flowering basil; around the windows scented stock. Wisteria grows thick and blue around the gate, the flowers already humming and nodding with bees. From somewhere high above and behind, the clear sound of running water.

He dresses, puts on his boots, takes from beside the fire the white enamelled water jug, and climbs the hill behind the house in search of water. There is an overgrown track which he follows until, a hundred yards or so above the house – which he can just see: a pink roof glimpsed between the green branches of a walnut tree – he finds, buried in deeper green vegetation, a spring.

Protected by stones, lined by ancient brickwork, deep enough to plunge into. A wide, deep pool, running onto an irrigation channel which disappears around the curve of the hillside. An enclosed, dark green space with high walls of mossy stone, a roof formed from the reaching branches of willows, a flat, dry stone to sit upon as he takes off his boots and his clothes and dips his feet into the freezing water; then, gathering handfuls of the cold, clear stuff, he drinks, then splashes his face, his back, his body, yelping as he does, quivering with the cold. He stands – spreads out his arms and his hands, lets the first of the day's sun, now just piercing the glade where he stands, caress and dry his aching limbs. The hills opposite are now obscured by the fine, morning mist, so he stands quite alone, enclosed.

Hair wet, still dripping, he returns to the cottage, carrying the jug, now heavy with water. He gathers armfuls of kindling and sticks from a wood-stack in a lean-to under the far gable, and feeds and lights the wood-stove, where the dry wood catches in a moment, crackling and blazing, the warmth reaching into his cold core, the room filling with the resinous scent of olive wood.

He fills a pan, boils water, makes coffee, fries four eggs taken from the food sack. He stretches out in a wooden armchair by the fire, warms his feet, drinks coffee and waits.

'Hello, Don.'

She speaks quietly, her voice flat. A timid, hesitant 'good morning.' He says nothing; notes a new humility in the voice. Fills her a cup of coffee from the pot, which she takes, frowning as she sips it, staring deep into the fire. The ghost of a smile. She thanks him.

She wears a plain white cotton nightdress. Her hair is wild around her shoulders, her eyes still slightly swollen from sleep. Don looks away from her, pokes the still-blazing fire, adds a few more sticks which swiftly flare up, and then stretches out, enjoying the warmth.

'This is your place? Your family's?'

She says nothing. He glances up at her again – lets his eyes rest a few moments on her tear-filled eyes, still cast down, the light from the dancing yellow flames reflected in her pupils.

'That guard should *not* have been killed,' she says, like a school mistress, her voice momentarily flaring into anger, a little fragile authority returned.

'No.'

Her voice drifts off again. 'You blame me for what has happened.'

'I don't.'

'He didn't have to die…'

'No.'

'He should never have attacked Horst.'

Don is silent. He *didn't* attack Horst.

'But Horst should never have shot him. Whatever.'

'No.'

'It's our fault. We should never have been there.'

He cannot find words with which to respond.

All day thereafter her silence is interspersed with this monologue:

'Why did Horst *do it?*'

What did you bloody well expect you stupid… But he doesn't say it.

Immersed in her own dark, solipsistic world, she sits alone and indolent by the fire, stirring from time to time to feed it. Even as the day grows into itself, as the sun pours down on the pantiled roof and the heat gathers its strength, even as the air thickens and the sun screams silently outside, she feels cold. She wraps her legs in her arms, squats bird-like on the chair, picking threads from her night-dress, shivering. She sighs. She mutters to herself, moans, gathers herself to speak, says nothing.

Driven from her self-absorption, repelled in turn by her rage and self-disgust, he puts himself to work. Stands on a wooden chair, reaches up deep into the roof space, and pulls down a rusty scythe, a long-handled axe, a shovel; finds a pot of grease and a grinding stone, and cleans and sharpens his tools in the shade of the porch.

He learns the rhythm in the long grass between the olive groves. Scythes a pathway free of hay between the trees, then sets to pulling free the fallen branches and the saplings, tearing up the young growth and piling it all in a clearing in the remains of an orchard below the house. He works a yard or so at time, making slow progress below the fierce sun, breaking every hour or so to drink water, to check upon the silent woman indoors beside the fire.

In the late afternoon he explores. Sets off back along last night's track, up a tight switchback to where they left the car the night before, onto the winding main road. Last night he'd seen a turn off to a town, Monte Rosa; seen lights flickering between trees somewhere off, high in the hills, and in the daylight sets off to find the place.

Under the sun the road is longer than he had anticipated: soon he's stumbling from shade to shade, labouring in the heat and wishing he'd brought water. The woodland clears. He sees that he's on the spur of the hillside at the end of which perches, on a white marble outcrop, a cracked old village. Hunched under the sun, he trudges to the next patch of shade and gathers himself for the last, exposed part of the walk.

The distance is short, but the last few hundred metres of the climb are a sweat even now as the sun sinks and the day grows slightly cooler. High broken walls protect the remains of the town from the cliffs below it. Deep scrub-filled ravines descend to the valley and the flatter, cultivated land below. The town itself is a nest of pink tiled roofs, a bell-tower and church in the centre, ravens calling to one another in the still evening; ragged vultures, brown, silent and sinister as dragons, hang and turn in the thermals high above the plain.

The town sign is rusted and broken, hanging half-detached from its post, pocked by bullets. The first houses, roofless, cracked in the walls and broken down, clearly abandoned. Ivy covering the walls, obscuring the red graffiti, cables and telephone lines draped across the streets, tangled weeds choking the gardens, long roots cracking the roads and pavements. The place is silent. A rusting 2CV truck rots beside the road, grass growing wild around its cracked tyres.

But there is life in the tiny village square. An old woman in black carrying a wicker-covered basket, full of fear and vulnerable as a little bird with a broken wing, scuttles from a little corner shop, across the square, round the corner, disappears. There is a little shuttered café opposite a medieval church, a grandiose brick front, crooked steeple and a shuttered oak door.

He enters the tiny shop; buys bread, rice, wine, a few spotted vegetables from a thin, saucer-eyed child dressed in a grey slip, a sleeping baby on her hip. He tries to talk to the child, smiling at the baby to pass the time of day, the silence beginning to wear him down; but the baby yells, and the girl doesn't reply – merely stares at him in fear, as if she doesn't understand a word of what he says.

He buys a paper, pays with a ball of crumpled notes and a few coins which he pushes with his finger over the counter and which the girl accepts, not bothering to count the change.

He walks back across the square; tries the door of the café, which is locked; sits a moment to rest on a plastic chair propped against the wall outside; shuts his eyes against the sun.

His eye is drawn to the paper. The word *Terroristi*. 'Red Brigade terrorists apprehended in Bologna…' Black and white pictures. '…After the murder of security guard Gianbattista di Ruffino, father of three…' Their faces, unmistakeable in the police mug-shots: Horst – dark, shadowed eyes, a snarl; Tini, the flashlight glancing off his pale, frightened face, hair still perfectly in place; their fat friend, Bergamo '…well-known to the authorities of Emilia Romagna; notorious killers…' Below their photos, that of their victim, Gianbattista, kneeling down beside his dog, smiling up at the camera, his name in the caption below, the word '*Assassinato!*'

He scans the piece for other names, other faces, his heart heavy with loathing as he reads '…*implorando pietá* – begging for mercy … *una pallottola alla nuca, stile esecuzione* – one bullet to the back of the head, execution style … apprehended after a brief struggle in their flat, later yesterday evening… "*Un colpo inferto alla minaccia del Terrorismo Rosso* – a triumphant blow against the scourge of Red Terror," says Police Chief Adolfo Ugoni…'

There is movement and the rattling of keys and locks from the café door behind him. Dry-mouthed, but no longer thirsty, Don stuffs his shopping and the paper into his canvas bag, scuttles guiltily back across the town, back to the safety of the house.

Where Maria still sits, eyebrows knitted, face tear-smeared, staring into a now-dead fire.

Don casts the paper lightly at her feet. She glances at it. The paper lies there; five faces look up: Horst, Tini, Bergamo, the only face still smiling that of the guard, arms still wrapped around the neck of his beloved dog. And a face half in shadow: curly brown hair, dark eyes. A blurred photo taken from a distance of a woman a year or two younger than Maria, sitting reading at a café table, a cup of coffee in front of her, a cigarette burning out in the ashtray. Maria seems unsurprised. Turns the paper face-down so that she needn't look at these pictures.

'You shouldn't have gone to town. You could have been seen.'

'They *killed* him...' is all he can manage. *Calm down. This doesn't help.* He goes to stand outside, gulping in the fresh, cooler air.

The far side of the valley is now in shadow, silhouetted by a startling, blood-red sun sinking behind the marble crags. Far off to his right, the village, the bronze clock-face of the bell tower shining back; a golden light cast back across the valley; the dead town glowing pink. *Monte Rosa.*

The floor of the valley is once again in near-darkness, though it's not yet late. A bird, darting between two trees below him, flashes its bright gold tail before it disappears. *Golden Oriole.* Rare. Only ever seen before dawn and at nightfall. Up high in a deep blue sky, the first of the night's stars emerge.

She stands behind him, at his shoulder. Says: 'I'm sorry, *Ton...*'

'They shouldn't have killed him.'

Silently she nods. She places a hand upon his shoulder – the first touch of her skin on his for many months. Says, nodding as she does:

'I'm *sorry, Ton.*'

He nods at her, gifts her a thin, watery smile, the best he can yet manage, then turns his back on the sunset, turns upon his heel and goes back indoors. He cleans the ashes from the fire, builds another, lights it.

He prepares food: a salad of bruised, over-ripe tomatoes which burst at the first touch of the blunt knife. Fries coarsely-chopped garlic in olive oil over the wood flame, a handful of dried olives, some herbs picked earlier from the over-run garden. Boils water for pasta. Pours red wine from a flagon into two tumblers and hands one to Maria who crouches down to sit with him. She takes it, drinks deeply, places the empty glass by his.

'This was my grandmother's. The tools you were using belonged to my great-uncles. The place is all mine, now. I used to come here often. Never recently. No-one other than Marco knows about it, and he hasn't been here since childhood. We can stay here.'

He places food on the plates and they eat and drink in silence. They eat last year's fruit, wrinkled and dry but still sweet enough, bought in the village shop. They throw the peel in the last of the fire and watch it flare sweetly up. They sit in silence, staring into the embers.

Then she says: 'I'm sorry, *Ton*' once more, and this time he forgives her. He places his hand on hers for the first time, and squeezes it. She turns to him, startled, and this time he leans over, gently, a little in fear, and kisses her softly on her dry mouth. He looks at her, examining her eyes for an answer, but there is nothing more than her silence and a far-off sad look. He kisses her again, and now, with a murmur, she put her arms around him, pulls his body to hers.

Part 4

20

'Tell me, Don,' says Gianmaria after a brief pause, fixing Don with those dark, slitted eyes. 'Did you ever see her again?'

Don, looking quickly away, stares down instead at his two familiar boots planted on the wooden floor. Looks up again, his face bunched up and squeezed, a little red, unconvincingly pugnacious. When he speaks, his voice is unsteady.

'Who? Did I ever see *who* again?'

'Rosie told me that when you were here … years ago … there was a woman…' Gianmaria, an unpractised liar, chooses his words with elaborate care. 'I wondered what had happened to her.'

'Then Rosie was wrong. Or lying.'

'Oh,' says Gianmaria, subdued, suspicious, yet not unfriendly. Don stands abruptly, points one angry, shaky finger, is about to speak but chooses not, leaves instead.

Gianmaria, all but certain now, watches him go.

In the early morning, in the hour after the sun has risen, but before it is high enough for its rays to pierce the fine canopy of leaves cast by the willows around the pool, the air is cool and Don shivers a little as he stands perched naked on the mossy brick wall, watching in silence as his lover's body makes wide circles under the water, and as her brown hair streams behind her, eddying over the pale skin of her back.

This brief time: a moment, isolated by circumstance from all before and all that is to come.

They have no towel with them. Don dries himself slowly using a sheet, his skin tensed and mottled by the cool air. The sunlight glancing through trees makes the surface of the water sparkle. She bursts through, shaking drops like crystals from her hair, scattering them on the black surface. Yelping with cold, she drags herself with an effort onto the stones and, blinded by the water flowing over her eyes, reaches up with open hands for the sheet which Don has clasped in his hand. Wrapping it around her body like a toga, she flicks the hair from her eyes and laughs at him, and the sound of her laughter is scattered around them like these brightly-glinting droplets of water that hit the surface of the pool. He puts his hand around her waist and feels the smooth surface of her skin under his hand.

She laughs at him. Says: 'You're cold!'

But he isn't, not really. At one with the water, the trees, the shade and the play of that delicate light scattering through the shade, he feels nothing but exhilaration at the touch of the air and the water on his skin, at the touch of her skin on his as he pulls her into him, as she buries her head into the root of his neck and offers him her mouth to kiss.

He pauses, allowing the moment its duration. Smiles, then beginning to feel the cold, bends to pick up his clothes.

❧

She is not dead. Although he cannot concentrate sufficiently on the voice that speaks to make out more than one word in ten, he can tell just by looking – by her colour, by the lines of tension flowing in her body, by her body's shape, the way it lies, although it lies quite still; he can tell by the slow intermittent rhythm of her assisted breathing; by the slow march of green lines and figures on the monitors above her cot – that death, for now – for the moment, at any rate – has been banished. That death – her death, which earlier he had sensed vividly as a presence there in the room with them, mimicking his movements: bending over the bed, solicitously, as he did; shrouded face tented in the flat palms of hands which cannot pray; or leaning back in the plastic hospital chair, easing the aching in its old bones, longing for rest – has left now.

Her head is shaved, wrapped mainly in bandage from which on one side a tube draining straw-coloured liquid emerges. Her eyes are taped shut and he finds himself longing to open them, to remind himself at least of their colour. A feeding tube in her nose. Her mouth is shut, and its shape – a wonderful wide, expressive curve, thinks Don, which he had never before appreciated or considered for its beauty – is distorted by the complex kit she needs to stay alive: the breathing tube which trails from the corner, held there by gauze strips; the filament of saliva pooling on the pillow beside her head.

Beyond that: the shape of her body, modestly concealed beneath a white sheet which passes over the upper part of her chest at the first rise of her breasts. Her arms lie on top, a drip in the back of one hand, the other hand free. A gold cross lies on her chest, which Don hadn't noticed her wearing before, and he wonders who had given it to her and what it represented – whether it was ornamentation or symbolic of a deeper religious or spiritual impulse of which he, her father, knew nothing. He thinks again, for the hundredth time, as he looks at the pale, clear skin of his daughter's chest, at the gold cross sitting on it, how little he knows her; how he longs to know her, and for how long he has yearned to be loved by her.

The doctor has stopped talking; his voice – '...*la pressione intra-cerebrale é normale...*' – has trailed off now into silence: whether because he has nothing left to say, or because he knows that he has no audience, Don doesn't know. But he stands there looking at Don, then leans across the corner of the cot and pats his shoulder. Don's face is grey with exhaustion, eyes red, skin lined, hair greasy. He glances at the clock: twenty to three. There are no windows, and the flickering bright light around them is purely artificial. He has no idea whether it is day or night.

Don thanks the doctor. Clasping his hands in an attitude of submission and gratitude, apologises for his rudeness, dismisses the tired man to his bed. He sits again, resumes his contemplation of his daughter's sleeping form.

❦

They rose early; they washed away the previous night's sleep in the spring water of the ancient stone pool, in the glade above Maria's grandmother's farmhouse. They descended from the place, picking their way bare-footed over the rutted path to the house, life now restored to them by the magical water, fresh for another day. They talked all the time – chatting, relaxed, like young lovers, talking in a way that had never been permitted them before. Talking of light and insubstantial stuff, of which little now remains to him. Beyond the simple physical content of their days, the fabric of the short time they spent together, his memories of that brief time are vague. He remembers the pool. He remembers the nights they spent together. He remembers the dream-like quality that these days had, even as he lived them.

He brought kindling for the fire from the stack cut the day before, and she boiled water for coffee, heating up yesterday's bread so that they might have breakfast. He spent the morning on the lands, clearing the tangled years of vegetation which threatened to choke the life from the remaining trees in the groves which extended in ancient terraces from the front porch of their house, all the way down the valley side to the river at the bottom. He sweated under the day's sun until he had cut living space around an apricot, peach or fig tree, had collected the fallen leaves and branches, all the fragrant wood to be burned during the cooler nights and the long, cold seasons which he imagined lay ahead of them.

She sat under the shade gazing at the hills opposite, either lost in thought or nowhere at all, or calling out to him as if to reassure herself of his continued presence – and her voice would come to him as he stood sweating in the shadows, catching his breath, and he would call back to her – '*Amore!*' – and carry on with the cutting and the hewing, the clearing, carrying and stacking to which he'd set himself.

From time to time she sang. When she thought she was most alone – perhaps when he had gone for the afternoon to buy provisions in the village, labouring up the path under the weight of bags or bottles; or if he was working the groves most distant from the house – those nearest the valley floor, where the noise of the river obscured any sound from the house, or the grove of citrus trees on the stony land above the spring – pausing in his work he would hear for a moment her clear voice drifting down to him. He would stand still, holding his breath, trying to catch and keep the tune that she sang, to keep for his own, to store in his memory.

And yet how little now remains to him of that precious time: the memory of the work; the taste of the cold morning water on his skin; their love-making on her grandmother's hard wooden bed, the thin sheet under them, and the tattered pale blue blanket they used to cover themselves after; the long nights spent together; the evening stars and the moonlight, and her clear voice singing, coming to him through the trees as he paused in his work. Mere fragments of memory, sense impressions, clear, yet obscure as a dream dreamt vividly the night before...

'…I have scarcely thought about that time, between then and now. I have kept these memories from my mind. And now, when I consider them once again, I find them to be no more than uncertain fragments: odd, snatched words, phrases, events, certain moments or even impressions of these moments which are as clear as if they had occurred yesterday – yet the rest unconnected, hazy and uncertain. And I fear most of all that this process of remembering will colour, contaminate and finally destroy the fabric of the memories themselves, and then I will be left with nothing at all…'

How long is it now since you last slept, Don? Two days? Three?

He is startled by the sound of his own voice talking, articulating his drifting thoughts while *he* sits still, mind elsewhere and long ago, holding his daughter's hand, watching the rising, falling of her chest.

The shadowy presence opposite has returned: barely perceptible to any of his merely corporeal senses, but present nonetheless: a shimmering in the air opposite, a form breathing as he breathes, leaning forward, leaning back, shifting its absent weight on the chair opposite, listening to his words, measuring each of them as he utters them.

Don gives form to this thought which has been growing in him since he heard of Rosie's injury:

'…What must I do to make certain that you will live, Rosie?'

He sobs, then swallows his tears.

She lies in silence, with never a flicker of response. The clock reads 4AM, the date August 2nd, the anniversary his daughter had originally come to Italy to mark.

The shadow opposite, the imagined shadow of his daughter's death, conjured by sleeplessness and grief, looks back down from the clock, its eyes meeting his, its grim, toothless snout settling into something like a smile. Don stares back.

'…To guarantee that you will live, and be happy?'

*

At night they sit together around the grate watching the yellow flames from the wood fire chasing themselves in scented, smoky spirals up the chimney. They drink wine, watch the fire as it burns down into a deep, slumbering red; they feel the night gather in, the rasping song of the crickets outside, the silent, regal moon sailing through wispy summer clouds, the long, falling cry of the night birds. They have been here for almost ten days.

'Tomorrow I'll clear the last of the land down by the river, where there is a grove of what look like lemon trees. I saw the fruit through the undergrowth: they're still green, but with a bit of work they should make a decent harvest. In a month or two. I don't know, when do lemons ripen?

'I need to check the roof as well. Although everything seems dry, when the winter comes it will be cold and we need to be certain that it's sufficiently water-tight to see us through the rain. I just need to check the tiles and replace any that are loose or have fallen. There's a stack of good tiles round the back, unused. I expect that this is something that they used to have to do every year.'

She nods. She remembers her grandfather doing exactly that: at the end of every summer, using the orchard ladder to climb up onto the roof to check the tiles. How did he, Don, know to do that?

'You'll find a ladder, somewhere, in the orchard...'

'I know, I have...'

They lapse into silence, watching as the embers of the fire settle.

'Don...' she says, after a while.

'Mmm?'

'We cannot stay here forever.'

Silence.

This thing has hovered in the background between them, unsaid since they arrived.

'I know,' he says eventually, although he had cherished this foolish, irrational hope... 'But we can stay here for a while. A month or two? We're safe here, at least. Nobody knows that we are here.'

'We have no money.'

'I will find work. I could sell the fruit from the orchard...' The idea, once articulated, is laughably impractical. She doesn't mock him, though. Just stares into the dying fire, sad, her fingers tight on the stem of her glass.

'I want to stay here with you forever. But there's something I need to do first.'

'Your comrades? They're in gaol.'

'No. Not them. I no longer care about them.'

'And your brother's safe…'

She shakes her head. Don waits in silence for her to speak. Then:

'I need to tell him that I am still alive.'

Don nods, staring into the fire, sensing hope, his happiness, this tender new life, beginning to fragment.

'I don't think you should speak to Manu…'

She takes his hand, squeezes it, a gesture of tender reassurance which serves only to remind him of what, whom, he stands so soon to loose.

'He cannot find us. One call. To finish this. To tell him that I am out. I need to do this.'

'And not going back?'

She pauses, considering this. Then says, with a tender smile in her voice:

'And not going back.'

Don thinks.

'Don't call him.'

'I have to.'

'I know.'

❧

'Let me tell you what happened, Rosie. This time I will tell you, but everything: right to the end…'

She is unresponsive still – still no movement beyond the movement of the machine which breathes for her; not a flicker of those taped-down eyes, nor a squeeze upon his hand when he squeezes hers. Yet Don is heard. As he gives voice for the first time to these wraiths which inhabit him, gives them shape, body, structure, makes a tale from those events which formed him, he knows that she listens.

'…so we set off for Monte Rosa on the morning of the first of August. She was frightened to leave. Although the suggestion had been hers and I resisted it, she had made it reluctantly, or so I thought at least, and it pained her. She was as much fugitive from the world as I. She had much to lose when she left her world, but, by returning, far more…'

§

There is a payphone in the middle of the village square. Don buys a handful of *gettoni* from the girl in the shop and then sits in the shade of a plane tree whilst Maria, her face turned from him, dials, waits, dials again. From the movements of her tensed shoulders, he can tell that she has made a connection, and from the angle of her head, that she is talking, and then that there is force in this conversation – that she is arguing, possibly pleading.

She stops talking, grips the phone between her cheek and her shoulder, scrabbling with the tokens in the palm of her hand, dropping one, stooping to pick it up from the floor of the phone-box, then pumping the last of the tokens in and resuming her conversation.

Don sits under the dappled shade of the leaves and branches of the plane tree, examining the moving patterns, the reticulated shadows cast on his body and legs. The comforting sun warms the skin on his face – his cheeks are warm but his eyes are in shadow. He sits very still as he waits.

Gently she replaces the receiver. Stands there a while, then with a toss of her hair she picks up her bag, opens the door and crosses the square to where he sits.

'So what did he say?'

Although she doesn't meet his eye, he can tell that something is changed. Something has been stolen from them.

'What's happened? What did he say?'

'Wait!' says an irritable Maria, looking around at the empty square before looking at him. 'Keep your voice down!'

She has been crying. She wears once again that haunted look. That cloud, which Don realises has been banished these last ten days, has returned. They walk in silence to the edge of the village.

'What has happened? What did he say? Does he know where we are?'

'No.'

Don is relieved. So long as no-one knows, they're safe.

'Marco?'

'In hospital. He's safe.'

'And the others?'

'Being held. Mariotti has disappeared.'

'So then we just have to stay hidden…'

She doesn't answer.

The house is as they left it. The air cool on their skins after the hot walk up from the village, the inside still deeply in shadow, the embers of their fire from the night before just dying. The bedroom door is open – he can see her clothes from the night before scattered on the floor, the sheet and the single blanket coiled on the wooden bed frame. He unloads the provisions he has bought – wine, flour, oil, vegetables, sugar, coffee – breathing in the intimate air of their occupancy. He has bought provisions sufficient to last them a week.

'And Manu? How was he?' He tries, and fails, to inject a note of tenderness into his voice, as if he cared, a little, for how Manu felt…

'Fine. Not surprised … by anything. Seemed to know perfectly well that we were … together. Didn't even ask where we were.'

'So we're safe. And everything is perfect,' he says, flatly.

Maria stands. As if she can no longer endure his presence, she walks briskly through the open door to the bedroom, throws herself face down on the bed. Don sits alone staring miserably into the ashes. Waits.

And soon she returns. Stands behind him, places a hand gently on his shoulder, stroked the shell of his ear between her finger and her thumb, sending tender ripples down his back.

'I have to go back to Bologna.'

'When?'

'Tomorrow.'

'Tomorrow! Why?'

A pause.

'The money. After the robbery, they dumped the bag in Manu's flat. That was the plan – the last resort. If everything else went wrong, we could leave the bag there, and it'd be picked up later. Manu was to be abroad. But they were arrested, and so it's still there. And I'm the only one left that can move it.'

'Leave it. It's a trap. You'll be picked up.'

'I have no choice.'

'Forget it. Stay here.'

'Sooner or later Horst or one of the others will talk. I need to pass on the money, before that happens. We haven't very much time.'

'Let Manu dispose of it! Let him burn the fucking money!'

'He will not touch this, Don. But if the contact isn't made – if the money isn't handed over – then they will assume that we have stolen it. And they are merciless. Believe me. I have to pass on that money.'

'You'll be stopped before you leave your flat. It's a trap. Your organisation – Martello – it's transparent. Everyone is spying on everyone else. No-one is innocent. Least of all Manu. Everything that you do is known about, weeks before you've even planned it. They just want YOU, Maria. So stay here with me.'

'If we don't do what he says, we will be pursued until we are dead. By both sides. Sooner or later they will find us. We will never be free. This is our only chance. Hand over their money, leave the country.'

'What will I do?'

She shrugs. An ugly, despairing gesture.

'You don't expect to get away at all, do you? You expect to be caught.'

A pause. She speaks:

'They will interrogate Horst and the others until they know where the money is, and everything else that there is to know about the organisation. If they can't find me, they will find Marco. If Marco doesn't tell them where we are, then the other side will take over, and he will eventually talk. We have had ten days of freedom. Now it's over. I suggest you return to England. I suggest that you go today. Give me a number. If they let me get away, I will come and find you.'

A pause.

'*You* go to England. I'll move the money. I'll follow you.'

A sigh. Yeah, yeah. A smile. A kind but patronising hand on his.

'You are kind. Thank you, Don, but this isn't your problem.'

'It is. Every policeman in Bologna will be looking for you. Your face is known. Your picture was in the fucking newspapers. You think we have to move the bag. Fine. But let me do it. I'm the virgin, remember? I'm the only one that can. You go to England. I will tell you where to go. I will meet you as soon as I've left the country. Then we can be free, and be together.'

A pause.

Don:

'Tell me what I have to do with the bag.'

'You can't do it. It's not right.'

'I love you, Maria!'

(Words uttered for the first time, eyes bright, and said with so much force that she flinches, as if she has been struck. He has never used these words before, nor has anyone ever used them to her. She doesn't handle it well. She looks away from him, grimacing, eyes filling with tears. Don tries again.)

'I want to spend my life with you, and if I can't, at least I want to have tried my best. This, now, isn't enough. If you go, you will be caught. If I go, then at least there is a chance. Then perhaps we can be together. What do I have to do with the bag?'

Maria, slowly, reluctantly:

'I don't know. It's lying in the hall of the flat. In the side pocket is an envelope containing some money, tickets and some instructions. That's all I know. Mariotti ... organised it.'

'Yeah. I bet he did. Have you the key to your flat?'

'Of course I do. Don?'

'What?'

'Do you have any idea how dangerous this is?'

'Yes. Of course I have...'

꧂

The story is an hour or two in the telling. At first Rosie is tranquil. The brief, happy time – those ten days spent with the woman her father had once loved, the days, the nights, the washing at dawn in the cold Etruscan pool in the grove above the farmhouse and the evenings under the stars, breathing in the warm air and listening to the noise of the insects and the birds – this story is a balm for the injured woman, who lies there listening, but quite unresponsive, breathing with the rhythm of the machine, her father's words falling upon her, soft and pale like moonlight upon her frozen, fragmented inner world.

꧂

She had woken with him at five that morning. The purple of the pre-dawn sky dissolving into clean, bright sunrise. They were silent, because they had nothing left to say. This was a morning like any other morning. She made coffee, the first of the day in a pot on the hob. Like any other morning ... but this was the morning chosen for their time to end. They had sat opposite one another at the wooden table, taken coffee, wincing at its strength, looking into one another's eyes, looking away, at their bare feet, their toes curling against the cool tiles. She was to stay put. He'd leave alone, walk the hour up to Monte Rosa, pick up the bus to town, then the train. They'd decided. He had to be away by quarter-past five. Time was tight. He stood, took his leather jacket from the peg inside the door, turned to her. Couldn't find any words. So just nodded. Turned to leave, but then she'd come rushing after him and broken his foolish silence.

'*Donald.*' Tonald, *in her voice.*
'*Yes.*'
'*Come back, please. Come back to me. Promise.*'
'*Yes.*'
And he'd left.

℘

Hearing is the last sense to go, and the first to return. She listens to her father's story. Conscious, but without being aware, her shadow accompanies him, step by step, as he walks through his remembered world.

That's before the sudden terror. Before the suffocation, the headache, the unendurable awareness of being bound down and strapped in and violated by a thousand alien tubes and tools – in her throat, her hands, her head, her bladder.

Before that: her father's calm voice, his story, and the experience, more vivid than a dream, of living in *his* world.

Although she lay there, paralysed, frozen, unconscious, asleep, yet she accompanied the two lovers as they swam in the morning, as he draped the towel, shivering, around her skin. She was the third, the silent presence, as he finished his coffee, as they sat opposite one another at the wooden table, toes curling on the cool, terracotta tiles. As he stood, tried to speak, but couldn't, then coughed and said his first and last farewell.

So she accompanies her father, heavy-hearted, premonitions billowing through her dawning consciousness like great, purple thunder clouds. *Daddy!* she thinks, in a fragmented and distant way, her heart filling with dread as she sits with the twenty-two year-old: like him, dry-mouthed, sweating, cold with fear; on a morning train, journeying back into the world.

At first Rosie is tranquil. But fear grows in her as it grew in him.

The world, as sooner or later it must, has chosen this day to end her sleep and intrude; to determine what of Rosie survives.

The sedative has been withdrawn. The paralysing agent has been stopped. The levels of these drugs in her blood fall, gradually at first, and her initial response is almost imperceptible – a twitching of her little finger, a little resistance to the ventilator which wasn't there before – but then it comes more rapidly: a cascade of sensation and movement which bursts upon her; which bursts out from within her.

She wakes suddenly, to find herself still asleep: suffocating, drowning, deep down in the green water of a well; paralysed by sleep and fighting with her hands and feet, kicking off from the bottom through green, murky water, gasping for air, using her hands to pull thick strands of pond weed from her face, blinking against her blurred vision, swimming up to where she can see the light, summoning all of her life power to struggle to break to the surface, coughing, retching, gasping for the cool, clear air of the world.

Don keeps his promise. He struggles through to the end of the tale, seeing with some fear and yet also with relief the effect that the story has upon her: at first, a tiny movement in her limbs, a twitching of her fingers against his fingers as he grips her hand; then an irregularity in the previously perfectly regular rhythm of her breathing; an increase in the rate of her heart; the appearance of sweat on her chest and forehead. But despite the pain it is clearly causing her, this story has to be told. The tremulous movement of her hands is like the fluttering of the wings of an injured bird which he holds firmly to prevent it from harming itself – yet it grows quickly to something more purposeful, and spreads down her wrists and forearms, shoulders. Her legs and feet and then her whole trunk begin to writhe as she struggles against the weight of the accumulated days that she has spent there.

Don tells his story in measured tones, word by word, drop by drop, titrated like strong medicine, yet hastening to its end.

Suffocating, she scratches at her face and mouth to be free of the tube in her throat, but lacking the coordination to both grip and pull, she falls back again. Don leans forward, half-embracing, half-restraining her, telling her in a loud, authoritative voice those secrets he should have told her years before, when she was still a child and he still her father.

Gathering her power again, she tears with both hands at her face, pulls the tube from her throat and disconnects the ventilator. Her airway obstructed by spasm, she coughs and wheezes, writhing in her cot; muscles of all four limbs now strong and coordinated, she pulls lines from her hands, scrabbles with long nails against the bandages round her head. Alarms ring in the room. Alarms sound elsewhere, alerting sleeping staff.

As Don finishes his story, a more detached, calmer part of Rosie listens still.

Two nurses enter followed a moment later by the doctor. Rosie is blue, coughing, breathing obstructed, fighting for her life in her cot; fighting against her father, who appears to be holding her down, embracing or smothering her, shouting at her in English, shouting her name as if he is pleading with her, weeping.

Rosie hears this shouting: the last of her father's voice, then voices speaking in Italian. The relief as her father's weight is lifted from her chest, then hands at the side of her face lifting her jaw forward, and another tube in her throat sucking out and clearing her airway. The release when she feels that she can breathe again. Then an overwhelming sense of drowsiness as she falls back into the frozen world which she has occupied for so many days.

This time, though, she is not alone. She is accompanied by the memory of her father's story, the horror of which doesn't leave her – but as she sinks, saturates her; swallows her, as she must swallow it; threatens to become a part of her.

The girl's airway is secured. Reattached to the ventilator, her colour now good, oxygen saturation one hundred percent, now heavily sedated once again. The nurse covers her naked body with the sheet, replaces the cross on the now-damp skin of her chest. The doctor is both frightened and relieved. Relieved because his patient is clearly neurologically intact, moving her arms and legs, fighting the ventilator, even vocalising – thus, against everyone's expectations, she is likely to make a rapid recovery. Frightened, though, by the rapidity of her return to consciousness, his management of which had clearly gone quite catastrophically wrong. It could have killed her.

And the father, that strange man lurking like a ghost at the periphery of the room, is now silent, rubbing his chin with his hand, staring wide-eyed and enraged at the sleeping girl.

'I think you should leave,' says one of the nurses, taking the arm of the grey and filthy man, leading him to the door. 'You need to get some sleep too…'

He tries to shake off her hand, wanting just to stand there, to stare at his daughter. The nurse tries again, gently insisting. He becomes angry, as she had feared he would, shaking her off with a little too much force, muttering something in English. Then turns his back on the room at last; walks out.

21

LUIGI FALCONE	56
DORA FALCONE	58
PETA FALCONE	8
LOTTI LEWINSKA	21
MICHAELA SALVATI	38
LIZABETA BIANCO	78
FRANCISCO SALVATIERRA	82
ANDREAS SCHUMAN	28
BETTINA KRAUS	23
PIERRE LAFEVRE	32
MARGOT LAFEVRE	33
JEAN-PAUL LAFEVRE	2
LILI LAFEVRE	4
MICHAEL STREET	28
RHONA MCKLUSKEY	26
DORA GALANTE	38
ALICIA GALANTE	6

By half-past nine it's already busy. Today will be a hot, bad-tempered day. A family of what look like gypsies have gathered by the stone: the mother, olive-skinned, with Albanian blue eyes, dressed in brightly-coloured printed rags, a cloth tied around her head and her bare-arsed, dusty toddler playing at her feet. Her three older children surround her, clinging to her skirts, fingers in their mouths, talking in subdued voices. Their luggage – cardboard boxes tied with twine, four heavy-duty plastic shopping bags stuffed and overflowing with clothes – has been stowed in the empty space behind the cordon which separates the crater from the rest of the waiting room. One bag has fallen, spilling its contents onto the stone itself, obscuring the two names that follow *Galante*.

The names organise themselves into their own categories: by family, by age, by nationality – and the longer he sits studying them, the clearer the mental images he forms of their owners.

Andreas Schuman and Bettina Kraus, for example – he with his short beard and glasses, a leather *pochette* where he keeps his pipes, pipe cleaners and tobacco, a studious, meticulous man;

she with her short, curling blond hair, her immaculately-pressed blue jeans, her tendency, meant well, to nag her unworldly, older boyfriend. Each sits guarding their respective rucksack – his, bright orange, nylon, framed; hers, blue, a sleeping bag and bed-roll tied securely on the top with elasticated straps. They were waiting for their connection to Pisa. A short holiday before the beginning of the university term.

Or Dora and Luigi, on the margins of their old age, perched like penguins around a solitary, borrowed egg: their treasure, their little Peta, eight years old and rather spoiled. The grandparents are privileged to be permitted to take her, their only granddaughter, for the weekend, to the beach. She, Dora, worries too much, fussing over the child, her perfect hair, her dress, is she too hot? Too cold? Hungry? Thirsty? He, Luigi, more instinctively in tune with the needs of the child, yet less confident of his ability to handle her, attempts to recruit her affection with a paper bag of toffees, bought earlier in the day for the purpose.

Lucia Fanfani	44
Mica Carabba	36
Paulo Amato	18
Paulo Sclavi	28
Maria Gorrieri	17

The stone itself is a highly-polished slab of black granite, the names inlaid, carved and painted over in gold-leaf. In front of the stone, an area of the original brick floor of the waiting room has been preserved; in the centre is a shallow crater, at the base of which the bricks have been fused by great heat into a slate-grey, smooth surface. Last year's flowers lie strewn still, withered around the base of the stone. They have lain there for a year, and no-one has touched or tampered with them. As he sits, silently, waiting, studying the stone, a woman in her early fifties, with silent reverence, stoops over the blue rope cordon, diffidently avoiding the gypsy woman and her bags, and lays a wreath of dark blue lilies in the crater. She stands, sighs, absent-mindedly wipes the sticky gold pollen from the flowers onto her creaking black nylon dress; wipes her plump cheek with the back of her hand, and sits, a space or two away from Don.

VALERIO FOA	37
DOMENICA FOA	24
HAMED AL'FAROUQH	36
MIRIAM AL'FAROUQH	32
TARREQ AL'ABADI	28
FATIMA AL'ABADI	4
CARITAS N'DEGWE	24
FABIANO ACCORNERO	52
GIOVANNA FIANELLO	28
TOMASO FIANELLO	4

Giovanna Fianello, a nurse, divorced, who sat with her over-hot and tetchy son, Tomaso, who was becoming a handful. She was taking him to Rome, to leave him with his grandparents while she took a holiday, alone: her first adult holiday, her first real chance to relax for over four years.

Outside, the trains come and go.

There are groups gathering, separating themselves out from the ordinary travellers. Many carry flowers, taking it in turns to pause a moment in front of the stone, stooping as did the first of them, the widow, before casting the flowers into the craters. They murmur greetings to one another. No demonstration of emotion other than the handshake, the discrete kiss on the cheek, between people who share nothing more than this common experience of loss. People who may, in the past – when the past was more recent and intense – have known one another well; who may have shared much, and whose lives have been involuntarily bound up with one another, as those of their loved ones were at the moment of their deaths. They murmur their greetings, and sit – a chair or two between each group – maintaining their distances and their differences, the privacy and separation imposed by the separate memories of their respective grief. A woman, Don's own age, pretty in a slightly faded, tired way, sits opposite him, catches his eye and smiles at him with an expression of open, shared concern, which in any other context would have warmed him.

'*Non mi sembra averti visto qui gli anni passati...*'

He blinks. Smiles back sadly.

'*Non. Non...*' Glancing up quickly, looking back down at the floor, feigning: a man apparently overwhelmed by this re-acquaintance with old sorrow. The woman's smile lingers upon his face.

RONALDO MATTEI	63
LAURA MATTEI	59
ZBIGNIEW JARUSELWSKI	49
EDDIE STROMBOLI	38
PAUL GRINGRASS	42
ANITA GRINGRASS	44
POPPIE GRINGRASS	16
BART GRINGRASS	13
SCONOSCIUTO	

Sconosciuto – the 'unidentified.' He pictures the charred bones of a young man, his burned flesh having contracted the bones into a *rictus* – an unnaturally-maintained, static, contorted pose; an artefact of those burns which would mimic, in death, suffering – although there would, for him at least, have been no suffering. He imagines him sitting close to the centre of the area where the blast would occur, staring mindlessly at the row of orange plastic chairs opposite, sitting as Don is now, doubtlessly bored, doubly-hot, waiting a long time – an eternity – for this train which will never come. Nothing remained of this man's face, his hands, his feet, his hair, or any of his possessions: nothing by which he could be identified. Perhaps he had been reduced to no more than a few fragments of bone, mixed with the fragments of others. Perhaps, in truth, he never really existed.

A spare, elderly man, who Don assumes to be a priest, stands and coughs for silence. Addresses those gathered with a smile of welcome. The group – the forty or fifty gathered in the busy waiting room, who have no bags and are not impatient – those gathered for a purpose other than waiting – become still, quieten their murmured conversations, look up expectantly at this man who coughs and smiles, and return his smile.

He talks in rapid, quiet Italian and Don doesn't get much of what is said, but at a signal they all stand, group quietly around the cordon, each with smiles and shuffling feet politely making space for the other, standing with heads slightly bowed, their hands clasped, each in a neighbour's. Don stands too but cannot join his hands with theirs, staying instead at the periphery, declining an offer to join the circle. Tries to pray but can't; watches the Gypsy woman, who has been supplanted by this circle of the grieving, standing with her little family, hauling away the boxes and the bags, shaking her head and muttering.

'*Pronto?*' asks the man with his embracing, all-inclusive smile.

'*Si, Signor Galante,*' mutters the woman standing in front, who, he realises, is the woman who smiled at him earlier.

Not a priest. Just another one of that dismal gathering.

They leave the waiting room in twos and threes, beginning again their quiet conversations. Don follows them out.

§

Galante speaks without notes.

The relatives are gathered in a knot at the front of the rood screen in the *Cattedral Santa Pietro*. Today they are insufficient to even quarter-fill the place. In the early years, these annual gatherings had attracted many hundreds: as well as relatives there were politicians, demonstrators – even tourists of grief who would come to be vicariously moved by the testimonies, thrilled by the touch of evil, authentically cold even at second hand. Now the relatives are half-swallowed by the shadows at the back. Time has winnowed them: many of the elderly parents are dead; the lovers of many of those lost have married again, have their own families, some of them divorced, and have moved on to other joys or pains. Some of those who live abroad can no longer afford to come every year, and for some the annual pain of remembering, of paying tribute, has become too much of a burden, and they have chosen to try to forget; to try, at least, to act as if they have forgotten.

Galante, standing alone at the foot of the steps, merely recites the names, from memory and without comment, barely stumbling over those of his own – *Dora Galante, Alicia Galante* – announcing each syllable of each name in turn in his firm, authoritative voice.

Giulia Veneto; Maurizio Volpi; Giovanni Capecchi; Pietro Ugolini; Fernanda Ramondino; Astrid Nicclasson

It was a walk, rather than a march, from the station to the church;

slow progress through the traffic, the smoke and dust, the gathering crowds of tourists come for the *Carnevale*. There was some pushing too, some swearing from those too uncouth, too unaware to recognise the pilgrims for what they were, as they made their slow progress through the mid-morning heat. Don kept himself half a pace apart, eyes on the heels of those walking ahead, rebuffing attempts to include him into the group.

'*Hai perduto un familiare?*'

'*Mi scusi, ma io non parlo Italiano...*' he mumbles.

Galante talks briefly. More table talk than oratory; more of a homily than a speech or diatribe. Don, his ear accustomed now to the man's quiet voice, or perhaps more attuned to the kind of thing he might say, understands more:

'*...Yet we, the family of the dead – their parents, children, spouses, lovers, friends – their last and only voice on this earth – we still wait. We cannot rest; we cannot forget...*

'*...For how long, bound as we are, hand and foot, by the dissimulation of those who seek with their lies to obliterate the memory of our dead, must we continue with this struggle, this quest of ours, to know the truth? Why are we not to know...?*'

And there's more:

'*...What do they want? Why do they hate us so? What must we do, that the living might be allowed once more to live, and that our dead might, at last, lie in peace...?*'

The families sit, heads bowed, listening in reverential silence.

Don leaves. Stands, half-crouched, picking his way through the semi-darkness, trying not to disturb the meditation of those in front of him, now sharing in communal silence, their heads bent in meditation and prayer for the peace of their loved ones.

But in his rush to leave behind him this thick, suffocating grief he stumbles, and tear-blinded, kicks the wooden edge of the pew. A number of heads in the rows immediately in front respond to the noise and turn, wondering who it is that cannot find it in themselves to share and respect their few minutes of silent contemplation. They see his silent shadow as it rushes to the back; the hush of leather over the tiled floor; the shaft of blinding sunlight as the cathedral door is opened for a moment; the slight creaking of its well-oiled hinge; the muffled slap as it closes upon them.

229

22

It had been hot on that day, too.

Don stands alone, neck bared to the unsheathed sun, eyes squeezed shut, blinded by the intensity of its light.

Don stands on the church steps, hands on his knees, gasping for breath, retching.

His breathing slows. He straightens up, blinking; feels suddenly exposed, as if he is watched from all sides. Rivers of tourists pass on the pavement below him. Few even glance his way.

But it was like that then, too, he remembers. He had had that same sense of suffocation. That same sense of being watched. Footsteps ringing on the pavement, always, everywhere he goes, just half a step behind. Stalked, even.

He looks around himself. Hurries down the cathedral steps, losing himself in the crowds on the pavement.

It had been hot on that day, too.

He stands for a long time on the pavement opposite the flat, looking for the signs: the people lurking on street corners muttering into walkie-talkies; the twitching of a curtain at a window, the glint of sunlight off the lenses of binoculars; the two grim-faced men drinking sweet coffee from plastic cups, sitting smoking in the front seats of their unmarked car, watching and waiting. His only experience and preparation for this is from television as a child. But Colombo or Kojak, he finds, are of no help in the real world. When they come for him – if they come for him – he knows he will not even see them.

He crosses the road, threading between the cars parked in front of the Palazzo, his head slightly bowed, trying to present a smaller target. He takes the two keys Maria has given him, remembers her voice telling him: the larger for the gate, the smaller for the front door. He struggles with the lock before the wrought iron gate finally yields, opening into the tiled courtyard within. The dark and the cool are a relief as he pauses in the shade amongst the silent terracotta pots, the dark green leaves of the plants, the smell of humus. He breathes in the damp air.

He takes the lift to the third floor, selects the name M. Boccaccio, presses the polished brass button, waits for the tug as the lift silently moves, feeling momentarily safe inside his brass cage. The lift stops at the 2nd floor, letting in a bald man with a grey suit and a polished scalp who examines Don from down the length of his long nose, narrowing his eyes, sniffing – as if he senses, from the tell-tale stink of Don, his fear. They share the tiny cubicle for a floor before Don gets out, breathes properly again.

He stands at the top of the stairwell outside the front door. He's alone. There's silence. Unless they are waiting for him in the flat, there is no-one else there but him. Don hears the opening and the shutting of the main door downstairs as the man – banker, lawyer, doctor, whatever – lets himself out.

He opens the door, the key almost silent in the oiled lock; braces himself, steps into the darkness of the flat.

Which sleeps. Which has the absolute, living silence of a place unvisited for many days. His eyes adjust. The black and white stone floor. The slight smell of dust in the air. The black canvas bag, sitting in the centre of the hallway. Dead flowers in a vase on a wooden stand in the corner, withered yellow petals cast onto the ground around it. No-one has been here since the bag was abandoned. Don can hear the sound of his own breathing amplified by the stone floor, the flat white walls, the high, glassed-in ceiling.

He stoops to open the side pocket of the bag, and removes the envelope. Slits open the pale blue airmail paper, removes a sheaf of banknotes – expenses, an awful lot: a train ticket from Ancona to Basle, leaving today at 13:05 – and he glances at his watch. And a note – the briefest of instructions – a place, a time, the description of a man who will take the bag, a contact number.

He places the envelope in the breast pocket of his leather jacket and examines the bag. Thinking as he does so: What if this is a trap? *and opens the zip to examine the layers of money, picking up a taped bundle from the top, feeling its unexpected weight in his hand.*

Thinks: My lover and I could live a year on this.

Thinks: And no-one would ever find us.

But he replaces the cash, closes the bag, lifts it, finds that he can't – the weight of all of that money is such that one hand is insufficient, and he must haul it in his two fists to hoist it onto his shoulders.

231

Even then he staggers under it.

He closes the flat door carefully behind him, makes sure he hears the latch click, presses the call button for the lift, waits a minute for it to come, is relieved to find it empty. Tries to step in, but cannot negotiate the clasp on the brass gate without putting the bag down on the carpeted lift floor, which he does, with a heavy 'thud.' Passes a woman in the foyer who scrutinises him and offers no assistance as he pulls the bag from the lift – heavy, inert and unhelpful as a corpse – and hauls it back onto his shoulders.

But time is limited. It's almost twelve-thirty. The contact's at one, his train leaves at five past. The timing is meticulous. He waits, half-hiding below a stand of poplars, exposed once again on the street outside, and hails a taxi.

It's twelve minutes to the station through the gathering crowds. The driver talks to him, and he attempts to follow the thread of a conversation in which he finds he cannot understand more than one word in three. Something about the carnevale. The procession. The tourists. A curse as the traffic stops, as a fleet of scooters cuts them up on the final freeway to the station.

At 12:45 place the money under the chairs numbered 12 and 13 in the second-class waiting room.
Sit opposite in chair 43 until the bag is picked up at 13:00 exactly, by an old man wearing a black suit.
Go immediately to join the 13:05 to Basle.

It is so hot in the waiting room. Fans in the roof turn slowly, barely stirring the soupy air. Don shows his ticket at the waiting room desk; a young man with black oily hair emerging from beneath his peaked cap, a five o'clock shadow and a uniform unbuttoned and stained with sweat, closes his eyes momentarily to indicate to Don that he has seen the ticket and that he may enter. He forces his way through the mass of people, the handles of his bag slipping on the sweat of his skin, stepping around the rucksacks and suitcases and the children who laugh at one another's games and scream.

12:45: chairs number 12 and 13 are empty, as is chair 43 opposite. Carefully he places the bag underneath, sits in the place opposite and waits. The seats are taken almost immediately: an arguing couple *sit down, intensely engrossed in one another, not interrupting their conversation, ignoring entirely the world around them.*

12:46: a train comes in; another load of passengers try to enter the waiting room, which is full now. There is shouting. The man at the desk raises his voice. Don sweats and slowly suffocates.

12:47: he stands, unable to breathe, heart pounding, mouth and fingers numb, a sense of pressure around his neck and throat, a pain in his chest which threatens to smother him. Looks around him, convinced that the fear on his face is obvious and must be read by anyone. The man at the desk catches his eye and looks away. A pregnant woman takes his chair and thanks him. Panicking now, he forces his way to the platform entrance, passes the desk without looking at the man, passes two policemen on the platform, stares at his feet, waiting, sick, for the hand on his shoulder or the shout or the gunshot. He runs through the main concourse, knocking over an old woman whose husband, a man wearing a black beret, shouts, berating him. He dodges through the taxis parked at the bottom of the station steps, crosses the station square and the road opposite, where the traffic has been stopped for the procession, the music of which he can hear advancing in the distance. He enters a bar opposite, sits at the bar stool, orders a coffee and water, catches his breath.

In an emergency call this number...

He leaves his coffee at the bar, picks up the phone in the corner, feeds in a couple of gettoni *when he hears a voice reply. Says, all in a torrent:*

'The station's watched. Let your guy pick up the bag, take your fucking money, whatever, but I'm out...'

Then realises that he's talking in English, tries to start over in Italian, but is interrupted:

'Don,' *says the voice,* 'you're not being watched. There's no danger. Calm down. Just go back to the station, make the pick-up, then get on the train. That's all you have to do.'

'Manu?'

'No. Michael.'

'How did you know that it was me?'

Silence. Then, calmly: 'Go back to the station. You still have *ten minutes…'*

Angry, he slaps the receiver back onto its cradle. The handset, swinging from its coiled metal wire, cracks against the aluminium bar…

Twenty-four years later, the single bell at the top of the *Torre degli Asinelli* sounds one o'clock.

Somewhere, far beyond the quotidian noise of the day – the roar of the traffic, the continual, wearisome sounding of car horns, the voices of citizens and tourists, the wistful noise, far-off, of trumpets – Don relives that long silence.

Remembers lying dazed at the foot of the station steps. The ringing in his ear. His absolute confusion. The choking smoke. The smell. The paper money which fluttered like brown leaves from an autumn sky, and those first few drops of rain. Then, after a long pause, the sounds of voices. Those first few cries.

Don has been standing, paused, outside the great offices of the *carabinieri*, waiting for that bell to strike, and for the last echoes of its voice to die away. And when it does, his decision is made. He enters through the heavy swinging doors, crosses the empty stone-floored courtyard, finds a desk in a public room, a man there waiting, a short queue in front of him. He stands a moment, waiting; then, emerging at the head, says:

'The *strage* – the slaughter – it was me. I left the bag there. It was me.'

He feels tears pricking his eyes; a black pool of anguish in his throat. He struggles to swallow.

23

The desk officer looks up.

A bullet-headed man in his late forties, tide marks spreading from under the arms of his olive-green uniform, oily black hair smeared across a shiny scalp, pebble-dark brown eyes, a tired, lined face, an ashtray always at his fingertips.

'*La strage,*' he says, without inflection.

'I'm sorry,' says Don, foolishly.

The desk officer looks immensely tired. Looks over his shoulder at the clock on the yellowing office wall. Five past one. He's thinking about lunch.

'You are … English?'

'No. Yes.'

'You claim responsibility for the *strage?* The *strage* of August 2nd 1980?'

'Yes.'

Big, big sigh. He picks out a battered file of forms from a drawer under his desk.

A small queue is growing behind them. A young woman with heavy, violet bruises on her face, crying; a man, her brother and an older couple, probably her parents, propping her up between them.

'This was more than twenty years ago. Are you sure?' His face bears an expression of desperate boredom. He glances over Don's shoulders at the others – the many others – behind him in the queue.

'Sure? *Of course I'm sure.*'

'Please complete this.' Hands a badly-photocopied sheet of A4 across the desk with a bitten pencil. Don stares. '*Auto-denunzia*' is what it says.

'Aren't you … ah…' *going to DO something?*

The desk officer lights a cigarette, takes a sip from a cup of cold coffee. Explains, in slow, careful Italian:

'Sir. The perpetrator of the *strage,* whoever he was, died at the scene. Nonetheless, every year, for so many years after the *strage,* on this day, at this time, we have people like yourself admitting responsibility for our tragedy. I do not understand why this should be, why people should wish to do this, but I am glad to say that in recent years this phenomenon has begun to die out. Nonetheless, *sir,* we must still have systems in place for processing ... ah ... *claimants.* So please to carefully complete and return the form.' *(But after I have left for lunch.)* He looks past Don, raising his eyebrows in a tolerant half-smile at the family pushing through from behind.

'No!' says Don.

Rapid, hysterical Italian from the bruised woman. The desk officer raises his hands, trying ineffectually to keep the peace. The woman weeping, her brother roaring, her parents denouncing the perpetrator of the bruises. Don soon gets shoved out of the way.

He pushes his way back to the front, shrugs off the angry brother, ignores the look of petulance in the eyes of the hungry desk sergeant. And then the man's shout of anger and surprise as Don reaches over his high desk for his collar; as he balls his fist and breaks the knuckle of his little finger on the man's startled, pug-like face.

§

He gets a cell to himself. Walls painted pale green. A bucket of water in the corner, a wooden chair, a metal bed with a hessian mattress and a crumpled sheet smeared on one corner with what looks like the last guy's shit.

Don sits on the bed, aching quietly. There is no mirror in which to examine the bruises on his face, or the gap in his smile where his front upper tooth once was. His back and his chest are bruised and he has a sharp pain in his side when he breathes in, which he attributes, correctly, to a broken rib. He can no longer breathe through his nose, which is clotted up with blood anyway.

None of this matters.

'Why do you choose *now* to give yourself up?'

Unable to find the right words, right now, he doesn't answer at all.

But it had something to do with Rosie. A *deal* he'd made to appease her, or the incarnate image of her death. Something he can't now bring to mind or articulate. Perhaps it was a simple emotional response to the words of the man called Galante, who'd lost his wife and child; or to that yearning which clung to him – like the suffocating stink of the burned bodies of his victims clung to him – for forgiveness. Or just an ending. A desire he'd too long suppressed. Something neglected, during all of these years.

Perhaps I have repented.

But that makes no sense. Not now, after fifteen hours of sound, unrouseable sleep – not now, today, in this cell; not here, in the company of this man who plainly believes not a word of what he is being told.

Because it wasn't my fault. It just wasn't my fault, whines a familiar voice from deep inside his head.

He says nothing.

His interrogator takes off his glasses, cleans them on the rolled-up sleeve of his shirt. His eyes, now unaided, blur and tire. He smiles, all world-weary, patient scepticism.

A kind man, thinks Don.

A watery-eyed alcoholic in his late forties with a lined, baggy face which was once handsome; bright blue, likeably-roguish eyes; a stained raincoat bunched over one arm; a rolled-up newspaper, a canvas brief-case. A man with time on his hands. Half-retired and hopeless, no longer a threat to anyone, he gets the job of debriefing the nut-cases. And, what's worse, he likes it. It's the opposite of real police work: trying to convince an endless chain of harmless penitents why *they* couldn't possibly be *guilty.* He paces around where Don sits, asking his questions, the tone of his voice more kind and curious than forensic.

'So why did you assault the desk sergeant, Don? He never did you any harm. You gave him *a black eye.*'

'I wanted him to arrest me.'

The interrogator – Ispettore Baggio – smirks at this senseless explanation, lights a cigarette and then offers one to Don, who wedges it in the new gap between his teeth, thus reinforcing Baggio's dominant impression: *un pazzo.* Nutcase.

'Have you been investigated before? For this? Or any other crime?'

'No.'

'Have you told anyone else of your alleged involvement in the *strage?*'

'No. Yes. My daughter.'

'Your daughter? Why?'

'It was time for her to know.'

'When did you tell her?'

'Today.'

'Why?'

Silence.

'So why did you do it?'

'Do what?'

'The *strage.*'

'I didn't know what was in the bag.'

'What bag?'

'The one with the bomb in.'

'What did *you* think was in the bag?'

'Money.'

'Money?' says Baggio, interest suddenly a little tickled. 'Why?'

'I was tricked. I thought the bag contained money.'

'Where did this … money … come from?'

'A bank robbery. Two weeks earlier. The *Banca Agricola Di Emilia Romagna* on *Universitá.*'

Baggio looks down at him. Frowns a little through his soft, nice brown eyes. Sits on the bed spot-on on the shit-stain, opens the canvas bag on his knee and takes out a file.

'Don, you are rehearsing information that was readily available in the papers at the time. I need more – much more – if I am even to *think* of charging you. I would like you to look at some pictures. Tell me if you can identify any of these people.'

He opens the first pages of the file. A mosaic of moody black and white pictures, mainly police mug-shots, the odd one taken outdoors. Don, experiencing a sudden, vertiginous nostalgia, lifts a brown, twitching forefinger. A hang-nail scratches the glossy black surface of the print.

'Go on,' says Baggio patiently.

'I never knew that one's name. He was some kind of student. Came from Bergamo. Least, that's what he said. What happened to him?'

'Name was Crespi. He was shot dead in a police raid on a terrorist hideout in 1982. No known connection with Bologna. Not in any way involved in the *strage.*'

Don shrugs.

'Any others?'

Points out another.

'He was one of the leaders.'

'Antonio Mariotti. Involved in the 1978 Collina kidnapping and murder. Turned *pentiti* in 1984; now off the page. No connection with Bologna. Try harder.'

Turns a few more pages. Points out two further faces, staring at him from the surface of the page, from out of the past: one, shaven-headed, snarling; the other close to tears: tears welling up in his limpid brown eyes. Don supplies their names himself.

'Horst Kleber. German. From Frankfurt. The other: Valentino Fioravanti.'

'You are *very warm*, my friend! These two were, indeed, arrested in Bologna. But one week *before* the *strage*.' Baggio looks at him through narrowed eyes, half-impressed, half-mocking. 'You have been hard at work. You have done your research.'

'What happened to them?'

'Suicide. They were found hung by their shoelaces in their cells. Presumably they were afraid that they would betray their comrades.' Baggio snorts, suppressing an ill-mannered burst of laughter. 'These men were … minnows. They all were. Just minnows. But still, better dead. More food for bigger fish.'

'Tino would *never* have killed himself.'

Baggio shrugs.

'Perhaps his friend *helped* him, hmm? Any others?'

Hesitates over the next: a small, blurred picture, three pages from the end, separated from the other pictures.

'Marco. I don't … I never knew his second name.'

Baggio raises his eyes; this time, for the first time, a little surprised.

'Why him? I wonder why you pick *him* out?'

'He was my friend.'

'But you don't even know his name…'

'Marco…'

Baggio shakes his head.

'Benito. Benito Francesco Calvi. Car thief. Mentally subnormal. Worked occasionally for the *Brigate* procuring vehicles. Sold information to the police in exchange for heroin.'

'He didn't!' Angry Don tries to stand, but Baggio stops him with a look. Shows just a flash, just a tiny, momentary glimpse of what he might be capable of. Don sits, winded. The bed-springs creak.

'What happened to him?' he asks after a pause, in a small, dry

239

voice.

'Dead. His ... friends ... killed him.'

Don waits, on his guard at last, though now it's far too late. He should not have underestimated this man. His face feels frozen; his jaws ache.

'He was in hospital, recovering from an amputation. He had been shot through the knee, as a punishment, by his comrades, presumably for talking. He was found dead, on the afternoon of the *strage,* in a lift, in another part of the hospital. He *might* have had some peripheral involvement Apparently he had been trying to run away. Which was remarkable, since he only had one leg. He must have hopped. Like a little bird.'

Another suppressed giggle from Baggio, who hops with the two fingers of his right hand before allowing it to collapse on its back, dead. A child's gesture. A game. Don stares, mouth half-open. The interrogator stares back, a disingenuous, unblinking smile.

'This ... coincidence of timing has never been investigated. Perhaps you might know of a connection?'

Don shakes his head. Baggio waits. Then sighs, turns a few more pages of snaps, leaves the book deliberately open on the back page.

'Anybody else?' he says, slowly.

This last is devoted to four prints of the same subject. The first, an old press photograph, a blurred image of a woman sitting at a café table, newspaper in her right hand, cigarette in the other. Her face is half-obscured by the curtain of her long hair, which she is about to brush back from her face with the fingers of her right hand. And how vividly Don now remembers that gesture. The second and third are university matriculation portraits: a girl in her late teens with smudged, black 1970s eye-shadow, an immaculate white schoolgirl blouse; a scowl on the face of one, a tentative little smile on the other. The fourth, taken more recently: an older woman – a woman in her mid-forties, though recognisably still the same person. Taken on the pavement of some European city – Paris, possibly: the road-signs are in French. She is looking half over her shoulder, the centre of her gaze just off the lens of the camera, her mind elsewhere, unaware that she is being photographed.

'Anybody else?' Baggio repeats the question.

'No.'

'Quite sure?' Baggio stands. Picks up the file, gathers his things. The bed groans and sighs.

'What will happen to me now?'

'You will be charged with the assault of the desk officer. You will be convicted. A few months, a year or two at most, then who can say?'

'And the rest?' he asks, losing hope. 'My ... confession?'

Baggio stands with one hand on his briefcase, the coat folded over the other, hand poised over the bell button to ring to be released.

'That? Who can say?'

Baggio waits.

'There *was* one other,' says Don, breaking eventually.

The interrogator's thick eyebrows patiently raised, mouth turned down, a bored face. A man who, understanding the inevitable nature of the truth, will wait forever if necessary.

'His name was Manu Boccaccio. He was an academic at the University of Rome. He was deeply involved, although I didn't know it at the time. I believe now that he was directing ... everything.'

A pause, then Baggio shrugs, says slowly:

'Sorry, Don. Never heard of him.'

A little, regretful smile as he pulls on his overcoat and rings the bell. The rattling of keys outside, a wave of his hand and he's gone.

❧

When they come, Don will die. He sits and waits for them.

He has had an hour or two to think about this. A little too long to turn over in his mind certain bleak images which linger and won't be suppressed. Of Horst and Tini, for example. He imagines Horst standing at the cell door, jaw thrust out, bellowing specious political demands to the warders whilst Tini sits with his face in his hands, weeping for his mother and complaining about the food.

Turning over in his imagination pages from Baggio's scrap book, he wonders briefly how many there would have been. How many policemen are needed to populate this photo? Four? Five? He moves them around his mental cell like toy soldiers.

And how many will it require, when the time comes, to hang *him*? He pictures the scene, the details. *Two? Three? How many?*

And when? *When?*

He wonders whether they had used the coat-hooks or the door frames or – casting his eye around the bare cell – the taps? The bed-frame? Is it possible to be hung from a bed-frame? He wonders whether they had fought, whether they had been able to struggle in any way, or whether they had been drugged to render the act safer for the killers. He wonders whether they had kicked out, wriggled or writhed, trying to loosen the ligatures around their necks with their thick, numb fingers as they suffocated, or whether their hands were tied; whether they had gone blue and twitched, their sad pricks poking up like tent poles, tongues swollen and eyes bulging; whether they had had time to know what was happening to them, or if it had been quick. He wonders if they wept and begged for mercy. He wonders whether they had even known which of their crimes it was that they were paying for.

He imagines Marco lying in a hospital bed, one leg a bandaged stump, bandages wrapped around both of his broken hands, hearing the news of the bombing. Perhaps he had heard the blast, the sirens of the emergency vehicles going to and fro between the station and the hospital. He would have heard the details on the radio, or watched the coverage from a chair on the ward television, and he would have understood the significance of what had happened. He, at least, had known that they were coming, because he had tried to escape. Standing on his one weakened leg, balancing on the bedside cabinet, supporting himself with his bandaged hands, then pushing himself off, hopping, as Baggio said, just like a little bird, leaning on the walls until he got to the lift. But there was someone waiting for him. Someone had sat smoking black tobacco in the relatives' room outside the ward, waiting for him to pass, quietly following him as he made his way through the hospital until they found a suitably silent place.

When eventually they do come, they are five.

The desk sergeant, who stares at him, sullen, through his swollen black eye. His two friends, who had first taken him to the interrogation room, solemnly ceding to their wronged comrade the privilege of kicking out Don's front tooth. A fourth, unknown; a fifth, more senior officer. They say nothing. They enter the room with the muffled rattling of keys, close the cell door and fan out around him, filling the space with their silence, their body smells, their threat. Two station themselves at either side of the bed where Don still sits frozen; a third stands behind him, in the space by his bucket; the fourth and fifth, the desk sergeant and the officer, stand in front.

There's your answer, sonny: five is the number required to reliably kill a sixth without leaving any marks...

They wait. The room quickly grows hot.

'Home, prick,' says the officer, while the others stare at him in silence.

Don looks up, surprised. The desk sergeant is kneading his fist in the palm of his other hand.

...But not now. Not in a prison cell. No need. Times have changed. Today things are done more ... hygienically.

'What?'

'We have orders to let you go. So go home, prick. Now. Run.' At a sign from the officer, the desk sergeant emits a tiny, flickering smile and opens the cell door with his keys. The smell inside the cell gradually dissipates.

Don tries to stand, but can't. His bruised muscles have stiffened up; his legs and back ache and he now stands, comically, half-bent in two like an arthritic old man. He grimaces with pain.

'Just. Don't. Fuck. Us. Around. Prick,' says the officer, without sympathy.

Don shuffles to the cell door, finds his way blocked by the smirking desk sergeant, who whispers to him, in English:

'Just wash your back...'

He glances behind him, sees the three others still staring at him, waiting for him to be gone.

'Wash ... your ... back,' threatens the desk sergeant in his hoarse, smoker's voice, before stepping aside to let him leave.

24

S he's been moved from intensive care. She has her own little side-ward now, where it's quiet and the blinds are down to keep her from the sun. She's sitting up in bed, supported by pillows, her eyes open, a magazine lying unread on her lap, staring into the middle distance at nothing. Her shaven head is shadowed by three days' new growth of hair. The bandages are gone and there is a fresh, purple scar across her left temple, staples still perforating its smooth margins. The drain has been removed and there's no drip in her arm now, no respirator, no vile urine bag hanging from the side of the bed. A jug of water sits half-empty on her bed-side table where the flowers should be. Gianmaria, who sits silently at her side, guarding her, looks up as he comes in.

'Rosie,' gasps Don, his voice harsh.

She looks up, startled by the new presence in the room, but stares right through him, a slight, curious look passing across her pale face. She says nothing.

'Rosie!' he says, all unshaved, stinking, unwashed; a ragged hurricane violating the peace of the shaded room where his daughter is recovering. He sits on the bed by her side. 'Rosie! I … I came to see you…'

She frowns, slightly shakes her head, staring at him.

'Rosie… Do you know who I am?'

A pause. She drifts off, then is suddenly startled awake by something. She stares, looking at him through widened eyes with an expression like fear. The pupils of her eyes flicker as she recognises him; the source of the voice. She nods, muttering to herself in a small, bewildered voice: 'I … I know who you are.'

Her voice. *Her* voice. For a moment Don is flooded with gratitude for the life that has been spared.

'Darling, Rosie – I … I have to go. I have to *leave* you,' he says.

She seems to shrink into herself. Without looking away from him, her hand moves slowly across the surface of the bed, seeking his. He lays his hand gently upon hers. She whispers something through her dry throat, and coughs. He squeezes gently upon her hand, and she says again, more clearly:

'Don't go … please … don't…'

'I must…' he whispers, glancing over at Gianmaria, who stares at him, a strange new look in his eyes. 'My life here is in danger. I'm putting *you* in danger, just by being here…'

But Rosie's drifting off again. She looks down at her hand, examining it as if it isn't hers, and then it goes limp in his. Her eyes flicker and begin to close. He squeezes her hand, shakes it, urgently this time, trying to wake her up.

'Wait, Rosie! Darling, listen to me: don't trust *anyone*…' he begins, but cannot finish. 'Rosie, my love, I'm *sorry*…'

But she is no longer listening to him. Her eyes are now fully closed, her body limp against the pillows, her mouth half-open, her breathing soft and even. Don lets go of her hand and stands, looking down; one last look at his sleeping daughter. 'I'm sorry, Rosie…' He looks at Gianmaria, who stares back at him through dark, suspicious eyes. 'Please look after her.'

'So you're leaving us,' says Gianmaria, interrupting quietly, staring up at him, angry now. Don can say nothing; doesn't meet his eye.

'Don, I hope you pray for yourself as well as for Rosie,' he says, simply.

'What do you mean?' asks Don, at once suspicious.

But Gian doesn't answer. Just stares him out; stares at his back as he leaves.

25

B ut despite the fear that clutches him, he finds in the end that
he cannot run.

LUCIA FANFANI   44
MICA CARABBA   36
PAOLO AMATO   18
PAOLO SCLAVI   28
MARIA GORRIERI   17

Gianmaria had been right. It wasn't his daughter's life that he
yearned for – it was her forgiveness. And the forgiveness of all
those others, too. And that could never happen. He couldn't forgive
himself. And so this ... atonement ... would never end.

The airport bus had carried him back across the whole arc of
his story. From the hospital where his daughter lay, through the
brightly-lit commercial street of *Ugo Bossi*, by the *Piazza Nettuno*
where Neptune's fountain still stood; the town hall with its faded
black and white photos of the town's war dead, and a new plaque
which wasn't there before, with the fresh flowers laid at its base that
morning, carrying the names – the familiar names – of those who
had died in his *strage*. He had passed the narrow entrance to the
via Poeti, where the *Café Usignol* is still open and where the now-
blind Sammi still buses tables. Then the trolley-bus had wheeled left
down *Indipendenza*, past the *Cattedrale San Pietro* with its bells
and its annual service for the relatives of his victims. There the bus
had stopped, picked up a group of American language schoolgirls
with bright nylon rucksacks strapped to their great chests, who had
laughed and chatted and brushed their fat arses by him where he
sat. They had passed the park where he and Manu had sat in the
early days of their friendship, playing chess; where this new friend
had confided to him his worries about the woman they had both
once loved. And past that place, at the bottom of *Indipendenza*,
the square – *Medaglie D'Oro* – and at the other side of that, the
railway station. From where it's open road, over the bridge on the
river where the boys had dumped their weapons and their masks,
to the airport. Half an hour at most, and then just a few hours – a
night, perhaps – to fix a flight home.

And they wouldn't dare to touch him at the airport.
But he changed his mind. Thinking:
It's better, in the end, not to run away.
At *Medagli d'Oro* he left the bus again. Crossed to the station. Found his own, special chair in the second-class waiting room; sat down and waited.

Now it's night-time, and far quieter. The guard at the door knocked off half an hour ago, ignoring him, probably assuming that he was a tramp. He sits alone in his place in front of his *lapide* and he contemplates the names.
It is better not to run, he reasons.
From the moment he had left the police station, they had been watching him. From the moment he had arrived in this country, possibly. There is nowhere to hide. They will come for him when they want to, wherever they want, and if he runs from them he will never be at peace. So he waits. Here. In this public place, sitting in vigil over the names of those that he – *they* – made victims. Reading their names over to himself, one by one, until they come to end it. And he knows, now, that he will not have long to wait.

ANDREAS SCHUMAN	28
BETTINA KRAUS	23
PIERRE LAFEVRE	32
MARGOT LAFEVRE	33

At least it is quiet. At least it is peaceful. At least, here, he has nothing left to fear.

❧

The door opens. Closes quietly: the subdued hush of compressed air, the bump of the rubber doorstop, almost imperceptible. Don keeps his head bowed, keeps his eyes on the names, lips moving in silence as he reads them.

FABIANO ACCORNERO	52
GIOVANNA FIANELLO	28
TOMMASO FIANELLO	4

To himself, like a prayer.

Concentrate on these names. Imagine their faces. Imagine their lives. Imagine their thoughts. Think what they were thinking in the instant before they died.

And *Sconosciuto*. Last of all. Of course.

Quiet footsteps. Solicitous, almost, for his privacy. His scalp tingles. He tries to swallow, but can't. There is movement in his own plastic chair as someone sits, two chairs down.

Concentrate on the names. Hold each of these names in your head. Say them to yourself, one by one, and try to picture their faces. Pray.

'Don.' *Ton*.

He looks up, startled by the familiar voice.

'I knew that you would come back.'

He stares.

At a woman in her mid-forties. Well-dressed: a black linen jacket, a patterned silk top, a necklace with a fine piece of hand-crafted jewellery in the form of a little blue flower – a forget-me-not. Her violet eyes stare unblinking into his, as if they look beyond their surface, deep within, seeing clearly the man within, and knowing him as he chooses now never to be known. She wears a black felt hat with a wide brim which shadows her face. Her black hair descends in curls to her shoulders.

'I didn't think that it would be you.'

'It *is* me, Don.'

'Then do it. Now.'

'What?' She frowns, as if she doesn't understand.

And it is true: her face is not the face of someone who means to harm him. It never was.

Apart from the leather bag over her shoulder, she carries nothing. There is nowhere a weapon could be concealed. She has nothing but a pair of deep violet eyes which look too deeply into his. Hands clasped, uncharacteristically Catholic, on her lap. Concerned eyes. The eyes of someone who cares. Don, unused to being read like this, flinches and looks away.

She says: 'I've been waiting for you.'

He stands, looks straight ahead, turns his back on her and starts to walk away.

'*Ton!*'

The tapping of those footsteps behind him. She catches him up. Her shoes are black, flat heels, soft, tooled leather. Expensive and comfortable. Everything about her radiates the same kind of money. Her own prosperity. Don becomes aware for the first time of how bad he smells. How ragged are his clothes. How evilly these last days and years have aged him. He forces himself to look into her eyes once more. Trying to control his voice, he speaks to her in English.

'Did you know? Did you know what was in that bag?'

She stands quiet for a moment as if she doesn't understand. Her mouth half-open, the new lines between her eyes knitting as she realises what it is he is asking.

'*Ton!* No! Of course I didn't know. Did you think I...'

She stumbles into silence. Tears fill her eyes. She wears black eye makeup. She never used to wear much makeup. She would despise women who wore heavy makeup.

'Tell me the truth. Just ... just tell me the truth. Did you know? What happened, Maria?'

She purses her lips. Her eyes are full of tears.

'I promise. I didn't know, Don.'

They stand like this, eight feet apart, two rows of orange plastic waiting room chairs between them, the door opening onto the platform at Don's back. On the wall, on the left, is a mounted photograph of that same hall before it was rebuilt. Roofless, the track-side wall demolished, the floor a mound of rubble and dust.

'I came back here to see my daughter. She was hurt. I would never have come back otherwise.'

'You have a daughter?'

He nods. They stare at one another, each fixing the new image of the other, as if trying to remember the faces of the people they had once been.

'I waited for you, Don. I waited for as long as I could. I had to leave in the end...'

'I'm sorry I never came...'

'*Ton,* it is for you to forgive me...'

The dam between momentarily breached, they step closer until only the chairs separate them.

'I thought that you were dead. *Sconosciuto.*' She nods at the stone. 'I thought that was you.'

'How did you know that I was here?'

'I saw you with the relatives. I come back every year. I stand at the back, and leave flowers after. For you. For us. For all of us. And then this year I saw you. I thought that you were dead. I wasn't sure. I followed you to the church. You left early. In a hurry. I knew, then. I knew that you would have to come back here.'

§

They cannot touch one another. At first, they barely even talk.

They sit in Maria's parked car, cocooned in the silence and the dark, faces lit momentarily by the lights of other cars that pass.

Don sits hunched, his bag on his knees, not quite able to look at the woman who sits beside him, staring out of the windscreen.

After many minutes:

'What is she called?'

'Who?'

'Your daughter.'

'Rosie.'

'Rosie...' She says the name to herself, turns it over in her mouth, trying it. She bites her lip.

'Do you have any...'

'No.' She cuts him off; returns to the contemplation of those many, separate years of their respective lives; the immensity of that gulf now between them which holds them fast in its silence. Don's body-stink gathers in the car and shames him. He has thought about this woman – conjured the image of her face, her body, the memory of her voice – for so long. He has tried so hard not to think of this woman, for all of the years of his adult life.

'I think I should just go,' he says, reaching for the door handle, then letting his hand drop. *Where?*

'We shouldn't wait here,' says Maria in the same instant, and arriving by some process at a decision, she turns the key in the ignition and moves out into the traffic.

The new car is fast and almost silent as it cuts through the night-time traffic on the autostrada that heads south-east out of the city. The last time that they had made this trip it was Don that had been driving the car, prompting the broken person at his side for directions. A young man had taken charge then: a bold man, mysteriously triumphant in all his love. He had been proud to drive her away that afternoon. 'Take us to the country. To your grandmother's house,' he had said, and with a quiet voice, hoarse from fear, she had told him the way.

Now he sits and stinks whilst this wealthy, well-dressed stranger-woman at his side drives him to wherever she may choose his end to lie.

He, for his part, resents it.

Her car. The smoothness of her skin, which smells of expensive oils. Bergamot. The softness of the fabric of the upholstery of the car seat. Her clothes: the smooth, black linen jacket which she has folded over the empty back seat; the shoes; the black curly hair which she must, by now, dye. He can't help noticing all this crap, and can't help but hate himself for it, too. The near imperceptible whine and jolt as the turbo kicks in when she hits ninety on the almost-empty road. The ring on her ring finger which she hadn't worn before. The thought of the man that must have given it to her, and their imagined history together. Those happy times, and the sad times, too, that she and this anonymous man must have spent, untroubled, together. Don cannot bring himself to ask her the story of those years which were stolen from him. He resents her pleated grey trousers, the perfectly-ironed silk blouse, the gold necklace with the pendant of the little blue flower; her still-bright eyes; her separateness from him, the casual way that she wears the trappings of her adulthood.

'What happened to *you*, Don?' Her soft voice, slicing through his dream, violates the integrity of his anger.

I picked myself up from the steps of the station, brushed that fine dust from my hair, and made my own way home. I married and had a daughter, and left them both before my presence could kill them too. For years after, I would find that fine, pale dust still clinging to my clothes and to my skin. I drank too much, for too long, and then stopped before it finished me, but far too late to undo any of the real harm. I worked as a gardener and lived in a shed. I taught gardening skills to young adults – boys and girls just coming out of care, and those who are sent to me by the courts. When I have been very lonely in the past, I have occasionally slept with the girls in my charge. It was too hard not too. The youngest of these children was fifteen. If I thought that you cared, I would tell you that, despite this, none of them now regretted me, and that I treated them all well, better than anyone else had, and that I was never the first for any of them, anyway. But how can I begin to tell you any of these things?

So he sits in his stinking silence instead, choked by acrid emotions that he can neither control nor stop.

'*I* became a journalist.' She talks, quite unaware of the nature of the monster sitting at her side. 'A writer. Mainly travel. I work under a pseudonym. I live in Brussels. I was married, but now I am divorced. I have no children, and I regret that. I have a little flat which I let in the summer, when I travel. No-one knows anything about my history, anything of what I really am. I feel sometimes that, because of this, I have no real friends.'

She glances at him as she drives. The shadows of the night outside play upon her face. There is a smile, delicate as a little flower, laid upon her lips.

'Are you happy?' he asks, suppressing the hateful urge to tear that flower away and crush it in his fist.

Pause. 'Yes.'

'You left it all in the past?'

Barely managing to control his voice. She nods, pensively. Staring out at the dark road as the miles pass beneath them. She says, as if it excused everything:

'I had no choice, Don. I thought that you were dead. I thought that you were all dead. You, Marco…'

'All of us?'

'I waited for a week, but I had no money. It wasn't safe. I had to leave the country. Even now, I sometimes feel frightened to be here.'

Twelve miles of silence pass. She pulls off onto the smaller road, turns towards the hills.

'*You* had a child.'

True. I had a child.

'And you love her.'

Not a question.

'Mmm.'

'We have to forgive ourselves, Don.'

He turns away, suddenly, as if he has been struck; looks out of the window; presses his burning face to the cooler glass. Elsewhere, far off in the hills, distant pin-points of light blur and swim.

❡

'Perhaps this is a mistake. Perhaps it is a mistake to return to the past, to lives which we once chose, or were forced, to abandon. Or perhaps we have no choice. Perhaps the force that drove us together when we first met is as strong now as then, and we as powerless to resist it. Everything changes, but our choices remain the same. And we two have been granted another chance. I see this very clearly.'

Appearing not to notice his silence, standing in the entrance of that magical place, she fixes him with her eyes, face as serious as life itself, and tells him, talking for them both.

'We must. We have no choice.'

The tiles on which he stands are the same. He remembers their coolness under his feet; the day's warmth still in the air, touching his skin. But the kitchen has a sink now, and the hand-pump has gone and has been replaced by taps. There is a cooker with gas rings, a new willow table, a place to eat, places to sit. The fire is there still, but unused – the grate is clean, the fireplace swept and there is no sign of ash. The roof-space is clear, the tools gone, and the eaves empty of bats. The walls are white-washed, and the windows cleared of vegetation. Where there was an alcove in one corner with a shrine bearing a plaster Christ and his mother, she has a computer; there's a phone, a fax machine, a flat-bed scanner on a table by her chair. She comes here when she can. A week or two in the summer; at Christmas time. Last year she had managed a couple of months, finished a book, spent weeks at that window, looking out at the valley and the hills opposite, watching day by day as the season changed.

'You can even wash, now!' she says, still wearing that smile which he both cherishes and longs to crush.

You have no right to smile!

'Wash!' she says, indicating the door.

So he stands under a powerful jet of hot water; squeezes his eyes tight shut so that the scented soap won't sting. He runs his fingers through his hair, scratches from the skin of his body what feels like years of sweat and grime.

It's all new. She'd built the bathroom four or five years ago, she said. The roof was threatening to fall in, so she'd done a lot of work on the place. She'd decided eventually that it was safe for her to return, from time to time. After a few tentative summers, she'd grown more confident that she was unnoticed, that no-one was looking for her any more. All the farms round about had been bought and sold half a dozen times. They're all tourists now. No-one sees her as she comes and goes. The place has become her escape. This is the only place in her life, she says, which has such memories.

He dries himself on the clean, white towel he finds on the rail. Feels, for the first time in months, strong. Clean again. A man. He wraps himself in a cotton robe he finds hanging behind the wooden door. A kimono. A Far Eastern *lungi*. Something like that. Something brought back from her travels.

'I want to try again, Don,' she says as he re-enters the room where she stands, a bottle of wine open on the table, two glasses, one in her hand, offered to him. 'I need to know whether it was all real, or just imagined. Just a memory, or actually our lives. Our whole lives.'

He takes the glass, drinks from its cool rim, and enjoys the taste of the wine as if it is the first time he has ever tasted wine.

'How long will we have this time?'

'I don't know.'

'Is it worth it?'

'Is it ever worth it?'

He thinks for a moment.

'Yes,' he says, 'always. It's always worth it.'

He places the glass back on the table, and then kisses her. With his hand gentle on her back, he pulls her to him, puts his mouth on hers and kisses her. As if it were the first time he had ever kissed her.

'Maria, I have loved you and hated you so much and for so long, I don't know whether I can ever come back to you.'

'I know,' she says, then laughs: a mysterious, wise chuckle. And kisses him again.

7

Waking beside her. An awareness: first of the quality of the light, then of the silence which surrounds them. The room where they sleep catches the morning light. Sunrise: the first beams of the new day catching the particles of dust which turn in the air above his half-closed eyes, and the slow dance of that dust. The new sensation of clean white sheets next to his clean skin, which propels from within him a contentment he hasn't felt for more than twenty years. Then the warm, living skin of the woman who lies next to him, still asleep, and her one arm which is trailed across his chest, rising and falling with his own breathing, and then the memory of how that skin and her body had felt next to his the night before.

In sleep, the years show more clearly upon her face. The line of her jaw and chin are less distinct. The skin around her eyes looser. There is some grey, too, in her hair which he hadn't seen the day before, and the lines between her eyes remain even after the frown has left her face. Her skin feels softer to the touch now, her whole body a little more vulnerable, a little more worthy of that wave of tenderness which now breaks over him. He runs his hand through her hair and concentrates on this new thought: that he is reunited with the woman that he loved and lost all of these years before, and that there is no reason right now, then and there, why that should ever change. Concentrate on that thought. *She wanted you back. She never forgot about you. She never stopped thinking about you.* Concentrate on that thought. *She never betrayed you.* She, also, was deceived. Don't forget it. Hold it with you. She never stopped loving you.

Gently, he lifts her hand from his chest; rises slowly, so as not to disturb her sleep. He stands naked in the morning light and contemplates the person still sleeping there, finally fixing in his mind forever the shape her body makes under the sheet, her face, the way her black hair spreads across the pillow.

He wraps himself again in the patterned cotton robe and, stepping lightly, leaves the room, standing a moment in the doorway to the cottage, watching the shadows in the bottom of the valley, the clouds rising from below him, the clear sky and the first of the sunrise above the hillside opposite.

His bare feet curling against the thorns buried in the red earth, he follows the path behind the house, up through the olive groves, trying to find the path they'd followed before, that first day, to the spring. It takes him longer that he had thought; the thicker vegetation, the change in the colour of the leaves of the trees which surrounds it, which marks its position, is less than he remembered it, or less this year than it was then. He tracks up and down the terraces above the house before he hears the sound of running water, finds the narrow irrigation channel where the water runs fast and deep across the line of the hillside. He follows the channel a couple of hundred metres upstream into the thicker vegetation, the copse of willow that he remembered still growing above the pool. He looks back, sees the red roof tiles of the little house half-hidden by the almond tree, the view he remembers now quite unchanged.

Unwraps himself. Stands quite naked, skin puckering against the morning cold, the night's moisture being burned off by the morning sun. The grey shape of the hill opposite, the first insects awakening, his own immense solitude.

To be a man again... To be a man...

He thinks in disconnected phrases, his skin absorbing the fresh light of that new sun as if it has thirsted for it.

Whole. Forgiven.

He turns his back on the valley; his toes curl on the cool moss growing on the ancient stones; he looks deep into the green water, anticipating its cold touch upon his skin; rises on his toes, falls back upon his heels, rises once again, and dives deep into the pool.

He reaches blindly ahead of himself, pulling himself further into the darkening water until the pressure grows on his temples and the shadows start to crush upon his chest. It is anger and joy, mixed, which propel him deeper; it seems to *matter* that his hands encounter, finally, smooth algae-covered rock at a depth beyond safety; it seems to matter that he has reached this spot, the stones lining and sealing the bottom, dry-fitted, fixed there two thousand years before, neither seen nor felt since. He runs his hands along the smoothly-curved contour of the great stone base of the cistern as if he is searching, as if perhaps there is a secret or a treasure down there for him to find. He sees no more than shapes and shadows, currents in the water, vegetation, rotting branches of a tree which fell last winter or a thousand years before.

His breath exhausted, the pressure building in his chest, looking up at the glimmering green day above his head, he kicks off from the bottom, struggling, hungry for air, beginning to panic at the depth, the cold and pressure of the water – then he bursts through the thin membrane of its surface, gasps, water like jewellery scattering around him. He gasps and shouts.

To be alive. To be a man again. To be forgiven.

§

He dries himself on the cotton wrap and covers himself, shivering a little despite the sun.

Thinks he hears a voice say something he doesn't catch, a phrase, cut off, the voice's owner distracted. In this still air, a voice could carry a mile or two, all the way across the valley. He looks at the woods on the other side of the valley, searching in vain for the source of that voice.

The smell of black tobacco, so faint in that fresh air that it could be just a memory.

Two sharp cracks like the branches of a tree, snapping.

He picks his way, slowly, finding the track back to the house.

The sharp clear light of the sun is reflected through the trees. From the shiny black body of a car, parked at the top of the lane. For a moment, it blinds him.

He hurries. He starts to run, barefoot, over the rough track, struggling not to fall amongst the tangled roots. He stumbles on sharp stones and last year's fallen wood. He bleeds, but doesn't notice the deep cuts on his feet. He bursts, raging like an animal, from the cover of the olive groves and, voice cracking, shouts her name.

Catching his breath, panting like a bear, he enters through the now-open door. Pauses, standing in the entrance of the big room, where he sees last night's glasses still standing on the table, the wine dry and purpled in the eye at the bottom of the cups, and a drop or two still on the wood, where it will leave its stain forever. A clawing, sweet smell in the air which wasn't there before. An artificial, expensive scent. The memory of a person.

He shouts her name for the second time. The house, crouching around him, absorbs his voice into its silence, guarding its secrets.

He paces into the bedroom, stands at the bedroom door and

gasps. Sees his beloved lying there, still at peace, still quite still, the white sheets upon which they had lain together that last night now blossoming with garlands of new, purple flowers. He flinches and looks away from those scorched holes where her eyes once were.

He shouts her name for the third and last time.

Part 5

26

All I have left of him is memory, and memory fades so quickly, always.

I have a childhood which was short, then a few angry years of truncated adolescence. I have the memory of a row one dismal afternoon last year in London, and lastly, the memory of a voice which haunted me during a long and troubled sleep. A story which was told to me in my father's voice as I lay sick. The rest I piece together from what I read and from what I have been told; from what is rumoured and from what I know in my heart must be so; from the voices of the memory of the man that I knew.

And I have his photograph still, on smudged newsprint, curling and yellowed already, pinned to the window-frame above the desk where I sit. Taken from the far corner of the room where he lies, taken in a hurry, and in bad light, because his face is not clearly visible: just the outline of his head, the shadow of stubble on his chin, two smudges of black for his still-open eyes, and the outline of the shape of his unclothed body under the bed sheet. It is not a picture that I like, or one that I can bear long to look at. My eye drifts constantly to and from it to rest once again upon the view outside: the tussocks of windblown sand-grass leading down to the narrow bay, the jaws of the bay, the rocks reaching into the Atlantic, the patch of sand on the cove where I sit in the afternoons when the weather is warm. I watch the tides come in and out, the weather as it builds far out at sea, clouds gathering to haul themselves over my black house at night when I sleep and the storms break. I watch the winds as they pass; the breathing seas. Yet it is this photograph which drives me forward. I need it for that – for the force and the anger that I borrow from it – but when I am finished, it will be burned.

During the mornings I walk and I think. I follow the same route, always: the path through the grass down to the cove which I comb for firewood; then back up to the hill where I stand and look for the smudges on the horizon. On a clear day, the Cuillins of Skye, and even the hills beyond Applecross. Looking north, the low grey hills of Barra; to the west, the sea. I cross to the far side of the island; walk the cliffs; watch for the puffins that dart through the wave-tops hunting for the little fish they feed upon. There is much to see walking these cliffs, and in the water too; and for many hours, here in this place, I can be happy.

I have conjured with many endings for my father's story.

Last night I had him face his lover's killer, and overcome him. So:

...He flinched and looked away from her. He called out her name for the third and last time...

...He stood waiting there in the doorway, staring, his skin tingling with anticipation, his breath coming in short gasps, half-suffocated by the heavy scent of her killer's aftershave.

'Manu.' Quietly saying the man's name.

Who stands there in the corner, waiting too.

'Lie down beside her.' His voice is hoarse. He wheezes. Twenty-four more years of those white-tipped, hand-made Turkish cigarettes have ripped through his vocal cords. He has the voice and the presence of an old man now.

He indicates with the weapon. Don, jumping in response, takes a step or two forward to the bed, as if there can be no question of disobeying this man's quiet, ruined voice. But then he stops. He turns and stares into that shadow in the corner of the room, seeks out the man's face.

Manu has not aged well. A life spent too long in the darkness, and his skin, the colour of onions, now has a deadened, pouched pallor. His thin hair lies close-cropped and grey against a smooth skull, and the face tells its own story. What once was a veneer of culture has long gone cold, and there are pebbles in these eyes which once glinted with such easy malice.

'Lie down.'

'I was the bait, wasn't I? I led you to her...'

Manu, saying nothing, just gestures impatiently again with the tip of his pistol.

'You've been waiting all this time, haven't you? How did you know that I was here?'

'Because we brought you here,' he says quietly.

'Rosie…'

The suspicion of a smile on the older man's face.

Which breaks the hypnosis which has held Don under the other's command, weak-legged, poised undecided between the doorway and the bed where his lover lies and where he must soon lie too.

But it's that last little smile that finally does it.

He balls himself and charges like a bull across the room, roaring with all of the rage that Manu's vain and too-human smile has unlocked in him. There is a shot – a muffled crack from the silenced pistol which Don feels snatching at the cloth that he still wears wrapped around him, burning his shoulder but leaving him otherwise untouched. His momentum carries him onto – through – his enemy, who, a small man, collapses there, winded, and Don uses his greater weight to crush him, and then break him, as he strikes upon the once finely-made face with his fists. The man under him makes no sound.

Don lifts the pistol from where it has fallen beside them, thrusts the tip under the man's chin, pushes hard, makes to pull the trigger, but can't.

Manu, struggling a little for breath, looks up at Don without much fear.

Some – very few – are capable of this: to kill another who at their mercy, from nothing, from cold, without hesitation. Don isn't one. Manu knows this. Manu has always known this. So Manu just waits. So does Don, who sweats, grimacing, his hand shaking, almost ready to weep. But he cannot, of course, kill.

'Let me … help you with this,' says Manu eventually, still struggling to breathe. 'It is not she who should concern you – she who betrayed you over and over again. Nor indeed is it I, who you betrayed, and who would have killed you.'

He fixes Don with his cold eyes, fearless as ever, still with that hint – that glimmer of a smile.

'It is for your daughter, whom you should not have left, that you should fear. You abandoned her, knowing what you now know. Even I, knowing you as I do, doubted that you would abandon her.' He shakes his head, despairing, it seems, of Don's fecklessness. Don pushes the pistol harder into the man's throat, wills himself again to shoot, but cannot.

'Now,' says Manu, still calm. 'Provided you have told her nothing, your daughter is safe. Gianmaria has a great sense of ... honour. He will spare her. He will see that she gets safely home. Provided, that is, that she knows nothing. If, on the other hand, you have...'

Don stands. Then, almost as an afterthought, crouches once again and shoots Manu through the left knee. That was for Marco! he thinks: a gift for my long-dead friend. That, at least, I can do.

Manu grits his teeth, barely flinching.

Don dresses; avoids looking at the face of the woman on the bed; at the eyes of the man that lies there at his feet bleeding, and their silent, piercing look of triumph...

§

But of course this fantasy just serves to make me more wretched. As I gather my armfuls of dried heather from the hillside to make kindling, stack driftwood, build my fire in the rusting metal stove, coax a little flame for the day's warmth, I let his gentle ghost pursue me. I listen as its cold voice blends with the undying sound of the wind, the story that it still whispers in my ear. Although I can imagine him miraculously, heroically, implausibly spared, I know at the same time that I simply lie to myself.

I know that he is dead. But I still sit all day in his imagined company, moving his image through his last days, hours, then seconds, like a child with her stick-figures in a doll's house. I listen to the memory of his voice, lodged deep within me, telling me how it was, and how it must have been. But I still yearn for the physical presence of the man, for his real, embodied self. To ask him: *Why?*

It was Gianmaria who finally told me that he was dead.

Gian hadn't left my side for the whole month of my recovery. He had slept in the chair; bought in food which he ate by my bedside; read while I slept; talked to me, to reassure me, when I was awake. I asked him many times to leave me – to go home, to rest, sleep properly, get something to eat, wash! But he said no. Shook his head, eyes grey and dead with exhaustion, said, 'No, Rosie, I'll stay. I'll wait here, with you...' I thought that it was simply because he was a good man; or that perhaps, as I slept, mysterious as this magic is, he had come to fall in love with me. I imagined myself a fallen fledgling, flight feathers not yet grown, held trembling and damaged, yet safe, in the cup of this man's warm hand.

Things, as they emerged, were not quite so simple.

When I was ready he walked with me, slowly, around and around the hospital, an old woman on sticks. At first just to the café, where he would drink coffee and I took my first tentative sips of bad Italian tea, and he mocked me for my choice. I wanted soon to walk further, but he denied me, shook his head, said no: I wasn't ready. It was only when I was strong enough and able to insist that he told me.

I was dressed in my old clothes. I had my shoes on; I was ready to leave. My headaches had lessened in the last days; I could talk, walk, care for myself in all ways without assistance. We had argued. He had said: 'A few more days, Rosie; just a few more days.' And I had said to him, a little angry, 'Why are you keeping me back?' And he had said, suddenly very quiet, very sombre, 'Rosie, there is something that you need to know...'

He gave me the newspaper, which he had kept for me in his leather case. I looked at it, not understanding. He pointed to the picture on the front page – the one that I keep with me – but I didn't recognise him at first, just shook my head again, and said that I didn't understand. 'Help me, Gianmaria. What is it?'

He translated it for me.

Two bodies were found. Dead, naked, shot in the face. They were lying together on a bed in a holiday villa in the hills of southern *Toscana*, arranged in an embrace. The man still held the gun which had killed them. It was placed in his right hand, in a crude attempt to simulate suicide. Crude – mockingly crude, because he, like the woman, had been shot twice.

The woman was known to the police: she had been a well-known *Brigate* terrorist in the late seventies, but had disappeared in 1980. She was named as Lara Focaccio, but my father knew her as Maria. The identity of the man in the picture was unknown to the police – *sconosciutto* was the word the newspaper used. His feet were cut and bloodied. His blood-prints led from the front door of the holiday villa through to the bedroom, where he had evidently stood for a little time, and then crossed to the bed, where he had lain down to die. It was apparent, according to the writer, that the man had been outside, barefoot, when he had heard the first shots; had run in, cutting himself on the flints and olive wood in the undergrowth.

I sat for an hour with the paper on my knees, studying the commentary, staring at the picture, which resolved itself under the pressure of my gaze into the image of my father and Maria, his lover. Whilst Gianmaria sat in silence, I wept. Until he broke his silence with a question.

'Rosie, how much of your father's story do you know? How much did he tell you?'

I stare at him through my tears but don't answer. He looks at me through those kind, brown eyes; looks straight down, deep into me; then takes my hands in his and says, 'There is something else that I have to tell you, Rosie.'

I stare at him, and say nothing. A confession.

'It was I that brought this upon you, Rosie. Upon you, and your father.'

I nod, a little sharp nod, and wait.

'In the course of my work for the *Lega,* I am often given information which casts light on the events of the *Anni di piombo.* Information which, from time to time, I have shared with ... old friends ... connected with government. This has led, in the past, to the unmasking of fascists or their sympathisers – even in the government, even high in the judiciary. For this reason, I have felt these actions to be justified. This country has changed a lot in the last years, and in some ways for the better. At least so I thought.

'When I met you, Rosie, I was suspicious that your father may have been involved in the events before the *strage* in ways that you didn't suspect. And I passed my suspicions on to my contact. I had no thought that my information would be misused in the way that it was. I am sorry. I have brought all of this upon you.'

I squeeze his hand back, as if to say, bright-eyed, *It's all right, Gian; you didn't mean it...*

'But now you must tell me exactly how much you know, Rosie. Your life here is in danger. To help you, I have to understand. You must tell me *everything* that your father told you.'

I nod again, open-eyed, my little hands shrinking from his. My eyes cloud over and I frown as I lie: 'I don't know, Gian ... I just don't remember.'

'We need to go, Rosie. I need to get you away from here. I will take you home to England. This is my fault, all my doing. But I won't abandon you.' His eyes fill again with tenderness; this unique and inimitable warmth which looks to me so much like love, this *facsimile* of love...

Are you lying to me, Gian? Were you always lying to me?

'We have no time. You're right, Rosie: you're ready. We should not have left it so late. I will get my passport, now. I have money. I will return in half an hour, and we will leave directly. I will ask the nurse to sit with you. Don't let anyone else into the room. Do you understand? No-one!'

I nod again. He kisses me, fretfully. He looks at me, as if he is about to say 'I love you, Rosie...' – which might have changed things – but he doesn't. Says instead, 'Half an hour, okay? You'll be okay...'

'Okay,' I say – the chirpy voice of a little bird.

As soon as he is gone, I gather together my things. There isn't much left: the computer, my notes, some clothes which I left in the *pensione,* which I resign myself to losing. Life, after all, is all that matters. I have a bag with stuff here: my money, credit card, my passport.

The nurse comes in as I pack the last bits and pieces: a book, a carefully-folded newspaper.

'Are you going?' she asks, smiling and slightly baffled. I am a favourite here. Hospitals like the miracle cases such as mine: they give so much hope. We are mascots; we're breathing, living shrines.

I smile, casual, and say 'Yes, Franka. And, Franka – thank you. Thank you so, so much...' And because we have become close over the month, we embrace, and I shed another tear.

'Your boyfriend? Gianmaria?'

'Downstairs,' I say, pointing to the door with my finger. 'He's waiting for me downstairs.'

Franka smiles; complicit, she thinks, in all this happiness.

And I casually sling my bag over my shoulder, and leave.

♀

I thought I heard a knock at the door.

I have just started what was to be the last page of my book. *'This is how it was. This is how it must have happened…'* was all that I had managed, after an hour or so of nothing.

I have started this half a dozen times already. Each version leaves me more dismal, more bereft, than the last.

I can imagine him standing there, naked but for the cloth around his waist. In the photo there is a smudge on the floor beside the bed, which *I* alone know is the cloth he would have been wearing. He is confronting three or four younger men. His death has been planned and practiced, well in advance. Manu is there, but possibly out of sight. Maybe he waits in the car at the top of the lane and will come down after, when the job is finished, to inspect his men's work.

No. Actually, in the scene which I contemplate he *is* there, present – but the two men do not speak. An exchange of looks, recognition, and no more. Each knows the role that the other must perform. I see the men's calm faces, the absolute authority with which they stare down my father's fear and rage. They have done this so many times before. One indicates the bed with the snub nose of his pistol, says, in English, 'There, over there. Lie down.' But my father still stands there, quite frozen.

'*…That was how it must have happened…*' I write.

But I cannot move them beyond that point. He, my father, standing there, blisters of sweat freezing on his face; the four men: two young ex-marines, two older, all armed, fanning around the room, blocking off any possibility for his escape…

When, suddenly, there is this knock upon the fabric of the here-and-now, a sharp blow which rocks the flimsy wooden door in its rotting frame and startles me out of my vision.

I sit in frozen silence, holding my breath. There is a gust of wind outside and the flames in my stove suddenly catch again with a roar. The air around me is warm; there will be smoke outside from the chimney, but it is dark.

No-one knows that I am here. I tell myself this, over and over again. My own mother doesn't even know whether I am alive.

The only person who knew of my connection with this place – my father, who brought me here when I was twelve – is dead. There is a fisherman on Barra who lends me a boat, but he doesn't even know my real name.

I stand, pause a second, then open the door to the cold and the wild weather outside.

A half-moon surfs the clouds. I hear the sound of the sea, which is constant, and the cry of birds far off in the night. No-one is there.

I have over two thousand pounds in cash in a bag under the mattress where I sleep. All of my savings. When I left Bologna, I was determined that I would leave no trace: no credit card bills, no mobile phone calls, no e-mail. No trace. At my current rate of expenditure, I can live here for over a year. Only through boredom, or the slow-burn yearnings of my heart, will I ever be found.

It's a warm night. The air smells of peat and heather – a dark, moist, honey-coloured scent.

I say his name, quietly, to the night.

'Gianmaria.'

Dark brown eyes, long curly hair which reached down to his neck. A splendid man.

I fell in love with him; he betrayed me.

I think.

'Gianmaria,' I say – enjoying, in a mad, lonesome sort of way, the sound of my voice.

I never knew whether he really cared for me.

He stayed with me when I was dying. He held my hand at night. He never left my side.

He used me for bait. He caused my Dad to be killed.

When I opened that door – whenever I open that door – my heart hammers, my mouth is dry, my stomach clenches. I tell myself that it is because I fear for my life. But I am lying. It's because I hope to see there the hunched, rain-drenched figure of a man, wrapped in a coat, big country boots on his fine Tuscan feet. For months I have been hoping for this impossible thing: that it will be him.

And whether he's here to tell me he loves me, or whether he's here to finish me, I hardly seem to care. It's all the same. I just want to see him again.

'Gianmaria.' I suck in the sweet, scented air. I turn my back on the night; sit again at my table, in this little circle of things that has been my home. My nearly-finished manuscript. My pencils. My candles. My few books. The yellowing newsprint photograph pinned to the window-frame. I look again at the picture of the dead man, his arm still wrapped around the body of the girl he gave his life to love.

'Gianmaria,' I say again, and watch a smirr of raindrops chase itself across the window-pane outside.

Fiction from Two Ravens Press

Love Letters from my Death-bed
Cynthia Rogerson

There's something very strange going on in Fairfax, California. Joe Johnson is on the hunt for dying people while his wife stares into space and flies land on her nose; the Snelling kids fester in a hippie backwater and pretend that they haven't just killed their grandfather; and Morag, multi-bigamist from the Scottish Highlands, makes some rash decisions when diagnosed with terminal cancer by Manuel – who may or may not be a doctor. Meanwhile, the ghost of Consuela threads her way through all the stories, oblivious to the ever-watching Connie – who sees everything from the attic of the Gentle Valleys Hospice.

Cynthia Rogerson's second novel is a funny and life-affirming tale about the courage to love in the face of death.

'Witty, wise and on occasions laugh-aloud funny. A tonic for all those concerned with living more fully while we can.' **Andrew Greig**

'Her writing has a lovely spirit to it, an appealing mixture of the spiky and the warm.' **Michel Faber**

£8.99. ISBN 978-1-906120-00-9. Published April 2007.

Parties
Tom Lappin

Gordon yearns for a little power; Richard wishes reality could match the romantic ideal of a perfect pop song; Grainne wants life to be a little more like Tolstoy. Beatrice looks on and tries to chronicle the disappointment of a generation measuring the years to the end of the twentieth century in parties.

Parties, the début novel by journalist Tom Lappin, is a scathing, insightful and profoundly human commentary on party politics and the corrupting effects of power. But above all it is a satire: a black comedy about young people getting older, and learning to be careful what they wish for, lest they end up finding it.

£9.99. ISBN 978-1-906120-11-5. Published October 2007.

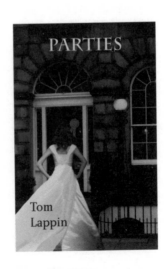

Prince Rupert's Teardrop
Lisa Glass

Mary undresses and wades into the boating lake. She dives and opens her eyes. In the blur, she perceives the outline of a head – she reaches...

A dead bird. But she will keep searching. Because Mary's mother, Meghranoush – a ninety-four year-old survivor of the genocide of Armenians by the Turkish army early in the twentieth century – has vanished.

Mary is already known to the police: a serial telephoner, a reporter of wrongdoing, a nuisance. Her doctor talks of mental illness.

But what has happened is not just inside her head. A trail of glass birds mocks her. A silver thimble shines at the riverbed – a thimble that belonged to her mother.

A glassblower burns a body in a furnace and uses the ash to colour a vase. Rumours circulate of a monster stalking the women of Plymouth. A serial killer who specialises in the elderly.

Has Mary's mother simply left – trying to escape the ghosts of genocide in her mind – or has she been abducted? It is left to this most unreliable and unpredictable of daughters to try to find her, in this moving, lyrical, and very powerful work.

'Lisa Glass writes with dazzling linguistic exuberance and a fearless imagination.' R.N. Morris

'A virtuoso stylist of the calibre of Rachel Cusk, Lisa Glass has created a powerful murder mystery, whose violent undercurrents flow from the bitter inheritance of the Armenian genocide.'
Stevie Davies

£9.99. ISBN 978-1-906120-15-3. Published November 2007.

The Most Glorified Strip of Bunting
John McGill

The United States North Polar expedition of 1871-73 was a disaster-strewn adventure that counts amongst the most bizarre and exciting in the annals of Arctic exploration.

Commanded by Charles Francis Hall, a romantic idealist with an obsessive interest in the frozen north, the converted river tug Polaris carries a multinational crew of scientists and sailors, assisted by two Inuit families, along the so-called American Way to the North Pole - the icy channels between Greenland and Ellesmere Island. For Hall, the planting of the Stars and Stripes on the top of the world is a sacred and patriotic duty, but his enthusiasm is shared by few of his companions, and the expedition, under the strain of conditions in the high Arctic, quickly disintegrates into warring factions. With their ship embedded in the ice, the explorers plunge into a maelstrom of anarchy and paranoia fuelled by the clash of two civilisations – Inuit and European – and the mutual misunderstanding and hostility that arise from it.

John McGill's novel chronicles the events leading up to the strange and suspicious death of the commander, and in a parallel narrative, tells the astonishing tale of the nineteen crew members separated in a storm and cast adrift on an ice floe.

Their story is one of the truly great Arctic adventures, a six-month drama of narrow escapes coloured by the ever=present threats of rape, murder and cannibalism, and acted out on a shrinking platform of ice exposed to all the horrors of the most inhospitable climate on earth.

£9.99. ISBN 978-1-906120-12-2. Published November 2007.

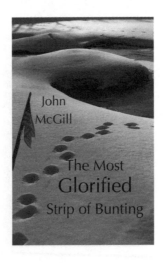

Short Fiction from Two Ravens Press

Highland Views
David Ross

Military jets exercise over Loch Eye as a seer struggles to remember his vision; the honeymoon is over for workers down at the Nigg yard, and an English incomer leads the fight for independence both for Scotland and for herself... This debut collection of stories provides an original perspective on the Highlands, subtly addressing the unique combination of old and new influences that operate today.

'I'm a big fan. A fine organic collection that advances a viewpoint, culture and history quite other than the urban central belt that still lopsidedly dominates recent Scottish literature.' **Andrew Greig**

'A view of the Highlands with a strong element of political and social comment. Ross explores these concerns in convincingly human terms through the lives of his characters.' **Brian McCabe**

£7.99. ISBN 978-1-906120-05-4. Published April 2007.

Types of Everlasting Rest
Clio Gray

From Italy and Russia in the time of Napoleon to the fate of Boy
Scouts in Czechoslovakia during the Second World War, Clio Gray's
short stories are filled with intrigue, conspiracy and murder. Laden
with sumptuous detail, each story leads the reader directly into the
compelling and sometimes bizarre inner worlds of her fascinating
characters.

'*Clio Gray is a master of atmosphere and sensuousness. She
combines historical realism with the bizarre, whimsy with the
macabre. Reading her is like being at a sumptuous feast in a palace,
just before it is stormed.*' **Alan Bissett**

£8.99. ISBN 978-1-906120-04-7. Published July 2007.

RIPTIDE
New Writing from the Highlands and Islands
Edited by Sharon Blackie & David Knowles

This diverse collection of new fiction and poetry from the Highlands & Islands showcases the work of established writers and new names to watch.

Contributors:
Pam Beasant, Sharon Blackie, Robert Davidson, Angus Dunn, Eva Faber, Alison Flett, Yvonne Gray, John Glenday, Clio Gray, Andrew Greig, Nicky Guthrie, Mandy Haggith, Morag Henderson, Elyse Jamieson, Laureen Johnson, David Knowles, Morag MacInnes, Anne Macleod, Kevin MacNeil, Daibhidh Martin, John McGill, Donald Murray, Alison Napier, Pauline Prior-Pitt, Joanna Ramsey, Cynthia Rogerson, David Ross, Mark Ryan Smith, and Peter Urpeth.

'*...a force of creation, the kind of irresistible tide into which we should dip.*' **The Scotsman**

£8.99. ISBN 978-1-906120-02-3. Published April 2007.

Poetry from Two Ravens Press

Castings: by Mandy Haggith.
£8.99. ISBN 978-1-906120-01-6. Published April 2007.

Leaving the Nest: by Dorothy Baird.
£8.99. ISBN 978-1-906120-06-1. Published July 2007.

The Zig Zag Woman: by Maggie Sawkins.
£8.99. ISBN 978-1-906120-08-5. Published September 2007.

In a Room Darkened: by Kevin Williamson.
£8.99. ISBN 978-1-906120-07-8. Published October 2007.

For more information on these and other titles, and for
extracts and author interviews, see our website.

Titles are available direct from the publisher at
www.tworavenspress.com
or from any good bookshop.